THE TEHRAN INITIATIVE

JOEL C. ROSENBERG

TYNDALE HOUSE PUBLISHERS, INC.  CAROL STREAM, ILLINOIS

ATIVE

Visit Tyndale online at www.tyndale.com.

Visit Joel C. Rosenberg's website at www.joelrosenberg.com.

TYNDALE and Tyndale's quill logo are registered trademarks of Tyndale House Publishers, Inc.

The Tehran Initiative

Designed by Dean H. Renninger

Some Scripture quotations and words of Jesus are taken or adapted from the New American Standard Bible,® copyright © 1960, 1962, 1963, 1968, 1971, 1972, 1973, 1975, 1977, 1995 by The Lockman Foundation. Used by permission.

This novel is a work of fiction. Names, characters, places, and incidents either are the product of the author's imagination or are used fictitiously. Any resemblance to actual events, locales, organizations, or persons living or dead is entirely coincidental and beyond the intent of either the author or the publisher.

Library of Congress Cataloging-in-Publication Data to come]

Rosenberg, Joel C., date.
    The Tehran initiative / Joel C. Rosenberg.
        p. cm.
    ISBN 978-1-4143-1935-3 (hc)
1. Intelligence officers—United States—Fiction. 2. Nuclear warfare—Prevention—Fiction.
3. International relations—Fiction. 4. Prophecy—Islam—Fiction. 5. Iran—Fiction. 6. Middle East—Fiction. I. Title.
    PS3618.O832T44 2011
    813'.6—dc23   2011026051

ISBN 978-1-4143-6492-6 (International Trade Paper Edition)

Printed in the United States of America

17 16 15 14 13 12 11
 7   6   5   4   3   2   1

To all our friends in Iran and the Middle East,
yearning to be free.

AUTHOR'S NOTE

Tehran, Iran, is one and a half hours ahead of Jerusalem and
eight and a half hours ahead of New York and Washington, DC.

CAST OF CHARACTERS

AMERICANS

David Shirazi (aka Reza Tabrizi)—field officer, Central Intelligence Agency

Marseille Harper—childhood friend of David Shirazi; daughter of CIA operative Charlie Harper

Jack Zalinsky—senior operative, Central Intelligence Agency

Eva Fischer—field officer, Central Intelligence Agency

Roger Allen—director, Central Intelligence Agency

Tom Murray—deputy director for operations, Central Intelligence Agency

Dr. Mohammad Shirazi—cardiologist, father of David Shirazi

Nasreen Shirazi—mother of David Shirazi

William Jackson—president of the United States

Mike Bruner—Secret Service agent, assigned to President Jackson

IRANIANS

Dr. Alireza Birjandi—preeminent scholar of Shia Islamic eschatology

Najjar Malik—former physicist, Atomic Energy Organization of Iran

Javad Nouri—senior governmental aide

Ayatollah Hamid Hosseini—Supreme Leader

Ahmed Darazi—president of Iran

Jalal Zandi—nuclear physicist

Firouz Nouri—leader of an Iranian terrorist cell

Rahim Yazidi—member of Firouz Nouri's cell

Navid Yazidi—member of Firouz Nouri's cell

Ali Faridzadeh—minister of defense

Mohsen Jazini—commander of the Iranian Revolutionary Guard Corps

Dr. Mohammed Saddaji—nuclear physicist (deceased)

ISRAELIS

Asher Naphtali—prime minister of Israel

Levi Shimon—defense minister

Captain Avi Yaron—commander, Israeli Air Force squadron

Captain Yossi Yaron—commander, Israeli Air Force squadron

OTHERS

Muhammad Ibn Hasan Ibn Ali—the Twelfth Imam

Tariq Khan—Pakistani nuclear physicist, working in Iran

Iskander Farooq—president of Pakistan

Abdel Mohammad Ramzy—president of Egypt

PREFACE
FROM *THE TWELFTH IMAM*

David Shirazi wondered if they'd even make it to the safe house in Karaj.

As he inched forward in Tehran's stop-and-go traffic toward Azadi Square, he saw the flashing lights of police cars ahead. Despite the roar of jumbo jets and cargo planes landing at Mehrabad International Airport, he could hear sirens approaching. Beside him sat Dr. Najjar Malik, the highest-ranking nuclear scientist in the Islamic Republic of Iran and the most valuable defector to the Central Intelligence Agency in a generation.

"They're setting up a roadblock," David said.

Najjar stiffened. "Then we need to get off this road."

David agreed. The problem was that every side street from here to the square was clogged with hundreds of other drivers trying to find their way around the logjam as well.

"We're going to have to get rid of this car."

"Why? What for?"

"The moment a police officer runs these license plates, he's going to come up with your name. We don't want to be in the car when that happens."

Without warning, David pulled the steering wheel hard to the right. He darted across two lanes of traffic, triggering a wave of angry honks.

Under no circumstances could he allow himself to get caught or implicated in the extraction of Najjar from the country. To do either would blow his cover and compromise all the work he'd done. The Twelfth Imam's inner circle would never use the new satellite phones he'd just provided them. The MDS technical teams would be thrown out of the country. The CIA's multimillion-dollar effort to penetrate the Iranian regime would be ruined. And given that Iran now had the Bomb, the CIA needed every advantage it could possibly get.

David heard a siren behind them. He cursed as he glanced in his rearview mirror and saw flashing lights about ten cars back. He guessed that a police cruiser had spotted his rapid and reckless exit from Azadi Road and gotten suspicious. Najjar, cooler than David would have expected under the circumstances, bowed his head and began to pray. David admired his courage. The worse things got, the calmer the man became.

The siren and flashing lights were getting closer. David turned the wheel, jumped the curb, pulled Najjar's car off the congested street and onto the sidewalk, and hit the accelerator. Pedestrians started screaming and diving out of the way as David plowed through trash cans. The police cruiser was left in the dust, and David let himself smile.

The escape, however, was momentary. By the time they reached Qalani Street and took a hard left, another police cruiser was waiting. David wove in and out of traffic, but despite blowing through one light after another, he was steadily losing ground. Najjar was not praying anymore. He was craning his neck to see what was happening behind them and urging David to go faster. The road ahead was coming to an end. David suggested Najjar grab the door handle and brace for impact.

"Why?" Najjar asked at the last moment. "What are you going to do?"

David never answered. Instead, he slammed on the brakes and turned the steering wheel hard to the right, sending the car screeching and spinning across four lanes of traffic.

They were hit twice. The first was by the police cruiser itself. The second was by a southbound delivery truck that never saw them coming. The air bags inside Najjar's car exploded upon impact, saving their lives but filling the vehicle with smoke and fumes. But theirs was not the only collision. In less than six seconds, David had triggered a seventeen-car pileup on Azizi Boulevard, shutting down traffic in all directions.

David quickly unfastened his seat belt. "You okay?" he asked.

"Are we still alive?"

"We are," David said, checking his new friend for serious injuries. "We made it."

"Are you insane?"

"We needed a diversion."

David couldn't get out his own door. It had been too badly mangled. So he climbed into the backseat, which was littered with shards of broken glass, and kicked out the back passenger-side door. He jumped out of the car and surveyed the scene. It was a terrible mess in both directions.

The police car was a smoldering pile of wreckage. Gasoline was leaking everywhere. David feared a single spark could blow the whole thing sky high. Inside, the solitary officer was unconscious.

Using all of his strength, David pried the driver's-side door open and checked the man's pulse. Fortunately, he was still alive, but he had an ugly gash on his forehead, and his face was covered in blood. David pocketed the officer's .38-caliber service revolver and portable radio. Then he pulled the officer far from the wreckage and laid him down on the sidewalk.

David hobbled back to Najjar's car, realizing his right knee had gotten banged up worse than he'd first realized. He looked down and noticed his pants were ripped and that blood was oozing from his leg.

"You ready to move?" David asked, coming over to the passenger side.

"I think so," Najjar said, his arms filled with the laptop and accessories.

"Good. Follow me."

They walked north about a hundred meters. Then David turned, pulled out the .38, aimed at the gas tank of Najjar's crumpled Fiat, and pulled the trigger. The car erupted in a massive ball of fire that not only obliterated the vehicle but all traces of their fingerprints and DNA as well.

"What was that for?" a stunned Najjar asked, shielding his eyes from the intense heat of the flames.

David smiled. "Insurance."

★ ★ ★ ★ ★

David walked north down the center of Azizi Boulevard.

He limped his way past wrecked cars and distraught motorists fixated on the fire and smoke, with Najjar close behind. He clipped the police radio to his belt and put in the earphone. Just then, his phone vibrated. It was a text message from his CIA colleague, Eva Fischer, telling him to call their boss, Jack Zalinsky, in the secure mode. He did so right away, but it was Eva who actually picked up.

"Have you gone insane? The entire Global Operations Center is watching you via a Keyhole satellite. What are you doing?"

The chatter on the police radio suddenly intensified. "I can't really talk now," David said. "Do you need something?"

"I found you a plane," she said. "It'll be in Karaj tonight."

Suddenly shots rang out, shattering a windshield beside them. Instinctively David hit the ground and pulled Najjar down with him between a Peugeot and a Chevy, dropping his phone as he did. People started screaming and running for cover. He could hear Eva yelling, *"What is that? What's going on?"* but he had no time to respond. He grabbed the phone and jammed it into his pocket. Ordering Najjar to stay on the ground, he pulled the revolver and tried to get an angle on whoever was shooting at them.

Two more shots rang out, blowing out the windshield of the Peugeot. David again flattened himself to the ground and covered his head to protect himself from the flying glass. He could see under the cars that someone was moving toward him. He got up and took a peek. Another shot whizzed by him and ripped into the door of the Chevy.

Dead ahead, maybe ten yards away, was a garbage truck. David made sure Najjar was okay, then made a break for the back end of the truck. His movement drew more fire. But it also gave him a chance to see who was doing the shooting. The blue jacket and cap were the giveaway. This was a Tehran city police officer.

Then the officer's voice crackled over the radio.

"Base, this is Unit 116. I'm at the crash site. One officer is down with multiple injuries. Witnesses say they saw someone steal the officer's service revolver. I'm currently pursuing two suspects on foot. Shots fired. Requesting immediate backup."

"Unit 116, this is Base—roger that. Backup en route. Stand by."

This was not good. David crept along the side of the garbage truck, hoping to outflank the officer from the right, then stopped suddenly when he heard the sounds of crunching glass just a few yards ahead.

David tried to steady his breathing and carefully choose his next move as the footsteps got closer and closer. He could hear more sirens rapidly approaching. He was out of time. He took three steps and pivoted around the front of the truck, aimed the .38, and prepared to pull the trigger. But it was not the officer. It was a little girl, no more than six, shivering and scared.

How did she get here? Where is her mother?

Three more shots rang out. David dropped to the ground and covered the girl with his body. He took off his jacket and wrapped her in it, then got back in a crouch and tried to reacquire the officer in his sights.

But now there were two.

David had a clean shot at one of them, but he didn't dare fire from right over the child. He broke right, hobbling for a blue sedan just ahead. Once again, gunfire erupted all around him. David barely got himself safely behind the sedan. He gritted his teeth and caught his breath, then popped his head up again to assess the situation. One of the officers was running straight toward David, while the other started running toward Najjar. David didn't hesitate. He raised the revolver and squeezed off two rounds. The man collapsed to the ground no more than six yards from David's position.

David had no time to lose. Adrenaline coursing through his system, he made his way to the first officer, grabbed the revolver from his hand, and sprinted toward the second officer. Racing through the maze of cars, he approached the garbage truck, stopped quickly, and glanced around the side. The second officer was waiting for him and fired. David pulled back, waited a beat, then looked again and fired.

The man fired three more times. David dove behind the Chevy, then flattened himself against the ground and fired under the car at the officer's feet. One of the shots was a direct hit. The man fell to the ground, groaning in pain. David heard him radioing for help and giving his superiors David's physical description. Then, before David realized what was happening, the officer crawled around the front of the Chevy, took aim at David's head, and fired again. David instinctively leaned right but the shot grazed his left arm. He righted himself, took aim, and squeezed off two more rounds at the officer's chest, killing the man instantly.

David's mobile phone rang, but he ignored it. They had to get out of there. They couldn't let themselves be caught. But Najjar was nowhere to be found.

Again his phone rang, but still he ignored it. Frantic, David searched for Najjar in, behind, and around car after car. This time, his phone vibrated. Furious, he checked the text message only to find this message from Eva: 3rd bldg on rt.

David suddenly got it. He glanced up in the sky, thankful for Eva and her team watching his back from two hundred miles up. He made his way up the street to the third apartment building on the right. His gun drawn, he slowly edged his way toward the entrance.

David risked a quick peek into the lobby.

Najjar was there, but he was not alone. On the marble floor next to him were the laptop and accessories. And in Najjar's arms was the six-year-old girl from the street. He was trying to keep her warm and telling her everything would be all right.

David began to breathe again. "Didn't I tell you not to move?"

"I didn't want her to get hit," Najjar said.

David wiped blood from his mouth. "We need to go."

★ ★ ★ ★ ★

At the safe house, David dressed Najjar's wounds.

Najjar ate a little and fell fast asleep. David unlocked a vault stacked with communications gear and uploaded everything on Dr. Saddaji's laptop, external hard drive, and DVD-ROMs to Langley, with encrypted copies cc'd to Zalinsky and Fischer. Then he typed up his report of all that had happened so far and e-mailed the encrypted file to Zalinsky and Fischer as well.

At six the next morning, word came that the plane had arrived. David woke Najjar, loaded the computer equipment into a duffel bag, and took the bag and the scientist to the garage downstairs. Ten minutes later, they arrived at the edge of the private airfield.

David pointed to the Falcon 200 business jet on the tarmac. "There's your ride," he said.

"What about you?" Najjar asked. "You're coming too, aren't you?"

"No."

"But if they find out you were connected to me, they will kill you."

"That is why I have to stay."

Najjar shook David's hand and held it for a moment, then got out of the car, duffel bag in hand, and ran for the plane. David watched him go. He wished he could stay and watch the plane take off as the sun rose brilliantly in the east. But he couldn't afford the risk. He had to dispose of the Renault he was now driving, steal another car, and get back to Tehran.

★ ★ ★ ★ ★

SUNDAY
MARCH 6
(IRAN TIME)

1

ISLAMABAD, PAKISTAN

"I have come to reestablish the Caliphate."

At any other time in history, such an utterance could have come only from the lips of a madman. But Muhammad Ibn Hasan Ibn Ali said it so matter-of-factly, and with such authority, that Iskander Farooq was tempted not to challenge the notion.

"I have come to bring peace and justice and to rule the earth with a rod of iron," he continued. "This is why Allah sent me. He will reward those who submit. He will punish those who resist. But make no mistake, Iskander; in the end, every knee shall bow, and every tongue shall confess that I am the Lord of the Age."

The satellite reception was crystal clear. The voice of the Promised One—the Twelfth Imam, or Mahdi—was calm, his statements airtight, Iskander Farooq thought as he pressed the phone to his ear and paced back and forth along the veranda of his palace overlooking northeastern Islamabad. He knew what the Mahdi wanted, but every molecule in his body warned him not to accede to his demands. They were not presented as demands, of course, but that's precisely what they were—and while the Mahdi made it all sound wise and reasonable, Farooq heard an edge of menace in the man's tone, and this made him all the more wary.

The early morning air was bitterly and unusually cold. The sun had not yet risen over the pine trees and paper mulberries of the Margalla Hills, yet Farooq could already hear the chants of the masses less than a block away. *"Give praise to Imam al-Mahdi!"* they shouted again and again. *"Give praise to Imam al-Mahdi!"*

3

A mere hundred tanks and a thousand soldiers and special police forces now protected the palace. Only they kept the crowds—estimated at over a quarter of a million Pakistanis—from storming the gates and seizing control. But how loyal were they? If the number of protesters doubled or tripled or worse by dawn, or by lunchtime, how much longer could he hold out? He had to make a decision quickly, Farooq knew, and yet the stakes could not be higher.

"What say you?" the Mahdi asked. "You owe me an answer."

Iskander Farooq had no idea how to respond. As president of the Islamic Republic of Pakistan, the fifty-six-year-old former chemical engineer was horrified that Tehran had suddenly become the seat of a new Caliphate. Though the Mahdi had not formally declared the Iranian capital as the epicenter of the new Islamic kingdom, every Muslim around the world certainly suspected this announcement was coming soon. Farooq certainly did, and it infuriated him. Neither he, nor his father, nor his father's father had ever trusted the Iranians. The Persian Empire had ruled his ancestors, stretching in its day from India in the east to Sudan and Ethiopia in the west. Now the Persians wanted to subjugate them all over again.

True, Iran's shah had been the first world leader to formally recognize the independent state of Pakistan upon its declaration of independence in 1947. But it had been a brief window of friendliness. After Ayatollah Ruhollah Khomeini had come to power in 1979, tensions between the two states had spiked. Khomeini had led an Islamic Revolution that was thoroughly Shia in all its complexions, and this had not sat well with the Pakistanis. Neither Farooq nor his closest advisors—nor anyone he had known growing up—had ever believed that the Twelfth Imam was coming to earth one day or that such a figure would actually be the Islamic messiah or that he would usher in the end of days, much less that Sunnis would end up joining a Caliphate led by him. Farooq's teachers had all mocked and ridiculed such notions as the heresy of the Shias, and Farooq had rarely given the matter any thought.

Now what was he to believe? The Twelfth Imam was no longer some fable or myth, like Santa Claus for the pagans and Christians or the tooth fairy for children everywhere. Now the Mahdi—or someone claiming to be the Mahdi—was here on the planet. Now this so-called Promised One was taking the Islamic world by storm, electrifying the masses and instigating insurrections wherever his voice was heard.

More to the point, this "Mahdi" was now on the other end of this satellite phone call, requesting—or more accurately, *insisting upon*— Farooq's fealty and that of his nation.

★   ★   ★   ★   ★

SYRACUSE, NEW YORK

David Shirazi faced the most difficult decision of his life.

On the one hand, despite being only twenty-five years old, he was one of only a handful of NOCs—nonofficial cover agents—in the Central Intelligence Agency who had an Iranian heritage. He was fluent in Farsi and had proven he could operate effectively and discreetly inside the Islamic Republic. He had no doubt, therefore, that he was about to be ordered to go back inside Iran within the next forty-eight to seventy-two hours, given how rapidly things were developing.

On the other hand, David simply wasn't convinced that the American administration was serious about stopping Iran from building an arsenal of nuclear weapons or stopping the Twelfth Imam from using them. In his view, President William Jackson was a foreign policy novice.

Yes, Jackson had lived in the Muslim world. Yes, he'd studied and traveled extensively in the Muslim world. Yes, Jackson believed he was an expert on Islam, but David could see the man was in way over his head. Despite years of hard evidence to the contrary, Jackson still believed he could negotiate with Tehran, just as the US had done with the nuclear-armed Soviet Empire for decades. He still believed economic sanctions could prove effective. He still believed the US could contain or deter a nuclear Iran. But the president was dead wrong.

The truth was chilling. David knew that Iran was being run by an apocalyptic, genocidal death cult. They believed the end of the world was at hand. They believed their Islamic messiah had come. They believed that Israel was the Little Satan, that the US was the Great Satan, and that both needed to be annihilated in order for the Twelfth

Imam to build his Caliphate. David had done the research. He'd met with and extensively interviewed the most respected Iranian scholar on Shia Islamic eschatology. He'd read the most important books on the topic written by Shia mullahs. He had found Iran's top nuclear scientist and smuggled him and his family out of the country. He had documented everything he had seen and heard and learned in detailed memos to his superiors at Langley. He had argued that they were severely underestimating the influence Shia End Times theology was having on the regime.

He knew at least some of his work had made it to the Oval Office. Why else was he being asked to come to Washington for a meeting with President Jackson at noon tomorrow? But he wasn't convinced he was getting through. Why should he risk his life and go back inside Iran if his superiors didn't understand the gravity of the situation and weren't willing to take decisive measures to neutralize the Iranian threat before it was too late?

★ ★ ★ ★ ★

ISLAMABAD, PAKISTAN

"I appreciate your very gracious invitation," Farooq replied.

Trying not to appear to be stalling for time, though that was precisely what he was doing, he added, "I look forward to discussing the matter with my Cabinet later today and then with the full parliament later this week."

Events were moving far too quickly for his liking. Someone had to drag his feet and slow things down. To Farooq's shock, he had watched as his dear friend Abdullah Mohammad Jeddawi, king of Saudi Arabia, had actually fallen prostrate before the Twelfth Imam on worldwide television, then publicly announced that the Saudi kingdom was joining the new Caliphate. Worse, Jeddawi had even offered the cities of Mecca or Medina to be the seat of power for the new Islamic kingdom should the Mahdi deem either of them acceptable. How was that possible? Despite his divinely appointed role as commander of the faithful and custodian of the holy sites, Jeddawi—a devout Sunni Muslim—had offered no resistance to the Shia Mahdi, no hesitation, no push back whatsoever. Farooq could not imagine a more disgraceful moment, but the damage was done, and in the hours since, the dominoes had continued falling one by one.

The prime minister of Yemen, a good and decent man whom Farooq had known since childhood, had called the Mahdi late last night to say his country would join the Caliphate, according to a report on Al Jazeera. Now the Gulf-based satellite news service was reporting that Qatar was also joining, a dramatic change from just twenty-four hours earlier. So were Somalia and Sudan. Algeria was in. The new government of Tunisia said they were "actively considering" the Mahdi's invitation to join the Caliphate. So was the king of Morocco. The Shia-dominated, Hezbollah-controlled government of Lebanon had made no formal announcement but was meeting in emergency session at that very moment. Turkey's parliament and prime minister were reportedly gathering the next day to discuss the Mahdi's invitation.

To their credit, the Egyptians under President Abdel Ramzy were resisting. So were the Iraqis and the Sunni king of Bahrain. These were good signs, but Farooq wasn't convinced they would be good enough. Syrian president Gamal Mustafa in Damascus was silent thus far, but Farooq had little doubt he, too, would soon cave.

"Is there a reason for this hesitation I perceive in you?" the Mahdi asked.

Farooq paused and considered his words carefully. "Perhaps only that this has all come so suddenly, and I do not know you, have not heard your heart, have not discussed your vision for our region or what role you envision Pakistan playing."

"History is a river, my son, and the current is moving rapidly."

"All the more reason that we should take caution," Farooq replied, "lest we be swept away by events beyond our control."

"Do you have a request of me?" the Mahdi asked. "If so, make it now."

Farooq struggled to find the right words. He had no desire to meet this pretender to the throne. He had more important things to do than to waste his precious time with a man so clearly consumed with blind arrogance and ambition. But Farooq knew full well that he was now walking through a minefield and that he had to be judicious with every step.

He looked out across the city and marveled at the majestic parliament building to his right and the ornate Islamic architecture of the supreme court facility to his left. Both served as tangible reminders of the great civilization over which he now presided. He dared not gamble with his nation's sovereignty, much less his people's dignity and honor. He felt a tremendous burden upon his shoulders. He governed more than 185 million Muslims. Precious few of them were Shias, like the Mahdi who had awoken him from his slumber at this ungodly hour. The vast majority of them were Sunnis, like him. Most were devout. Some were passionate. Some were fanatics. A week ago, Farooq would never have imagined that any of them would embrace the teachings about the Mahdi, much less take to the streets to call for Pakistan to join the Caliphate with the Twelfth Imam as its leader. But now the people were on the move.

From Karachi to Cairo to Casablanca, millions of Muslims—Shias and Sunnis alike—were on the streets demanding change, demanding the immediate downfall of "apostate regimes" like his own, demanding that the *ummah*, the community of Muslims around the world, join forces to create a new, unified, borderless kingdom, a new Caliphate stretching from Pakistan to Morocco.

And that was just the beginning. The masses wanted what the Twelfth Imam was preaching: a global Caliphate in which every man, woman, and child on the face of the planet converted to Islam or perished in a day of judgment.

It was lunacy, Farooq thought. Sheer lunacy. Yet he dared not say so. Not yet. Not now. To do so, he knew, would be political suicide. Abdel Ramzy could publicly defy the Mahdi from his secure perch on the banks of the Nile, backed by all that American money and weaponry. But one word in public from the Mahdi that he was unhappy with the "infidel of Islamabad," and Farooq knew he would have a full-blown and bloody revolution on his hands. The protesting masses—notably peaceful in their first twenty-four hours—could very well turn violent.

He had seen it before. He had been part of such mobs before, back in his youth. If that happened, he genuinely doubted the military would stand with him, and then what?

"I appreciate your call very much, Your Excellency," Farooq told the Mahdi. "There are a few more questions I have, ones that I would prefer not to discuss over the phone. Perhaps we could meet in person? Would that be acceptable to you?"

"It must be soon. Coordinate details with Javad."

"Very well, Your Excellency," Farooq said before being put on hold.

As he waited for Javad Nouri, the Mahdi's personal aide, to come on the line, Farooq tried not to think about the consequences if he were deposed and his nation descended into anarchy. If he didn't bide his time and plan his steps very carefully, this self-appointed Twelfth Imam would soon gain control of his beloved Pakistan, and with it, control of 172 nuclear warheads—the nation's entire arsenal—and the ballistic missiles to deliver them.

2

QUEENS, NEW YORK

Air Force One was now on final approach.

As they descended through the clouds into John F. Kennedy International Airport, the military crew and Secret Service detail on board the presidential jumbo jet were unaware of the threat materializing on the ground below. For them, this was just another mission, carefully scripted and exacting in detail, one of hundreds of similar missions they flew every year for their commander in chief. Thus far it was indistinguishable from the rest. Half a world away, tensions were mounting, to be sure, but for now, in the blue, cloudless skies over the Big Apple, they had a beautiful Sunday afternoon with unlimited visibility and unusually warm temperatures for the first week of March.

Flying over the Bedford-Stuyvesant section of Brooklyn, the pilots could see Runway 13R—at more than fourteen thousand feet, one of the longest commercial runways in North America—three miles ahead and closing fast. "Wheels down" was scheduled for 5:06 p.m. eastern time, and they were on track for another picture-perfect, on-time landing. All other air traffic was on hold. Ground traffic at JFK was on hold. Marine One and her crew were on standby.

"It's time, Mr. President."

Special Agent Mike Bruner, thirty-eight, head of the president's protective detail, made sure he had his boss's attention. Then he stepped out and quietly closed the door behind him, leaving the leader of the free world alone with his thoughts.

William James Jackson, about to turn fifty, fastened his seat belt, adjusted the air vent above him, and looked out the bulletproof window at the strobe lights guiding them in. They were now steadily descending over Queens. He could see Jamaica Bay off to his right, but none of it registered. It was all a blur. Having just finished reading the latest eyes-only briefing paper sent to him by the Central Intelligence Agency, the only thing he could think about was Iran.

According to the Agency's best analysts—including their top man inside Tehran, an agent code-named Zephyr—the mullahs had done it. They had crossed the threshold. They had built an atomic bomb. And they had just successfully tested it near the city of Hamadan. The world had just taken a very dark turn.

Now what? Would Israel respond? Should his own administration? The sobering reality that he had no answers made him physically ill.

To the world, he would put on a brave face—particularly tonight. In less than an hour, he would headline a black-tie fund-raiser for 1,500 well-heeled donors in the posh grand ballroom of the Waldorf-Astoria. It was going to be an exceptionally rare evening, and the photos would dominate the front pages of newspapers around the world. Joining him would be both Israeli prime minister Asher Naphtali and Egyptian president Abdel Ramzy. Together they would explain the urgency of striking a comprehensive peace deal between Israel and the Palestinians once and for all. Together they would call on men and women of goodwill to hold fast against the forces of extremism, particularly in the Middle East. Together they would raise nearly $8 million in a single evening to complete construction of the new Anwar Sadat Institute for Peace in Cairo. The center had been in the planning for nearly two years. The fund-raiser had been in the works for eleven months. The timing could not have been more appropriate, Jackson believed. They had to present a united front. They had to believe peace was possible, no matter how impossible it seemed. They had to reach through the television cameras to a billion Muslims and appeal to the better angels of their nature.

But would it be enough? Despite his optimistic can-do visage, Jackson feared he wasn't ready for what was coming. He wasn't sure anyone was.

He had graduated first in his class at MIT. He held a master's in international relations from Oxford and read voraciously, mostly history and classic literature. He was fluent in French and conversational in Arabic, having studied for a year at the American University in Cairo as an undergraduate. He had traveled the globe extensively, particularly in the Muslim world. He certainly understood Islam better than any American president in living memory, perhaps in the nation's history. But this was not why he had run. The tasks already on his plate were daunting enough. He had an economy to fix, millions of jobs to create, an out-of-control budget to balance, an approval rating to boost, a hostile opposition party to silence, and his own party to placate and rebuild. This was no time for another war. The people hadn't sent him to Washington to accept—much less launch—another trillion-dollar Mideast adventure. The nation wouldn't stand for it. Nor would he.

At the same time, Jackson was palpably aware that he was no longer in control of events. The situation in the Middle East was teetering on the edge of disaster and was beginning to consume the White House's already-limited bandwidth. He couldn't ignore it. He couldn't wish it away. Just that morning, he had spent more than five hours with his National Security Council when he should have been meeting with his Council of Economic Advisors or the Fed chair. Jackson was increasingly aware of the broad range of grave threats now forming against the United States and her allies. One thing he knew for certain was that his entire agenda—his entire reason for running for president in the first place—was in peril unless he could navigate a way out of this latest Middle East disaster, and fast.

★　★　★　★　★

Firouz answered his cell phone on the first ring.

"They just touched down," a voice at the other end said.

Firouz thanked the caller, hung up, then turned to his men. "Rahim, Jamshad, come with me. Navid, you know what to do."

"Six o'clock," Navid said.

"Not a minute later."

"Don't worry, Firouz. I'll be there."

Firouz grabbed his gear from the back of the rented SUV and motioned for the other two to follow him out of the parking garage to the bank of elevators. It felt good to be out, good to be moving after waiting in that parking garage for nearly six hours.

A moment later, they were out on street level, crossing East Fiftieth Street to the alley behind the Colgate-Palmolive Building. The streets around them, blocked off for half a mile in every direction, were empty. From their vantage point, there was not a soul to be seen. It was eerily quiet, save for the sound of an NYPD helicopter making another sweep overhead. And it was unseasonably warm. The snow was all gone now. The temperature topped sixty. Firouz couldn't stop sweating.

Using a passkey they had pickpocketed off a janitor the night before—he wouldn't miss it until the next morning at the earliest—they slipped into the Colgate building through a service entrance. They proceeded directly to the stairwell and double-timed it to the corner office on the fourth floor.

"Stay away from the windows," Firouz reminded them in a whisper, "and don't turn on the lights."

★ ★ ★ ★ ★

The gleaming blue-and-white 747 taxied for a few moments.

When the front wheels came to a halt on the white X taped on the tarmac by the White House advance team, Secret Service agents and a contingent of New York's finest moved in to secure the perimeter. The stairs were lowered. A greeting party stepped out of a nearby terminal and took up their positions. Marine One began powering up, just a hundred yards away.

"Renegade is moving," Agent Bruner said, surveying the scene and coming down the ramp behind Jackson.

"It's good to see you again, Mr. President." New York mayor Roberto Diaz shook Jackson's hand vigorously and shouted to be heard over the roar of the green-and-white VH-3D Sea King. There was bad blood between the two. Diaz hadn't endorsed Jackson in the primaries even after privately promising that he would. But Diaz's approval rating in the Big Apple was in the sixties. Jackson's was in the forties. If Jackson was going to run again, he needed New York, which meant he needed Diaz. Which meant he needed to make amends.

"You, too, my friend—thanks for all you did on this thing."

"It is my honor, Mr. President. Anwar Sadat is one of my personal heroes. Anything my good offices can do to spread his legacy of peace and reconciliation, especially at this time, well, I'm in."

"Very good. So, full house tonight?" Jackson asked, now shaking hands with several city councilmen and their wives, who had joined the mayor.

"Standing room only, sir."

"And we're going to get the $8 million you promised?"

"No, sir, I'm afraid we're not."

Jackson finished shaking hands and turned back to the mayor, trying to mask his displeasure. "Why not? I don't understand."

"Looks like we'll hit $10 million instead."

Jackson broke into his trademark smile, then began to laugh. "Good work, Roberto," he said, slapping the mayor on the back. "Very good. Come on, my friend, ride with me."

The two men made their way to the helicopter and climbed aboard. A moment later, they were airborne.

★　★　★　★　★

Any idiot could use them, which was what made them so deadly.

The unclassified version of the US Army's training manual on them was even on the Internet, for crying out loud. But that wasn't where Firouz and Rahim had learned to use rocket-propelled grenades. They had been specially trained by the Iranian Revolutionary Guard Corps in Dasht-e Kavir, the great salt desert of south-central Iran. In fact, they had become so proficient in inflicting severe damage and large numbers of casualties in various IRGC operations that they had been sent into Iraq to train members of the Mahdi Army to use RPGs against Iraqi forces and Americans. Neither man had ever imagined the honor of being sent to the heart of the Great Satan to apply their craft against the president of the United States. But they were ready.

On the floor before them lay two Russian-designed RPG-7V2 launchers, along with six 105mm TBG-7V thermobaric warheads. Specially designed for antipersonnel and urban warfare operations, thermobaric weapons were essentially fuel-air bombs, built to dramatically expand and intensify the blast wave of a standard RPG. The goal was not so much to destroy a car, truck, or tank with one of these—though that was likely too—but to kill as many people as possible. Firouz thought they'd be lucky to get off three shots before someone stopped them, but he had ordered that six be smuggled across the Mexican and Canadian borders through various channels, hoping that at least three would make it into the US. He'd been stunned when he had arrived the night before to learn that all six had arrived without a scratch on them.

Firouz and Rahim went to work checking every detail. Soon they were loading the weapons and checking their watches. Jamshad, meanwhile, patrolled the hallways with a silencer-equipped pistol, making certain no one stumbled in. It was Sunday. No one was working. But they weren't taking any chances. The stakes were too high.

"Nighthawk is inbound. Hold all radio traffic."

Three identical choppers flew low and fast over the East River. Any of them could have been Marine One; only a handful of senior government officials knew which one actually carried the president at that moment. And that was precisely how Mike Bruner wanted it. No surprises. Just one evening event, a late-night return flight to DC, and he'd be having breakfast in the morning with his young wife.

As he sat directly behind his commander in chief, Bruner stared out the window and went through his mental checklist of all that would happen on the ground in just a few moments. In a city of eight million people, he knew it was impossible to safeguard against the possibility, however remote, of terrorists acquiring shoulder-mounted ground-to-air missiles and trying to shoot down the president's chopper. Even though each of the Marine helicopters was equipped with state-of-the-art countermeasures, the safest bet—and it was a bet, though so far it had always paid off—was to create uncertainty. Bruner and his colleagues believed it would be difficult for al Qaeda or other terrorist groups to obtain and smuggle into the continental United States even one Stinger or its equivalent. Obtaining two was exponentially more difficult. Obtaining three or more, they believed, was virtually impossible. So even though each chopper cost about $150 million, and it cost about $27,000 an hour to operate all three, this was how it was done.

The heliport on East Thirty-Fourth Street had been closed down for the past three months for renovations, and the one at West Thirtieth Street had been the scene of a giant traffic accident a few hours earlier.

So one by one, the Marine choppers made their way to the Wall Street heliport and landed at the tip of the Financial District. A moment later, Nighthawk's side door opened, and Jackson and his entourage disembarked and headed to their assigned vehicles in the presidential motorcade lined up along Pier 6. Mayor Diaz and the councilmen were shown to a black SUV behind the lead vehicles. Jackson's chief of staff and press secretary joined a group of White House advance men in Halfback, the follow-up limousine. The president, meanwhile, stepped into Stagecoach, and Bruner quickly closed the door behind him.

"Renegade secure," the lead agent said, getting in the front passenger seat.

"Status check on Architect and Sphinx?" the command post director asked.

"They're inside with Renegade."

"So we're good to go?"

"We're good. Let's roll."

"Roger that. All posts, be advised. Freight Train moving. ETA to Roadhouse, fifteen minutes."

The motorcade began to move, and Bruner relaxed, if only imperceptibly. Moving the president by air worried him most, particularly over a city this size. But on the ground, in an eighteen-vehicle motorcade, riding inside a brand-new Cadillac specially built to exacting Secret Service specifications, Bruner felt safe. He always preferred to have the president buttoned up in the White House or Camp David. Home-field advantage was without question his ideal. But the limousine they were now in was impenetrable by small-arms fire, machine-gun fire, or even an antitank missile.

Sphinx was quiet. That was Bruner's code name for Egyptian president Abdel Ramzy. Architect was his designation for Israeli prime minister Asher Naphtali. Both leaders had arrived on earlier flights. Both were glad to be riding to the event with the president. But even while keeping his eyes on the police cars and motorcycles taking them up FDR Drive on the Lower East Side, Bruner couldn't help but notice that neither foreign leader wanted to talk about the fund-raiser to which they were heading.

★ ★ ★ ★ ★

"You need to hit the Iranians hard, fast, and now."

Jackson was taken aback. He had fully expected to hear the sentence on this trip, but he had expected Naphtali to be doing the requesting. To his surprise, however, the words came from Ramzy.

"Abdel," the president replied, "we must be patient."

"The time for patience is over, Mr. President," the octogenarian Egyptian leader insisted, his portable oxygen tank at his side. "The mullahs now have the Bomb. The Twelfth Imam has come. It means only one thing: they're going to use it, and they're going to use it soon. And when they do, millions of people are going to die. Mr. President, we have a moral obligation to prevent this catastrophe from happening. *You* have that obligation."

"You're getting ahead of yourself, Abdel. Our job is to make sure no one or nothing destabilizes the region."

"Mr. President, with all due respect, the Iranians have just tested an atomic bomb—illegally, I might add, as they signed the NPT."

"Yes, they tested," Jackson confirmed. "But we don't even know if the test was successful or not. We don't know how many bombs they have. There's a lot we don't know, which is why we need to keep our heads, try to ratchet down tensions in the region, and certainly not do anything provocative. That's why tonight is so important."

"Provocative?" President Ramzy asked. "Did you not see the television coverage out of Mecca? King Jeddawi was *bowing* to the Mahdi. *Bowing.* The Sunni leader of the House of Saud was lying prostrate before the Shias' so-called messiah. A nuclear-armed Iran and the oil-rich Saudis have formed a single country. Kuwait has just joined the party. And my intelligence chief says Prime Minister Azziz of the UAE will announce tomorrow that he has joined as well."

Jackson hadn't heard this about the Kuwaitis yet. "What about Bahrain?" he asked.

"I spoke to the king less than an hour ago," Ramzy said. "He's still with us. I was close to his father. The family trusts me. They will stick with us, but only if you come out strong and make it clear you're going to take action."

"What kind of action?" Jackson asked.

"You must take out the nuclear facilities from the air, Mr. President. You must hit the regime in Tehran as well. How else can you neutralize the threat?"

"You want me to raise $10 million tonight to finish building the Sadat Institute for Peace by announcing that I'm going to launch a first strike against Iran?"

"I'm not asking you to give up the element of surprise," Ramzy said, "but you have to lay the groundwork, and quickly. You have to make it clear just how dangerous a moment this is. And, Mr. President, I must tell you this—and, Asher, I'm sorry if this offends you, but it must be said—tomorrow Egypt will begin a nuclear weapons development program."

Jackson recoiled.

"We have no other choice," Ramzy pressed. "Egypt cannot be dictated to by the Twelfth Imam or whoever this charlatan is. We must be strong. We must be able to defend ourselves. It may be too late. But Egypt will not be a slave to anyone, least of all the Persians, least of all the Shias."

★ ★ ★ ★ ★

The cell phone rang again.

"Where are they?" Firouz asked.

"They're about to turn on East Forty-Second Street," said the young woman, another member of his team.

Firouz hung up. "Four minutes," he whispered to Rahim.

They checked their weapons one last time. This was it.

★ ★ ★ ★ ★

The president looked at Naphtali. "Did you two plan this little ambush together?" he asked, only half in jest.

The Israeli premier didn't smile. "There's no conspiracy; it wasn't necessary," Naphtali replied. "Abdel and I have been telling you for two years this was coming. We have both wanted you to hit Iran. We wanted your predecessor to hit Iran. Abdel's actually pushed for it harder than I have. You haven't been listening."

"I have been listening," Jackson insisted. "I just haven't liked what I've heard. The Indians have nukes. The Paks have nukes. Pyongyang has nukes. It happens. We can't always stop it. But nobody's crazy enough to use them. They're purely defensive. We can't go starting a war every time another country joins the nuclear club."

"Look, Bill, you and I have known each other for a long time," Naphtali countered. "I've always been honest and direct with you. Now listen to me. First of all, you've promised publicly and countless times that the United States would never allow Iran to acquire nuclear weapons. Well, now they have. Second, Muhammad Ibn Hasan Ibn Ali—this 'Twelfth Imam'—just might be crazy enough to use these weapons. He's not a Communist. He's not an atheist. He's not part of the Soviet politburo or some corrupt bureaucrat in Beijing. He thinks he's the messiah. He might even think he's a god. He just said he's trying to build a unified Islamic government. If he's successful, the Caliphate could stretch from Morocco to Indonesia. Who's going to stop him if you don't? Nobody. And remember: the Shias think the Twelfth Imam is *supposed* to use nukes. They believe that's why he's here—to bring an end to Judeo-Christian civilization, to end the era of the infidels, to bring about the end of days. He's already got millions of Muslims following him, and he's just emerged. Most of them think he's doing miracles, healings, and he's uniting Shias and Sunnis faster than any Muslim leader we've ever seen."

Jackson looked out the window, unconvinced but trying to stay calm.

Agent Bruner turned and looked back at him. "Two minutes, Mr. President."

Jackson nodded. They were almost at Roadhouse, the Waldorf-Astoria. But this was not the conversation he wanted to be having. He had scheduled a meeting for noon the following day with the director of central intelligence and his top Iran experts, including Zephyr, whom they had temporarily pulled out of Iran. They were going to review the latest intel and evaluate their options. But Jackson didn't enjoy being pushed into a corner. He didn't like to have his course of action dictated to him. He had come to New York to give a major address laying out a game plan for peace in the Middle East, not a new road map to war.

He turned back to Ramzy. "You're a good Muslim, Abdel," he said, looking the Egyptian Sunni in the eye. "You really think this guy wants to bring about the end of days?"

"There's no question in my mind," Ramzy replied. "Anyone who has studied Shia End Times theology—and I have in recent years because Hosseini and Darazi are so obsessed with it in Tehran; they seem to talk about it all the time—knows that the Twelfth Imam is going to hit Israel, the 'Little Satan,' first. Then he's going to hit you, America, because you're the 'Great Satan' in their view. He's going to hit you when and where you least expect it, and he's going to hit you in such a way that you'll never recover, in such a way that you'll be unable to ever hit back—which is why you need to hit Iran first. You have a very narrow window, Mr. President. History will not forgive us if we don't act right now. This is a rare convergence. Think of it. Arab leaders, starting with me, are willing right now to unite with America, even with Israel, against the Shias of Persia for one brief moment. It's never happened before in all of recorded history. But it's happening now. And if this moment slips away, if we squander it, if we miss our chance to stop Iran from unleashing a genocidal apocalypse, then I fear we are about to plunge into a thousand years of darkness."

4

Firouz could hear the sirens approaching.

The motorcade was almost there. It was time. He carefully poked his head up and looked across the street. To his left stood St. Bartholomew's Church, at the corner of Park Avenue and East Fiftieth Street. Straight ahead he could see the Park Avenue entrance of the Waldorf-Astoria. Using a laser range finder, he calculated the front doors at precisely 110 meters away, near-optimum distance for the weapon at his side and the one now in Rahim's hands.

Though his view was slightly obstructed by several trees growing in the median, there were no leaves on the trees this early in the year, which helped. When he had scoped out the twenty-five-story office building, he had briefly considered a higher office, above the trees and with a broader and arguably more commanding view of the street below. But in the end he had opted not to sacrifice distance for a clear sight line. He needed to be close. That was the primary issue. He couldn't see perfectly, but it would do.

The mob of media types was obvious enough in a roped-off area on the sidewalk to the right of the main doors. Reporters, still photographers, TV cameramen, and producers—they were all there, making final preparations of their own as the first of the police motorcycles rolled in. With red and blue lights flashing everywhere, Firouz counted a half-dozen NYPD uniformed officers standing with or near the press and another fifteen to twenty officers in key positions on both sides of the street, holding back a small crowd and making sure the adjacent streets remained sealed off. He also counted at least a dozen plainclothes agents, a mixture, he assumed, of the Secret Service, the State Department's Diplomatic Security Service, and the city's VIP protective unit, as well as Israeli Shin Bet and an Egyptian contingent.

Little did they know they were going to have a front-row seat.

★   ★   ★   ★   ★

The motorcade roared up East Forty-Seventh Street.

But Ramzy was not finished. As they turned right onto Park Avenue, the Egyptian leader explained that his intelligence services had two sources inside the royal palace in Riyadh. Neither knew the other's identity, but that morning, each of them—unbeknownst to the other—had sent urgent messages back to Cairo indicating that the Ayatollah Hosseini, Iran's Supreme Leader, had personally called the Saudi king twenty-four hours earlier and told him that Iran's nuclear weapons were operational and that one would be detonated on Saudi soil within the month if His Excellency didn't welcome the Twelfth Imam, show him proper deference, and prepare a lavish welcome ceremony in Mecca.

It was news to Naphtali, but Jackson was not impressed.

"The NSA picked up the same calls," he replied. "But if I had a dime for every lie Hosseini has told, the US wouldn't have a national debt."

"That's not the point, Mr. President," Ramzy pushed back.

"Then what is?"

"The Saudis—keepers of Mecca, keepers of Medina, commanders of the faithful—are being blackmailed by their worst enemies, the Persians. Why? Is it because King Jeddawi, the most devout Sunni Muslim on the planet, has suddenly, secretly converted to Shia Islam? No. It is because he is terrified for his life, for his riches, for his kingdom. He's convinced Iran has the Bomb, and that has changed everything. And now the neighboring nations will start to fall. First the Saudis, then the Kuwaitis, then the Emirates."

The car was silent for a moment, save Agent Bruner issuing commands on his wrist-mounted radio. Then the specially designed Cadillac pulled up to the Waldorf's famous art deco entrance and drew smoothly to a halt. A team of agents jumped out of two black SUVs in the rear of the motorcade and began taking up positions around Stagecoach and Halfback. Bruner issued more instructions, making sure all his men were in place, then turned and caught Jackson's attention.

"We're here, Mr. President."

"In a moment, Mike," Jackson replied. He had a question he wanted answered before they headed inside. Turning to Ramzy, he asked bluntly, "Abdel, tell me one thing. Why are you more obsessed than Asher here with this whole Twelfth Imam thing?"

Abdel paused for a moment, seeming surprised by the question. "I wouldn't call it an obsession, Mr. President. I don't think that's a fair characterization. Am I concerned? Yes. Deeply. But even more than that, I believe the pharaohs are watching me. I believe all my forefathers are watching me. I will go to them soon. This I know all too well. And when I see them face to face in the afterlife, I don't want to be received as the man who lost Egypt."

Jackson pondered that answer, and as he did, he discerned something he had never considered before. "It was you who ordered the assassination of Dr. Saddaji in Hamadan the other day," he said, looking Ramzy in the eye.

Until just a moment ago, Jackson had been convinced that Naphtali and the Mossad had been responsible for the car bombing that had killed Iran's top nuclear scientist just two weeks earlier.

Ramzy motioned out the window at Agent Bruner, ready to open the limousine's back door and usher them past the crowd of journalists and inside the Waldorf to greet the 1,500 guests eagerly anticipating their arrival. "They're waiting," the Egyptian said softly.

"So am I," the president said.

Ramzy looked back at both of them with a twinkle in his eye. "I actually don't know who did it exactly," he demurred. "It was a beautiful hit, I agree. But whoever ordered it waited too long. It should have been done six months ago."

There it was, Jackson realized. A classic nondenial denial. Ramzy wasn't formally accepting credit or blame, and yet he was. Six months earlier, Jackson remembered, the eighty-two-year-old Egyptian had been undergoing open-heart surgery. He had been bedridden nearly ever since. This was his first foreign trip in almost a year. But just because he hadn't been traveling didn't mean Abdel Mohammad Ramzy hadn't been on the move.

★ ★ ★ ★ ★

Firouz summoned Jamshad on his radio.

"Make sure the stairwell is clear."

"I'm on it."

"And make sure Navid is in place."

"Of course—absolutely."

Firouz then turned to his closest friend and nodded. Each man pulled a black balaclava ski mask over his face and donned protective eyewear.

"Are you ready, Rahim?"

"I serve at the pleasure of the Promised One, Firouz. And you?"

"Yes, my friend, and I count it an honor to complete this mission with you, of all people."

★ ★ ★ ★ ★

Agent Bruner saw Jackson give him the signal.

Immediately he opened the back door of the limo, which at nearly eight inches thick was as impenetrable as a vault door.

"Look sharp, everyone," he said into his radio, once again scanning the faces in the media section and the crowd across the street. "Renegade's moving."

The president stepped out of the car and smiled for the cameras. Then he turned back and helped President Ramzy out of the car as well, carrying his portable oxygen tank for him.

In the harsh glare of the TV lights, Ramzy looked even older than he was, Bruner thought. He moved slowly and with a limp. But to his surprise, even though he knew Ramzy hated the media and typically dodged the press at almost all costs, tonight the Egyptian president seemed drawn to the blizzard of photographs being taken. Indeed, even before the detail of Shin Bet agents could run up from the back of the motorcade, take their positions, and help Prime Minister Naphtali out of the limo, Ramzy hobbled over to the press section and actually took a question shouted out by the New York bureau chief for Al Jazeera.

"What is Sphinx doing?" one agent asked over the radio.

"I don't know," Bruner said, "but get two men up at his side—*now*."

★ ★ ★ ★ ★

Firouz poked his head up one more time.

It was a risk, he knew, but he had no choice. He had brought with him a portable Sony TV and a small satellite receiver. He'd been hoping to watch live coverage of the president's arrival. He'd hoped that would enable him to see precisely what was happening across the street. But none of the networks—American or foreign—was carrying it live, including Al Jazeera, and he was out of time.

Through a pair of high-powered binoculars, Firouz could see Ramzy talking to the press. It was a shocking sight. Firouz had grown up watching television coverage of Abdel Ramzy ruling Egypt with an iron fist. But he couldn't remember a single time the man had willingly spoken to the press corps. Still, it was a good development. It meant the three leaders would be motionless for a few moments, at least, and that was all they needed.

Firouz scanned further and could see President Jackson a few steps to the Egyptian's left, closer to the front door of the hotel, which someone was holding open. He could see two Secret Service agents beside the president and several more just a few steps back. There were other men in suits standing there too. One of them looked like Prime Minister Naphtali. Firouz couldn't be sure, not with the trees obstructing his vision. He desperately wanted absolute confirmation. He realized he should have positioned someone on the ground, another spotter who could have given him more information from a better vantage point. But this was it. He didn't dare wait any longer. They'd never have a better opportunity than the one now before them.

"Now!" Firouz shouted.

Both men yelled praise to Allah. Then, across the room, Rahim detonated two small packages of explosives the two men had installed on the windows, blowing them out instantly. In a seamless motion, Rahim jumped to his feet. Ignoring the shattering glass, he aimed his RPG-7 at the crowd across the street and pulled the trigger.

5

Ramzy heard something behind him.

Distracted, sensing something was amiss, he turned to see what was happening. At that moment, he heard glass shattering on the sidewalk across the street. He found his dimming eyes drawn to the fourth floor, to the corner office. He saw the flash and the rocket emerging from the window, slicing through the trees, and heading straight for them.

★ ★ ★ ★ ★

Bruner heard the glass shatter behind him.

But unlike Ramzy, he didn't turn. He didn't need to see what was happening. Everything in him knew it was wrong.

Moving purely by instinct refined by years of training and fueled by a sudden burst of adrenaline, Bruner pivoted hard to his left. He grabbed the president and shoved the man through the Waldorf's entrance. Then he threw his body on top of Jackson just as a deafening explosion erupted behind them.

Looking back, he watched in horrified amazement as an enormous, searing ball of fire and smoke engulfed the crowd outside. Ramzy's oxygen tank exploded. Burning wood, molten glass, chunks of brick and plaster were flying everywhere. Huge flames—eight, maybe ten feet high—surged into the lobby, licking the ceiling and setting everything in their path ablaze. A huge glass chandelier came crashing down just yards away from them.

Outside, Bruner could hear the shrieks of men and women being burned alive. He, too, was on fire, but for a split second he didn't feel a thing. All he could think about was getting the president to safety.

★ ★ ★ ★ ★

Rahim instantly dropped to the floor, taking cover.

But now Firouz was on his feet. He pointed the weapon in his hands out the shattered window and tried to aim at the door of the Waldorf. Everything was obscured by leaping flames and thick, black, acrid smoke, which the wind was blowing his way. His eyes began to sting and water even behind his goggles, causing him to hesitate for a moment. But only for a moment. Then, aiming into the center of the chaos, he pulled the trigger and fired anyway.

The nine-pound rocket-propelled grenade exploded from its launcher, and time almost stood still. Everything seemed to go in slow motion. Firouz watched the contrail. He saw the rocket arc over Park Avenue on a trajectory higher than he'd planned. But he wasn't worried. The impact still had its deadly effect. He saw the grenade slam into the hotel's exterior wall just above the press corps and erupt into another ghastly ball of fire and death. He could see part of the facade of the historic building beginning to crumble. Better yet, he could hear the screams of the dying intensifying, mounting to a grisly crescendo that sent shivers of ecstasy down his spine.

For a moment, he found himself completely mesmerized by the scene of death and destruction below. But then he heard Rahim screaming at him to get down, and he snapped back to his senses and hit the deck.

Rahim had already reloaded and was back on his feet. Firouz watched as his comrade in arms scanned the scene, pivoted to the right, and pulled the trigger. He desperately wanted to see where the rocket was headed. He wished he could see the results. But at least he heard the explosion. He heard the wrenching sound of burning, twisted, crashing metal and the secondary detonation of a gas tank. He knew immediately that Rahim had fired at one of the Secret Service SUVs. The limousines, after all, were impervious to RPG fire. So Rahim had clearly done the next-best thing. He was faithful. He was fearless. He was striking a blow against the Great Satan in the heart of Manhattan. Soon the Twelfth Imam would know, as would the entire world.

★ ★ ★ ★ ★

Bruner could hear automatic gunfire outside.

He could also hear the squealing tires of Stagecoach and Halfback racing away from the scene. He had no idea what the status of President Ramzy or Prime Minister Naphtali might be. Had they died in the attacks? Had someone gotten them to safety? Given all that had just happened, he couldn't imagine how either man could have survived.

The smoke inside the hotel's entrance was thick and low. Above him, the sprinkler system had immediately activated. Water sprayed everywhere, but the entire lobby was still engulfed in flames. A fellow agent sprayed him and the president with a fire extinguisher. The pain on Bruner's back, legs, and arms was unlike anything he had ever experienced, far worse than the time his Humvee had been nearly blown to smithereens by an IED just outside of Baghdad. But Bruner refused to think of himself.

"Mr. President, are you all right?" he shouted above the commotion as he carefully turned Jackson over and quickly checked him for injuries.

The president didn't answer. He was coughing up blood.

★ ★ ★ ★ ★

The corner office erupted with gunfire.

Secret Service sharpshooters had found them. They laid down a withering blanket of suppressive fire, and Firouz felt a wave of fear ripple through him for the first time. He pressed himself to the floor, against the front wall—out of sight, or so he hoped—pleading with Allah for mercy.

But Rahim was not so lucky. Firouz looked on in horror as his best friend's body was ripped to shreds by dozens of the 7.26mm rounds that came crashing through the windows. He watched as Rahim collapsed to the ground, blood spraying everywhere, his eyes rolled back in his head. His first instinct was to crawl to Rahim's side to see if he was still alive, but the fire kept coming, and from a high angle—most likely from the roof of the Waldorf.

When the shooting paused—just for a moment—Firouz made his move. He scrambled across the floor and dove into the hall. Almost immediately the gunfire erupted again. But Firouz rolled around a corner unscathed. Breathing hard, his shirt soaked with sweat, he pulled a silencer-equipped pistol from his jacket, jumped to his feet, and raced for the stairwell.

★　★　★　★　★

"We're going to get you out of here, Mr. President."

Gritting his teeth, Bruner forced himself back to his feet. With the help of three other agents, he hauled Jackson to his feet as well. That was when he first saw the blood trickling down the side of the president's face. But this was no place to do a proper assessment. Parts of the ceiling were already starting to collapse. They had to move. Nearly choking on the smoke, Bruner considered their options. The flames were the thickest to their left and right. The only way forward was to head deeper inside the hotel. He had no idea who or what lay ahead, and he couldn't rule out the possibility of a multiple-front ambush. But at the moment, he didn't have a choice.

With their guns drawn, agents were racing toward them from all over the building. Bruner shouted orders to his men to surround and cover them and then began moving the president down the hall and around the corner to an unmarked freight elevator as quickly as they could. Inside, he hit the button for the basement level and cursed until the doors shut and they started descending.

"Six-One, Six-One, I have Renegade," Bruner shouted into his radio. "I repeat, I have Renegade. We are Code Red and inbound. Hold all radio traffic and prepare to evacuate immediately."

When the elevator door opened, they were met by four more agents brandishing Uzis. Together, they raced Jackson through the narrow passageway deep underneath the Waldorf until they reached Track 61. There, waiting for them, was an idling Metro-North train. It was already running and loaded with more heavily armed agents and a medical crew. Bruner got the president on board and directed his men to put him on the floor, out of sight. Two physicians began treating him immediately. But Bruner refused to be a sitting duck. He ordered the train to pull out.

The doors closed. The agents around them took up their preassigned positions. Engine One began to move. They had practiced this for years, beginning in 2002 when the Secret Service had run an extensive exercise using this escape route in the lead-up to President Bush's stay at the Waldorf during the opening session of the UN General Assembly.

But Bruner had never really imagined having to get the president of the United States to a secure, undisclosed location underneath Manhattan via the tracks leading to and from Grand Central Station. Now it was happening, and everything was moving so fast. People lay dead and dying above them. Friends of his. World leaders, perhaps.

Bruner realized his hands were covered in blood, and he could taste more blood in his mouth. Then he heard one of the doctors shouting for silence.

"The president's blood pressure is dropping fast."

SYRACUSE, NEW YORK

David Shirazi had been born for this moment.

With a photographic memory, a 3.9 GPA, and advanced degrees in computer science, the Syracuse native could have been recruited by the CIA's Technical Services Division or the Agency's information-management team and would have been exceptional working for either. Instead, fluent in Arabic, German, and Farsi—the language of his parents' native Iran—David had been recruited and trained to serve in the Agency's National Clandestine Service, formerly known as the directorate of operations.

For his first two and a half years in the field, he had served faithfully in a variety of posts inside Iraq, Egypt, and Bahrain. Each assignment had been fairly mundane, but they had proven good training grounds. They'd allowed him to make mistakes and learn from them, allowed him to learn from more-seasoned operatives in the region, and allowed him to understand the dynamics of Mideast politics and the rhythms of the "Arab street."

That said, his last assignment had been his most effective and personally rewarding to date. On orders from Langley, he had infiltrated Munich Digital Systems (MDS), getting himself hired by the German computer company, which developed and installed state-of-the-art software for mobile phone and satellite phone companies, and establishing himself as a young gun—hardworking and willing to take risks. He'd then been assigned by MDS as a technical advisor working closely with Mobilink, the leading telecommunications provider in Pakistan.

Once on the Mobilink account, David had done whatever it took to get the information asked of him by Langley. He'd penetrated Mobilink's databases, bought off key employees, hacked his way past advanced security protocols, and mined mountains of data until he began to track down the mobile phone numbers of suspected al Qaeda members operating on the Afghan-Pak borders or living in the shadows of Islamabad and Karachi. One by one, he began to funnel the numbers back to Langley. That allowed the National Security Agency to begin listening in on the calls made from those particular numbers and triangulating the locations from which they were being made. The goal, eventually, had been to track down and kill Osama bin Laden and his top associates, and they had gained real ground. In less than six months, David's efforts helped his colleagues capture or kill nine high-value targets. In the process, he got himself noticed on the seventh floor, the inner sanctum of the Agency's senior staff.

But during that time, the Agency's priorities had shifted significantly. While neutralizing bin Laden had certainly been high on the list at that time, at the top of the list was neutralizing Iran's ability to build, buy, or steal an arsenal of nuclear weapons. The Israelis were increasingly convinced that they were facing an existential threat from the mullahs in Tehran, that once Iran got the Bomb, they would launch it against Tel Aviv to make good on their repeated threats to "wipe Israel off the map." The Jackson administration was publicly committed to preventing Iran from acquiring such lethal capabilities. But David knew the president was privately worried even more about an Israeli first strike against Iran.

In January, Jackson had quietly signed a highly classified national intelligence directive authorizing the CIA "to use all means necessary to disrupt and, if necessary, destroy Iranian nuclear weapons capabilities in order to prevent the eruption of another cataclysmic war in the Middle East." The problem was that while the Agency had a half-dozen special operations teams on standby, ready at a moment's notice to sabotage nuclear facilities, intercept shipments of nuclear-related machinery and parts, facilitate the defection of nuclear scientists, and so forth, what it didn't have was someone inside giving them hard targets.

That was why David had been pulled out of Pakistan and sent inside Iran with orders that were as clear as they were nearly impossible to achieve: penetrate the highest levels of the Iranian regime, recruit assets, and deliver solid, actionable intelligence that could help sink or at least slow down Iran's nuclear weapons program. The good news was that in just a few short weeks, he had already impressed his superiors back at Langley with actual, measurable, demonstrative results, working with Iran Telecom and distributing specially engineered satellite phones to several key government officials. The bad news, from David's perspective, was that it was all too little, too late. The Iranians had just tested a nuclear warhead in a research facility in the mountains near the city of Hamadan, a facility previously unknown to the CIA. A figure claiming to be the Twelfth Imam, ostensibly resurrected from the ninth century, was convincing a rapidly growing force of Muslims throughout North Africa, the Middle East, and Central Asia that he was, in fact, the Islamic messiah, yet few inside the CIA had thus far taken seriously the notion of the coming of the Mahdi, much less understood the implications of his arrival to the region or US interests there. The president's wishes notwithstanding, Israeli leaders seemed poised to launch a preemptive strike at any moment, and David wasn't sure Prime Minister Naphtali was wrong to be moving in that direction. He vastly preferred that the US take the lead in stopping Iran, but the truth was the president didn't get it, and even the CIA—himself included—had been behind the curve for years. Now they were out of time.

David was seriously contemplating the possibility of resigning. But it wasn't merely political weakness and organizational inertia that weighed on him. His personal world was imploding.

For the past six and a half hours, David hadn't been briefing his superiors in the Bubble, the secure conference room on the seventh floor of CIA headquarters in northern Virginia. Nor had he been preparing his presentation for the White House Situation Room the following day. He hadn't been reviewing transcripts and recordings of the latest intercepts of phone calls, the fruit of his work in Iran.

He had, instead, been sitting at his mother's bedside at Upstate University Hospital in his hometown of Syracuse, New York, not far from the house he had grown up in. He was watching the woman who bore him, the woman he loved so dearly, steadily and rapidly deteriorate. She'd been battling stage 3 stomach cancer for months. In recent days, however, things had taken a turn for the worst. David was doing everything he knew to comfort her. He'd held her hand. He'd brought her ice chips. He'd filled the sterile hospital room with the yellow roses she so loved and read Persian poetry to her from a slim volume of verses that was the only personal possession his mother still had from her youth in Iran.

At the same time, David was trying—in vain, it seemed—to comfort his grieving father. He brought him fresh coffee every few hours with a splash of half-and-half and four cubes of sugar, just as he liked it. He returned all of his father's phone calls, working with his office to reschedule his many appointments for the next few days, and told his father again and again that somehow everything would be okay when he knew very well that wasn't true.

All the while, David silently cursed his two older brothers, who weren't here at all, despite his messages imploring them to come quickly. Azad was the serious one. A successful cardiologist like their father, Azad was a busy man, to be sure. But it wasn't as if he lived on the other side of the country, much less the planet. Azad lived in the suburbs of Philadelphia, for crying out loud. David had MapQuested it. He knew Azad's house was a mere 257 miles away, door to door. He had spoken to Nora, his brother's wife, just last night, with the only result being his further frustration.

"David, you know we'd be there if we could. We are grieving at this situation, but it's just impossible. Your brother is in back-to-back surgeries until late tomorrow afternoon. And I'm scheduled to be induced in two days. Once I'm settled in with the baby, Azad will come right away. He just wants to meet our child. Can't you understand, David? I know *Pedar* understands. *Maamaan* knows we love her."

How could it be that his mother's greatest dream—grandchildren—was preventing her from having her firstborn son by her side as she suffered?

Saeed, on the other hand, was the playboy of the family. He probably made more money than the rest of them combined, but he seemed to spend it as fast as it came in. He owned a lavish apartment in Manhattan, was always dating someone new and wasting his money by jetting off on extravagant vacations. Saeed hadn't been home in ages and only kept in touch if you counted the occasional text message. David didn't have the slightest idea why Saeed chose this frantic, rootless lifestyle. But he had given up trying to figure it out a long time ago.

All he knew was that as the youngest of the three boys, he had done almost an equally lousy job of being a loving, devoted son. None of them knew the life he was really living. None of them knew he worked for the CIA or that he was spending most of his time inside Iran. They all thought he was a computer programmer based in Munich, working sixteen to eighteen hours a day, traveling constantly, never having a girlfriend, with few serious prospects for getting married and having kids. Not that it mattered much to his brothers, but to his parents it mattered a great deal.

At least he felt guilty about it, David told himself. At least he had actually been home for the past few days, trying desperately to make up for lost time.

Yet he was palpably aware that he was not in control of events. Over the course of the past fifteen minutes or so, he had witnessed his mother slipping into a coma from which, the doctors explained, she would likely never recover. If that weren't painful enough, it was becoming increasingly clear that he was simultaneously watching his father slip into a deep depression.

"Excuse me, Mr. Shirazi?"

David was startled by the voice of a nurse at the door.

"Me or my father?" he asked.

"Are you David?" asked the older woman running the late afternoon shift.

"I am."

"You have a phone call at the nurses' station."

In all the sadness unfolding around him, David had completely forgotten that he'd turned his phone off when he had entered the hospital just before noon. Cell phones weren't permitted in the ICU. He thanked the head nurse, patted his father on the back, and whispered that he would be right back. His father, sitting in a chair beside his wife, face buried in his hands, barely responded.

David stepped into the hallway and around the corner. It felt good to stretch his legs, he thought as he reached for the phone, and good too to take his mind off his parents' troubles, if only for a moment. He hoped it was Azad, telling him he was on the road, that he'd rescheduled the surgeries and was heading north up 81 toward Syracuse, coming to give his younger brother some relief. Even more, he hoped it was Marseille, saying she'd gotten back to Portland safe and sound and wanted to catch up or just check in on his mom. Hers was the voice he needed to hear just then.

It wasn't to be.

7

"David, it's Jack—we need to talk."

Hearing the voice of his mentor and handler caught David off guard.

"*Jack?* What's the matter? You sound terrible."

"Not on this open line. Call me back secure. You know the number. And get somewhere private."

"Will do—I'll get right back to you."

David handed the phone to the nurse and headed quickly for the stairwell, powering up his Agency-issued phone on his way. Never had he heard Jack Zalinsky sound as rattled. Angry, frustrated, ticked off? More times than David cared to remember. But rattled? Not in all the years since Zalinsky first recruited him. You didn't spend four decades in the Central Intelligence Agency, much less climb the ladder from lowly field operative fresh out of training at the Farm to become clandestine operations manager of the Near East Division, without a cool head and ice in your veins.

David burst out an exit door to the roof and headed toward one of the large air-conditioning units, where he would be unlikely to be seen by anyone on the ground. He punched in a ten-digit clearance code to make his call secure, then speed-dialed Zalinsky's office number on the sixth floor at Langley.

"Jack, what's going on?"

"Are you alone?"

"I am."

"Are you watching the news?"

"No, I've been with my mom. Why? What's happening?"

"You need to get back to Washington immediately."

"I'm on the first flight out in the morning."

"No, tonight; something's happened."

"What?"

"There's been an attack."

"Where?"

"Manhattan."

David knew immediately it was the fund-raiser.

"The president—is he okay?"

"I don't know," Zalinsky said. "Not yet. But President Ramzy is dead."

David could feel his anger rising. "How? What happened?"

"We're still piecing it together," Zalinsky said. He explained the attack and the sequence of events leading up to it as best he understood it at the moment.

"What about Naphtali?" David asked. "Did he survive?"

"Miraculously, the prime minister escaped relatively unharmed— minor burns but nothing serious," Zalinsky replied.

"Thank God."

"I know. It's strange, actually. The president got out of the limo first and was followed by Ramzy. But as it happened, the terrorists fired the RPGs before Naphtali ever got out of the car. One of his Shin Bet guys was standing in front of the open door to the limo. When the first RPG hit, the agent was immediately engulfed in flames, but his body blocked most of the blast and he somehow managed to get the door closed, probably saving Naphtali's life. The driver immediately pulled away and got out of the kill zone."

"Where's the PM now?"

"On a flight back to Tel Aviv."

"And the Shin Bet agent?"

"Pronounced dead at the scene—one of forty-six, with another twenty-two wounded, most of them severely burned and unlikely to make it through the night."

David could barely comprehend what Zalinsky was telling him. The casualty count was horrifying enough, but so was the fact that the CIA had just failed the nation again. Another terrorist attack had just been unleashed on American soil—in the heart of New York City, no less—and the Agency not only hadn't done anything to stop it but hadn't even known it was coming. What else was coming? Who else was in the country, ready to strike?

These were the first thoughts running through his head, but more followed. David shuddered at the implications of Egypt's aging, ailing, authoritarian leader assassinated. The government of the world's largest and historically most stable Arab country had suddenly been decapitated. Who would take over? Would it be a peaceful transition of power? Having spent nearly a year working in Cairo, reporting first to the economic attaché and later directly to the CIA station chief in the Egyptian capital, he knew full well that President Ramzy had never developed a clear or orderly or legal transition plan. The old man had always wanted one of his sons to assume power when he was gone. But few others in the country wanted that—not the majority of the legislature, not the leaders of the Muslim Brotherhood, and certainly not most of the rank-and-file Egyptians. This raised the chilling prospect of a chaotic, even violent transition that risked igniting into a full-blown revolution in a country of eighty million, 90 percent of whom were Muslims, the vast majority of whom were deeply discontent. Such a revolution could be massively destabilizing. It could unravel the three-decade-plus-long peace treaty with the Israelis. It could theoretically bring leaders of the Muslim Brotherhood, or others sympathetic to the Radicals, to power. Such forces would almost certainly be willing, even eager, to build stronger alliances with Hamas, Hezbollah, and Iran to confront Israel. What's more, a takeover by the Radicals could provide an opening for the Twelfth Imam to try to lure the country—or even force it—to join his emerging new Islamic Caliphate.

The implosion of Egypt after the sudden death of the man they called the Pharaoh on the Nile had long been one of the Agency's greatest fears. Now they were about to discover how it would all play out, and the timing could not have been worse.

"Any suspects at this point?" David asked, forcing himself to concentrate on gathering the facts rather than letting his mind run away with what-if scenarios.

Zalinsky said that Roger Allen, the Agency's director, was privately speculating that the attack was most likely payback from al Qaeda after the killing of so many high-level figures in recent months. Dr. Ayman al-Zawahiri, for years the number two man in the al Qaeda organization, was Egyptian and had long vowed to topple the Ramzy regime and replace it with an Islamic Republic. However, Zalinsky noted, his immediate boss, Tom Murray, deputy director for operations, suspected the Muslim Brotherhood, the radical Islamic group founded in Egypt in 1928. The Brotherhood, which operated in the shadows because it was legally banned in Egypt, had hated Ramzy for years, in part because he kept imprisoning their top operatives and in part because he understood their true mission—the establishment of Egypt as the epicenter of a revived Islamic kingdom, the imposition of Sharia law, and the exporting of their Sunni brand of jihad throughout the region and eventually the world. Their motto: "Allah is our objective. The Prophet is our leader. Qur'an is our law. Jihad is our way. Dying in the way of Allah is our highest hope." Al-Zawahiri, David knew, was not only Egyptian born but had been a member of the Brotherhood before he'd formed the even more radical group Egyptian Islamic Jihad, which had then merged with al Qaeda. "Murray thinks it's possible that this was a joint operation between the Brotherhood and al Qaeda and could even have a Hezbollah angle, although you'd think we would have picked up on the plot if there was that much coordination between groups."

"What do you think?" David asked.

"I don't know," Zalinsky replied. "It's too early."

"But you don't think it's actually al Qaeda or the Brotherhood, at least not by themselves, do you?" David pressed.

"We don't have enough data yet."

"Jack, come on; this is Iran. This is being directed by the Twelfth Imam. It's got their fingerprints all over it. The timing? The targets? The weapons? The fact that the attack happened so soon after the assassination of Iran's top nuclear scientist in Hamadan?"

"Why would Iran pick a fight with us now?" Zalinsky countered.

"With Israel, sure. But why hit us, our city, our leader? Why take such a risk when doing so could push the White House into going to war with Iran? It doesn't make sense. It's not rational."

"Based on whose perspective?" David asked. "Look, Jack, do you really believe the president is ever going to go to war with Iran? You hear what he's telling the director behind the scenes. You know he doesn't have the Pentagon developing a serious plan. You saw the advance text of the speech for the Sadat Center. He's dreaming of peace. He still thinks he can negotiate with Iran. Now he thinks he might be able to talk with the Twelfth Imam. He barely mentioned Iran in the State of the Union address. He's not signaling to the country that he's about to get tough with Iran. Meanwhile, he's cutting the defense budget in the name of deficit reduction. He's pulling forces out of Iraq and Afghanistan. Nobody believes he's going to launch a war with Iran, least of all the Iranians."

"But don't you think an assassination attempt by Iran could change the calculus, push a reluctant warrior onto a war footing after all?"

"Not if the hit worked," David said. "Or even if it was close."

"Look, David, the whole reason you're in this thing is because the president gets it. He's listening to the director. He's listening to us. He signed the directive authorizing the use of 'all means necessary' to stop Iran's weapons program. He's giving us everything we asked for. Your job isn't to make policy. Your job is executing it. Don't forget that."

The line was silent for a few moments.

"Now, you need to get back here tonight," Zalinsky said.

"I can't," David replied.

"You have to."

"Jack, my mom is dying."

"I know, and I'm very sorry. You know how far back I go with your parents. But—"

"No, Jack, you don't understand," David interrupted. "My mom slipped into a coma less than an hour ago. The doctors say she hasn't got much time left. They don't think she's going to make it through the week. And my dad's a mess. I can't leave them. Not now."

"What about Azad?"

"He's AWOL."

"Then what about Saeed?"

"Tell me you're kidding."

"Look, David, your president was nearly assassinated in the last hour, and the Middle East is about to explode."

"I get it, Jack; I do. But I need more time."

"There is no more time."

"You said the president wanted to meet with us tomorrow at noon. Why can't I fly down there tomorrow morning? I already have the ticket. That's what my father's expecting. Please, Jack. I need this favor."

"I'm sorry, David. I understand your situation, but your country is under attack. The meeting with the president is off. Honestly, I can't even tell you at the moment if the president is alive, much less capable of a briefing. But Director Allen is ordering all of the Near East Division to be here tonight—no exceptions. He's pushing for us to go hard after al Qaeda, and we've got a team drafting new options on that front. But he's also terrified that the Israelis are going to use this assassination attempt against Naphtali to order a first strike against Iran. He wants options. He said he wants to 'take the gloves off.'"

David could see there was no point arguing any longer, but the pressure on him was excruciating. He was tempted to offer his resignation right then and there, but with his country under attack, that felt like a betrayal.

"Look, David," Zalinsky continued when David didn't respond, "you've been doing amazing work. You've given us a new set of targets in Iran. You've given us a bunch of new leads. But we don't have much time. Eva and I have some ideas, but there are gaps only you can fill."

Zalinsky paused for a moment, and David wondered how their colleague, Eva Fischer, was faring with her in-depth interrogations of Dr. Najjar Malik, the senior Iranian nuclear scientist whom David had helped smuggle out of Iran and into the United States along with his family. Malik was critical to the Agency's ability to truly understand Tehran's capabilities and intentions.

Zalinsky cleared his throat. "Believe me, if there was another way, any other way, I wouldn't ask you to do this. But this is why I recruited you in the first place. I think your parents would understand."

David wasn't buying it. "You're wrong, Jack. There's nothing about this my father will understand. He's watching the love of his life slip away from him forever. He won't eat. He's not taking his own medication. I'm worried he might harm himself. My brothers aren't here. Besides, I can't possibly get a flight to DC tonight. It's Syracuse, not Munich."

"There's already an Agency plane en route," Zalinsky said. "It will touch down in less than an hour. There'll be a car waiting for you when you arrive. Come to my office the moment you get in. I've got to go. I've got the director calling on the other line."

With that, the call went dead.

8

Thick, dark clouds were rolling in.

Thunder rumbled in the distance, and lightning strikes were getting closer. The winds were picking up, and David could feel the temperature dropping steadily. Another storm was approaching, and it wasn't safe to stay on the roof. But David couldn't bear the thought of going back inside and telling his father he was leaving.

He knew the Agency had invested heavily in his training. He knew that Zalinsky and Murray and Director Allen were counting on him to do everything possible to protect the people and interests of the United States from all threats, foreign and domestic, and particularly from the regime in Iran. What's more, he had taken an oath. He had given his word to his country.

But now his parents needed him to stay. He didn't want to disappoint them—particularly his father—yet again. They deserved better.

And then there was Marseille. It already felt like a lifetime ago, but he had eaten breakfast with her that very morning, after so many years, after so much history, and he still couldn't quite believe it. Just seeing her come into the restaurant all bundled up against the late-winter chill with her red scarf and turtleneck sweater had stirred up emotions he had long tried to suppress. When he closed his eyes, he could vividly picture her, looking more like a graduate student than the elementary school teacher she had become. She had endured so much pain in the years since he had seen her last. Yet with those large green eyes and that dark brown hair pulled back in a loose braid, Marseille was more beautiful than he'd remembered or imagined, and he missed her already.

It embarrassed him to admit such a thing, if only to himself, but he couldn't help it. He wanted to talk to her again. He wanted to hear her voice. She'd invited him out to Portland, and he wanted to go. To see her again. To spend some real time with her. To see if something was possible between them. There had been a warmth in her eyes and a tenderness in her embrace that had surprised him. He would never forgive himself if he didn't find out for certain who she really was now and what she really wanted.

There was no time, of course, to ponder any of this, certainly not on the roof of Upstate University Hospital. But the notion of going back to his mother's room, pulling his father aside, and telling him there was an "emergency at work" and that he needed to leave town immediately made him physically ill. What fictional emergency could he possibly concoct in the next two minutes that would persuade his father he really had to leave at a time like this?

David knew he was stalling, but he wasn't sure what to do next. He stared down at his phone and was tempted to call Marseille, just for a moment, just to make sure she had gotten back to Portland okay. If she seemed eager—or even simply willing—to talk a little longer, well, that would be good too. And maybe a sign. At least she would know how he felt right now. She would know what to say to him. After all, she hadn't lost only one parent; she'd lost two.

David thought better of it and abruptly put the phone away. This was not the time or the place. He had to stay focused. He glanced at his watch and winced. He needed to be at Hancock Field in less than an hour, and he still needed to get back to his parents' house to pack.

He headed back downstairs. As he approached his mother's room, he could see his father sitting in a rocking chair, rocking back and forth in an almost-hypnotic rhythm. He wasn't crying anymore. He was just sitting there, staring at his beloved wife, who lay in her bed motionless and hooked up to all kinds of life-support systems. The entire scene was hard to bear, but it was the vacant look in his father's eyes that pained David most of all.

His parents had been married for more than three decades, and they were inseparable. It seemed like nearly every kid David had grown up with had divorced parents. But throughout all of his own trials and mistakes and disappointments growing up, one thing he had always been able to count on was the deep and abiding love of his parents. Mohammad Shirazi had been born in 1952, just a year before Nasreen Vali, in adjacent towns. They had both grown up in Iran under the Shah. Theirs had been an arranged marriage, but their parents loved them and had chosen carefully and wisely. Mohammad and Nasreen had spoken their vows in the early seventies and escaped from Iran together during the Islamic Revolution of 1979, losing all of their material possessions, including a thriving medical practice, in the process. When they'd arrived in the US, they'd had to rebuild their lives from scratch, but they had done so without complaining. Mohammad had studied hard to get his American license to practice cardiology. The couple had made friends, bought a home, raised three sons, put them all through college, and lived the American dream without a handout from anyone. They were proud of that. They had done it themselves. They had done it together. They were more in love today, David was certain, than ever before, and it was clear his father couldn't bear the thought of losing her.

Would she be lost forever? Would they ever see her again? None of them had ever taken religion seriously. Though born Shia Muslims, David's parents had always prided themselves on their rejection of Islam. Now his mother was about to find out the truth about heaven and hell. David suddenly felt cold and scared in a way he'd never felt before. He was staring into the abyss, without a single answer, without a single shred of hope.

Abruptly he realized his decision had become clear. He could no longer lie to his father. Whatever the consequences, David was going to tell him the truth. Not all of it. He would not betray state secrets or operational security. But his father had to know that his son worked for the Agency. He had to know David was fighting against the great evil that had driven them from their beloved land of Persia in the first place, the very evil that had cost them so dearly before and might very well cost them even more. He had to know why his son was leaving tonight. David wasn't sure his father would believe him, but he needed to try.

"Hey, Dad," he whispered, poking his head in the door, "can I talk to you about something?"

★ ★ ★ ★ ★

TEHRAN, IRAN

Tehran was eight and a half hours ahead of central New York.

Hamid Hosseini, Iran's Supreme Leader and Grand Ayatollah, finished his early-morning prayers. He had been caught off guard by Javad Nouri's predawn call informing him of the Twelfth Imam's sudden and unexpected decision to visit Beirut rather than return directly to Iran. But who was he to question the Lord of the Age?

Hosseini asked Allah to bless every detail of the Mahdi's trip, to give him safety and success, and to give him the infinite wisdom needed to build the Caliphate longed for by a billion Muslims. Then he rose to his feet, left the small mosque in the palace without saying a word, made the short walk with his bodyguards back to his enormous corner office, and shut the door behind him. He planned to stay in seclusion for the next several hours.

Pulling out an unmarked folder, he began reviewing the latest assessment from his chief of intelligence. The good news was that Iranian scientists had mastered the nuclear fuel cycle and now had a small but significant stockpile of highly enriched uranium (HEU) ranging from 95 to 98 percent purity. As a result of such efforts, design teams had finally completed building nine nuclear warheads and had tested one just two weeks previously.

Hosseini was not a physicist, and he skimmed over much of the technical detail contained in the report. But the bottom line was clear enough. The warhead had worked perfectly. The blast yield had been extraordinary. The design they had bought years before from A. Q. Khan, the father of the Pakistani nuclear program, had been a good investment after all. They weren't ready to attach any of the warheads to the high-speed ballistic missiles they had built themselves or bought from the North Koreans. Indeed, the report indicated the team still felt they were many months away from perfecting a missile delivery system. But that was okay. For now, Hosseini concluded, he had what he needed. What's more, the report promised him that within roughly another three weeks, six more warheads would be built and ready for use.

Not all the news was good, however.

For starters, Dr. Mohammed Saddaji, Iran's top nuclear scientist, was dead, killed by a car bomb in Hamadan just days before. Saddaji's death was a huge blow to the weapons program. The pioneer of Iran's clandestine Bomb-making program, Saddaji was nearly irreplaceable. It was still unclear to Hosseini how Saddaji's activities had been discovered by whoever had assassinated him. He had held the fairly innocuous title of deputy director of the Atomic Energy Agency of Iran and had ostensibly been in charge of day-to-day operations at the Bushehr reactor, the nuclear power plant located near the Persian Gulf that was about to go online that spring after years of delays and technical complications.

Most of Hosseini's closest advisors were convinced that the Israelis were responsible for Saddaji's death. The charge made for good propaganda, and the Supreme Leader encouraged them to feed those rumors to the blogosphere and the Western media. But Hosseini had a source he trusted who told him it was the Egyptians who had murdered Saddaji. What's more, the source indicated that the order for the hit had come directly from President Abdel Ramzy. Was it true? He had no idea. How could Ramzy have found out? It did not matter. All that mattered to Hosseini was retribution, and now he had taken it.

But there was more bad news. Saddaji's death, the nuclear test beneath Alvand Mountain, near Hamadan, and the subsequent earthquake in the area had drawn unwanted attention. Now Hosseini's intelligence chief believed that Facility 278, Iran's top-secret nuclear weapons development complex, located forty kilometers west of Hamadan and built into the side of the 11,000-foot mountain, had been compromised. The site was surely being watched twenty-four hours a day by spy satellites from nearly every country possessing such technology, and most definitely the Americans and the Zionists. This was a huge problem, the report in Hosseini's hands noted, because most of the warheads were still being housed there—not all, but most. They needed to be moved fast and without international detection. They needed to be moved into position to be used, in accordance with the Mahdi's explicit instructions. But how?

★ ★ ★ ★ ★

SYRACUSE, NEW YORK

The stunned look on his father's face pained David.

He hadn't wanted to hurt his father or add to his many burdens. He hoped he had done the right thing. But as the two men sat together in silence, David's anxieties began to grow. Was it anger he detected in his father? Disappointment? Resentment? The man was hard to read.

One thing was clear: Dr. Shirazi clearly believed his son's story, even if David had left out a few key elements. David hadn't shared with his father the fact that Jack Zalinsky had been the one to recruit him to join the CIA, nor that Zalinsky had been responsible for his training. He hadn't revealed any of the operational details of his life in the CIA, like the fact that his apartment in Munich was just a front or that the name most people knew him by these days was Reza Tabrizi.

"So how long have you been in the CIA?" Dr. Shirazi asked.

"A few years," David said. "I'm not allowed to say exactly."

"And you think Iran is behind the attack in New York today?"

"I don't have proof, Dad, but yes, that's where I think the trail of evidence will eventually lead."

"So you're going back into Iran tonight?"

"Well, no, not exactly. I'm flying to DC tonight to meet my colleagues at Langley and compare notes and develop a plan. And then we'll see."

"But they're probably going to send you back into Iran?"

David nodded, his stomach in knots, and there was another long, uncomfortable pause.

"Dad, I'm not even sure I should stay with the Agency."

"What are you talking about?"

"I'm thinking of stepping down."

"Why?"

"I want to be with you and Mom. I want to help you, not leave you all alone. And honestly, I'm not sure whether I really—"

But his father cut him off. "No, no, David; you have to go. You have to. Your country needs you, especially now."

"But, Dad, there are others who—"

But Dr. Shirazi would have none of it. "I'm so proud of you, David."

"You are?"

"Of course. Your mother would be too."

David bit his lip. This wasn't a reaction he'd even considered.

"Honestly, I wish I was young enough to do the same thing." Dr. Shirazi smiled faintly and put his arm on David's shoulder.

"Join the CIA?"

"Of course."

"But why?"

"Because America saved my life, and your mother's. The CIA and the State Department saved our lives. I'll never forget what Jack Zalinsky and Charlie Harper did. They risked their lives to get us out of Iran. They adopted us into this country. Don't get me wrong, Son; I love Iran for giving me birth, but I'm disgusted by what the mullahs are doing to the people. I loathe Ayatollah Hosseini and President Darazi. I despise everything they stand for. They're suffocating Iran's economy. They're devouring Iran's children. They're strangling Iran's future, and they don't care. They're cult members and murderers, both of them. They deny the Holocaust, and they want to murder six million Israeli Jews. And that's not even their main goal. Israel is just the small devil. America is the big devil. Hosseini and Darazi want to annihilate us all. They want to murder Christians along with Jews, plus every Muslim who doesn't believe what they believe. They want the whole world to bow down and worship the Twelfth Imam, all to bring about their Caliphate and the end of the world. They are evil, David, sheer evil. Someone has to stop them. Someone has to go in there and cut through all their lies and all their defenses and find a way to put an end to all this madness. And believe me, David, if I were younger, I would join the CIA and go back to Iran and put a bullet through both their heads. I thought about that many times over the years, but I'm ashamed to say I never had the guts to do it. But I will die a happy man—your mother will die a happy woman—if that someone is you. At least our lives will have meant something. At least we'll have done something right."

9

TEHRAN, IRAN

Hosseini set down the folder and turned on the television.

He soon found himself glued to Iran's state-run news channel, showing alternating coverage of the Twelfth Imam's inaugural address in Mecca only four days before and the news out of Manhattan. As he stared at the mesmerizing images and listened to the reporting and analysis, Hosseini found himself in near disbelief. For decades he had prayed for this moment—dreamed of it, studied for it, prepared for it. But though he didn't dare confide this to any of his subjects or staff, the Supreme Leader of the Islamic Republic of Iran wasn't sure if he had ever fully believed such a moment would truly happen in his lifetime, much less that he would be so intimately involved. It was one thing to believe oneself to be living in the end of days, but it was quite another to be certain.

As a child, his parents and teachers had taught him that one day, Muhammad Ibn Hasan Ibn Ali—aka the Promised One, the Mahdi, the Lord of the Age, the Twelfth Imam—would return from hiding or "occultation," bring Jesus as his deputy, force all Jews and Christians and other infidels to convert or perish, destroy the leaders of enemy nations, and then reestablish the Islamic Caliphate once and for all. Seven decades later, he could still remember word for word a passage from one of his grandfather's books on Shia eschatology that his father had required him to memorize. The words were seared into his psyche forever, and as he watched a montage of video clips, they began to tumble involuntarily from his lips.

"'He will appear as a handsome young man, clad in neat clothes and exuding the fragrance of paradise. His face will glow with love and kindness for the human beings. He has a radiant forehead, piercing black eyes, and a broad chest. He very much resembles his ancestor, the prophet Muhammad. Heavenly light and justice accompany him. He will overcome enemies and oppressors with the help of God, and as per the promise of the Almighty, the Mahdi will eradicate all corruption and injustice from the face of the earth and establish the global government of peace, justice, and equity.'"

How poor even the blessed Farsi language was at painting the portrait of the man who had come to save them, Hosseini thought.

With an estimated fourteen million faithful breathlessly awaiting his first formal public appearance, the Twelfth Imam had emerged from the shadows and taken center stage. He appeared significantly younger and strikingly more good looking than Hosseini had imagined growing up. But there was no question it was him, and what a contrast to Hosseini's old nemesis, Abdullah Mohammad Jeddawi. The Sunni Saudi king looked positively ancient as he bowed in his standard white robes before the Shia messiah. What's more, the man looked ashen, his face gaunt, his hands trembling. Hosseini couldn't remember a single word Jeddawi had uttered in his brief and pathetic introduction, but he hadn't forgotten a single syllable of the Mahdi's brief and powerful message—nor would he.

"It is time," the Twelfth Imam had said with a strong, booming voice that instantly seemed to command both reverence and respect. "The age of arrogance and corruption and greed is over. A new age of justice and peace and brotherhood has come. It is time for Islam to unite."

The crowd in Mecca had erupted with an intensity Hosseini had never witnessed in any public event, not even the Friday sermons delivered by his own mentor and guide when the Islamic Revolution had first begun in 1979.

"No longer do Muslims have the luxury of petty infighting and division. Sunnis and Shias must come together," the Mahdi had continued. "It is time to create one Islamic people, one Islamic nation, one Islamic government. It is time to show the world that Islam is ready to rule.

We will not be confined to geographical borders, ethnic groups, and nations. Ours is a universal message that will lead the world to the unity and peace the nations have thus far found elusive."

Men were spellbound. Women wept. And Hosseini felt a pang of regret that he had not insisted upon being there to experience this historic, transformative event in person.

"Cynics and skeptics abound. But to them I say, it is time. Time for you to open your eyes and open your ears and open your hearts. It is time for you to see and hear and understand the power of Islam, the glory of Islam. And today, let this process of education begin. I have come to usher in a new kingdom, and today I announce to you that the governments of Iran, Saudi Arabia, and the Gulf States are joining together as one nation. This will form the core of the Caliphate. My agents are in peaceful, respectful discussions with all the other governments of the region, and in short order we will be announcing our expansion. To those who would oppose us, I would simply say this: The Caliphate will control half the world's supply of oil and natural gas, as well as the Gulf and the shipping lanes through the Strait of Hormuz. The Caliphate will have the world's most powerful military, led by the hand of Allah. Furthermore, the Caliphate will be covered by a nuclear umbrella that will protect the people from all evil. The Islamic Republic of Iran has successfully conducted a nuclear weapons test. Their weapons are now operational. They have just handed over command and control of these weapons to me. We seek only peace. We wish no harm against any nation. But make no mistake: any attack by any state on any portion of the Caliphate will unleash the fury of Allah and trigger a War of Annihilation."

★ ★ ★ ★ ★

EN ROUTE TO WASHINGTON, DC

The Agency-owned Citation climbed rapidly and banked southeast.

David sat alone on the eight-seat business jet, ensconced in a Corinthian-leather seat, staring down at the city of his youth as it shrank in the distance behind them. He was shocked by, but grateful for, his father's unexpected blessing. He had never dreamed of doing any of this when he was growing up. When he'd joined the Agency, he certainly had never imagined his parents approving. Just the opposite. He'd been certain they'd be furious, and he'd been glad that he was not legally allowed to tell them. But now he wished he'd broken the law earlier, telling them from the beginning. Finding out that he actually had his parents' full support would have relieved a lot of stress.

The conversation with his father had gone much better than he'd thought on so many levels. After talking awhile longer about the CIA, David had even told him a little about his breakfast with Marseille and about the feelings he was having for her again. To his surprise, his father had actually encouraged David to keep in touch with her and try his best to, at the very least, rebuild the friendship. "Even if nothing else comes of it," his father had said, "you could do worse than having a Harper for a friend." His father had even mentioned not once but twice how grateful he'd been when Marseille sent flowers and a note to the hospital, and when David asked if it would be appropriate if his father added Marseille to the list of those he was e-mailing with occasional updates on his mother's condition, he'd agreed.

Now, however, it was time for David to shift gears. Before him lay a folder of classified cable traffic and raw intel reports from throughout the Middle East, including Iran. As they reached cruising altitude, he felt completely overwhelmed by the thought of how desperately he needed to catch up on all that had happened in the past few hours and how urgently he needed to develop a plan. Was he really going back into Iran within the next twenty-four hours? It was an order he both expected and worried would be issued the moment he arrived at Langley, and if it was, he wouldn't simply be going in to "oversee" the team of Munich Digital Systems technicians already on the ground and working around the clock in Tehran. Events were spinning out of control. War was coming too quickly. They needed an entirely different approach. But what?

David forced himself to sift through the contents of the folder. The Twelfth Imam's decision to head from Saudi Arabia to Lebanon caught his eye first. David had expected the Mahdi to return to Tehran after his big coming-out party in Mecca. But he'd been wrong, and that worried him. He'd been distracted for the past several days. He was having trouble focusing. He stared out the window for several minutes, saw nothing but a black night sky, then closed his eyes and tried to recalibrate.

What is the Mahdi doing? What does he want? How will he try to get it? What is driving him? Vanity? Power? With so many nations and leaders joining the Caliphate so rapidly, why is he heading to Lebanon, of all places? Isn't Lebanon already controlled by Shias? Isn't Hezbollah the wholly owned subsidiary of Iran? Haven't Hezbollah's leaders and rank-and-file members been pining for the coming of the Twelfth Imam for decades? Why spend precious time shoring up his base?

David chewed on that awhile. Yes, the Mahdi had the passion of the masses in Lebanon, particularly the Shia-dominated southern tier. But perhaps he was trying to make sure Hezbollah was truly ready for war with Israel and would be loyal to him when he ordered them to strike. Perhaps he was going to review the troops. Perhaps he was going to make sure Hezbollah's fifty thousand–plus rockets and missiles aimed at Israel were in place, fueled, armed, and ready to go. Maybe this wasn't public relations but final preparations for war.

If that were true, where might the Mahdi go next after Beirut? David quickly scanned through the folder to see if there was any intel about the Mahdi's schedule for the week. Unfortunately, there was none. Even details about the day ahead were sketchy.

But something else struck David as odd as he forced himself to focus on the intel before him. He noticed that neither US spy satellites nor the NSA was picking up any evidence that the Israel Defense Forces were mobilizing for war. Why not? Hadn't Prime Minister Naphtali nearly been assassinated just hours ago? Hadn't the Iranians tested an atomic bomb just days before? Wasn't Shia Islam's so-called messiah heading for the northern border of Israel? Why weren't the Israelis moving to a higher-alert status in anticipation of more attacks? Something didn't add up.

His phone vibrated. A text message was coming in. He checked it immediately, hoping it was from Marseille or his father. Instead, it was from Eva Fischer, letting him know that she would be the one picking him up from Reagan National once he landed. She hoped he was doing well, she said, and she had news, though she left it unspecified.

David set the phone down and stared out the window. He was still struggling to clear his head of the cancer consuming his mother, his father's crushing grief over her seemingly imminent death, and his own grief as well, not to mention thoughts of Marseille. He was a professional, he told himself. He could not let himself be encumbered or bogged down. He had to sharpen his focus for the mission ahead. It was for Marseille and his parents that he had joined the Central Intelligence Agency in the first place, was it not? To avenge them. To defend them. It was for them, not for himself, that he had left the comforts of home and been willing to go into the heart of darkness. He would never have chosen this life for himself. He wasn't that brave. He wasn't that adventurous.

Unchecked, David knew his love for his parents and for Marseille might threaten to divert him from his destiny, tempt him to renege on his duty, all out of a desire to remain with the ones he cared for so deeply. But now, in no small measure because of the talk with his father, he realized that it was precisely because he loved them that he had to leave them. Such love had to compel him to keep his word and return to the battle, to fight for those he loved, to protect them, to honor them, and to give them the freedom to live their lives without fear or regret—even to lay down his very life if necessary.

It was time. He was ready. Now there was just one piece of unfinished business—he had to decide whether to tell Marseille what he was doing and why.

10

WASHINGTON, DC

Eva Fischer was waiting for him as promised.

As David stepped off the jet and into the chilly night air at Washington's Reagan National Airport, Eva gave him a long hug and asked about his mother. David appreciated the gesture and filled her in as best he could as they got in her car and headed to Langley. He felt like he should reciprocate, but David realized he knew hardly anything about Eva's personal life, and at that moment it somehow felt awkward to ask. He was certain she wasn't married. She wasn't wearing a ring, and in all the time they'd worked together, she'd never mentioned a boyfriend, much less a fiancé. He wondered why. Blonde, blue-eyed, in good shape, and attractive, she was certainly one of the most eligible single women in their division, maybe in the entire Agency. He'd been interested in her since the first day they'd met, and if Marseille weren't suddenly back in the picture . . .

It was not a thought he wanted to finish. He realized that work typically dominated all of their conversations. Perhaps it should again, he decided.

"So what's your news?" he asked, running his hands through his hair and shifting gears. "Is it about the president?"

It wasn't. She had nothing new to report on Jackson's condition beyond what the media was reporting. He was alive and was still in surgery. Beyond that, the doctors were keeping tight-lipped. Eva said the White House press secretary had announced she would do a briefing at the top of the hour. The National Security Council had just finished meeting with the vice president, but apparently the twenty-fifth amendment was not being invoked. Not yet, at least.

"Let's hope that's a good sign," David said.

Eva agreed, then shared the news she'd hinted about in her text. "I just talked to one of my friends over at the Secret Service. They're all under strict orders not to say anything. They don't want it to leak to the media yet. But they killed one of the terrorists in Manhattan during the attack, they captured another, and a third escaped. There's a massive manhunt under way for him at the moment."

"You're serious?"

"Jack wants me to head up to New York after our meeting tonight to be part of the interrogation team."

"That's phenomenal."

"Thanks. I know. I'm excited. Whoever this guy is, we need to squeeze him hard. Are there other attacks coming? Who sent them? Where'd they get their weapons? How did they get into the country? Is there anyone else involved in the cell? All that."

"What's your sense of it?"

"There've got to be more people involved," she said. "The Service and FBI guys think so too. They found a cell phone on the guy they captured. They're running the LUDs now and seeing who he called and when."

"Do you know their nationalities yet?"

"Nothing definitive. Just 'Middle East origin.' That's it so far."

★ ★ ★ ★ ★

"Excuse me, ma'am, do you have any updates on the Portland flight?"

Marseille Harper's flight out of Syracuse had been repeatedly delayed and hadn't landed at Washington Dulles until just after 6 p.m. She'd missed her 5:35 p.m. connection back to Oregon, though it had been canceled anyway. She had been standing in line at the United customer service desk ever since.

Massive late-season snow and ice storms in the Midwest and Northwest, some of them quite severe, had caused dozens of major airports to be shut down, and hundreds of flights were canceled. United wasn't alone in routing flights to its Dulles operations hub, and now thousands of passengers found themselves stranded, frustrated, and trying to figure out another way to their homes, businesses, or other destinations.

"Portland?" the harried customer service rep asked above the din.

"Yes, I really need to get home tonight," Marseille said, trying to imagine twenty-three little faces showing up in her classroom the next morning without her being there to greet them.

"Good luck, honey. Nothing's moving to the Northwest today. Probably not even tomorrow. Haven't you seen the news?"

About the storms in the Midwest and Northwest, the woman meant. But the truth was, Marseille hadn't paid much attention to the storms. She'd been riveted to the coverage of the attack on the president, and it made her heartsick. Until now, it had been such an amazing weekend. Being in her best friend Lexi's wedding. Hanging out with so many friends from college she hadn't seen in so long. Seeing David Shirazi for the first time since she was fifteen. Now her country was under attack, and she felt disoriented and unsure where to turn.

"How close can you get me?"

"At this point?" the heavyset woman asked, typing furiously into her computer. "Phoenix."

"You're kidding."

"Wish I was, darlin', but believe me, I have neither the time nor the energy."

"How about San Francisco?" Marseille asked, thinking maybe she could rent a car there and drive to Portland.

"Everything's booked. Look, dear, I can give you vouchers to stay at a hotel tonight. I can give you a free flight anywhere in the country you want to go in the next twelve months. But I can't book you on anything right now unless you want to go south."

"Ma'am, really, you don't understand. I'm a teacher. I have kids waiting for me. I really need to get home."

"You and ten thousand other people, missy. Look, it's not going to happen. Not tonight. Now, here's your vouchers. Pick up your luggage downstairs in the main terminal, carousel two. Then we've got a free shuttle bus that will take you to a hotel."

"Then what?"

"Call this 800 number tomorrow, and we'll try to get you home as fast as we can. But I wouldn't hold my breath. These storms are killers. If you ask me, you're going to be here for a few days."

The words hit Marseille hard. She had no desire to be stuck in Washington. She didn't know anyone here. She hadn't been here since an eighth-grade social studies trip. And given the terrorist attacks in Manhattan just a few hours earlier, she wondered if DC might be the next target. She wanted to be home in her own bed, safe and secure, if all alone.

With no choice in the matter, however, she thanked the United rep, gathered up her vouchers, and headed for the baggage claim area. As she did, she found herself thinking about David. She'd been so anxious for weeks leading up to that day, anxious about seeing him again after so long, anxious about all she had to say to him, about how he would respond. She feared he'd be angry with her, or worse, disappointed. She feared he'd never want to see her again. But their meeting had gone better than she had hoped. He had actually seemed glad to see her. He'd been a good listener. He'd been kind and gentle when she told him about the miscarriage, about the recent death of her father, about all that she'd faced since she'd seen him last.

What meant the most to her was what David had said right before they had parted. He said he wanted her to know that he'd "like nothing more than to sit here with you for hours, take a long walk with you, even fly back to Oregon with you, for that matter." He said that he didn't want to be cut off from her again, that he was going to wrap up this business in Europe and then, if it was all right with her, "come to wherever you are" because there was so much more to talk about. It was true. There was so much more to say. She'd told him the truth—yes, she'd like him to come see her whenever he could. She hadn't wanted to seem forward, but she had no desire to play coy either.

Marseille picked up the pace so she wouldn't miss the shuttle that would take her from the United gates over to the main terminal, and as she did, she passed an advertisement on the wall that caught her eye. It was for some DC-based consulting firm. "Where are you headed next?" the copy read in big blue letters. She boarded the crowded shuttle just before the driver closed the doors, then inched her way forward and stood in the corner since there was no place to sit, pondering that question.

What did she want with David? For months since writing him to say she was coming to Syracuse for the wedding of her college friend, she had simply wanted David to agree to have coffee with her, and for their first meeting in eight years not to be a disaster. But it dawned on her in that moment that she had never really thought much beyond that. She had no idea where she wanted their relationship to go. She hadn't seen David in so long that she didn't really know who he was anymore. But she wanted to get to know him again and find out who he had become. She hoped they could be friends. She sensed in him a kindred spirit. She wanted to spend time with him again, to hang out with him and let him make her laugh. She wanted a friend who had known her before September 11, before she lost her mom, before her father melted down, before her world came crashing in. There was something safe about being friends with David, something nostalgic—not more than that, necessarily. For now that seemed enough.

She took a moment to pray for David. She asked the Lord to keep him safe and give him favor with his boss and his work, but most of all she prayed what she had prayed every night before she went to sleep, that the Lord would open David's eyes and draw him to His Son. And as she did so, she felt a pang of guilt. They had talked at breakfast of so many things. Why hadn't she talked with him about the Lord? Why hadn't she at least shared the many changes that were under way in her life, what had happened to her in college and since? Was she afraid of what he would think? Was she afraid he might think her too religious? She remembered that David had prided himself on being an agnostic. But what did her pastor and his wife keep telling her? *"If you love someone, you need to share Christ with them."* She believed that. Why was it so hard to do it? And so, for no particular reason, she pulled out her cell phone and dialed David's cell phone number just to say hi, and found herself surprised by how sad she felt when she got voice mail instead of him.

★ ★ ★ ★ ★

BROOKLYN, NEW YORK

Sean Taylor couldn't wait for his shot at him.

In twelve years with the FBI, he had interrogated hundreds of suspects in all kinds of criminal cases. But he had never had the opportunity to grill a suspected terrorist during a real-time investigation of an attack on American soil. It was what he'd joined the FBI to do. Now he had his chance. He was under orders—and under enormous pressure—to extract as much information as he could, as rapidly as possible. The Bureau now had reason to believe that the cell that had attacked the president had at least four members, possibly as many as six. But only one had been shot dead, and only one was in custody, which meant there was still a high risk that more attacks were coming unless he could get this guy to talk.

Taylor could hear the roar of the rotors as the Bureau helicopter touched down on the roof of their Brooklyn facility. He felt a jolt of adrenaline move through his staff as the stairwell door opened and three burly agents dragged their prisoner—face covered by a black hood—through the bull pen of cubicles and desks and secretaries on phones and locked him down in Interrogation Room D. Taylor signed the paperwork acknowledging he now had custody, then quickly scanned the notes from the arresting agents.

The suspect had been captured with a Glock 9mm pistol, but he hadn't used it or even been holding it at the time. The 1982 Plymouth Gran Fury he was captured in was stolen. He had no ID on him at the time of arrest. They had taken his fingerprints at the scene and digitally transferred them to FBI headquarters in Washington, where they were being run against the Bureau's entire criminal and terrorist database. But that would take time, and time was not something they had much of.

Taylor asked the agents to step out of the room, then closed the door behind them. He figured the suspect for about six feet two inches tall and about 160 to 180 pounds. His hands were cuffed to the chair behind him. His feet were shackled to the floor.

"I'm going to give you one chance to cooperate, and that's all," he said quietly, noticing that the man's breathing was labored and quickening. "Let's start simple. What's your name?"

No reply.

"Where are you from?"

Again, no reply.

"How many were part of this mission to kill our president?"

Silence.

"Where is the rest of your team heading now? Is there another team? Who are they going to attack next?"

Still nothing.

So Sean Taylor was done talking. First he began to beat the suspect with his fists until blood trickled down through the hood and all over the suspect's shirt. When that didn't work, he unlocked a small box on the wall about the size of a telephone book and pulled out two long wires, which he proceeded to attach to various parts of the suspect's body. One way or another, this suspect was going to talk.

11

David felt his phone vibrating but couldn't take the call.

They were pulling up to the gate at CIA headquarters in Langley, Virginia. Both he and Eva flashed their photo ID badges, were asked a few questions, and then were waved through.

"How's it going with Najjar Malik?" David asked as they found a parking space. He hoped he'd be able to see the man again, under much different circumstances than the last time they'd been together. He remembered the scientist's gentle nature and quiet bravery. He'd been practically peaceful in the midst of uncertainty and danger. Najjar intrigued him—not just because of the valuable information he possessed but because of the character and heart he'd exhibited during the chaos of escaping from Iran.

"Amazing," Eva said. "I'm supposed to brief the director on that in a few minutes."

"Good."

They locked the car and hurried inside. They passed a full security checkpoint, complete with 100 percent ID check, retinal and fingerprint scans, and the passage of their personal belongings through an X-ray and themselves through a magnetometer. When he retrieved his phone, David checked and saw that there were two missed calls. One was from Zalinsky, presumably checking on their progress. The other was from Marseille. The problem was, they were now in a restricted area where all radio frequencies were jammed and no cell calls or text messages could be sent or received. David felt a pang of regret. He wished he had time to hear Marseille's voice and make sure she was okay, but it would now be hours before that was possible.

"Hey, more good news—NSA just picked up an interesting intercept from one of the satphones your friend Esfahani asked for," Eva said when they finally boarded an elevator and pushed the button for the seventh floor. "Somebody really high up."

"Really?" David asked. "Who?"

He was surprised but grateful to hear that the phones were being used. Only a few weeks earlier he had been approached by Abdol Esfahani, the deputy director of technical operations for Iran Telecom, the government-run telecommunications company of Iran, to see if he could obtain twenty encrypted and totally secure satellite phones for senior members of the Iranian regime. It was a key development. The Iranians had previously purchased satellite phones from Russia, then discovered they had all been bugged. Now they wanted state-of-the-art phones that Nokia, the Finnish communications giant, and Thuraya, an Arab phone company, jointly produced. Esfahani, of course, thought David was actually Reza Tabrizi, working for Munich Digital Systems as a subcontractor for Nokia. Senior Iranian officials wanted the same "clean" phones used by members of the EU, prime ministers, and parliamentarians, and they were willing to pay top dollar. With Langley's help, David had delivered satphones that weren't bugged but whose numbers could be intercepted by the National Security Agency. He had been skeptical that the phones would actually be used so soon, but he was glad to be wrong.

Eva turned and looked him in the eye. "Ali Faridzadeh."

"You're kidding."

"I'm not."

"The Iranian defense minister?"

"The very same."

"Who did he call?"

"The French defense minister. Apparently the two went to some private high school together in Switzerland, and they've stayed close," Eva said.

"What did they talk about?"

"Well, that's just it. The interesting thing was that Faridzadeh said he needed to relay a private message from the Twelfth Imam to President Jackson."

The doors opened. They stepped off the elevator and turned left.

"The Mahdi wanted to send his personal condolences to the president for this 'terrible tragedy' and said he would get to the bottom of it and find out who was responsible. When I read the call transcript, I honestly didn't believe it at first. I made the guys at NSA send me the audio of the call, but when I finally listened to it myself, they were right. Their translation was precise. And there was more. The Mahdi wanted the president to know that 'now is the time for peace, not more bloodshed.' He asked for a phone call with the president and said that now that the Iranians had the Bomb, they felt they were finally in a position to come back to the table and talk about a regional peace accord. He ended with what seems to be an ancient Persian saying: 'A promise is a cloud; fulfillment is the rain.'"

"Meaning?"

"That's what the French defense minister asked," Eva said. "Faridzadeh told him it meant 'The sky is full of dark clouds just now, but they hold the promise of peace. The Promised One has come to bring peace, and his peace will soon cover the earth.'"

★ ★ ★ ★ ★

ARLINGTON, VIRGINIA

All of the hotels near Dulles Airport were booked.

In fact, because of the storms in the Midwest, there were so many thousands of stranded passengers in DC that Marseille had had trouble finding a vacancy anywhere. When she finally had found a room available at the DoubleTree in Crystal City, she'd booked it instantly. She'd had no idea it was a forty-minute cab ride away from Dulles, and she'd blanched at the fare on the meter when they pulled up. But she had paid without complaining, checked in, and collapsed on the king-size bed in her room.

What was she going to do now? She'd been able to reach her principal back in Portland on his cell phone, and he'd been sympathetic. He'd make sure there was a substitute in her classroom the next morning and asked simply that she stay in touch. If it took a few days for her to get back, it was okay.

"You could use the break," he said. "Try to enjoy it. Just stay safe."

Grateful to have a boss who wasn't a tyrant, she took a few deep breaths and tried to relax. She didn't want to watch a movie or even turn on the television. The news out of New York was far too depressing, and she'd seen so much of the coverage for the last few hours, she was exhausted by all of it. She wished she could call Lexi and debrief about the wedding and the old friends who'd come. But the woman was on her honeymoon.

How amazing would it be to travel to Jerusalem and Nazareth and Bethlehem and Jericho? Marseille thought. She knew Lexi's itinerary and couldn't help but be envious.

Raised Catholic, Lexi hadn't been particularly religious growing up. But she had been a Near East studies major and had always dreamed of traveling around Israel. After she had prayed to receive Christ with Marseille as a freshman, Lexi had developed an insatiable hunger to study the Bible and visit the lands where Jesus and Paul had walked. Now, with her new husband, Chris, who had just graduated from seminary and was preparing to become a pastor, she was actually seeing her dreams come true.

Marseille wondered if she would ever get married. She wondered if she would ever get the joy of going on a honeymoon with a man she really loved, ever get to travel around the world like her parents used to do. But the very question made her feel worse.

Trying to shake off encroaching feelings of jealousy and loneliness, Marseille got up and walked over to the windows. She half expected to see another office building or an air shaft but was pleasantly surprised by the sight of the Pentagon, such a striking symbol of power and mystery along the Potomac River. Immediately, her thoughts turned to her father and the information she had uncovered upon his death that he had once actually worked for America's spy agency.

It was a puzzle she wanted to solve. She wondered where the CIA's headquarters was located. Was it right downtown or out here near the Pentagon? She genuinely had no idea and was too tired at the moment to look it up. But it had to be close, she figured.

That's when the name Jack Zalinsky crossed her mind. He was the CIA operative who had engineered the rescue of her parents out of Tehran during the Iranian Revolution of 1979. David had been the first to tell her Zalinsky's name years before, when she practically begged him to tell her more about how their parents had met and escaped Iran together. She could vividly remember saying the name to her father and seeing him wince, almost recoil. He'd refused to discuss it, any of it, but his reaction had confirmed David's story.

Marseille wondered. It wasn't possible, was it? Could Zalinsky still be at the CIA? It didn't seem likely. It had been more than three decades. The guy was probably living on a beach near Miami or in a retirement home in Phoenix or Sun City. Perhaps he had passed away. But it was worth a shot, she decided. She didn't have anything else to do for the next few days.

With a new focus, she felt a little better now. She changed into her nightgown, washed her face, and climbed into bed. She prayed for her students and for her grandmother, suffering from Alzheimer's. She prayed for the president and all those wounded in New York. She prayed for David's mom, that the Lord would heal her, and for Mr. Shirazi, that the Lord would comfort him in his grief.

Then she prayed for David again, and as she did, she wondered if he was the one. Yet how could he be? By his own admission, he was an agnostic Shia Muslim. She was a girl who had made a lot of mistakes, but she was a follower of Jesus and determined to go wherever He led her. How could He lead her to David? That couldn't possibly be His will. Friends? Yes. But no more. In so many ways they were kindred spirits, she felt. But not in the way that mattered most. So she prayed again for the Lord to protect him and open his eyes to the truth of the gospel. And she wondered if she was really praying for David's sake . . . or for her own. A little bit of both, she admitted to the Lord; a little bit of both.

Marseille lay back on her pillow and stared out at a full moon bathing Washington in its glow. She had to get her mind off David, or she'd never get to sleep. She would call the CIA first thing in the morning, she decided. In her quest to truly understand her father's past, she would see if the name Jack Zalinsky was still in their system.

What she couldn't know, what she could never have imagined, was that Jack Zalinsky and David Shirazi were sitting together in the same room at that very moment.

★ ★ ★ ★ ★

MONDAY
MARCH 7

(IRAN TIME)

12

BEIRUT, LEBANON

IranAir flight 001 from Mecca was late.

But when the Airbus jumbo jet finally touched down at Beirut International Airport, it was greeted by throngs of cheering crowds, a phalanx of Lebanese soldiers and policemen, and hundreds of local and international journalists, all covering the event live. Some commentators speculated the delayed arrival was meant to build drama. Whether that was true or not, TV ratings had certainly spiked throughout the Islamic world.

Though it was not clear where the rumor had started, it was widely anticipated that the Twelfth Imam would deliver a sermon or some extended remarks on or near the airport grounds. That, however, turned out not to be true. Aided by the security detail, Javad did his best to steer the Mahdi past the crowd of reporters and cameramen waiting for them on the tarmac. Javad was a small, wiry man, nervous by nature. But his chest puffed out considerably to be the right-hand man to the Lord of the Age, at the center of the spectacle. He glanced sideways at the Mahdi and found himself impressed all over again by the man's charisma and authority. His dark eyes were full of intensity and plans.

But then, to everyone's surprise, the Mahdi stopped in his tracks, paused for a moment, and turned to respond to a question from a French reporter.

"Your Excellency, the Egyptian Foreign Ministry has just confirmed that President Abdel Ramzy died in the attacks in New York yesterday," the chief diplomatic correspondent from Agence France-Presse shouted.

"Do you have any comment on this development and on the attempted assassinations of the American president and Israeli prime minister?"

"Sorry, no time for questions," Javad said.

But the Mahdi ignored him and responded anyway. "Islam is moving across the earth. A new Caliphate is rising. This is mankind's destiny. It is the will of Allah, and no mere mortal can stop it."

"Are you saying you are happy about the death of the Egyptian leader?" the reporter followed up.

"We have come to the end of days," the Mahdi replied. "The presidents and prime ministers and kings of the world are ignoble relics of an ancient, passing age. They do not concern themselves with the poor or the common man. Their societies are corrupt. Their debts are crushing. Their currencies are collapsing. Their armies are emasculated. Their evil systems are dying, and so they should. Only Islam can give us hope."

"What message do you have for the people of Egypt?" an Al Jazeera reporter asked. "Hundreds of thousands are taking to the streets of Cairo, Alexandria, Suez, and Aswân, cheering the death of President Ramzy. But now the army is moving against them, deploying tanks and armored personnel carriers."

"Allah is our objective," the Mahdi said. "The Prophet is our leader. Qur'an is our law. Jihad is our way. Dying in the way of Allah is our highest hope."

"Does this mean you want to see the Egyptian people engage in jihad to join you, to join the new Caliphate you are constructing? Are you calling on the Muslim Brotherhood to rally to your cause?"

"If the Arab states and peoples had relied on Islam instead of relying on the Americans and the Zionists—if they had placed their eyes on the luminous and liberating teachings of the noble Qur'an, had memorized those teachings, embraced those teachings, and had practiced them with true conviction—they would not be slaves today. They would not be poor. They would not be beggars. They would not be shamed in the eyes of the *ummah*, the greater Islamic community. It is the great chasm between those who call themselves Muslims and the teachings of the Qur'an that has plunged so many millions of Arabs into this dark and catastrophic situation. It is time to awaken the people, to call them to a higher purpose, to show them a purer path."

"Again, just to be clear," the Al Jazeera reporter pressed, "are you calling the people of Egypt to join this new Caliphate?"

The Mahdi stood still for a moment and kept silent, a peaceful smile playing on his lips. He waited an extra beat, glancing at the crowds and cameras before fixing his eyes on the young reporter. "I am calling on *all* the countries of the world to join the Caliphate. This is why I have come. To liberate the oppressed peoples of the earth and lead them to a path of victory and unity. I have come to declare that Islam is the answer to all the world's ills. Islam will bring you peace. Islam will bring you freedom from fear, freedom from want, freedom to know Allah and to submit to his will. Not simply saying you're a Muslim. Not simply going through the motions. Submission. This is the heart of the matter. Will you truly submit to the will of Allah? Will you live for him? Will you die in his service? The time has come for nothing less. Mine, therefore, will be no ordinary government. It will be a purely Islamic government. It will be based upon Sharia law. It will give honor and dignity to all who submit. But make no mistake: opposing this government means opposing the Sharia of Islam, and this cannot be tolerated. To revolt against Allah's government is to revolt against Allah. And to revolt against Allah has its punishment in our law. And let there be no misunderstanding; it is a heavy punishment."

"We still don't know the fate of the American president," a BBC reporter said, "but were you disappointed to learn that the Israeli prime minister escaped from the attack relatively unscathed?"

"The Zionist regime is heading toward annihilation, one way or the other."

★ ★ ★ ★ ★

LANGLEY, VIRGINIA

David had never met CIA director Roger Allen.

Not in person. Not even over the phone. But as he entered the director's secure conference room on the seventh floor, where Tom

Murray and Jack Zalinsky had arrived moments before, he immediately recognized the graying, somewhat aristocratic sixty-four-year-old former senior senator from Connecticut who had long served as chairman of the Senate Select Committee on Intelligence before President Jackson had nominated him to run the Agency. Introductions were made quickly, and then David took a seat with Eva on one side and Zalinsky on the other.

"I want to begin with good news," the director said. "The president is out of surgery and is in stable condition at George Washington University Hospital. I just talked to the First Lady and the president's physician. They both say it looks like he's going to be just fine."

David breathed a sigh of relief, along with the others. He deeply disagreed with Jackson on policy matters, especially those related to the Middle East, but he just as deeply respected the office of the president and wished no personal ill toward his commander in chief. Just the opposite—he was willing to sacrifice his life, if necessary, to protect the president and the country.

"How's he feeling?" Murray asked.

"It's somewhat of a mixed bag," Allen conceded. "The First Lady told me he is taking President Ramzy's death hard, though obviously he's very glad Prime Minister Naphtali is okay. As for himself, he suffered a combination of second- and third-degree burns. He also cracked a rib when the Secret Service agents tackled him. But on balance, he's lucky to be alive."

"And Agent Bruner?" Eva asked. "How is he doing?"

Allen lowered his eyes. "The White House isn't ready to release that information to the public yet. They're still looking for his wife, to inform her. But I'm afraid Mike passed away about thirty minutes ago. The president wants all of you to know that his number one priority is making sure another war doesn't erupt in the Middle East," Allen said. "He knows there will be all kinds of calls, especially from the Republicans on Capitol Hill, for retaliation, for reciprocity. But he wants us all to know our jobs are to keep cool heads, go about our work carefully and methodically, identify who was responsible, and develop options for him. But war, he stressed, is not one of them. Moreover, the president wants the Israelis to be kept on a tight leash. Naphtali is going to take this personally, and he's going to be inclined to hit Iran. The president insisted we do everything in our power not to let that happen."

David was stunned. Not go to war? What were they talking about? Of course they were going to war. Someone—probably the Iranians—had just tried to kill the American president and the leaders of the nation's two key allies in the region. They needed to hit somebody, hard and relentlessly.

"Sir, with all due respect, dozens of Americans have just died in the worst terrorist attack on American soil since this president took office," David said. "How can the Agency—and the entire US government, for that matter—not be going into war-planning mode?"

"Agent Shirazi, that's out of line," Murray said.

"No, no, that's all right," the director said. "Look, David, I understand your point. But we don't make policy here. We follow the orders of the commander in chief. And our orders are to stop the next war."

"Director Allen," David replied, "if we don't move fast and hard, the next war just might wind up with mushroom clouds over New York, Washington, and Tel Aviv. This fire is already burning. It is spreading rapidly. Everyone in this room feels terrible about the attacks that happened today in New York. But what's coming is ten thousand times worse if we don't use this moment to hit Iran's nuclear weapons program with everything we have."

"We haven't confirmed who is responsible for the attack in New York," the director said.

David was incredulous. "Does it matter? Sir, this was a decapitation strike, designed to cut off the heads of the only three countries on the planet with the will to stop both the mullahs in Tehran and now the Twelfth Imam from building their Caliphate and annihilating Judeo-Christian civilization forever. Of course we should go after the specific terrorist cells responsible for this attack when we find them. But we don't need to wait to hit Iran. We already know Iran has tested nuclear weapons. And the fact is, if we don't hit the Iranians in the next few days, we may never have the chance again."

Tom Murray was livid. "David, that's enough," he said, barely able to keep his voice down. "You weren't invited into this room to lecture the director of the Central Intelligence Agency or try to goad him or the president into a war with Iran—or with anyone else, for that matter."

"Tom, we're already at war," David said. "The president authorized this Agency to use all means necessary to stop Iran from getting nuclear weapons. Now they have at least eight, after their test. Doesn't the same national security directive not only authorize but command us—those of us in this room—to find those weapons and the people who built them and neutralize them before it is too late?"

BEIRUT, LEBANON

Jacques Miroux was Reuters's chief Mideast correspondent.

"Your Excellency, on Thursday in Mecca, you said, 'We seek only peace. We wish no harm against any nation,'" Miroux shouted. "But you also said Iran now has nuclear warheads, of which you have full control. Just now you spoke of the annihilation of Israel, saying it is coming and implying that it is inevitable. A moment ago you spoke of jihad as your goal. Is it your intent to threaten a thermonuclear war against the Jewish state?"

"I bring a message of peace. That is my message, and that is all. To those who want peace, I welcome you with open arms."

"Well, at the very least, Your Excellency," Miroux followed up, "are statements like these provoking the Israelis into what could be a massive first strike on their part?"

"Islam cannot be defeated. Period. Islam will be victorious in all the countries of the world. The teachings of the Qur'an will prevail all over the world. Even in Palestine. Especially in Palestine and the holy city of al-Quds. Why should a lion fear the mosquito, so tiny, so annoying, but so inconsequential?"

With that, the Mahdi flashed a smile and turned to wave to the masses. Then Javad guided him into a white armored SUV for the brief drive north from the airport to the Camille Chamoun Sports City Stadium, where an estimated 160,000 Hezbollah members were eagerly awaiting the Twelfth Imam's address in a facility built for a third that number, at best.

★ ★ ★ ★ ★

LANGLEY, VIRGINIA

David could feel the tension in the room spiking.

But he didn't care. Their country had been attacked. The president was too weak to respond. The director of central intelligence was covering his behind. Someone had to speak up. Why wasn't Murray? Why wasn't Zalinsky?

"Director Allen, may I speak?" Eva suddenly asked.

"Of course, Eva; what is it?"

"Well, sir, I've known Agent Shirazi for some time now. You know full well that Jack and I worked together to design his cover story. We worked hard behind the scenes to get him hired at Munich Digital Systems along with me, working undercover. We designed and oversaw his operations in Pakistan. And Jack and I designed this mission for him in Iran and are running it together. You know that I've traveled into Iran with David, and you know that if it wasn't for him, the entire operation would have been blown the first day."

"Your point, Agent Fischer?"

"My point, sir, is that I know the extraordinary risks David is taking. Every moment of every day that he was inside Iran, he was putting his life on the line for his country, for this Agency, for each one of us. Because he believes in this stuff. His family wouldn't be here in the US, or probably even alive, if it weren't for this Agency, and for Jack in particular. So this is very real and very personal for him. David takes his job very seriously, and I am absolutely amazed by how well he's doing it. My expectations were quite high from the beginning, but they've been blown away. And I'd submit that none of us—not a single one of us—could be doing what he's doing. He's gotten us inside Esfahani's operations. He's gotten us inside the defense minister's office. Inside the Revolutionary Guard Corps. Inside the Supreme Leader's office . . . and quite possibly inside the inner circle of the Twelfth Imam. He found us Dr. Najjar Malik and got him out alive. He got us Dr. Saddaji's computer and all his backup discs—intact. And much of what we know about how serious this situation is, we know because of what David has done. It wasn't his plan. I grant you that. It was Jack's plan and mine. He's made some mistakes. But so have we. David isn't an experienced strategist yet, but in my view he's an unbelievable tactical operator . . . and the best shot we have right now to get back inside Iran and stop this nuclear program while we still have time. But we can't send him back in—and that's our plan, is it not? That's what we're about to do, right?—well, we can't send him inside and ask him to risk his life day after day unless he has a reasonable expectation that his country and this Agency are going to back him up every step of the way. Director, my point is this: if the president isn't serious about having us execute his own national security directive, then you need to tell us that right now so we can readjust our goals and retask our team, and that would start with not sending David back in."

The room was silent. Murray fumed. Zalinsky maintained a poker face. David was about to speak for himself, but the director cut him off.

"Agent Fischer, I appreciate enormously what you and your colleagues have done, including Agent Shirazi. You all have this Agency's highest thanks, and particularly mine. I know the risks you're all taking, and I assure you that I don't take those lightly. What's more, I can promise you that if I make the decision to ask any of you to put his or her life at risk, you will be fully backed by all the resources at this Agency's disposal."

Allen let that sink in for a moment.

"That said," he continued, "perhaps it's a little premature to talk about sending anyone to Iran at the moment. There are a range of questions we need to answer first. Starting with this one: was Iran's nuclear weapons test near Hamadan successful, and if so, how are we defining *success*? The answers make a big impact on how we proceed. The president is asking specifically about this. What do we know so far?"

"Well, sir, from everything we can gather," Murray replied, "from the magnitude of the blast as determined by the Richter scale measurements of the earthquake the blast triggered, the damage that earthquake did, and the readings from the Constant Phoenix flight over Hamadan, the guys in the analysis division are judging the test successful. They believe the warhead is likely based on the Pakistani designs sold to Iran by A. Q. Khan."

"Weren't they tinkering with North Korean designs as well?" the director asked.

"They were, but based on a bunch of technical readouts I won't bore you with now, the analysis guys say the warhead they tested was the Pakistani version," Murray explained. "Now, by *successful*, what they mean is that they believe the bomb was built properly, detonated as expected, and had a two-hundred-kiloton yield. We're not talking about a suitcase nuke here. That's a pretty hefty warhead. If it was detonated in the center of Tel Aviv or London or Manhattan or here in DC, it would completely obliterate every structure within a mile radius of the blast. It would destroy most civilian buildings and kill every person within about three miles. It would also set every structure on fire another mile after that, and anyone within five to ten miles—possibly more, depending on the prevailing winds and other factors at the time—would receive massive radiation doses. Many of them would die within days or weeks."

"So pretty successful," Allen said.

"I'm afraid so."

"The president also wants to know if the Iranians can deliver one of these warheads by missile at the moment," Allen said.

Zalinsky took that one. "We don't think so, sir—not yet."

"How confident are you in that assessment?"

"Ninety-five percent."

"So there's still a chance."

"There's a chance, sir—it's small, but I agree it's something we need to push on and find out for sure."

"Director Allen, if I may?" Eva asked.

"Please."

"The reason we're as confident as we are on the missile issue is the material David here was able to acquire from the computer of Dr. Saddaji, the head of Iran's nuclear weapons program."

"The one who was assassinated two weeks ago."

"Correct. And what we've learned from our subsequent interrogations of Saddaji's son-in-law, Dr. Najjar Malik—"

"The scientist David smuggled out of the country."

"Yes, sir."

"He was Saddaji's right-hand man?"

"Correct."

"Okay, proceed."

"Well, sir, while it's true that Saddaji wasn't running Iran's ballistic missile program, the fact is we now have volumes of highly classified e-mail correspondence between Saddaji and the head of the missile program. When you go through it all, it becomes clear that Saddaji was being told that his colleagues were still several months—possibly even a year or more—away from perfecting the detonation of a warhead on an incoming ballistic missile."

"A few months isn't that much time," Allen noted.

"That's true, sir," Eva agreed. "My point is only that we're highly confident that the Iranians aren't there yet—though you're right, they're not far off. What's also troubling is that we have e-mails between Saddaji and high-ranking military officials with plans and memos discussing how to transport the warheads by truck, what kind of safeguards need to be in place, how many men would need to be part of the transportation team, whether detonation control would be in the hands of the on-the-ground commander or could be with someone more senior back in Tehran, and so forth."

"Good. Now, the next thing the president needs to know—and this is his highest priority—is the exact location of all eight warheads at the moment."

"Right—Jack, you want to talk about that?" Murray asked.

Zalinsky nodded and leaned forward in his seat. "Sir, we have retasked a Keyhole satellite over Hamadan," he began. "We're watching all movement in and around that nuclear facility and have been since the earthquake. If all the warheads were built there—and based on all the documentation we have from Dr. Saddaji's computers, we believe that's the case—then some, if not all, could still be there."

The director interrupted. "I thought David had a highly placed source who told him all the warheads had been moved."

"Yes," Zalinsky agreed. "You're referring to the source we've code-named Chameleon. He is a longtime personal friend and advisor to President Darazi and Ayatollah Hosseini. The three had lunch recently—we don't have the exact date, but it was about three weeks ago—and Chameleon obtained direct intel that 'large nuclear bombs' had been dispersed to secure locations all throughout the country."

"How reliable is the source?" the director asked.

Zalinsky looked to David.

"Very," David said. "Chameleon is the one who said we needed to find Dr. Malik because Malik was the key to understanding exactly what Iran had."

"And he was right."

"He was."

"But you guys don't believe him when he says the weapons aren't in Hamadan anymore. Why not?"

Zalinsky answered that. "That's not exactly what we're saying, sir. Chameleon could be right. We certainly believe that Darazi and Hosseini told him that the warheads were no longer in Hamadan. But we still have questions."

"Such as?"

"Was the president being told the whole truth by Saddaji and his team? Were they planning to move the weapons but hadn't yet? If they were really moving the warheads, were they fully assembled, or were parts being moved? It's dangerous to move fully assembled nuclear warheads, not so much because they might go off but because someone could hijack the convoy and suddenly a fully assembled warhead is in the hands of a rogue element of the military or a terrorist group or whatever."

"Bottom line?" Allen asked.

"The bottom line, sir, is that maybe all the weapons were scattered. Maybe they weren't. We simply don't know, which means Iran has eight operational two-hundred-kiloton nuclear warheads, and we don't have any idea where they are."

14

BEIRUT, LEBANON

The motorcade finally departed the airport grounds.

Jacques Miroux, following the Mahdi in a rented compact Renault, expected the entourage to head directly up Hafez El Asad Drive, where hundreds of thousands of Lebanese lined both sides of the street, hoping to catch a glimpse of their beloved Twelfth Imam as he made his way to Beirut's largest stadium to deliver a major address. But at the last moment, to his surprise, the Mahdi's SUV and the six other vehicles filled with heavily armed bodyguards diverted off the expected path, heading north on Al Imam El Khomeini Boulevard. A few minutes later, they turned northwest and made an unscheduled detour and stop inside the Shatila refugee camp.

It was a brilliant move, Miroux realized instantly—bold, risky, unconventional, and populist to its core. It was exactly what a typical head of state wouldn't do. Indeed, he couldn't think of a single world leader—especially an Arab leader—who had ever visited the twelve thousand impoverished souls crammed into the one square kilometer that was the Shatila refugee camp. The Mahdi was going to identify directly with the Palestinian cause. He was going to see and feel and touch and smell the misery of these refugees, and in so doing he was likely to win not only the hearts of the four hundred thousand or so Palestinians living in Lebanon but of the nearly four million Palestinians in the West Bank and Gaza, the nearly three million in Jordan, the million and a half living in Israel proper, the million living in Syria, and the pockets of Palestinians living in nearly every other country in the Middle East and North Africa.

Sure enough, as word spread through the camp of what was happening, Miroux watched the place become electrified. Thousands of Palestinian boys and girls, dirt-poor but smiling and cheering, came running to the motorcade, shouting, *"The Holy One has come! The Holy One has come!"*

The bodyguards assigned by the Lebanese government to protect the Mahdi scrambled to take up positions and attempted to build a corridor of protection around their principal. But as the Mahdi stepped out of the SUV, he ignored their movements and their counsel and immediately plunged into the throng. The crowd went wild. Mothers, clad head to foot in black chadors and holding babies in their arms, came running, as did fathers and sons, all of them unemployed, few of them sacrificing anything more important to do.

The crowd pressed in closer and closer. They tried to touch the Mahdi. They tried to kiss his hands and feet. The elderly and infirm tried to get close, hoping to touch the hem of his garment, that their ailments might be healed, and Miroux wrote furiously in his notepad to get it all down.

He noted that the Mahdi didn't try to speak but for a few words of thanks and appreciation to those nearest to him. The crowds wouldn't have been able to hear him anyway, but they loved him.

★ ★ ★ ★ ★

Ahmed was only eleven.

He was playing soccer with his friends near the trash dump when he heard the rumor come rifling through the camp. *Could it really be?* he wondered. *Could the Lord of the Age be near us? Could he really be walking among us?* It seemed impossible.

Ahmed had no access to a television. His parents could not afford any books. All they had was a Qur'an, and he studied it morning and night. He knew he was not that bright; his father told him constantly. Still, he was trying to memorize it all. His memory was terrible, certainly compared to his older brothers. But he wanted to learn. He wanted to be faithful. What more could he do? He prayed constantly for Allah to have mercy on him. It seemed impossible. He was only a poor Palestinian refugee. Forgotten by the world. Alone and scared. What could he do for Allah but perhaps one day join Hezbollah and become a martyr waging jihad against the Zionists?

He picked up his soccer ball and took off running, leaving his less-devout friends bewildered and screaming after him to come back or at least leave them the ball. But the ball was his only worldly possession. And he knew what he had to do. Down one muddy, sewage-filled alley after another he ran, as fast as his little legs could take him. He was smaller than most children his age, and when he saw the enormous crowd near the center of the camp, his first instinct was to cry. He would never get close enough to see the Mahdi.

Fighting back tears, determined not to give up, Ahmed pushed together several empty crates lying nearby and used them to climb up on the corrugated tin roof of a makeshift medical clinic. Scrambling to the top, he stood on his tiptoes and found himself in awe of what lay before him. There were masses of people as far as the eye could see—and more coming from every direction. People were chanting praises to Allah at the top of their lungs. He counted six—no, wait, seven—white vehicles in the center, nearly engulfed by the crowd, and figured that had to be where the Mahdi was. Try as he might, though, he couldn't see the one he had come for. Nor could he imagine a way to get closer.

Suddenly, he saw in the swirling dust something hovering in the sky over the center of the crowd, something almost glowing, right over where he was sure the Mahdi must be standing. It was a figure of some kind, Ahmed realized, bathed in a yellowish-white light. He had never seen anything more beautiful. Then, to his amazement, the apparition seemed to turn and look at him directly. And then it began to speak.

"Ahmed, do you know who I am?"

"I do not, my Lord," the boy replied, trembling.

"I am the angel Gabriel, Ahmed. I have come to proclaim to you the one you seek, the one over whom I now stand, is the Promised One, and you shall be his servant, the servant of the ruler of the Caliphate now rising. Submit to him, Ahmed, and you shall live."

★   ★   ★   ★   ★

Miroux saw it and was mesmerized.

Not that he wanted to be. He didn't. He wasn't religious. Far from it. He'd been raised near Lyon by atheist parents, who taught him from his childhood that religion was dangerous, anti-intellectual, a crutch for the masses, and a game for the foolish, the poor, and the hypocrites. For him, covering the Twelfth Imam was a fascinating diversion from typical stories about wars and rumors of wars and peace talks that never went anywhere. This story, he believed, was about the rise of a new political leader in a tumultuous political environment. The man was building a new Caliphate, an Islamic kingdom, or so he claimed. Few people in the West had ever heard of Muhammad Ibn Hasan Ibn Ali even a month earlier. Now he was a rock star.

But this was different. This was strange. This was news, but would anyone, his editors included, actually believe him? He grabbed his digital camera and started snapping pictures, and to his shock, when he checked the result on the viewfinder, the ghostly image hovering over the Mahdi was as plain as day.

★   ★   ★   ★   ★

LANGLEY, VIRGINIA

Director Allen turned to Eva.

"Now let's get back to Dr. Najjar Malik, whom you referenced earlier. I take it your interrogations of the good doctor are bearing fruit, Agent Fischer?"

"They are, sir. Very much so."

"He's cooperating?"

"Absolutely."

"What can I pass along to the president and the NSC?"

Eva got up and handed out a black folder marked *EYES ONLY*, containing a five-page summary of key findings from her several days' worth of interrogations. "Dr. Malik, as we've already established, is the highest-ranking living Iranian nuclear scientist at the moment, and thanks to David, he is presently secured in a CIA safe house in Oakton, Virginia. We've covered a lot of ground in the last few days. You've got the highlights there. But the headline would be this: Dr. Malik has helped us identify two new high-priority targets, both of whom were the senior deputies to Dr. Saddaji in the Iranian weapons development program. The evidence we have suggests these two scientists were doing most of the actual technical work day to day on building the warheads."

"Do you have names?" Allen asked.

"Yes, sir. The first is Jalal Zandi. He's forty-seven. An Iranian national. Born in Tehran. Holds one PhD in physics from Tehran University and another PhD in nuclear physics from the University of Manchester in the UK."

"And the second?"

"The second is Tariq Khan. Fifty-one, Pakistani national. We don't have a bio on him yet, but we know he's a nephew of A. Q. Khan and worked closely with his uncle on the Pakistani nuclear program during the nineties. These are the guys who know where the bodies are buried. Find them, and I think we find the warheads."

"So how do we find them?" the director asked.

"I don't think we have any choice," Eva said. "We need to send David back into Iran immediately."

15

Ahmed stared and couldn't look away.

He tried to speak but couldn't. He tried to swallow but his throat was bone dry. After a few moments, however, he realized that he was not the only one to see this angel of light. Suddenly everyone was pointing into the air and a hush fell over the crowd, and at that moment, Ahmed snapped out of the trancelike state he had just been in. He realized that the motorcade was getting ready to depart and that with everyone else focused on the angel, he had a chance.

Scrambling down from the roof of the clinic, careful not to drop the soccer ball he held in a vise grip, he began running once again as fast as he could. Zigzagging through alleyways filled with garbage and a stench he had never grown used to, Ahmed did his best to outflank the crowd and reach the northwest exit of the Shatila refugee camp. His heart pounded. His little lungs were sucking in as much air as they possibly could, but it didn't seem to be enough. Sweat poured down his face and down his back. His bare, calloused feet ached terribly. But finally he reached the checkpoint just as the crowds reluctantly parted and the Twelfth Imam's white SUV began to wind its way ever so carefully through the narrow streets toward Tarik Jdideh, the road that led to the sports complex.

Panting fiercely and trying desperately to catch his breath, Ahmed ran ahead of the crowd to a highway overpass just in front of the camp entrance. Standing in the shadows, listening to the cars and trucks rumbling overhead, he waited for the motorcade to pass by. He waved at the tinted windows, not knowing who—if anyone—was watching or caring. Then suddenly, one of the vehicles stopped right in front of him. One of the tinted passenger-side windows in the back rolled down, and there, staring directly into Ahmed's eyes, was the Twelfth Imam.

"Peace be with you, my son."

Ahmed fell to his knees and bowed low.

"Are you coming to hear my sermon?" the Mahdi asked.

"No, my Lord."

"Why not?"

"I do not have a ticket, my Master. I waited in line all night, but when morning came, they told me there were no tickets left."

"Come and see," the Mahdi said.

"How, my Lord?"

"Come with me, little Ahmed, and I will show you great and mighty things you do not know."

A rear passenger door opened. The Mahdi told an aide to get out and find a seat in the last SUV in the motorcade. Ahmed could not believe it—the Mahdi knew his name and was inviting him to join him for the most important event in the history of Lebanon, maybe in the history of the world. And yet he hesitated.

"You do not want to come?" the Mahdi asked.

"I do, my Lord, more than anything. It's just my parents. I don't want them to miss me. I'm not always a good boy, but I . . ."

Ahmed stopped in midsentence. His eyes went wide, and he turned pale as a sheet. For as he peered into the SUV, there sat his father and his mother waiting for him in the backseat, tears streaming down their faces. How was this possible? Ahmed wondered. It was simple, he figured. The Promised One could do all things. All he needed to do, Ahmed decided, was to believe and to submit, without asking questions. Questions, he feared, might mean he didn't really believe or perhaps believe as deeply as he should.

Nodding his head without saying a word, he gratefully climbed into the vehicle, kissed his mother, and sat beside the Twelfth Imam, his hands shaking, his lips quivering.

"Do not be afraid, little one," the Mahdi said. "I will take care of you. And once we are inside, I have a surprise for you, young man, something I think you will enjoy very much."

"What is it?" Ahmed asked, surging with anticipation.

"Be patient, and you will see."

★ ★ ★ ★ ★

Miroux saw Javad exit the Mahdi's vehicle.

He saw the aide walk to the back of the motorcade and climb into the last SUV, already jammed with Iranian intelligence operatives. But from his vantage point, Miroux could not see why any of this was happening. The highway overpass cast such deep and dark shadows that it was virtually impossible to get a good look at what the holdup was.

Not that it really mattered. His main job at the moment was to not lose the motorcade. His editors had been explicit. They wanted wall-to-wall coverage of the Mahdi and his movements. Interest in the UK was off the charts, and it was spiking worldwide as well. Editors of newspapers and news websites around the world were seeing readership of Twelfth Imam–related articles surge beyond anything they had ever witnessed in their lifetimes. Miroux was tasked with filing three stories a day—at least.

So he laid on the horn, tried to maneuver his tiny Renault through the crowd, and prayed desperately to a God he did not believe in that he wouldn't run anyone over.

★ ★ ★ ★ ★

Ahmed smiled, for he did not know the dangers just ahead.

He dutifully put on his seat belt, and someone shut the door. The motorcade started moving again. As they left the camp, they took a right and then a quick left, and he could soon see the gigantic steel-and-glass stadium rising before them. Ahmed pressed his face against the window, fascinated by the sights and sounds of helicopters hovering overhead, of police motorcycles—lights flashing and sirens wailing—leading the motorcade and bringing up the rear, of well-armed Beirut policemen and Hezbollah militia members blocking off every street and providing a secure corridor. No longer were they surrounded by regular people. No longer was the Promised One being mobbed by commoners or refugees. Now he was being treated like a president, like a prince, like royalty, Ahmed thought, and he had never been more excited.

The side street they were on now was narrow and lined on both sides with small homes and parked cars and trucks. Ahmed realized he had never been this far away from the camp, and he began to wonder what the rest of Beirut looked like. He had heard there were beaches. He had heard that the Mediterranean lapped gently along the shoreline and that the waters were warm and tasted salty, and he wondered what that must be like.

Ahmed's attention was drawn to a silver Mercedes, old and somewhat rusted and parked just a few yards ahead of them on the left. He didn't know why it caught his eye. It just did. At that moment, the Mercedes exploded in a massive fireball. Flames shot high into the air. Shards of glass and twisted, molten metal flew in all directions. Ahmed's arms instinctively covered his head, and he leaned right, away from the blast. But just then a green Volkswagen they were passing on the right exploded as well. Then so did the SUV ahead of them and the one right behind them.

The enormous force of the four blasts in rapid succession rocked their own SUV, lifted it, and sent it soaring through the air, flipping it completely over. They landed hard. Every one of the bulletproof windows blew out, and the roof scraped along the pavement, sparks and tongues of flame flying everywhere.

Thick, black, acrid smoke filled the interior. Covered in blood, his own and others', and choking uncontrollably—gasping frantically for oxygen—Ahmed wanted to scream for his mother but couldn't. He tried to turn to see her and his father, but he couldn't move. He strained to hear them but the crackle of the flames and the screams and shouts of people on the streets nearby made it impossible. He was hanging upside down, tied in by his seat belt, which he couldn't unfasten. He could feel the searing heat. Through his tears he could see the flames licking around the edges of their vehicle. He could see the driver hanging limply, blood pouring from his head. He could see the bodyguard in the front passenger seat shaking violently, an engine part driven deep into his chest. He knew he had to get out of this car as fast as possible or he was going to die. So he tried to turn and see if the Twelfth Imam could help him, but as he did, a pain more intense than anything he had ever felt before went shooting through his neck and down his spine like a thousand volts of electricity. Then everything went silent and black, and little Ahmed lost consciousness.

★   ★   ★   ★   ★

Miroux slammed on the brakes and bolted from his car.

His camera and notebook in hand, he began running toward the Twelfth Imam's SUV. What he found when he got there and would relay to the world minutes later was a horror show unlike anything he had ever witnessed before.

The stench of burning human flesh was overpowering. The entire street seemed to be covered in blood, and yet oddly it also seemed like autumn, he noticed. Most of the trees lining the narrow street were now in flames, but the force of the explosions had stripped them bare, and leaves lay scattered everywhere, as if it were October or November and they needed to be raked.

Policemen, militia members, and ordinary citizens came running from everywhere. A crowd started forming, making it difficult for fire trucks and ambulances to reach the scene. Women were sobbing. Several of the men standing nearby looked dazed and confused. Miroux tried to ask people questions about what they had just seen and heard, but few could bring themselves to speak. He started shooting pictures until a soldier ripped the camera from his neck and smashed it to the ground. Then suddenly there was a loud gasp from the crowd, almost in unison.

Miroux turned quickly to see what everyone else was seeing. He couldn't believe it. Someone was actually emerging from the wreckage. To his shock, he realized it was Muhammad Ibn Hasan Ibn Ali, covered in soot but apparently uninjured. In his arms he held a small boy, no older than ten or eleven, Miroux figured. The child, too, was alive, though badly bloodied. No one else, it seemed, from the Mahdi's vehicle had survived. Nor had anyone in the SUVs in front of or behind his.

At first the crowd erupted in applause and cheers that seemed like they were going to go on and on. But then, without warning, everyone grew quiet. One by one, they got down on their knees and bowed to the Mahdi. Miroux tried to write it all down but felt a cold shiver run down his spine. The hair on the back of his neck was standing. Something bizarre was in motion, he told himself. It finally dawned on him: this was not a political story.

16

Najjar Malik tossed and turned continuously.

Trying to fall asleep in a bedroom on the second floor of a beautiful split-level home in a quiet cul-de-sac somewhere in northern Virginia, he desperately missed the company of his wife, Sheyda, their baby daughter, and Sheyda's mother, Farah, all of whom had defected with him. To the best of his knowledge, they were in another CIA safe house, apparently somewhere in Maryland. He had not been told when they would be reunited. For now, it was nearly as though he had been sentenced to solitary confinement. He'd been told to try to stay upstairs and in his room as much as possible. The bedroom was more spacious than the apartment he'd shared with his small family in Iran. There was a sitting area with two large overstuffed chairs, a basket piled with fleece blankets, and a huge spalike bathroom he couldn't quite believe was for normal people. Still, he couldn't say he was enjoying it. If only Sheyda were sitting in one of the chairs, holding the baby and sharing her heart with him.

He had asked for a Bible and been given one. So for now, all he could do was read and pray and think and try not to worry about the future— his own, his family's, or his country's—but it wasn't easy. There was no television, no radio, no computer, and not a newspaper or magazine in his room or anywhere in the house. There was a phone in the kitchen, but it required a code his caretakers would not give him.

Going outdoors was out of the question. Eva Fischer didn't want him to have any contact with the outside world until their interrogations—she called them "conversations"—were finished, though he couldn't imagine what else she could ask. They had covered every conceivable topic, and he had done his best to be forthcoming. He had thoroughly studied and exhaustively explained all the information he could find in his late father-in-law's computer files. He had given them Zandi and Khan. He had given them detailed floor plans of the nuclear facilities not only in Hamadan, but also in Bushehr, Natanz, Arak, and Esfahān, all of which he had been to many times and knew by heart. He had even described the execution of the Arab nuclear expert from the University of Baghdad and explained his theory on why an expert on UD3, or uranium deuteride, was even in Iran.

But it was not Iran's nuclear weapons that burned Najjar Malik's heart. The threat of their use against the US or Israel was real and serious, to be sure, and he was genuinely grateful for the opportunity to help the Americans unravel Tehran's weapons program in any way he could. But what kept him up night after night at this safe house in the town of Oakton, what forced him to his knees in prayer for hour after hour—at least when Agent Fischer wasn't there to ask him so many questions—was the haunting reality that once again war was coming to the Middle East and that millions of his countrymen could very well perish and spend eternity burning in the fires of hell, with no hope of escape.

Najjar prayed desperately for peace. But the more he prayed, the more he sensed somewhere deep in his soul that the Lord's answer to this heart cry was "no." No, the Lord was not going to bring peace, security, or calm to the Middle East. No, He wasn't going to restrain those who were determined to bring bloodshed. No; not yet; not now.

Najjar had been raised a devout Shia Muslim and a Twelver. For all his life, he had prayed for war. He had believed what his fellow Twelvers believed, that the more chaos and carnage and bloodshed that occurred in the Middle East, the more likely it was for the Mahdi to come and establish justice and peace. To pray for war and even genocide, especially against the Jews and the Christians, had been his religious duty, he had always believed, because it would hasten the coming of the Promised One. But now Najjar was a completely different person. Jesus Christ had appeared to him personally in a vision in the mountains of

Hamadan. "Come and follow me," Jesus had said. Jesus had shown Najjar the scars in His hands and feet, where nails had been driven during His crucifixion. And at that moment, Najjar had known beyond the shadow of a doubt that all he had ever been taught by the mullahs and the ayatollahs was a lie. He believed at that moment that Jesus truly was King of kings and Lord of lords, that Jesus was the Alpha and the Omega, and that He was coming back soon. And at that moment, at the very instant his eyes had been opened to the reality of Jesus' love and compassion and forgiveness for him, Najjar had bowed down and worshiped Him and vowed to follow Him forever.

Ever since, he had been devouring the Bible. He had read it for hours each day, beginning when he first opened his eyes in the morning and making sure he did not go to sleep without meditating more on God's Word and even memorizing large passages of it. He couldn't get enough of the Scriptures. He was like a man who had been groping through the desert, parched beyond belief, had stumbled into an oasis of palm trees surrounding a spring, and was now gulping down fresh, clean, sweet water as fast as his system would allow.

And hour by hour, it seemed, Najjar felt his perspective on life, on the world, on the future changing dramatically. Now he knew that the prophet Isaiah had taught that the Messiah would be the Prince of Peace. Now he knew that Jesus had taught His disciples, "Blessed are the peacemakers, for they shall be called sons of God." Now he knew that David had written in the Psalms, "Pray for the peace of Jerusalem." So he spent hours on his face before his God, often in tears, praying that war and chaos and genocide would *not* come, and yet he had the strongest sense that they were coming anyway.

He couldn't see how events could turn out any other way. The Twelfth Imam was going to launch simultaneous nuclear attacks on Tel Aviv, New York, and perhaps London and Paris as well. Or Washington was going to attack Iran first using all the intelligence he himself was providing. Or the Israelis were going to hit first because they felt President Jackson and his advisors were too cowardly or were dragging their feet too long.

The question, Najjar thought, was no longer *if* war was coming but *when.* Which prompted a second and more pressing question: *Why?* Then again, the more Najjar studied the Scriptures, particularly Bible prophecy, the more he saw that Jesus and the prophets and the apostles all said that wars and rumors of wars would be prevalent in the last days before His return. Nations would rise against nations. Kingdoms would rise against kingdoms. Revolutions and lawlessness and death and destruction would come like birth pangs, the holy Scriptures foretold. Followers of Christ weren't supposed to cause or foment or desire such traumas, but they were not supposed to be surprised by the fiery trials that were coming. To the contrary, they were supposed to be ready and be prepared, for the Day of the Lord was coming at a time when the world would be caught off guard. Indeed, if Najjar was reading the Scriptures correctly, it seemed to him that in the last days the Lord was going to allow great trials and tribulations to occur to shake people out of the notion that anything but faith in Jesus Christ could save them.

Before their escape from Iran, Sheyda had told him she was convinced that God had chosen Najjar not only to know the truth of salvation and full redemption through Christ Jesus but to proclaim that truth to all of Iran. Their people had to know the Good News of God's love and free gift of forgiveness, she had insisted. Every single one of the seventy million people in his beloved country needed to hear—in Farsi—that Jesus Christ was the Way, the Truth, and the Life and that no man or woman could come to the Father except through faith in Jesus Christ. Time was short, she had said, but the message had to go forth, and even though it went against every natural instinct within him, Najjar Malik had begun to wonder if Sheyda was right.

Was his Lord really calling him to preach the gospel without fear? And if so, how? He was a stranger in a strange land. He was a prisoner of the US government. How could he possibly get out? Where would he go? And how could he spread the Word before it was too late?

★ ★ ★ ★ ★

Word of the events in Beirut ricocheted across the globe.

Reuters moved the story first, without a byline, just nine minutes after the first explosion, noting simply that "the motorcade carrying the Twelfth Imam and his entourage was attacked by a series of car bombings in Beirut" and that the casualty count and condition of the Mahdi were "at present unknown." Miroux's intention wasn't to deceive or even necessarily to heighten the suspense of an already-extraordinary global drama, though he would later be accused by some media critics of both. The truth was he simply didn't know how to write what he had seen. The world needed to know about the attack first and foremost, he told himself, so he dictated a four-hundred-word story by satellite phone to his editor at Reuters headquarters at Canary Wharf in London.

Twelve minutes later, Reuters posted the first of what would become multiple updates. This time, the story was bylined—*Jacques Miroux in Beirut*—and this was the story that took the world by storm. Seventeen people were dead. Twenty-three were wounded. "But the Twelfth Imam emerged from the crumpled, blazing wreckage with barely a scratch on him, holding a boy covered in blood, but according to two police officials interviewed by Reuters, the boy was either 'uninjured' or 'healed.'" The article quoted no fewer than six bystanders saying they were certain they had just witnessed "a miracle." There was no mention, however, of the "angel" sighting in the Shatila refugee camp, not because his editors in London wouldn't include it but because Miroux had not yet told them.

The Associated Press was the first to publish grisly still photographs from the scene, as well as exclusive photos of the Mahdi holding little Ahmed—photos taken on a bystander's mobile phone—sixteen minutes after the first explosion. Within thirty minutes, Al Jazeera was the first network to broadcast live images from the site of the attack, plus exclusive videos of the actual explosions themselves and even of the Mahdi emerging from the wreckage of his SUV with the boy in hand. These, too, had been shot by several different witnesses and residents of the neighborhood near the stadium; Al Jazeera had purchased them for a rumored six-figure sum in US dollars.

An hour later, Agence France-Presse became the first international news service to report on the "angel" sighting in a story headlined, "Thousands Claim to Hear, See 'Angelic Being' Hovering over Mahdi in Beirut Refugee Camp." The report quoted more than two dozen people, all unrelated and unknown to each other, who said they had been in the crowd in Shatila and had both personally seen the heavenly figure and heard him call their name and tell them to follow "the Promised One." The wire story moved with photographs of the "divine apparition," one taken by an AFP reporter, the other two taken on mobile phones by witnesses.

★ ★ ★ ★ ★

EN ROUTE TO TEHRAN

David was now forty-one thousand feet over the Atlantic.

Upon Director Allen's orders, he was heading back into Iran aboard the Agency's Citation. But to get there, he had to make sure it didn't appear as if he had just been in the US, much less kibitzing at CIA headquarters. Thus, he first had to return to Munich, reassume his identity as Reza Tabrizi, and only then catch two Lufthansa flights, first to Frankfurt, and then into Tehran.

For the last several hours, David had been poring over transcripts of Eva's interrogations of Dr. Najjar Malik. He'd dutifully read the five-page summary that Eva had written for Allen and the NSC. But as much as he respected Eva, he wasn't interested in her analysis. He wanted to study every page of the transcripts for himself so he could draw his own conclusions. David found every word of the transcripts riveting, and he wished he'd been there with Eva for any or all of the sessions.

Malik had not been captured. He wasn't being forced or pressured to tell the American government what he knew. He was a defector. He had been eager to leave Iran. He felt betrayed and deeply hurt by Dr. Saddaji and the Iranian government, and he wanted them exposed. The more he read, the more convinced David became that Malik had answered every single one of Eva's questions as honestly and thoroughly as he could. He was impressed by the fact that when Malik didn't know the answer to something, he just said so. He didn't seem to be trying to impress anyone with his knowledge. He didn't seem to be trying to say he knew more than he really did. Unless he was a world-class liar,

Malik seemed to be telling them the truth, and one truth was crystal clear: they needed to hunt down and bring in Jalal Zandi and Tariq Khan as rapidly as possible, for at the moment they held the keys to the kingdom.

As useful as that information was—and it was very useful indeed—David was struck even more by Malik's personal story. The scientist had been remarkably candid about his conversion from being a Twelver to being a follower of Jesus Christ. Eva had rightly pressed into his conversion, asked lots of questions, and gotten lots of details.

The CIA's reactions were mixed. Zalinsky and Murray were clearly put off by all this spiritual talk. For them, Malik's depiction of his encounter with Jesus on the road to Hamadan called into question the validity of everything else he said. Murray went so far as to mock Malik's claim of seeing a vision of Jesus. But for David, the opposite was true. Everything else Malik had told them had proven to be accurate. Indeed, they were basing much of their current strategy on what they'd just learned from him and from his interpretation of the files on Saddaji's computer. Didn't that enhance the credibility of Malik's spiritual claims? They were strange, to be sure. It wasn't often one met someone who claimed to have met God face-to-face, and David privately conceded that in another context he might have dismissed Malik as well. But what about Sheyda? She claimed to have seen Jesus too. So did Farah Saddaji, Sheyda's mother. And what about Dr. Birjandi back in Iran? He was arguably the most respected authority on the Twelfth Imam in all of Iran, probably the world, yet he had told David point-blank that he and his wife, before her death, had renounced Islam and become followers of Jesus. Could they *all* be crazy?

David needed a break. He got up, went to the back of the plane, and made himself a cup of coffee. Then he returned to his seat, buckled up again, leaned back, and shifted gears. His thoughts turned to Marseille, and he replayed her phone message in his mind.

"Hey, David, it's Marseille. Hope you're good. I really enjoyed breakfast with you. It was so great to see you again and to talk with you and give you a hug. I knew I missed you. Guess I didn't even fully realize how much until I was sitting with you again after all these years. Anyway, I hope your business

emergency gets worked out. I'll be praying everything goes better for you than for me right now. I'm stuck here in DC. All the flights out to Portland are canceled due to the storm. So I'm at a hotel for a few days with nothing to do. I'd love to talk again. Call me when you get a chance. And let me know how your mom is doing. I'm praying for her. See you. Bye."

David had wanted to call her before takeoff, but it was the middle of the night and he didn't want to wake her up. Nor had he wanted his call to be picked up by the NSA. He felt sensitive enough about this relationship. The last thing he needed was the US intelligence network eavesdropping on his personal life. At this point, the best he figured he could do was call her from a pay phone in Germany before heading back into the abyss that was Iran.

17

Eva Fischer was on a CIA jet to New York.

Her mission for the next twenty-four hours was to link up with the FBI team interrogating the only suspect they had in the attempted assassination of the president and help the Agency determine who exactly was responsible for the attack and what they might be plotting next.

Midflight, Eva received an urgent flash-traffic message from Zalinsky and learned for the first time of the attack against the Twelfth Imam in Beirut. Zalinsky also forwarded links to the latest stories off the wires and ordered her to log on to a secure conference call with him at Langley. The message indicated that David, on his way to Iran, had received the same directive. Both complied immediately.

Zalinsky briefed them on what he knew, which so far was precious little more than what the media was reporting.

"The stop they made in the refugee camp," Eva said. "You're saying that was unscheduled?"

"That's right," Zalinsky said.

"So they weren't scheduled to be on the street they were going down when the attack happened?"

"Not that we're aware of."

"Then how could someone have known to plant all those car bombs and IEDs in that particular place to go off at that particular time?"

"No idea," Zalinsky conceded. "None of us here have come up with any viable explanations."

"What if they weren't car bombs or IEDs?" David said.

"What do you mean?" Eva asked.

"What if the attack was designed to mirror the attacks in Manhattan?" David continued.

"Not possible," Zalinsky said. "We've been monitoring all police and military radio traffic in Beirut. There's no indication of RPGs, grenades, nothing like that. The Lebanese intelligence services have canvassed the entire neighborhood. They've talked to hundreds of witnesses. No one saw anything out of the ordinary. And believe me, the police were out in full force. If someone had fired at the motorcade, someone would have seen something. And besides, I'm looking at live Keyhole satellite images of the scene. These were car bombs, David. You should see the craters that they left. RPGs and grenades don't leave craters like this."

"What if it was a drone attack?" David said.

Eva hadn't considered that before, but she was intrigued.

"Think about it," David continued. "What if someone was using a UAV to track the Twelfth Imam's movements in real time?"

"Go on," Zalinsky said.

"They would have seen him enter the camp. If they were a terror group, they probably would have attacked right then. But if it was a foreign intelligence agency . . ."

"They wouldn't have wanted all the collateral damage," Eva said.

"Exactly. Too many civilians. So what if they waited for the motorcade to leave the camp and then saw him head through a residential area? Risks there, too, but more if they waited for him to get to the stadium."

"Then they fired missiles from the drones," Eva said.

"Right."

"The cars parked along the side of the road would have provided a perfect cover," Zalinsky added. "To the world it looks like a series of car bombs and IEDs. But a drone strike is far less complicated to plan and far more precise."

"It's just a theory," David said.

"It's a good one," Eva said, increasingly impressed with David's quick mind and sharp instincts.

"Can you get the analysts to review all the videos of the first explosion?" David asked. "If you slow them down enough, you might actually be able to see the incoming missile and its initial impact."

"We'll get right on it," Zalinsky said. "But let's say you're right. It wasn't us, so who was it?"

Does he really have to ask? Eva wondered. She knew exactly what David was going to say: the Israelis.

"It was the Israelis," David said without a trace of doubt in his voice.

"I hope you're wrong," Zalinsky said. "The president is going to go ballistic."

"Why?" David asked. "The Mossad is trying to avenge the attack on their prime minister. They're trying to cut off the head of the snake. Personally, I'm surprised they hit back so fast, but I don't blame them one bit."

"The president is doing everything he can to avoid a new war erupting in the Middle East," Zalinsky said. "This now almost guarantees the war will happen anyway."

Eva strongly disagreed. "Jack, come on; if a war is coming—and I grant you it probably is—it was Iran's nuclear bomb test that was the straw that broke the camel's back, not this."

She tried to picture David on the Citation, looking out the window of the jet at the blackness below, smiling, thinking he couldn't have said it better himself. They made a good team, she thought. She just wished she were traveling back into Iran with him.

Zalinsky, however, had a different perspective. "If you take a shot at a man in control of eight nukes, he'd better not make it off the pavement," their boss said with an intensity she hadn't anticipated. "If it was the Israelis, it was an enormous gamble—and it failed."

★ ★ ★ ★ ★

ALEXANDRIA, VIRGINIA

The phone rang in the darkness.

Roger Allen fumbled for the light and his glasses. He'd been home less than an hour and asleep for no more than thirty minutes. But just seeing the caller ID gave him a jolt of adrenaline. It was the White House Situation Room.

"Allen speaking. . . . Yes. . . . Right now? . . . I understand. . . . Of course. . . . I'm on my way."

His wife rolled over and tried to rub the sleep from her eyes. "Who was that?" she asked.

"The chief of staff," Allen said. "They've got a plane waiting for me at Andrews."

"Where are you going?"

"Israel."

"But you just got back."

"The president is terrified Naphtali is going to launch a preemptive strike on Iran in the next few days."

"Can you blame them?"

"Not entirely, but he wants me to talk them off the ledge."

"Can you?"

"I serve at the pleasure of the president."

"No, no, obviously you're going to go. But can you persuade Asher not to go to war after all that's happened?"

"I've known him since college, but honestly, sweetheart, I have no idea."

"Did they give you new instructions of what to say?"

"No. They just said get moving. We have the entire flight to figure it out."

★ ★ ★ ★ ★

ARLINGTON, VIRGINIA

Marseille was up at the crack of dawn.

She got on her knees, prayed for a while, and began her morning devotions. She was trying to follow a plan her pastor had asked everyone in their church to do: read through the Bible in a year. But she was way off. She was supposed to have covered Paul's second letter to the Thessalonians the previous October, along with everyone else. But here it was March and she was only in chapter two.

There were lots of reasons. Sometimes she was just plain lazy. It was hard to get up so early and study the Word before going in to teach, and at night often she either was too tired or just wanted to curl up with a movie or a novel. Other times, she was so fascinated by a particular passage that she would hunker on it for several days rather than sticking to the plan. That had been the case all the way through 1 Thessalonians and in the first chapter of the second letter as well.

Who could not be fascinated with—and deeply concerned by—verses like "the Lord Jesus will be revealed from heaven with His mighty angels in flaming fire, dealing out retribution to those who do not know God and to those who do not obey the gospel of our Lord Jesus. These will pay the penalty of eternal destruction, away from the presence of the Lord and from the glory of His power, when He comes to be glorified in His saints on that day"?

As Marseille began chapter 2, however, she found herself entering into an arena she had never studied before.

Now we request you, brethren, with regard to the coming of our Lord Jesus Christ and our gathering together to Him, that you not be quickly shaken from your composure or be disturbed either by a spirit or a message or a letter as if from us, to the effect that the day of the Lord has come. Let no one in any way deceive you, for it will not come unless the apostasy comes first, and the man of lawlessness is revealed, the son of destruction, who opposes and exalts himself above every so-called god or object of worship, so that he takes his seat in the temple of God, displaying himself as being God. Do you not remember that while I was still with you, I was telling you these things?

And you know what restrains him now, so that in his time he will be revealed. For the mystery of lawlessness is already at work; only he who now restrains will do so until he is taken out of the way. Then that lawless one will be revealed whom the Lord will slay with the breath of His mouth and bring to an end by the appearance of His coming; that is, the one whose coming is in accord with the activity of Satan, with all power and signs and false wonders, and with all the deception of wickedness for those who perish, because they did not receive the love of the truth so as to be saved.

For this reason God will send upon them a deluding influence so that they will believe what is false, in order that they all may be judged who did not believe the truth, but took pleasure in wickedness.

As best she could tell, these were prophecies about the coming of the Antichrist. But as she read, she found the description reminded her of things she had seen and heard about the man calling himself the Twelfth Imam.

She had never really done a study on the Antichrist, she realized. She had heard the term many times in sermons and from other Christians, but she had never bothered to consider the term carefully or figure out what it really meant. As for the Twelfth Imam, she didn't know much about him either, except for what she had been reading in the papers and seeing on television in recent days. But she was curious about both, and for the first time in a long while, she actually had some time on her hands. She wasn't teaching. She wasn't home. She was stuck in a hotel room indefinitely. Maybe the Lord was giving her a gift, the freedom to spend time in His Word today.

She eagerly got out her notebook and wrote at the top of a clean page: "What the Bible says about the Antichrist." Then she jotted down a few observations based on the text.

1. The Antichrist will come before the Day of the Lord comes.
2. A period of apostasy will precede the coming of the Antichrist and the Day of the Lord.
3. The Antichrist will be thought of as the man of lawlessness and the lawless one and will be connected somehow to the mystery of lawlessness.
4. He will also be the son of destruction.
5. He will oppose all other gods and religions.
6. He will "exalt himself above every so-called god or object of worship."
7. He will sit down "in the temple of God, displaying himself as being God."

8. He will be revealed—this is mentioned three times (2:3, 2:6, and 2:8).
9. He will come "in accord with the activity of Satan."
10. He will come with "all power and signs and false wonders" and will be engaged in deception of wickedness.

Marseille shuddered. She had only just started developing her list. There was so much more to learn, so many more passages to explore. But it was clear that a great evil would rise, and she was beginning to wonder if it was already here.

BROOKLYN, NEW YORK

Eva shouldn't have been thinking of David at that moment.

She had far more important matters before her. But she couldn't help it. The arrest report she was quickly reviewing said the suspect was six feet two inches tall, about 180 pounds, with black curly hair, brown eyes, olive skin, an athletic build, and an apparent Middle Eastern heritage. It made her think of David, to whom she found herself increasingly drawn. She wondered what David thought of her and why, to the best of her knowledge, he wasn't seeing anyone.

"You ready?" asked Sean Taylor, the FBI agent in charge.

Eva wasn't, but she said yes. She was letting herself be distracted by a guy, and she cursed herself for it and refocused. Then the massive, vaultlike steel door was electronically unlocked, and she entered the small, cold, barren room alone.

As the locks reengaged behind her, she felt her heart rate quickening. She'd conducted a lot of interrogations over the years, in Baghdad and Fallujah, in Kabul and Marrakesh, at Gitmo and in CIA safe houses around the world. But each encounter had its unique twists. She never knew what was coming. And though she'd never admit it even to her closest colleagues, she got the jitters every time. She didn't know why exactly. She was in no danger. The suspects were always locked down. This morning there were a dozen armed agents outside the door ready to burst in and help her at any moment. There was just something about being alone in the room with pure evil that she never got used to. She wasn't a religious person, but sometimes she wondered why not.

The floor of this particular cell, in an unmarked FBI field office in a seedy section of Brooklyn, was tiled with white porcelain, as were the walls. A box about the size of a phone book hung on the far wall, opposite the door. The ceiling was higher than others she'd seen, about twelve feet, with fluorescent lighting and a small video camera recording every sound and movement. That, she reminded herself, had its pluses and minuses.

The suspect was properly shackled and wore a thick black hood and a clean, brand-new orange jumpsuit, like he was already in prison. Wasting no time, Eva stepped behind the man, yanked off the hood, and recoiled at the gruesome mess. She had seen beatings in her years of doing this, but none quite like this. The man's face was severely bloodied and bruised, as were his arms and hands. His eyes were nearly swollen shut. His hair was matted with blood. He had been under the hood since his capture nearly twelve hours ago. He hadn't been offered any food or water. He hadn't been allowed to use a restroom. And for what? Taylor hadn't gotten a single shred of information out of him and had told Eva to her face that she wasn't going to get any either. Maybe he was right, but she certainly wasn't going to follow his lead. It had gotten them nowhere.

"I'm sorry about your brother," Eva began, remaining behind the suspect and not letting him see her face. "We will make sure he has a proper funeral."

The young man flinched. Eva waited a few moments, letting the words and their meaning sink in. Finally she began talking again, but only in a whisper, just behind his right ear.

"Your brother Rahim was only thirty-two years old. That's pretty young, isn't it?"

There was no reply.

"I see Rahim held an Iranian passport. Was employed by the Iranian Revolutionary Guard Corps. Was wanted in six countries—Great Britain, the Netherlands, Denmark, Spain, Thailand, and Venezuela. We know all about him. We know he was your older brother. We know he recruited you into the Revolutionary Guard. And now you know he was shot dead by the US Secret Service before he even got off a third shot."

The swollen hands of the unshaven, swarthy young man with jet-black hair and angular features were shaking. Eva wasn't yet sure if that was sorrow or rage, but she decided to find out.

"Now what about you? We ran your fingerprints through our system and learned quite a bit. We know your name is Navid Yazidi. We know you're twenty-eight years old. We know you grew up in Tehran. You lived in an apartment on Ghazaeri Street, just off Piruzi, around the corner from Fajr Hospital."

Eva paused for a moment, then heard Agent Taylor—watching and listening to the proceedings via video from the room directly adjacent to hers—speaking into her earpiece. "His blood pressure is spiking," Taylor said. "He's surprised you know all this. Keep going."

"Even as we speak, Navid, we are sending people to your parents' apartment to deliver the news of your brother's death," Eva said, ignoring Taylor, whom she considered a sadist. "We don't want them to have to hear it on Al Jazeera."

★ ★ ★ ★ ★

ARLINGTON, VIRGINIA

Marseille turned to the book of Daniel.

The editor's notes in the margin of her study Bible provided cross-references from 2 Thessalonians 2 to several related passages in the Old Testament book. The first was Daniel 7:25.

He will speak out against the Most High and wear down the saints of the Highest One, and he will intend to make alterations in times and in law; and they will be given into his hand for a time, times, and half a time.

The next was Daniel 8:23-25.

In the latter period of their rule, when the transgressors have run their course, a king will arise, insolent and skilled in intrigue. His power will be mighty, but not by his own power, and he will destroy to an extraordinary degree and prosper and perform his will; he will destroy mighty men and the holy people.

And through his shrewdness he will cause deceit to succeed by his influence; and he will magnify himself in his heart, and he will destroy many while they are at ease. He will even oppose the Prince of princes.

The third was Daniel 11:36-37.

Then the king will do as he pleases, and he will exalt and magnify himself above every god and will speak monstrous things against the God of gods; and he will prosper until the indignation is finished, for that which is decreed will be done.

He will show no regard for the gods of his fathers or for the desire of women, nor will he show regard for any other god; for he will magnify himself above them all.

Marseille was making notes as fast as she could. As she did, she found herself backing up and reading all the way through Daniel 11 and learned that this future king was described by the prophet as a despicable person who would arise during a time of tranquility and would seize global power by intrigue and by overflowing forces in the End Times. What horrified Marseille most was that Daniel indicated that this future tyrant would eventually "enter the Beautiful Land." That had to be Israel, she thought. Daniel even wrote that this tyrant would "pitch the tents of his royal pavilion between the seas and the beautiful Holy Mountain." Did that mean he would set up his global headquarters between the Temple Mount in Jerusalem and the Mediterranean? At first glance it seemed so. But why would God let that happen? Marseille had no idea. She had been a believer for only a few years. She'd never taken the time to study Bible prophecy, and she felt overwhelmed. One thing, however, was unmistakably clear: this evil dictator, whoever he was, would "go forth with great wrath to destroy and annihilate many." The only good news Marseille could find came in verse 45: "yet he will come to his end, and no one will help him." But at the moment, such a promise seemed to offer little solace.

Checking the cross-reference notes again, she turned to Revelation 6:1-4.

Then I saw when the Lamb broke one of the seven seals, and I heard one of the four living creatures saying as with a voice of thunder, "Come." I looked, and behold, a white horse, and he who sat on it had a bow; and a crown was given to him, and he went out conquering and to conquer.

When He broke the second seal, I heard the second living creature saying, "Come." And another, a red horse, went out; and to him who sat on it, it was granted to take peace from the earth, and that men would slay one another; and a great sword was given to him.

The more Marseille read about the four horsemen of the apocalypse, the more fearful she became. For after the white horse bearing a conqueror and the red horse bringing global war came a black horse unleashing global famine and a pale horse with death in so many forms that a fourth of the earth, the text said, would perish. Marseille quickly did the math. If there were nearly seven billion people alive today, that meant something like 1.75 billion people could die in the early years of the Tribulation of which the prophecies spoke. Had that time come? Was the arrival of the Twelfth Imam going to trigger the release of the four horsemen?

She set aside her Bible and notebook and decided to take a break. She ordered some oatmeal with brown sugar and a glass of orange juice from room service and then opened her door to pick up her complimentary copy of *USA Today*, which was waiting in the hallway. Checking the front-page headlines below the fold, she was relieved to see the president was improving and might be released from the hospital in another day or two, though she grieved for the families of the slain Egyptian president and all the others who had perished in the attacks in New York.

As she turned the paper over, she was startled by the lead headline: "Twelfth Imam Miraculously Survives Assassination Attempt, Says Nothing Will Stop Rise of Global Caliphate." Marseille stared at the large color photo of the unscathed Mahdi carrying a badly burned little boy in his arms. She read how everyone else in the Mahdi's vehicle and the SUVs in front of him and behind had been killed in the attack; only the Twelfth Imam and the eleven-year-old boy had walked out of the burning wreckage. How was that possible? How had they survived? It made no sense, Marseille thought.

What struck her most, however, were the quotes by the Twelfth Imam toward the end of the article, from the impromptu press conference he had given in Beirut just prior to the attack. "I am calling on all the countries of the world to join the Caliphate. . . . I have come to declare that Islam is the answer to all the world's ills. . . . Will you truly submit to the will of Allah? Will you live for him? Will you die in his service?"

He added that his would be a purely Islamic government based upon Sharia law. He warned that opposition would not be tolerated and that "to revolt against Allah's government is to revolt against Allah. And to revolt against Allah has its punishment in our law. . . . It is a heavy punishment."

The most chilling line of the article was the last, Marseille thought. Asked if he was disappointed that the Israeli prime minister had survived the attack, the Twelfth Imam had simply replied: "The Zionist regime is heading toward annihilation, one way or the other." The word *annihilation* jumped out at her and drove her again to her knees in prayer.

"What does all this mean, Lord?" she cried out. "What does it mean for me? I'm just a schoolteacher. And hardly a very good one. I feel all alone in the world, Lord, and I fear a great evil is rising. But I love You, and I know You love me. Show me what You want me to do. Please show me what would please You. This is what I want, Father, until You take me home . . . or send Your Son to get me."

19

Eva stood behind Navid.

She was still not yet ready for him to see her face. That would come in due time. He was hooked up to all kinds of physiological sensors that were streaming data to the analysts in the next room. They sent her periodic updates through her earpiece, keeping her in control and him guessing.

"We recovered your cell phone, Navid. Prepaid. Disposable. Untraceable. Smart choice. Very smart. Except that you made a little mistake, Navid—just one. But then again, it only takes one."

"His blood pressure just spiked again," Agent Taylor said in her ear.

She nodded and kept going. "Now, Navid, I know you want to be a martyr," she said calmly. "Like your brother. I'm sure you're very proud of him. I'm sure that you've always looked up to him. But he died in action. I oppose everything he stood for and everything he did, obviously. He gave his life for something he believed in. I'll give him that. You, on the other hand—I'm curious about you. The FBI caught you sitting in a car doing nothing. I mean, presumably you were waiting for the others. You were supposed to drive the getaway car. But you were just sitting there. You didn't put up a fight. You didn't try to escape. Of course, you were surrounded by two dozen guys with automatic weapons. But hey, you could have gone down in a hail of gunfire like your brother, shouting, *'Allahu Akbar!'* I guess I'm just curious why you didn't."

She paused a moment, then changed course. "That's all right. Don't answer that. We'll get back to why you gave up so easily in a little while. Let's focus on your execution."

"His blood pressure is off the charts now," Taylor said.

"I'm figuring at this point that you want to go to the electric chair. Heck, you're probably looking forward to it, which is good, because you will. Believe me, you will die. This is an easy case. You were part of a terrorist team that killed dozens of people, including the president of Egypt. I doubt there will even be an appeal. I give you two weeks, maybe three, before they execute you."

She was lying, of course. She couldn't remember the last time the feds had executed anyone with the electric chair. What's more, she figured they'd be lucky if they could give Navid Yazidi any type of death sentence in less than a decade. More than likely, they would cut him some ridiculous deal in exchange for information. But his reactions were proof he didn't know any of that. She thought the fact that he was so nervous strongly suggested he'd never seriously considered the prospect of being caught. She guessed he had figured he would likely be killed in action or—more likely, in his mind—somehow slip through the American dragnet and escape capture or punishment entirely because he was a servant of Allah and Allah took care of his own.

Uncertainty clearly unnerved him. So did the prospect of death. That was good. Those were his Achilles' heels. She needed to exploit them.

"I'm afraid I won't be there, though, Navid. There's a lot I can handle, but watching a man be electrocuted to death is not one of them. But you'll be fine. You want to be a martyr like Rahim, right? You'll probably be grinning ear to ear when they strap you into the chair." She stopped talking, and all was quiet, save the hum of the fluorescent lights. She waited awhile for everything to sink in, then continued.

"You got caught, Navid. You didn't resist. You didn't try to escape. Maybe you weren't really so committed to this mission, like Rahim was. And you were drinking alcohol—lots of it—the night before the attack. That's right, Navid. At one point you called your hotel with your disposable phone. That was your mistake; we found the number, went to the hotel, and saw your room. I was there myself. And I personally saw the hotel security tapes. I know you checked into that Sheraton. I saw you get into the elevator and push the button for the ninth floor. I saw you key into room 919. I went to room 919, Navid; I saw that you ate everything in the minibar. And you drank everything in the minibar. Had they ever let you be in a room by yourself with a minibar? I'm guessing not. Because you really went to town. Which is fine. Don't get me wrong. I mean, you all paid your bills with cash. I'm just thinking Allah might not be too pleased. And I'm guessing he was watching. And I guess if I were sitting in the electric chair soon, waiting to pass from one world to the next, I'd be wondering where I was going. Because it's one thing to be executed in one of the most painful ways imaginable—did I mention your whole head is going to explode into flames?—but that might be nothing compared to what's coming the moment you leave this world and enter the next."

Again she paused for effect. She shook her head so Taylor would keep his mouth shut. She didn't need an update. She knew exactly what she was doing. She unbuttoned her blouse an extra button and smoothed out the wrinkles of the skirt she was wearing, then stepped around the chair and met the nervous gaze of Navid Yazidi with a gentle smile as she put her blonde hair in a ponytail.

"I want to be your friend, Navid," she said softly. "There are people in this building who want to put you in that chair, but I just want you to know that I'm not one of them. I want to help you. But first you have to help me. I don't want anyone else to die. I don't want anyone else to get hurt, especially you. But they're only going to give me a few more minutes with you, Navid. And if you don't help me, then I can't help you. And then those men who beat you are going to come back in here and do what they do best. So tell me what you know about Firouz. Tell me what you know about his driver, Jamshad. That's right. We know the names of your accomplices—that's another mistake you made. You left them both voice messages in their hotel rooms, and you used their real names."

★ ★ ★ ★ ★

OAKTON, VIRGINIA

Najjar stared out his bedroom windows.

He watched some nameless couple and their two children who lived in the house just behind the safe house packing up their minivan with suitcases and beach blankets and all kinds of toys, headed off on a vacation of some kind. The image made him miss his own family all the more. He wanted to play with his daughter. What he wouldn't give to get away with them on a vacation. He couldn't remember the last time he'd taken a break and gotten away from all the cares of life. His father-in-law had worked him like a slave, and he was constantly exhausted.

He turned away and flopped back on the bed and stared up at the ceiling. He couldn't talk to his family or hold them, much less go on holiday with them. So he began to pray for them. He prayed they wouldn't worry too much about him or about their future. He prayed the baby was being peaceful for Sheyda, that she and her mother could laugh together and not be too lonely without him. Eventually he drifted off to sleep with their faces crossing his mind's eye and a prayer on his lips.

And as he slept, he had a dream.

"Najjar, do not be afraid," a voice said. "I, Jesus, have sent My angel to testify to you about these things. I am the root and the descendant of David, the bright morning star. Behold, I am coming quickly, and My reward is with Me, to render to every man according to what he has done. Yes, I am coming quickly. You must speak to the sons of your people. Say to them, 'If I bring a sword upon a land, and the people of the land take one man from among them and make him their watchman, and he sees the sword coming upon the land and blows on the trumpet and warns the people, then he who hears the sound of the trumpet and does not take warning, and a sword comes and takes him away, his blood will be on his own head. He heard the sound of the trumpet but did not take warning; his blood will be on himself. But had he taken warning, he would have delivered his life. But if the watchman sees the sword coming and does not blow the trumpet and the people are not warned, and a sword comes and takes a person from them, he is taken away in his iniquity; but his blood I will require from the watchman's hand.'"

Still dreaming, Najjar was careful to remember the words, just as they had been spoken. He somehow knew this was more than just a dream and that he would remember these words even after he awoke.

He also realized he knew the sword was coming soon, and his heart quickened at what he sensed was coming next.

"Now as for you, Najjar, I have appointed you a watchman for the nation of Persia. When you hear a word from My mouth warn them from Me. When I say to the wicked, 'You will surely die,' and you do not warn him or speak out to warn the wicked from his wicked way that he may live, that wicked man shall die in his iniquity, but his blood I will require at your hand. Yet if you have warned the wicked and he does not turn from his wickedness or from his wicked way, he shall die in his iniquity; but you have delivered yourself."

20

"Is Rahim really dead?"

Eva looked up from the magazine she was reading as she sat patiently in a wooden chair on the other side of the cell. It had been quiet for too long. She was beginning to think Navid Yazidi wasn't going to take the bait. But now he was nibbling, and Eva was determined to hook him and reel him all the way in.

"I beg your pardon?" she asked, though she had heard every word.

"Rahim? Is he . . . is he really dead?"

Eva nodded. "I'm afraid so. Didn't anyone tell you when they first brought you in?"

"No."

"I thought they did."

"They didn't."

"I'm very sorry, Navid," Eva said gently. "It's hard to lose a brother, I know. My older brother died four years ago next week. Drunk driver. Never saw it coming."

It was a lie. Eva had three sisters, all younger, but not a single brother. But she certainly sounded convincing and empathetic. Navid nodded and hung his head. It was working. The ice was beginning to crack.

"May I have some water?" he asked, his tone subdued but his eyes pleading with her for mercy.

"Of course, Navid. Would you like something to eat as well? Have they fed you yet? You must be famished."

"No, no, just some water, please."

This was a good sign. She got up, knocked three times on the steel door, and stepped out for a few minutes. While she was gone, guards gave the prisoner several sips of water and a few bites of warm pita bread dipped in freshly made hummus, then led the man to the facilities to allow him to relieve himself. Only when Navid was locked down again and given a bit more water and pita did Eva return.

"How are you feeling?" she asked.

"A little better," he said softly, his voice hoarse, his spirit nearly broken.

"Good," she said and then went back to her reading, knowing all the while that he was staring at her, sizing her up, trying to understand who she was and whether he could really trust her.

After several minutes, she lowered her magazine, looked him in the eye, and asked, "What did you love most about Rahim?"

The question seemed to take Navid completely by surprise. He quickly turned away and closed his eyes. So Eva went back to reading. But after another few minutes, it seemed Navid couldn't help himself.

"Rahim was always more devout than I."

"Son of a . . ." Taylor said in Eva's earpiece. "He's desperate for human contact, just like you said."

Eva resisted the temptation to nod or glance at the video camera. But she was glad Taylor and his colleagues were taking notice.

"What do you mean?" Eva asked Navid.

"Rahim was always the strong one, always the one who submitted to Allah faster and more faithfully than I. He memorized all of the Qur'an by the age of ten. I still haven't done it. He got straight As in the madrassa. I got Cs and Ds. When it was time to get up for morning prayers, Rahim would hear the muezzin call and jump right out of bed. Most of the time, I slept in . . . or wanted to."

"What was his favorite passage?"

"In the Qur'an?"

Eva nodded.

Navid hesitated for a moment as if trying to determine whether she was sincere or not. He must have finally concluded that she was because all of a sudden he said, "He really loved Sura 3, verses 185 and 186."

"What do those say?"

"'Every soul is bound to taste death. So you will be repaid in full on the Day of Resurrection for whatever you have done in the world. Whoever is spared the Fire and admitted to Paradise has indeed prospered and triumphed, if you are patient, steadfast, and keep within the limits of piety.'"

"Is your brother in paradise now, Navid?"

"I hope so."

"And you?" Eva asked, pushing the envelope. "Will you see him when it's your time?"

There was a long pause. "I don't know." Another long pause. "I hope so. I miss him."

"I'm sure you do," Eva said. "Were you always close?"

"No," Navid said, staring off into space.

"Why not?" she asked, trying to bring him back.

He shrugged his shoulders and stared down at the floor. "Rahim was four years older than I. So when I began junior high school, he was already in high school. When I was a freshman in high school, he was already done and in the army. When I was drafted, he was in college. It was only about six months ago that we began to connect again after so much time."

"What happened?"

"I . . ."

"What?"

"I shouldn't be telling you this."

"Why not?"

"They told me not to say anything."

"Who did?"

"The commander. He said if we were caught, we shouldn't say anything, just keep our mouths shut."

"Does it really matter now what he said, Navid?" Eva asked. "You're never going to see that commander again. He can't hurt you. He's half a world away."

"He will kill my family."

"You mean your parents?"

Navid nodded, his eyes glassy and fatigued.

"They still live in Tehran, in the apartment on Ghazaeri Street, right?" Eva asked.

Navid nodded again.

"It's okay, Navid. I told you. We've already sent people to make sure they're okay and to let them know that you're safe. No one can hurt them now. No one."

It was another lie. But it seemed to work.

"Really?" Navid asked.

"I promise," Eva said.

Navid closed his eyes for several minutes. His breathing was light and shallow. She wondered if he had actually dozed off, but then he opened his eyes again and resumed staring at her.

"You look a lot like her."

"Like who?"

"His sister."

"Whose?"

"Firouz's sister."

"I do?"

"Except her hair is dark brown, almost black, not blonde. And her eyes are brown, not blue. But your face, your hands, your smile, your mannerisms . . . you look so much like Shirin. She is very beautiful."

Eva didn't know what to say. He was, after all, a prisoner, a terrorist, a murderer.

"Is she around my age?"

"No."

"Younger or older?"

"Younger. Much younger."

"Younger than Firouz, too?"

He nodded.

"How much younger?"

"At least ten years."

"So how old does that make her?"

"She'll be eighteen in July."

"Pay dirt," Agent Taylor exclaimed. "Now we need a last name."

Eva ignored the request. It was a distraction. She knew what she had to do, and she knew how to get it done. She wasn't interested in being coached by novices.

"Is she married?" she asked.

"Shirin?"

"Yes."

"Not yet."

"So there's hope."

"What do you mean?" Navid asked.

"For you," Eva said. "There's hope for you, right?"

He shook his head and looked back at his feet. "No."

"Why not?"

"I could never win the heart of a girl like her. Not now."

"Why not?" Eva said. "Does she know you?"

"A little."

"How does she know you?"

"Rahim was engaged to her sister."

"Really?"

"And if he had come back from this mission, they were going to marry."

"And now?"

"There will be great joy in that family, and ours, over Rahim. He is a martyr. His name will be praised forever. Everyone will be so proud of him."

"And you?"

"I will be cursed."

"Why?"

"I am a failure. You said so yourself. And Mr. Nouri will agree with you. He will say, 'Rahim was killed, but you were caught. Rahim gave his life to Allah. But you betrayed the regime, betrayed the Mahdi.'"

"Who is Mr. Nouri?"

"Mohammed Nouri, Shirin's father. He will never let me see his daughter again or even set foot in his home. He is a mullah in Qom. He is a very hard man. He is devoted to the Mahdi. It's all he can think about, all he can talk about. He will not allow an infidel like me to marry his daughter."

Firouz Nouri.

There it was. Now she had the suspect's name, his father's name, his father's profession, and the city of his birth. She had something to research, facts to check, leads to follow. It was all good, and it was a lot more than they'd had before she got there. But something wasn't right. Something about that name bothered her, and she couldn't figure out why.

★   ★   ★   ★   ★

ARLINGTON, VIRGINIA

Marseille got up from her knees and stared out the window.

She looked out over Washington and wondered what the president was thinking. She wondered what his advisors were thinking. What were they going to do? So many of her friends were in awe of President Jackson. They'd voted for him. They supported him enthusiastically. They couldn't be more excited about where he was leading their country. But Marseille wasn't one of them.

She wasn't especially political, but she didn't trust Jackson. She sensed weakness in him or, more precisely, an odd combination of arrogance and indecisiveness. He acted like he understood the Muslim world, but did he really? He said he would never let US national security interests in the Middle East be threatened, but was that really true? Why wasn't he doing anything to stop the rise of the Twelfth Imam? Why wasn't he doing something decisive to stop the rise of this new Caliphate? Why hadn't he done more to stop Iran from getting the Bomb? Now that they did have the Bomb, was he going to do something? Anything? Now that he'd almost been killed—presumably by Mideast terrorists, if the early media reports were accurate—was he going to retaliate?

She didn't want another war in the Middle East. Nobody she knew did. But America was under attack and being run out of the region. America's leaders looked weak and feckless. That didn't strike Marseille as a formula for peace. It struck her as blood in the water, and she was certain the enemies of the United States could smell it and were preparing to strike again. Was there any doubt that the Iranians were going to use the Bomb now that they had it? Not in her mind. At the very least, she figured they would give some of their nukes to Hamas or Hezbollah or al Qaeda or some other terrorist group to attack Israel and the United States. It was just a matter of time. Why wasn't the president doing anything to stop that?

She suddenly realized she was thinking like her father—like both of her parents, actually. That's how they used to talk around the dinner table when she was growing up, she recalled. They were always interested in her classes and her plays and musicals and the boys that caught her eye. They always seemed to have time to listen to her, and they loved to encourage her and came to every school event or activity to which she invited them. But their world was geopolitics and economics. They were always quizzing her on the names of countries, the names of their leaders, the names of their currencies. They were forever teaching her obscure little tidbits of history. *Who was the head of the KGB under Brezhnev?* Yuri Andropov. *Yasser Arafat claimed to be born in Jerusalem, but he wasn't. Where was he really born?* Cairo. *What was another name by which Arafat was known?* Abu Ammar. *What world leader was recorded in the* Guinness Book of World Records *for having the largest funeral in history?* The Ayatollah Khomeini, with nearly twelve million people attending. *Where was he buried?* In Qom, the religious capital of Iran. *What's the Turkish currency called?* The lira. *What's the Iraqi currency called?* The dinar. *What's the largest country in Africa?* Sudan. *What's the most beautiful city in France?* Paris, she would always say, but her parents always said Marseille.

She wondered what her father would have been thinking if he were still alive, and she felt a lump forming in her throat. What would he have advised the president to do about the Twelfth Imam? What would he have advised the president to say to Israel? Had he ever had that chance? she wondered. Had he ever met an American president while working for the CIA under the guise of working for the State Department?

Shifting gears, she checked her watch, then set up her laptop, logged on to the hotel's wireless network, and clicked over to the Weather

Channel's website. The lead headline did not bode well: "Monster Storm Rips through Midwest, Northwest: 125 Million Americans Affected, 10,000 Domestic Flights Canceled, Governors of 16 States Declare Emergencies." Portland, she read, had been hit with more than a foot and a half of snow overnight. Winds were gusting up to fifty and sixty miles an hour, making temperatures feel subzero and bringing the city to a complete standstill. Denver had more than two feet of snow, as did Chicago. Forecasters said more was coming over the next twenty-four to forty-eight hours. She wasn't getting home. That much was clear.

So was her next step. It was now a few minutes after 9:00 a.m. So she picked up the phone in her room, dialed nine, and then dialed Langley.

"CIA switchboard. How may I direct your call?"

"Yes, I'm trying to track down a gentleman who works there by the name of Jack Zalinsky."

"One moment, please."

Marseille's pulse quickened. Was she really about to talk to the man who had saved her parents' life? She had so many questions for him. Would he be willing to give her answers? Would he even be allowed to?

The receptionist came back on the line. "I'm sorry, but we have no one by that name."

Caught off guard, Marseille tried to keep the woman on the line. "How about John Zalinsky or possibly James?"

"I'm sorry, nothing."

"Could I have the personnel department?"

"Sure, one moment and I'll transfer you."

That, however, was a dead end as well. She explained who she was and how her family knew Mr. Zalinsky, but the young man in the personnel office said he was looking in the Agency's database, and there had never been anyone there by that name.

21

It was true, Najjar thought.

War was coming. He didn't know how. He didn't know when. But the Lord was calling him to warn his people and tell them the truth. That much he knew. He also knew the Lord Jesus was coming back soon, which meant he had to move fast.

Najjar was fully awake now. All fear had left him, as had all fatigue. He was pacing his room again, trying to come up with a plan. Was he supposed to go back to Iran? Was that what the Lord wanted? He would be arrested immediately upon arrival at Imam Khomeini International Airport. Maybe the Lord wanted to use his trial for him to speak to his nation. But what if the trial wasn't televised? What if the war started before the trial did? Was it faith or foolishness to put his fate into the hands of the Iranian intelligence services? And what about his family? Was he really going to leave them behind? He loved Sheyda more than life itself. He was willing to obey Jesus no matter what. Still, something in his spirit didn't feel right. He didn't really believe the Lord was asking him to leave them. What, then? How was he supposed to proceed?

★ ★ ★ ★ ★

ARLINGTON, VIRGINIA

Frustrated, Marseille googled *Jack Zalinsky CIA.*

Nothing.

She tried *John Zalinsky* and *James Zalinsky.* Still nothing. She tried *J.*

139

Zalinsky and other possible spellings of *Zalinsky* but still found nothing. Something didn't add up. She was absolutely certain she had the correct name. She had written it in her diary the same day David told her the story long ago when they were teenagers.

She looked up from her laptop and out the window at a line of planes on approach to Reagan National Airport. The morning was dark and gray. A light freezing rain was pelting the capital and building up a thin sheet of ice on the roads and on her window.

She could still recall begging David to tell her the story of how their parents had met in revolutionary Iran in 1979 and how their parents had helped each other during their escape when the Shah was toppled and Ayatollah Khomeini rose to power and the American Embassy was captured and its staff taken hostage. Her parents had been annoyingly resistant to talking about that period of their lives, even though she'd asked them time and time again for more details. At that point, she knew only the basics—that at the age of twenty-six, her father, Charlie Harper, had been a junior political officer for the State Department, fluent in Farsi, newly assigned to the US Embassy in Tehran in September 1979. She knew her mom, Claire, had been an assistant to the economic attaché at the embassy. She also knew her parents were then newlyweds in a new country, full of adventure with no kids, no debts, and lots of freedom. In the first few months in Tehran, they'd become friends with their next-door neighbors, Mohammad and Nasreen Shirazi. He was an up-and-coming cardiologist with his own clinic. Nasreen had worked for the Iranian Foreign Ministry under the Shah as a translator and later became a translator at the Canadian Embassy in Tehran. But that was it. That was all they would say.

She'd been electrified when she discovered that the Shirazis' youngest son knew the rest of the story, and to this day—despite all they'd been through—she still vividly recalled David's kindness at finally telling her the story that her parents had never shared.

He'd begun by explaining how Marseille's mother had vetoed at least three different plans that the CIA and the State Department had drawn up, schemes that in her view ranged from the impracticable to the suicidal, and to Marseille's amazement, he explained how her father had actually devised the plan that was finally accepted and executed. The Harpers and the Shirazis, along with the other American FSOs, would be given false Canadian passports. This would take a special, secret act of the parliament in Ottawa, since the use of false passports for espionage was expressly forbidden by Canadian law. They would also be given false papers that identified them as film producers from Toronto working on a new big-budget motion picture titled *Argo*, set in the Middle East, in conjunction with a major Hollywood studio. Their cover story would be that they were in Iran scouting locations. The CIA would set up a front company in Los Angeles called Studio Six, complete with fully operational offices, working phone lines, and notices in the trade papers announcing casting calls and other elements of preproduction. The Americans and the Shirazis would then further develop and refine all the details of their cover stories, commit them to memory, and rehearse them continually. Eventually, the CIA would send in an operative named Jack Zalinsky to go over the final details and to see if they were ready for any interrogation they might encounter. When the time was right, Zalinsky would take the team to the airport and try to get them through passport control without getting caught—and hanged.

"You're saying my father came up with this idea?" Marseille remembered asking David when he was finished.

"Actually, your mom helped quite a bit," he'd replied.

"That doesn't make sense," she protested. "How would my parents even know . . . ?"

She closed her eyes, and it was as though she were fifteen all over again. She could hear the wind rustling through the pines and see the dark thunderclouds gathering overhead. She could still feel the temperature dropping as the next storm front came in, and she would never forget any detail of the dilapidated A-frame cabin they'd found in the woods, their own private hideaway from their fathers and David's brothers and the others during the days they spent in the north.

David had explained that D-day was set for January 28, 1980.

"Zalinsky got the team to the main airport in Tehran. They were going through passport control, and my parents were absolutely terrified.

They weren't convinced your parents' plan was going to work. But your father and Mr. Zalinsky kept insisting that if the tickets and passports said they were Canadians, then the guards at the airport would accept it. And they did. So before Khomeini's thugs knew what was happening, your parents, mine, and the others were taking their seats on board Swissair flight 363, heading for Toronto via Geneva."

Marseille felt her eyes misting. She had finally gotten the story she'd always wanted to hear, but she had never been able to talk about it with her mom. That very Tuesday morning when their fishing party was supposed to be picked up from the island in the middle of the desolate Gouin Reservoir, deep in the interior of the province of Quebec, had been September 11, 2001. Under orders from Osama bin Laden, nineteen Middle Eastern terrorists had hijacked four American civilian jetliners. They'd flown two of those planes into the Twin Towers of the World Trade Center in Manhattan. Marseille's mother had worked in the South Tower and had perished in the attack.

She'd never been able to talk about it with her father, either. After his wife's death, he had emotionally imploded, quit his job, sold their family home in Spring Lake, New Jersey, and moved them to his parents' farm just outside of Portland. She'd never seen her friends again. She'd been forbidden to have any contact with David. She'd lost not only her mother but her childhood and her past, and it had left a gaping wound from which Marseille had never fully healed. And then her father had committed suicide—on September 11, just last year—and she was essentially all alone in the world. Free from her father's consuming and debilitating pain, but alone nonetheless.

Now she was on a personal quest of sorts to make sense of it all, to get answers, to find closure, and to figure out where she was going to go from here. Reconnecting with David was part of the journey. She didn't think she'd have had the courage to reach out to him on her own. But then fate stepped in. A wedding was planned. Her best friend from college wanted her to be a bridesmaid. In Syracuse, of all places. It gave her a reason to see David again after all these years, and to her astonishment and relief, he had graciously accepted her invitation. It was a step, and a good one. But that was not all.

Unraveling the mystery of her father's secretive past had to be part of the quest as well. After his death, she had taken care of his estate and sifted through his personal papers. In doing so, she had come across a key to a safe-deposit box she'd never known he had at a bank in downtown Portland. Upon opening the box, she'd been surprised to find it empty but for one yellow piece of paper. Written on CIA stationery was a letter of commendation for Charles Harper for his valor under fire in Iran. It mentioned the crisis of 1979, thanked him for his crucial work for the Agency, and was signed, *Tom Murray, Director of the Near East Division*. She had shown it to David at breakfast that morning. She had wanted his thoughts, his advice, but they'd been interrupted by an emergency call from his boss, and suddenly he'd had to leave.

Marseille reached into her pocketbook and pulled the paper out again. She'd memorized it by this point, but she read it again several times. Then she turned back to her laptop and googled *Tom Murray CIA* and was stunned by what she found: Thomas A. Murray was not only alive and in Washington, but he was still on active duty at the CIA and was now the deputy director for operations.

She picked up the phone and hit redial.

"CIA switchboard. How may I direct your call?"

22

"Mr. Murray?"

Out of the corner of his eye, Tom Murray—his headset on, pacing his office overlooking the CIA's Global Operations Center—could see his secretary sticking her head through his door, trying to catch his attention. But he quickly held up a hand and made her wait. Whatever she had, he had no doubt that Zalinsky's call was far more important.

"What time did it happen?"

"Sunday morning, Islamabad time," Zalinsky said.

"Saturday night our time?"

"Correct."

"So why am I just hearing about it now?"

"NSA says they're all backed up. They intercepted the call. They recorded it. But no one had time to translate it until about an hour ago."

Murray cursed under his breath. The American taxpayers were spending $80 billion a year on intelligence. They had a right to better than this. "You're sure it was to Farooq?"

"Absolutely. NSA confirms it was his personal cell phone number. My team says voice analysis confirms it was definitely his voice."

"So just to be clear, Jack, you're telling me that Iskander Farooq, the president of the Islamic Republic of Pakistan—the *Sunni* Islamic Republic of Pakistan—received a direct phone call from the Twelfth Imam?"

"Yes, sir."

"And you're saying Farooq is giving serious consideration to the Mahdi's 'invitation' for Pakistan to join the Caliphate?"

"Correct."

"And that Farooq seemed inclined to agree but has a few last questions that he would like to discuss in person, face-to-face, not over the phone?"

"That was my impression."

"And you're saying the entire call was in Urdu, not Arabic?"

"Well, most of it. Some was in Panjabi."

"Did we even know the Twelfth Imam was fluent in either Urdu or Panjabi?"

"No, sir, we did not."

"And our translation is accurate?"

"The original translation comes from NSA," Zalinsky said. "I don't speak either language myself. But I had my team double-check everything, and it seems solid."

Murray ran a hand through his thinning gray hair. "What's your best guess?"

"If I had to bet," Zalinsky said, "Farooq is scared. He's a Sunni Muslim. His country's Sunni. But he's got millions of Pakistanis on the streets worshiping the Mahdi. He sees millions more throughout the Muslim world doing the same. They're all demanding their governments follow the Mahdi and join the Caliphate or their days are finished. He sees one Muslim government after another bowing down and kissing the Mahdi's feet. On the one hand, he's thinking if he doesn't do the same, he's going to have a bloody revolution on his hands. But if he capitulates, he's going to be handing Pakistan's nuclear arsenal over to the Twelfth Imam. And that was yesterday. Now Farooq sees the Mahdi survive a sophisticated assassination attempt against all odds, an attack that killed everyone else . . ."

"Except the little boy," Murray said. "Don't forget the little boy."

"Right, the little boy," Zalinsky said. "Every Muslim in the world, practically, is calling it a miracle. They're openly speculating about whether the Mahdi was sent from Allah or is Allah incarnate. Farooq doesn't know what to do. He's stalling for time. In fact, on the call, the Mahdi actually asked the president why he's hesitating."

"What did Farooq say?"

"'Perhaps only that this has all come so suddenly, and I do not know you,'" Zalinsky said, reading from the English transcript, "'have not heard your heart, have not discussed your vision for our region or what role you envision Pakistan playing.' Then the Mahdi replies, 'History is a river, my son, and the current is moving rapidly.' And Farooq says, 'All the more reason that we should take caution, lest we be swept away by events beyond our control.'"

"Is the Mahdi going to Islamabad?" Murray asked.

"No," Zalinsky said. "Farooq wants to meet privately, discreetly, one-on-one. They're scheduled to meet in Dubai on Thursday night at ten."

"Where?"

"TBD."

"I thought the Sunnis didn't even believe in the Twelfth Imam," Murray said. "I thought Zephyr's memo said this was a Shia thing."

"For the last ten centuries it was," Zalinsky said. "Something's changed. Something's different. I wish I could tell you where we're headed now, but I can't. Look at Egypt. Ramzy's gone, and now you've got a million Egyptians out in the streets, demanding the VP step down and the military give the reins of the country over to the Mahdi. None of it makes any sense. But one thing's clear."

"What's that?"

"The Twelfth Imam has the initiative. Everyone else in the region—us included—is reacting to him."

"Okay, write it up; get it to me. I'll get it to the director and the president. Keep me posted, Jack."

"Will do."

Murray hung up the phone and turned to his secretary.

"Mr. Murray, you have an odd phone call, and I'm not sure how to respond to it."

"I really don't have time for anything new today, Laura."

"I know, but . . ."

"But what?"

"A woman named Marseille Harper called. She said she's the daughter of Charles D. Harper."

Murray was stunned. He hadn't heard that name in decades. "Charlie Harper?"

"I looked him up in the database, sir. He was a NOC from '79 to '85, then shifted over to the analysis division."

"I know who he is."

"Well, sir, Mr. Harper committed suicide in September."

Murray recoiled. "Charlie Harper? I don't believe it."

"I'll e-mail you the obituary. Anyway, his daughter says she has a letter from you to her father on CIA letterhead, a commendation of some sort for his work in Iran during the Revolution. She only recently discovered it in his papers. She's in town and would like to come in and discuss it with you."

Murray stared out his window at the ice forming on the pine trees of the Virginia countryside. "Charlie Harper," he said, shaking his head.

"I told her there was no way for you to meet with her, given the current situation. But I took her number and asked her to call back in a few months."

"No, I'll meet with her."

"But, sir—"

"How long is she in town?"

"A few days."

"Wednesday morning, 9 a.m. Have her bring the letter."

"Of course, sir."

"And what was her name again?"

"Marseille," the secretary said. "Like the city."

★ ★ ★ ★ ★

FRANKFURT, GERMANY

Call Marseille.

That was David's primary objective for this layover. That, and to not miss his next plane. His flight into Frankfurt from Munich had touched down more than an hour late. Now he had less than fifteen minutes to get to the next gate and catch his connection to Tehran. Zalinsky would all but take a contract out on his life if he missed this flight, he knew, and he was determined not to let that happen. But that was business, and as important as it was, there were other things that were important too.

It took several minutes for the plane to taxi over to the terminal and several minutes more for the ground crew to connect it to the jetway. But the moment the seat belt sign went off, David jumped up, grabbed his carry-on, and begged, pushed, and pleaded his way through economy class and then through business class in order to be the third person off the plane. Sprinting flat out was impossible given the large crowds in the airport that day, but by weaving in and out of little old ladies and high-priced businessmen and young families headed south for their holidays, David finally made it to his gate with four minutes to spare and found a pay phone.

The first three rings gave him a chance to catch his breath. The next three got him worrying again. Where was she? Why wasn't she picking up? David had no idea when he'd have another chance to call her. It would be impossible from inside Iran, and he could very well be there for weeks, if not months.

"Hello?"

David was startled. He'd just resigned himself to leaving a message. "Marseille? Hey, it's David."

"David, how are you?"

"I'm good now. It's nice to hear your voice."

"Yours too. Guess you got my message?"

"I did. I'm so sorry you're stuck in DC. Probably the last place you'd want to be."

"Well, yeah—but actually . . ."

A Lufthansa rep was now calling first-class passengers to begin boarding and giving a number of other instructions. It wasn't anything David needed to hear for the moment, but the woman was speaking so loudly it was almost impossible for him to hear what Marseille was trying to say.

"Sorry, I missed that last part," he said.

"That's okay. I just said it wasn't my first choice, but now I'm thinking it may be a gift."

"Why's that?"

"I decided to call the CIA and track down Jack Zalinsky."

David's heart nearly stopped. Had he heard her right?

"Jack who?" he asked.

"Zalinsky," she replied. "You know, the guy who helped rescue our parents out of Tehran in 1980. Wasn't that his name?"

"Uh, yeah, I guess it was."

"I thought that was right. I'd written it down in my diary that night you told me. Remember up in Canada?"

"How could I forget?"

"So I called the personnel department at the CIA."

David couldn't quite believe this was happening. "And?"

"And they said they'd never heard of him—said no one by that name had ever worked there."

"Really?"

"But I didn't get discouraged. I asked them about Tom Murray."

"Who's that?" David asked, not wanting to lie but so caught off guard he was simply reverting to his training back at the Farm when he'd first joined the Agency.

"Thomas A. Murray—he was the guy who signed the letter of commendation for my dad, the one I showed you at breakfast."

"Right, right. So did you find him?"

"You wouldn't believe it," Marseille said. "He still works there."

"Wow."

"In fact, he's been promoted several times. Guess what he does now?"

Deputy director for operations, David wanted to say but didn't. "I give up," he said instead.

"He's the deputy director for operations."

"Who knew?"

"And guess what else?"

David couldn't even begin to imagine. "What?"

"I'm meeting with him at Langley—that's what they call CIA headquarters, you know—anyway, I'm meeting him tomorrow morning at nine. I told his secretary I want to learn as much as I possibly can about what my dad did when he worked for them. She told me to bring the letter. David, I'm so excited. I don't know where it's all going to lead, but I've been searching for answers about my parents for as long as I can remember. And ever since my dad took his life . . ."

David heard her voice catch and wished he could be there to comfort her. Instead, the Lufthansa lady was calling for all passengers to board. He had only a few moments left to talk with Marseille, and he genuinely had no idea what to say. He didn't want to keep lying to her. He wanted to tell her everything, like he'd told his father. He wanted her to know that he knew Zalinsky and Murray, that he'd love to help her learn everything she could about her father. But that was impossible. Not here. Not now. Which meant maybe not ever. There were no guarantees he was ever coming out of Iran alive, much less making it all the way to Portland. And that's what hurt him most—not risking his life for her sake but being unable to tell her he loved her.

"Marseille?"

"Yes, David?"

"I'm afraid I have to catch this plane."

"I know. I'm sorry. I shouldn't have been jabbering on all this time."

"No, no, it's good. I wish I could listen all day. I love to hear your voice. I love that you're trying to figure out your dad's past. That's good. You should. It's the right thing to do. I just . . ."

"What, David?"

He was tongue-tied. His heart was racing, but he couldn't find the words, and he didn't dare miss this flight. The Lufthansa rep was giving a final call, saying all ticketed passengers needed to be on board as the door to the Jetway was going to be shut in one minute.

"Is everything okay, David?"

"Yeah, I just wish we had more time to talk."

"It's okay. Just call me when you land."

If it were only that easy. David sighed. "Marseille?"

"Yes?"

"It may be a while until I can call you again. Not because I don't want to. It's just the way my business works. It's hard to explain. But I want you to know how much I enjoyed seeing you yesterday. It really meant a lot to me. And I meant what I said. I can't tell you how much

I'd like to up and quit my job or take a few weeks of vacation and spend some time with you and catch up. It's hard for me to say because . . . well . . . it's embarrassing, but I miss you. I have to go, but . . . well, I just wanted you to know that."

★ ★ ★ ★ ★

TUESDAY
MARCH 8
(IRAN TIME)

23

The Airbus A310-200 touched down in Tehran without fanfare.

To the casual observer, it was a typical IranAir flight. But while the twin-engine, wide-body jet typically carried more than 230 passengers, this particular inbound flight from Beirut carried just eight—the Twelfth Imam, his personal aide, and six Iranian intelligence agents, now doubling as a personal security detail after the death of all the Mahdi's bodyguards.

No crowds were on hand to greet the Mahdi. No press. No official welcome delegation. In fact, the Ayatollah's office had issued a statement that the Mahdi was going to stay in Beirut for at least another day and hold a series of private, off-the-record meetings with Hezbollah party leaders and senior military commanders. It was a lie, but it had been issued at the Mahdi's direct command, and it bought them time to get him back safely and quietly to Iran, where he could regroup with his most trusted servants.

From Imam Khomeini International Airport, the Twelfth Imam and Javad were taken by a Bell 214 Huey military helicopter to the Qaleh, the Supreme Leader's heavily guarded retreat complex on Mount Tochal, one of the highest peaks in the Alborz mountain range, far above all the smog and noise and congestion of the capital. Waiting for them were his closest advisors: the Ayatollah Hosseini, President Ahmed Darazi, Defense Minister Faridzadeh, and General Mohsen Jazini, commander of the Iranian Revolutionary Guard Corps.

They all fell prostrate the moment the Mahdi walked into the main dining room. Each one praised him lavishly and thanked Allah that he had not suffered from the attack.

The Twelfth Imam warmly welcomed their worship. Indeed, to Hosseini it seemed he reveled in it, gained strength from it. Then the Mahdi instructed them to once again take their seats and proceed with the briefing for which he had come. Javad, meanwhile, sat against the wall in the back of the room and took notes.

The Ayatollah cleared his throat and assumed command of the meeting. "First, as you directed, we are selecting deputies to form a group of twenty. You said they must be men of honor and courage, men willing to die for your sake and for the sake of Allah. This is almost complete. We now have seventeen of the twenty. A copy of the names and bios for each is in the folder in front of you. We hope to have the other three on board within the next few days."

The Mahdi nodded but said nothing, looking neither pleased nor disappointed.

"*Inshallah,* we will hold our first meeting—quiet, discreet, without any press attention—of this high command next Monday. We would be honored, of course, if you chose to join us. Meanwhile, we have directed the seventeen to begin recruiting their quota of a total of 313 disciples. Some are mullahs that we implicitly trust. Most are military commanders and leaders of business and industry, and most are Iranian, though we have some well-trusted Arab members, a few Turks, and a handful of Pakistanis. As you requested, they are extraordinarily gifted in the areas of organization, administration, and warfare. We will be careful not to ever gather this Group of 313 in one place but are instead creating a cell structure. None of the members will know that there are 313 of them in total. None of them will be privy to any details except those that are necessary for completing their own operations. This should all be in place by the end of next week."

Again the Mahdi nodded. Hosseini waited for a moment, hoping for something clearer, more demonstrative, but it was not forthcoming, so he proceeded with his briefing.

"Now, with those basic details out of the way, it is with great pleasure that I inform you that our first operation—the one to assassinate

Egyptian president Ramzy—was highly successful," Hosseini continued. "While I wish I could say that the American president and the leader of the Zionist entity were also killed in the attack, some of the events were beyond our control. Still, we proved how vulnerable the Americans and the Zionists are, and we have put them on the defensive without their tracing the attack back to us."

"Foolishness!" the Mahdi shouted. *"Pathetic and childish!"*

Everyone in the room was stunned, Hosseini most of all.

"How dare you initiate any action against our enemies without clearing it through me?" the Mahdi fumed. "This is not a democracy. You are no longer the Supreme Leader. *I am.* I will tell you when we are going to strike. Do I make myself clear?"

"Yes, my Lord," Hosseini half whispered.

"What's that?" the Mahdi demanded.

"Yes, my Lord!" Hosseini repeated, stronger this time, though still with a tremor in his voice.

The rest of the group followed Hosseini's lead.

"I thought I had made myself clear," the Mahdi continued. "We will proceed to annihilate the Little Satan first and all the Zionists with it. This and this alone is your first objective. I told you: you must bring me the blood of the Jews on the altar of Islam. You must wipe the ugly, cancerous stain of Israel from the map and from the heart of the Islamic Caliphate. I told you that this was only the first step. I told you not to be distracted or confused. This was not the ultimate objective. Destroying the Little Satan alone is too small a thing. The main objective is to destroy the Great Satan. But we must move methodically. We must move systematically. I am not interested in merely assassinating their petty leaders. We are going to annihilate the Americans. Extinguish them. Obliterate them. Vaporize them. In the blink of an eye. Before they know what has hit them. The Americans are a dying empire. A sinking ship. Their time will soon come. But first we must hit the Zionists and rip them from the beating heart of the Caliphate. You must hit them before they strike, but with your gutless act of cowardice, you have endangered my entire plan. You have pushed the Zionists to attack me personally. And I guarantee you it's only a matter of time before they launch a massive first strike on this country. This could have been avoided if you had listened to me, if you had obeyed me. Now we must rapidly change course."

Hosseini and his colleagues fell to the ground again, imploring the Twelfth Imam to forgive them and give them a second chance. The ayatollah, for one, feared his life was in danger. He had slaughtered servants for lesser crimes than this.

★ ★ ★ ★ ★

TEL AVIV, ISRAEL

Roger Allen still had no idea what he was going to say.

When his plane landed at Ben Gurion International Airport in Tel Aviv, he still had heard nothing from the White House Situation Room and nothing from the secretaries of state or defense. He didn't blame them. They had multiple crises on multiple fronts, and this was why they paid him the big bucks, he told himself before remembering that he had actually been making nine times his current salary in the private sector and used to leave his office in Naples, Florida, each day no later than three o'clock, often to play a round of golf before going home to the missus. It all felt like a million years ago.

They still had an hour-long drive up Highway 1 to Jerusalem, so the director, two of his senior aides, and his security team linked up with the chief of the CIA's Tel Aviv station and climbed into a convoy of three bulletproof SUVs.

"Two key things before we get there," the station chief began as they departed the airport grounds. "First, the Israeli media is reporting that Naphtali wasn't injured in the attack."

"That's not accurate?" Allen asked.

"Not exactly."

"What do you mean?"

"The prime minister actually suffered second- and third-degree burns on his back and the backs of his legs. From what we can gather, he heard the RPG fire, instantly recognized the sound, and hit the deck of the limousine. His lead Shin Bet agent was standing in front of the open door. As reported, he did block most of the blast and clearly saved his boss's life. But the fireball did penetrate the interior of the car and scorched the PM more badly than any of us knew."

Allen tensed, knowing this was going to make a delicate conversation all the more difficult. "How'd you find out?" he asked.

The station chief said nothing.

"On second thought, never mind," Allen said. "What's the second thing?"

"Zephyr's hunch on the Twelfth Imam attack."

"A drone strike?"

The station chief nodded. "When you watch the video frame by frame, you can actually see the blur of one of the incoming missiles."

Allen exhaled. "That's not good."

"No, sir."

"How many countries have UAVs at this point?"

"Forty-five or so."

"How many of those had a motive to hit this Mahdi guy?"

"Three."

"The Israelis, the Egyptians, and us?"

"Right."

"And we didn't do it."

"Right."

"So it's the Egyptians or the Israelis."

"It seems unlikely, sir, that the Egyptian high command would have made a decision to retaliate militarily so quickly after a decapitating strike against President Ramzy. They're still trying to figure out who's in charge in Cairo. The VP is the one on television speaking for the government, but under the Egyptian constitution, the line of succession actually goes to the speaker of the People's Assembly, who hasn't been seen in public since this crisis began."

Allen nodded and looked out the window as they began climbing the Judean Hills toward the Holy City. He didn't have proof that the Israelis were responsible for the drone attack, but he certainly had strong circumstantial evidence. The problem was, he was heading into his meeting with the Israeli prime minister with nothing. He couldn't just tell Naphtali not to launch a massive preemptive strike against Iran's nuclear facilities. He needed leverage. There had to be consequences. But for that, he needed a presidential directive.

The secure phone in the backseat of the middle SUV rang. The station chief answered it, then turned to Allen. "It's for you," he said.

Allen took the phone.

"Director Allen, this is the White House operator. Please stand by for the president."

★ ★ ★ ★ ★

OAKTON, VIRGINIA

Najjar spotted a satellite dish on his neighbors' roof.

His first thought was what he wouldn't give to sneak into their house to watch some television and find out what was happening in the outside world. That, however, was quickly replaced by a second thought far more useful. He remembered a satellite TV program he had stumbled onto one night in Hamadan when Sheyda and the baby had been visiting her parents. He could still see the man on the program speaking so boldly, so powerfully. The message had stunned him, frightened him. Even now he could clearly remember how ashamed he had felt for pausing on that channel and listening. But now that he recalled the message, his heart began to race.

"It's time," the man, a priest of some kind, had said, "for the church to stand up with courage and conviction and say in the power of the Holy Spirit, 'Islam is not the answer; jihad is not the way. Jesus is the way. Jesus is the truth. Jesus is the life. And no man or woman can come to the Father except through faith in Jesus Christ.' This is the message of John 14:6. This is the message of the entire New Testament. And this message of faith is filled with love, not with swords."

Remembering, Najjar felt electrified, just as he had when he'd heard the words.

"Now is not the time to hide in fear from the Muslim world," the priest had declared without hesitation. "Now is the time to take the gospel of Jesus Christ to every man, woman, and child on the planet and proclaim Him as the hope of mankind, the only hope for the troubled world."

Najjar had never heard anyone talk like that before or since.

"The God of the Bible is moving powerfully in the Muslim world today," the man had continued. "He is drawing Muslims out of Islam to faith in Jesus Christ in record numbers. Yes, there is much bad news in the Muslim world today. But there is also much good news; more Muslims have come to faith in Jesus Christ in the last three decades than in the last fourteen centuries of Islam put together. This is the greatness of our great God."

At the time, Najjar had questioned every word. Now he had no doubt this was all true. Muslims really were leaving Islam and becoming followers of Jesus Christ like never before. He certainly had. Now everything was different. And still, one phrase echoed in his heart again and again: *Jesus is the way. Jesus is the truth. Jesus is the life. And no man or woman can come to the Father except through faith in Jesus Christ.*

Satellite television. That was the answer, Najjar realized. He needed to get himself to a TV studio that could beam his message into Iran. But first he had to escape the "hospitality" of the Central Intelligence Agency.

24

Zalinsky answered the call on the first ring.

"Jack, it's Eva."

"What do you have?"

"David was right—the cell is Iranian."

"You're positive?"

"One hundred percent. The dead guy is Rahim Yazidi, Iranian national and member of the Revolutionary Guard Corps. The guy we have in custody is Navid Yazidi, his younger brother. Also Iranian. Also part of the Revolutionary Guard. The guy we're looking for, the head of the cell, is named Firouz Nouri. His father is Mohammed Nouri, a leading Twelver mullah in Qom, Iran, author of several books on the Twelfth Imam. I'm sending you all the paperwork by secure e-mail as we speak. But there's more."

"What?"

"The name Nouri—does that ring a bell?"

"Vaguely. Why?"

"I'm pretty sure this guy Firouz is related to a guy named Javad Nouri."

"It's still vague. Keep talking."

"Remember David delivered a bunch of satellite phones to a guy we suspected was close to the Supreme Leader?"

"That was Javad Nouri?"

"Yes."

"You're sure?" Zalinsky asked.

"I'm sure his name was Javad Nouri," Eva said. "Was it the same Javad Nouri? Is he related to Firouz? I'm going to need some more time to pin all that down for certain. But it fits—the father's a true believer, his older son is a senior government aide, his younger son on a mission for the Supreme Leader. It's still circumstantial, but it definitely doesn't point to al Qaeda or the Brotherhood running this attack. This came from Tehran, Jack. David was right."

It appeared he was, Zalinsky realized. He thanked Eva for her work and ordered her to catch the next flight back to DC. He needed her back at Langley, for things were about to get very difficult. Then he speed-dialed Murray's office.

"I have something for you, Tom, and we need to get it to the director and the president immediately."

★ ★ ★ ★ ★

OAKTON, VIRGINIA

"Dr. Malik?"

The agent, making his hourly check on the doctor, stopped pounding on the door of the master bedroom for a moment. He could hear the shower running, but there was no response.

"Dr. Malik? Can you hear me?"

Still nothing.

He radioed downstairs to the watch commander and explained the situation.

"Go in," the commander said.

"You're sure?"

"Absolutely."

"Very well." The agent tried the handle, but it was locked. So he drew his pistol, put his shoulder to the door, and broke it down. Then he pounded on the bathroom door and called out a few more times. When there was still no reply, he gave one last warning, then broke down that door as well.

To his astonishment, Najjar Malik was not to be found.

★ ★ ★ ★ ★

JERUSALEM, ISRAEL

Roger Allen arrived at the Knesset building early.

He cleared security and was taken directly to the prime minister's office, only to learn that Naphtali was not going to be available for another hour. There was no explanation from the PM's chief of staff other than that dinner wasn't going to work any longer, that Naphtali had been "unavoidably detained" and "would appreciate Mr. Allen's patience." He also said that when the meeting did occur, it would take place with principals only. Staff, even senior aides, were not invited.

Allen was furious but did his best to keep his legendary temper in check. He knew exactly what was happening. Naphtali was trying to send him a message that he didn't take orders from the United States, least of all from a man who ran the very agency that had failed to detect or prevent an attempt on his life and was doing precious little, in his view, to punish the country he considered directly responsible. Allen was tempted to thank the PM's chief of staff, say he had other business to attend to, go check into the King David, and get some work done until the leader of the Jewish State could deign to meet with a senior representative of Israel's only serious friend left on the planet.

But now was not the time for a diplomatic temper tantrum. That would surely get picked up in the Israeli media—and then the Arab and Iranian media—and cause more harm than good. So he sat alone in an electronics-clean anteroom down the hall from Naphtali, unable to make calls, unable to use e-mail, and without any of his staff.

★ ★ ★ ★ ★

OAKTON, VIRGINIA

Najjar knew he didn't have much time.

He climbed out the bathroom window of the safe house, then lowered himself onto the garage roof and jumped to the ground. Then he sprinted through the backyard of the safe house and into the side yard of the neighbors who had just gone on vacation, crouching behind a row of shrubbery and praying that he couldn't be seen. He'd fully expected to be caught. The fact that he hadn't been, he hoped, had to be the hand of Providence.

Glancing around to make sure no one was looking or within earshot, he wrapped a hand towel he had taken from the master bathroom around his fist and smashed through a basement window of the neighbors' house. Then he scraped away all the remaining glass and climbed inside.

Najjar landed in a sea of Barbie dolls and toy cars. He paused for a moment, wondering if a security alarm was about to go off. When it didn't, he started breathing again and hastily proceeded to the main floor.

Staying low and away from any of the windows along the back of the house, he found his way to the laundry room and through it to the garage. Sure enough, the subcompact he'd seen drive in and out every day was still there, right beside the empty space for the minivan. Now all he needed was the key. He checked the wall by the door but found only rakes and tools. So he moved back through the laundry room and into the kitchen, furiously riffling through drawers and cabinets but finding nothing. Next he headed into the main foyer. Unfortunately, though there was a small table with a vase of roses by the front door, there were no keys. Nor were there any hanging near the door.

Najjar's heart was racing. He'd never broken into anyone's house. He had certainly never borrowed anyone's car without their permission. He was terrified of getting caught.

He raced upstairs, past the children's rooms to the master bedroom at the end of the hall, grateful that the layout of the house was exactly the same as the one from which he had just come. And there, to his relief, on the nightstand by the bed he found a spare set of keys—along with a cell phone. He grabbed both, found a pad of paper and a pen on the dresser, and scribbled out a short message—a thank-you—and his name. He was ready to go to jail for this if need be. He wasn't going to hide what he had done. He just hoped he could stay ahead of the CIA and the police long enough to do what he had to.

Najjar raced downstairs, through the laundry room, and back to the garage. He unlocked the driver's-side door of the red Toyota Corolla, got in, and quickly acclimated himself to the dashboard. Then he adjusted the mirrors, turned on the engine, hit the garage door opener clipped to the visor, and backed out as carefully as he could, half-expecting the house to be fully surrounded by American agents by that point. But it wasn't. He could hear a siren in the distance, making his heart beat even faster. Then he put the garage door down again and pulled out of the neighborhood, not exactly sure where he was headed but determined not to look back.

★ ★ ★ ★ ★

EN ROUTE TO TEHRAN

David couldn't wait to get on the ground in Tehran.

Having been cooped up on one flight after another for nearly twenty-four hours, he was eager to get to his hotel, take a shower, and get an early start on the day. In the meantime, he made a mental checklist of his next moves.

His top priority was hunting down Jalal Zandi and Tariq Khan. His best shot, he figured, was to reconnect with Dr. Alireza Birjandi, code-named Chameleon. Thus far his most useful asset, Chameleon was essentially a mole inside the upper echelons of the Iranian regime. It was from Birjandi he had learned that Iran now had eight operational warheads, and it was Birjandi who had pointed him to Najjar Malik, an absolute treasure trove of intel for Langley. Perhaps the eighty-three-year-old professor, scholar, author, and leading expert on Shia eschatology—widely described in the Iranian media as a spiritual mentor or advisor to several of the top leaders in the Iranian regime, including Ayatollah Hosseini and President Darazi—could help him track down Zandi and Khan as well.

Birjandi regularly met with both Hosseini and Darazi, and he'd been willing to share with David information from these meetings—information that had proven invaluable. If David remembered correctly, Birjandi was scheduled to have lunch with one of the leaders the following day. He was determined to be the last person Birjandi talked to before going into that lunch and the first person Birjandi spoke to when it was over. At the very least, he hoped he could gain critical insight on the regime's latest thinking, especially after the assassination attempt on the Twelfth Imam. Whom did they hold responsible—the US, Israel, or someone else? How were they planning to respond? How quickly were the Iranians—or the Mahdi—planning to use the eight warheads in their possession? Was Israel the first target? Had they truly been unable to attach the warheads to ballistic missiles yet? Would the Iranian missile boats heading through the Suez Canal in the next few days be carrying nuclear warheads? The list of questions David needed answers to was growing by the hour.

25

JERUSALEM, ISRAEL

It was 8:12 p.m. Jerusalem time.

Roger Allen was finally ushered into the prime minister's spacious, wood-paneled office. He was in a foul mood and more than ready to have a very candid conversation about the importance of maintaining good professional relations between two allies. But the moment he saw Naphtali, a man he had known personally for more than four decades, Allen's tone changed completely. He suddenly realized that not a single photograph of the PM had been released since the attack, and now he knew why. The official government spokesman had told the international press corps that Naphtali had "miraculously" received only "minor wounds." Nothing, it was now clear, could have been further from the truth. The man's entire face was bandaged, as were his hands. He was wearing not a suit but light-blue scrubs, like a surgeon would wear. Hovering in the background was Naphtali's personal physician, and a bed specially designed for burn victims was set up in the corner, alongside an array of monitors, medical trays, and various other types of equipment.

"Asher, I heard you'd suffered more than publicly known," Allen blurted out, dispensing with formalities, "but I had no idea how serious it was. Why didn't you tell us?"

"You know exactly why," Naphtali said, clearly unable to shake hands but gesturing to the couch for Allen to sit down.

"The Iranians."

"They would think we were coming for them tonight."

"Didn't you just do that?" Allen said, choosing to stand instead when he realized Naphtali was unable to sit.

"The hit on the Twelfth Imam?"

"That was a mistake, Asher."

"It wasn't. He killed Abdel. He tried to take out your president. He tried to kill me. We didn't have a choice."

"You nearly killed an eleven-year-old boy."

"We didn't know he was in there."

"You killed his parents."

"We didn't know they were in the car either."

"Then you shouldn't have ordered the shot."

"We didn't start this war, Roger. Look at me."

"I know, but it was a foolish move. You've made a hero out of him."

"Roger, the Muslims think he's the messiah. He was a hero the moment he stepped out onstage in Mecca and King Jeddawi bowed down before him."

"Now you've made him look invincible."

"I was promised he wouldn't survive. No Mahdi, no Caliphate. The IDF told me it was going to be a surgical strike."

"They never are."

"No, not always," Naphtali said, asking his physician to give them the room for a few minutes before continuing. "I'm sorry to make you wait."

Allen held his tongue.

"I'm sure you think it was personal," the prime minister said.

"Not at all," Allen said.

"Don't lie to me, Roger. We've known each other for forty years. You think I'm mad at you. But I'm not. Well, okay, I am, but that's not why I kept you waiting out there so long."

"Why, then?"

"We just had an emergency meeting with the Security Cabinet. The Mossad says the Iranians are moving five warships into the Med. They're heading north up the Red Sea right now and are set to pass through the Suez Canal tomorrow. We think two are heading for Turkey, while the other three will go to Syria. They're destroyers and missile boats, and I don't have to tell you what a provocative act this is right now."

"I haven't heard definitive intel on that."

"Given the last twenty-four hours, you're not exactly instilling me with confidence that the US is on top of things."

"I'll look into it," Allen said.

"You'll do better than that," Naphtali said. "I want the president to block the Suez Canal and refuse the Iranian warships entry into the Med."

"Asher, please, we can't do that. It's tantamount to an act of war."

"And Iranian missile boats off the coast of Tel Aviv and Haifa aren't?"

"This isn't the first time the Iranians have sent warships into the Med."

"This is the first time those ships could have nuclear warheads on board."

"You don't know they do."

"I can't take the risk, Roger. This is a red line for me and my government."

Allen felt like he was being backed into a corner, and he didn't like it. "You're preparing for war, Asher."

"I don't want war. That's not my intention."

"But you see one coming."

"You don't?"

"It doesn't have to come to that. We're actually opening a back channel with the Mahdi. We have reason to believe he wants to contact the president directly and talk peace and find a way to de-escalate the situation."

"Assassination and warships don't signal de-escalation."

"Look, Asher, we don't know for certain who is responsible for the attacks in New York. We certainly don't know it was Iran."

Allen knew full well that wasn't true. He'd gotten off the phone with Tom Murray less than an hour ago. He knew all about the Yazidi brothers and their connection to the Nouri family. But he was under strict orders from the president to keep the Israelis from launching a preemptive strike. He hadn't had time to discuss the latest intel with the president, but he had no doubt Jackson would not permit him to disclose such information to the Israelis, for fear that such proof would provide the *casus belli* for an Israeli attack.

★ ★ ★ ★ ★

LANGLEY, VIRGINIA

"What do you mean you can't find him?"

The more Eva Fischer heard from the watch commander at the safe house, the more furious she became. "How do you lose the most important defector in a generation?"

There was nothing the commander could say that could possibly calm her down. So she cut him off and told him exactly what to do. "Call Fairfax County police. Get them his name and photo and tell them he's wanted by federal authorities. Don't tell them he's a defector or that he's an Iranian national. Got that?"

"Yes, ma'am."

"Get the neighborhood sealed off. No one goes in or out without a full search. He can't have gotten far. He's never been to the US. He's obviously not familiar with the area, he's on foot, and he's not danger-ous. He's not a threat to the neighbors. But he is smart, and he has had at least a forty-five-minute head start. So have the cops put checkpoints up at every major intersection for ten miles in every direction. And you'd better catch him fast, Commander, or your career is finished."

★ ★ ★ ★ ★

JERUSALEM, ISRAEL

Allen continued his case to the prime minister.

"We're doing everything we can to investigate what happened in Manhattan, Asher. But at this moment we don't know exactly who was responsible, and the stakes are too high for guessing. We can't slide or drift or lurch our way into war with Iran or with the Twelfth Imam based on guesses and hunches, and neither can you."

"You're kidding, right?"

"What do you mean?"

"Roger, please tell me you're kidding."

"I'm not."

"You think I need to know who tried to kill me to take the State of Israel to war? That would merely be the proverbial straw. Please tell me you're not forgetting the nuclear weapons test in Hamadan. Please tell me you're not forgetting the Twelfth Imam's assertion in Mecca that Iran has nuclear weapons, and that command and control of those weapons are being transferred to his authority. Please tell me you didn't miss the Mahdi's press conference in Beirut in which he told the BBC, 'The Zionist regime is heading toward annihilation' whether I'm dead or not."

"The president called me on my way to see you," Allen said.

"How is he?"

"About the same as you, as it turns out."

"I'd like to call him and tell him I've asked all the people of Israel to pray for his speedy recovery."

"That's very kind. I'll let him know. In the meantime, he wanted me to pass on to you a very specific message, in person, face-to-face."

"I'm listening."

"You know the people of Israel have no greater friend than the American government."

"But . . . ?"

"But under no circumstances can the president tolerate an Israeli first strike against Iran."

The words just hung in the air, as incendiary as they were direct.

"I don't want a war with Iran, Roger. I thought I had made that clear."

"You don't want one, Mr. Prime Minister, but you might be tempted to order one anyway. I am here as a personal representative of the president of the United States to make it unequivocally clear that our government wholly, completely, and utterly opposes a preemptive strike by the State of Israel on the Islamic Republic of Iran."

"Under any circumstances?"

"The president opposes a preemptive strike under any circumstances."

"He wants to dictate to a sovereign nation how to defend her people and prevent a second Holocaust?"

"The president is ready to make it worth your while."

"Meaning what?"

Allen pulled out of his suit pocket a page of handwritten notes with a deal dictated by the president over the phone less than ninety minutes earlier. He offered it to Naphtali, but the PM couldn't hold it in his hands, so Allen read it from beginning to end. It was an extraordinary deal, the most sweeping and lucrative ever offered by the US.

1. $250 billion in advanced new fighter jets, missile defense systems, and two Los Angeles–class submarines to help Israel maintain her "qualitative edge" over her enemies
2. A pledge of aggressive US support for Israel to join NATO as a full member in the next six months
3. A pledge for the US to sign a full alliance treaty with Israel should the NATO deal stall or be denied, promising to go to war alongside Israel if the Jewish State were ever attacked by Iran
4. A pledge for the US to build a new American embassy in Jerusalem within eighteen months of acceptance of this deal, and for the president to publicly declare Jerusalem the "eternal, undivided capital of the Jewish State of Israel"

There was, of course, a price: Israel had to forswear any preemptive strike against the Islamic Republic of Iran for at least the next five years.

"It is a very generous offer," the prime minister said, "but it doesn't solve the problem. Iran already has several nuclear warheads. Next month, it will have more. The month after that, it will have even more. This growing arsenal of annihilation is controlled by madmen who have specifically and repeatedly and publicly threatened to attack us—and you, I might add. Now the president is asking us to accept this American largesse on the hope—some in my government would say the false hope—that Iran or the Mahdi can be deterred or contained over the next five years. I'm not certain this is possible."

"Well, that's the president's offer," Allen said. "I'm afraid it's not open for negotiation."

"And if we decline?" Naphtali asked.

Allen had hoped he wouldn't be asked. He was not comfortable with the answer, but he served at the pleasure of the president.

"Asher, as a friend, I cannot stress how strongly the president opposes an Israeli first strike."

"I understand," Naphtali replied. "But if we find ourselves with no other choice?"

"There is always another choice."

"But if we get to a point where we don't see it that way, what happens then?"

"Please don't ask me that."

"Roger, there's an ultimatum here. I can feel it. Just tell me what it is."

Allen looked away and took a deep breath, then looked back in his friend's eyes. "Should the government of the State of Israel defy the wishes of the president and thereby endanger American national security and the security of the entire region by launching a preemptive strike or series of strikes against Iran, then my government would have no choice but to halt and rescind all foreign military assistance indefinitely."

26

David landed in Tehran late Tuesday night, local time.

He powered up his phone and found a rare e-mail from his brother Azad.

> Hey, David—not sure where you are right now but thought you'd like to know you're an uncle. Nora delivered a beautiful, healthy, strapping baby boy this morning. We've named him Peter Alexander Shirazi, after Nora's grandfather. He's seven pounds, six ounces, with thin little wisps of black hair. Nora's labor was difficult, but overall she's doing well. I'll take her home tomorrow. Her mom came in from Ohio last night and will be here for as long as we need her to help out. I just talked to Dad to tell him the good news. I'm sure he's glad to be a grandpa, but I don't think he can focus so much right now. He said Mom's condition seems to be worsening, and the doctors aren't sure there is anything else they can do for her. Thought you'd want to know I'm driving up there tonight to be with him and to see Mom and bring them some pictures before coming back for Nora in the morning. Anyway, call me when you can. Thanks.
> —Azad

David smiled. He needed some good news. There had been far too little of it in the last few weeks. Part of him wished Azad had named his firstborn son after his own father or grandfather, but did the world really need another Mohammad Shirazi? As much as he loved his father, David couldn't quite imagine naming his own son Mohammad, if he ever married and had a son, so he could hardly blame Azad for not doing so.

It was time to move. David grabbed his jacket and briefcase from the overhead compartment and followed the crowd off the plane to a long line for passport control. Just then, however, someone tapped him on the shoulder.

"Excuse me; are you Reza Tabrizi?" asked an airport official wearing a dark suit, starched white shirt, dark tie, and a security badge of some kind.

"Yes, I am. May I help you?"

"Please, Mr. Tabrizi, come with me."

"What about passport control?"

"I will take care of that."

"And my luggage?"

"One of my colleagues will collect your bags and bring them to me."

"Where are we going?"

"We just have a few questions. It should only take a moment."

David complied. He had no choice. But he did not have a good feeling about what was going to happen next. They stepped away from the crowd, turning many heads in the process, and proceeded through several locked doors, along several nondescript hallways, down a stairwell, and into a small, windowless, cinder-block room. There were no furnishings, save two wooden chairs on either side of a simple wooden table.

"Please, have a seat," said the man, who, from his receding hairline and slight paunch, David guessed was in his midfifties. "May I have your passport?"

David handed it to him.

"You are twenty-five?"

"Yes."

"You are a German citizen?"

"Yes."

"But this says your city of birth was Edmonton, Canada."

"My parents were both Iranians, born in Tehran. They immigrated to Germany, where they became citizens. My father worked for an oil company. He was assigned to work in the oil sands industry in Canada. That's where I was born."

"In Edmonton?"

"Yes."

"So you grew up there?"

"Mostly, yes. But just before I graduated from high school, my parents were killed in a plane crash. After that, I moved back to Germany to go to college."

They were simple questions, but David wondered why they were being asked and where they were leading.

"And whom do you work for now?"

"Munich Digital Systems."

"What is that?"

"We develop and install software for mobile phone and satellite phone companies."

"And what do you do for them?"

"A little bit of everything. I'm a technical advisor, but right now I'm the project manager on a new deal signed recently with Iran Telecom. I have a letter in my briefcase, if you need it, describing—"

The security official cut him off. "That won't be necessary. Just tell me what you do."

"That's actually a long story, but basically we're helping your country dramatically expand its telecommunications capacity."

"Meaning what?"

David did not detect any hostility or suspicion in the man's voice. Not yet, anyway. He reminded himself that spot checks like these happened all the time, not just coming into Iran but into many countries he had traveled to over the years. It was hard to believe that he, of all people, had been chosen randomly out of more than 250 people on that plane. But it was possible, he told himself and tried to stay calm.

"Well, you see, the telecom sector in your country is exploding. For example, in 2000, Iran only had 5,000 miles of fiber-optic cable networks. Today there are more than 48,000 miles of fiber-optic cables crisscrossing Iran. In 2000, there were fewer than four million mobile phones in Iran. Now there are fifty-four million. Your systems aren't designed to handle that much traffic. Your government is now investing heavily in modernizing and expanding its civilian communications networks. That's why I'm here."

This didn't seem the appropriate time to add that the Iranian regime was also spending aggressively on a parallel track to create a secure and far more robust military communications system. Nor did it seem wise to mention that the regime wanted to create a high-tech operations center that would allow their intelligence services to monitor calls and text messages using certain keywords. Hosseini wanted to maintain an iron grip on his people and crush any dissent with speed and lethality, and for the right price, European technology companies like MDS were apparently happy to oblige.

"How many people are working on your project?" the official asked.

"That depends."

"On what?"

"On how broadly you define my 'project.'"

The two men just stared at each other for a moment.

"Let me put it this way," David explained. "Iran Telecom recently awarded a huge contract to Nokia Siemens Networks, which is a joint venture between the Finnish cell phone giant and the German engineering conglomerate. The contract supports several hundred Nokia technical staff members to come here—live here, really—for the next year to eighteen months to make specific telecommunications upgrades and train their Iranian counterparts. Two months ago, my company, MDS, won a subcontract from NSN. At this point, we have forty-two technicians in Tehran whom I oversee."

"Why, then, do you keep leaving Iran and coming back a few days later?"

"The execs at Iran Telecom keep expanding the scope of the work," David replied. "I keep going back to talk to my superiors to see if we can meet the demands and to see how quickly we can get more technical staff here."

Fortunately, David thought, all that he had said so far was true. It wasn't the whole truth, of course, but it didn't have to be. The best cover story, he knew, was one that contained the fewest lies.

Just then, however, the tone of the conversation began to change.

★ ★ ★ ★ ★

JERUSALEM, ISRAEL

Asher Naphtali stood alone in his office.

The CIA director had just departed. Now he needed time alone, time to think, time to process this unprecedented turn of events. He ordered his secretary to hold all his calls and not allow anyone in to see him.

With Israel facing an imminent second Holocaust, in light of a fresh terrorist attack, in light of all the instability and turmoil metastasizing throughout North Africa, the Middle East, and Central Asia, was the president of the United States actually threatening to cut off $3.09 billion in annual military aid to America's only truly democratic and secure ally in the entire region? How was that possible?

Naphtali's first instinct was to call the Speaker of the House and the Senate majority leader. Surely Congress would stand with Israel in a war with Iran. Surely the American people would as well. The latest poll the prime minister had seen, just two months before, showed that 58 percent of Americans would approve an Israeli military strike against Iran if sanctions and diplomacy failed. Only 27 percent disapproved.

What's more, the poll found that a stunning eight out of ten American voters said they did not believe President Jackson's policies of economic sanctions and repeated attempts to engage the mullahs diplomatically would stop Iran from getting nuclear weapons. They'd been right. The exact same number of American voters said they believed that once Iran got nuclear weapons, Tehran would launch annihilating nuclear missile attacks against the State of Israel. Fully 85 percent of American voters said they were also concerned that Iran would give nuclear weapons to terrorist groups once they got the Bomb.

Naphtali hadn't seen new polling numbers since Iran had tested its first nuclear warhead. However, he suspected American support for an Israeli first strike in light of all that was happening would go up, not down. Still, even if Congress continued voting for substantive military aid packages for Israel, if the president chose to veto such aid, the question was whether congressional leaders had the muscle to override the veto—and continue to do it year after year. Would they do so if the Middle East went up in flames and a new wave of terrorism broke out around the world? Would they do so if oil prices hit one record high after another and the American economy was further damaged by spiking gasoline and home heating oil prices?

★ ★ ★ ★ ★

TEHRAN, IRAN

"Who are the satellite phones for?"

"The executives at Iran Telecom," David replied.

"Why so many?" the security official asked.

"There are only twenty."

"But you brought in twenty last time and five before that."

"You have all the paperwork. It's all legitimate."

"That's not what I asked."

"Then I don't understand the question."

"Why are you bringing in so many?"

"I'm bringing what is being ordered," David said. "I have no idea what the phones are for, nor do I care."

"Did you know that Abdol Esfahani has been arrested?"

David was genuinely stunned. He had heard no such thing. "No," he replied. "What for?"

"He was arrested while you were gone, Mr. Tabrizi, on espionage charges."

"Espionage? That's impossible. He's not a spy."

"Actually, he is. We have proof that he has been working with the Central Intelligence Agency. And now we suspect you are too."

David felt a wave of fear flash through his system. How could they know? How had he slipped up? "I don't know what you're talking about."

"Why was Esfahani trying to buy more than three hundred satellite phones?" the official asked. "What use could he possibly have for so many?"

David's mind scrambled for an answer. He had been sworn to secrecy by Esfahani not to mention the connection to the Twelfth Imam or the Group of 313. "I have no idea. You'll have to ask him."

"We did. He said it was your idea."

"Mine?"

"He said you also worked for the CIA, that you were paying him a quarter of a million dollars to get these satellite phones into the hands of all the top officials in Tehran. Under torture, severe torture, he showed us how the phones have bugs in them that allow them to be listened to by the NSA's Echelon signals intelligence system."

"That's crazy!" David shot back, jumping to his feet and putting his finger in the man's chest. "I'm not paying him for these phones. He's paying me. And none of these satphones are bugged. I've checked each one of them myself. And I'm a German, you moron, not an American. I wouldn't work for the thugs and imbeciles who run the CIA for all the money in the world!"

"Sit down, Mr. Tabrizi."

"I will not sit down."

"I said, sit down, Mr. Tabrizi."

"Look, you fool, I'm not one of your stooges. I'm not going to be accused of spying or bribery or anything else. Now, I was hired to do a job for your government, and I expect to be treated with respect. *So let me go, or I demand to see someone from the German Embassy immediately.*"

27

Two large men rushed into the room.

Before David realized what was happening, they moved quickly around the wooden table in the center of the room, punched him in the stomach, dragged him to the floor, gagged him, and tied him up. He struggled as best he could, but they kicked him repeatedly, and eventually one of them pressed his boot down on David's face to keep him from thrashing around any further.

Next they kicked the chairs aside and dragged in a large wooden board that looked almost like a stretcher, roughly seven or eight feet long and several feet wide. They propped one end on the desk so that the board was inclined like a child's slide. Then they grabbed David and strapped him to the board with thick ropes, his feet at the elevated end, his head toward the floor, and his arms stretched over his head.

That's when David knew exactly where they were headed. He was about to be waterboarded. He struggled all the more to get free, but it was impossible. Everything was happening too fast. They knew he was CIA. He had no idea how. But they were going to brutalize him until he told them everything. Fear gripped him. Sweat poured down his face and up his back. He gritted his teeth and willed himself not to break. He would rather die than betray his family or his country.

They placed a dirty towel over his face. It had been soaked in something, alcohol or possibly gasoline. Either way, his eyes began to sting and water. He began to gag as well. He knew what was coming. He sucked in a lungful of air and shut his eyes and mouth. Without warning, they hoisted a large can over his head and began to pour water over his face in a steady, controlled fashion. The water soaked the towel, making it heavy and limp. As more and more water poured over it, the towel settled around the contours of David's face and sealed up his nose and mouth. Now, even if he wanted to breathe, he wouldn't be able to. His arms tried to thrash but couldn't move. His legs struggled to break free but could not. David knew he shouldn't be expending the extra energy. He needed to save every ounce of strength, every bit of oxygen, to stay alive. But he couldn't help himself. His movements were involuntary.

From the moment the water started, he was counting.

Fifteen, sixteen, seventeen, eighteen . . .

The water kept coming.

Twenty-eight, twenty-nine, thirty, thirty-one . . .

He wasn't going to make it. His lungs were going to explode. He didn't want to die. He had no idea where he would go, and it scared him more than anything else he had ever faced. *Thirty-five, thirty-six, thirty-seven . . .*

Suddenly the water stopped. The towel came off. David exhaled. The overhead lights were so bright he couldn't see his captors. He knew he had only a moment. He breathed in and out and in and out and in one more time.

Then they smashed the towel back down on his face and began pouring buckets of water over him again.

One, two, three, four, five, six, seven, eight . . .

His lungs burned. His hands and feet were shaking. Was he about to go to hell? Was hell real? Was he going to spend eternity burning and writhing with no way of escape?

Nineteen, twenty, twenty-one, twenty-two, twenty-three, twenty-four, twenty-five, twenty-six . . .

The more he writhed, the more he could feel the burning of the ropes as they cut into his wrists and ankles. And because his body was strapped to the board at a downward angle, water finally began seeping into his nasal passages. This instantly triggered a gag reflex to keep him from drowning.

Thirty-two, thirty-three, thirty-four, thirty-five . . .

"Okay, he's ready," one of them said.

The water stopped. The towel came off.

"How long have you worked for the CIA?"

David shook his head. "I don't."

"Stop lying! We know you do. We've been tapping your calls. We've been following you. We just want to know how long you've been with them."

"I'm a businessman. I work for MDS. You have my papers."

"Forget it," the leader said. "Do it again."

Again they covered his face. Again they poured gallons of water over his mouth and nose. David couldn't take any more. He was suffocating. He was drowning. He'd never experienced such terror. He knew he was going to die any moment, and if not now, then by hanging or firing squad later that day or the next day.

He tried to fix his mind on an image of his mother or father but couldn't do it. He tried to picture Marseille, tried to achieve one last moment of sweetness before he crossed into eternity. But he couldn't do it. Everything was black.

And then he saw a tunnel. He was heading down this tunnel, and all he could hear was screaming, shrieking unlike anything he had ever heard before. He could no longer feel the water pouring over his face. All he felt was heat, rising up through the tunnel as he descended. Intense, scalding, searing heat. It was real. It was happening. He had to make it stop, but he didn't know how.

Then suddenly the water stopped again. The towel came off, and the blinding light was in his eyes once more.

"We have Fischer in custody. We were going to torture her. We were going to make her suffer too, but she sang, almost from the start. She's told us everything. She admitted she was CIA. She said that you were too. She told us MDS was a front organization. She told us you were sent to penetrate the Revolutionary Guard Corps. So stop lying. Tell us what we want to know. How long have you been working for the CIA?"

Every molecule in his body screamed for him to tell them what they wanted to hear. They already knew. Why prolong the agony?

"I don't. My parents were Iranian. I'm German. You know that. I would never betray Iran. I'm not a traitor."

David had been through SERE training—Survival, Evasion, Resistance, and Escape—but it had been nothing like this. He was terrified. He was ready to tell them anything to make them stop.

Dr. Birjandi's face suddenly flashed in his mind. He could hear the man saying, "David, you need to receive Christ as your Savior. You need to be forgiven. Don't wait. Give your life to the Lord before it's too late. Only He can save you."

But they were shouting at him again. They were firing question after question at him. He couldn't think, couldn't react. David felt a sharp blow to the stomach and then another to the kidney. The combination knocked out of him what little air he had in his lungs. Wincing in excruciating pain, he forced himself to breathe in and out, deeper and deeper, and then sucked in a final lungful as the towel came down again and the water began crashing down all over his face, all over his head and body.

One, two, three, four, five, six, seven . . .

David forced himself to stop moving, stop thrashing. How could they have captured Eva? How could they have interrogated her? She was in New York. She was interrogating one of theirs. They couldn't possibly have captured her. There was no way they had her. So they were lying. But how, then, did they know about the three hundred phones?

Thirteen, fourteen, fifteen, sixteen . . .

The pain was intense, but using every ounce of energy, he focused on counting, not resisting.

Twenty, twenty-one, twenty-two . . .

Why hadn't they taken shots to his face? Why were they hitting him in the stomach and sides?

Twenty-five, twenty-six, twenty-seven, twenty-eight . . .

They didn't want his face to be bloodied or bruised. They were professionals. They were doing everything they could to break him without letting him look like he'd been tortured. Maybe they were lying. Maybe they were fishing.

Thirty-eight, thirty-nine, forty, forty-one . . .

His lungs were burning again. He was about to explode.

Forty-two, forty-three, forty-four, forty-five . . .

David couldn't hold out much longer. Maybe he was wrong. Maybe they did know. Maybe they were going to kill him after all. Then once more, without warning, the water stopped. Someone pulled the towel off.

"Why are you asking so many questions about the Mahdi?" one of them asked. "Why do you care about who he is and what he's doing?"

"I love the Mahdi," David cried, half-choking in the process. *"Everybody wants to know who the messiah is. I do too. How is that wrong? How can that be wrong?"*

"Were you part of the plot to kill him? Why were you out of the country when someone tried to kill him?"

"I would never betray him," David replied, willing now to say almost anything he thought they wanted to hear. *"I'd follow him anywhere. I'd pledge my life to serve him!"*

28

BROOKLYN, NEW YORK

Firouz Nouri could not wait any longer.

He had been given a number to call if all else failed. He had waited several days, but time was running out.

"Code in," the voice at the other end said.

Firouz recited two lines from a famous Persian poem and then waited.

"Cousin, is that really you?"

"It's me, Javad," Firouz said.

"Are you all right?"

"Yes, yes, thanks to Allah, I'm safe—for now, at least."

"Are you alone?"

"No, Jamshad is with me."

"What about Rahim and Navid? Are they safe too?"

"No. I'm afraid I have bad news for you."

"What?"

"Rahim was martyred in the operation," Firouz said. "We think Navid was captured."

"They're not saying anything about that on the news."

"I know, but I saw Rahim die. Navid I'm not so sure about."

"I never trusted him."

"I know. You were right."

"He was too young, too green."

"We should have listened."

"Where are you now?"

"In the flat."

"In Queens?"

"Yes."

"Why so long? We need you. You must get moving."

"We cannot, Javad. The police have set up roadblocks and check-points on all routes in and out of the city. It is safer just to lie low until things calm down a bit."

"Very well. Do what you must."

"May I speak to Shirin?"

"I'm not at home right now. I'm with the Mahdi."

"Really? Is he okay?"

"Of course. I have so many stories to tell you. Miraculous stories. Allah's favor on him is palpable, little one."

"I cannot wait to meet him."

"I cannot wait to introduce you. So get back safely. And watch your back."

"I will, Javad. And please send Uncle my love and let Shireen know I miss her."

"Of course."

"You don't think she will miss Navid too much, do you?"

Javad erupted in laughter. "I don't think she will miss him at all."

★ ★ ★ ★ ★

JERUSALEM, ISRAEL

"Get Shimon over here quickly and discreetly."

"Yes, sir," the prime minister's personal secretary said. "Right away, sir."

Naphtali didn't have many men in his government he trusted implicitly. But Levi Shimon, his defense minister, was one. Naphtali didn't dare explain the American ultimatum with his entire Cabinet, or even his Security Cabinet. They would all be livid. Even the doves among them wouldn't take kindly to such pressure from Washington. Someone would leak the story to the Israeli media within the hour. He couldn't take that risk. He, too, was furious, but Shimon had a cool head and a strategic mind. He would not let his emotions overwhelm him, which was why Naphtali valued his counsel.

Less than an hour later, the defense minister arrived alone in an unmarked car, with a single bodyguard and no aides. He was immediately ushered into the prime minister's office, where Naphtali briefed him on the situation.

"Unacceptable," Shimon said. "Absolutely unacceptable."

"Of course it's unacceptable," the PM replied. "The question is, what do we do about it?"

"Jackson is weak. He's going to get us all killed. We need to strike quickly, before the Americans can find a way to stop us."

"You may be right. But how?"

"You must call him back immediately," Shimon said.

"The president?"

"No, Allen. You must call Roger Allen right now."

"And say what?"

"Tell him that you've spoken with me—they've got to be watching; they know I'm here—tell him you've spoken with me and that the president may be right."

"What?" Naphtali asked. "He's not right."

"Of course he's not right. But the president needs to think you believe he *may* be right."

"Go on."

"Tell him we need twenty-four hours to discuss amongst ourselves. Tell him if it's going to work, we need two things. First, we need an iron-clad alliance with the United States. Any attack on Israel by the State of Iran or any other state or entity in the Middle East must be regarded as an attack on the American people, and the US must immediately respond with us in a joint military operation. We'll need lots of language explaining how that would work, a workable mechanism to trigger very specific American assistance in case of terror attacks or war."

"And the second thing?"

"Second, we need absolute silence about any of this prior to a formal announcement. Tell him that any leak would destroy the deal. We need time to fully develop the language with his team in private—at least a week—and time to discuss individually with members of the Cabinet to get their input and approval. Tell him we will need to move quickly, or all of Israel will be demanding we attack. But we also need things to be quiet so we can gain internal support before it leaks. Oh, and one more thing."

"What's that?"

"We need the president to visit Jerusalem and address the Knesset within a week, or there is no deal."

"Why is that?" Naphtali asked.

"Tell Allen we need a show of American support. We need Iran to know we are joined at the hip. We need the region to know America will never let us down. And tell Allen that as long as the president of the United States is on Israeli soil, we won't be able to launch an attack. See if the president can get here by next Monday."

"You think we can launch the attack before then?"

"All I need is your word, Mr. Prime Minister, and forty-eight hours."

Naphtali thought about that for a moment, then dismissed the idea entirely. "No, we can't do that."

"What do you mean?" Shimon asked. "We have to."

"We're not going to deceive the president," Naphtali said. "We're Israelis. That's not how it's done."

"So what, you're just going to tell the president that we're attacking this weekend? You're going to put the lives of all our pilots in danger, not to mention the lives of six million Jews whom you've sworn an oath to protect?"

"Of course not, Levi," Naphtali responded, fighting hard to keep his emotions in check. "But we have to keep two goals in mind. We are going to employ all means necessary to stop the Twelfth Imam and the Iranian regime from annihilating us or having the capacity to do so in the future; that I assure you. But at the same time, we have to do everything we can to maintain a strong strategic alliance with the United States. We certainly can't start by lying to them."

"And if the two objectives are incompatible?" the defense minister asked.

Naphtali turned and looked out his office window at the skyline of Jerusalem. "Let's hope to God they're not."

★ ★ ★ ★ ★

WASHINGTON, DC

Oil prices were skyrocketing.

The president scanned the latest briefing from his secretary of energy as he limped around the Oval Office, still in severe pain, still wrapped in gauze soaked in various medicinal creams and ointments. Brent Crude was now trading at $143.74 a barrel, up from $69.41 before the attacks in New York. That was a 107 percent increase in just two days. If the Israelis launched a first strike against Iran, there was no telling how high oil prices would soar. And then gas prices. And airline fuel prices. And home heating oil prices. And then inflation, as the shock waves from spiking energy costs spread through the already-weak economy.

The campaign was only a year away. He had enough challenges to getting reelected. He didn't need the Israelis making more. The American economy had stalled. Growth in the last quarter was barely over one percent. Stock markets were tanking worldwide. One out of ten Americans were out of work. Union workers out of work. Hispanics out of work. African Americans out of work. Women out of work. His base was screaming at him to do something, but what was he supposed to do? His OMB director was projecting another trillion-and-a-half-dollar budget deficit. If he couldn't turn things around and get the economy moving again, the country's debt would top $25 trillion by the end of the decade. But how was he supposed to get the economy moving again if it was dragged down by exploding fuel costs?

"Mr. President, I have CIA director Allen on line three for you."

Jackson thanked his secretary and reached for the phone behind the desk. He wasn't supposed to be in the office at all. He was supposed to be upstairs, resting in the residence. The White House physician was going to have a fit when he found out. But the world was on the brink of war, and he had no desire for sleep. He picked up line three, crossing his fingers for some good news.

"Roger, how did it go?"

"Hard to say, Mr. President."

"Meaning what?"

"Let's just say Naphtali was noncommittal."

"You gave him my offer?"

"Yes, sir."

"Every detail?"

"Yes, sir."

"Including the Los Angeles–class submarines?"

"Every detail, sir."

"And what did he say?"

"Honestly, sir, the first question he asked was what you will do if he respectfully declines and feels he has no choice but to deal with Iran directly."

"You told him I'd sign a formal alliance?"

"Of course, and to be honest, Mr. President, I think if we had offered him this package six months ago, he might very well have accepted it."

"But he turned us down?"

"No, sir, I wouldn't say that. I'd say he's still weighing the offer very seriously."

"You're sure."

"Absolutely," Allen said. "I've known Asher Naphtali for a long time, Mr. President. He's a smart guy and a shrewd operator. Believe me, he doesn't want to hit Iran alone if he doesn't have to. He now knows for certain—without any doubt—that you are 100 percent opposed to an Israeli first strike. He surely had to know that before. You had made it pretty clear in Manhattan on the drive to the Waldorf, as you said. But now he knows the costs. He knows that he risks fundamentally rupturing the special relationship between the US and Israel. So I don't think he's eager to go to war."

"But . . . ?"

"But obviously the last few days have dramatically changed the calculus for him and his government."

Allen took a few moments to brief the president on just how seriously Naphtali had been wounded in the attacks. Jackson was stunned by the news. He was distressed because of the personal, physical toll on Naphtali but also because of the rising potential political cost to forcing an ally not to defend herself when her leader had nearly been assassinated on American soil.

"I feel terrible for Asher, and I don't want it to look like I'm turning against the Israelis," the president said after a long pause, "but we simply cannot have a war. It will dominate the international agenda and domestic agenda for the rest of my presidency, and that's unacceptable."

There was another long pause. Allen apparently wasn't sure how to respond.

"Is there anything else I can do to stop Naphtali from going to war, without making him look like a martyr to his own people and triggering congressional backlash here in Washington?" Jackson asked.

Allen thought about that for a moment. "You have a lot of tools in your toolbox, Mr. President," he finally replied. "But let's let the PM chew on your proposal overnight and see what he says in the morning. In the meantime, I'll make sure my team is watching the Israelis closely to see if they detect any signs they are moving toward a preemptive strike."

★ ★ ★ ★ ★

TEHRAN, IRAN

David was blindfolded, and a rag was stuffed down his throat.

Then he was dragged down several hallways and up some steps before being thrown into the trunk of a car. He could hear voices but couldn't make out what they were saying.

Still bound, he could hardly move. And he could still barely breathe. He was obviously being taken away from the airport, but he had no idea where. Then he felt a needle shoved into his arm. The last thing he heard was the trunk slam shut.

TEHRAN, IRAN

When he came to, David found himself dressed in a fresh suit.

One of his own.

He was shaven. His hair was wet and combed. He was sitting across a large conference table from Abdol Esfahani. *Smart,* he thought, trying to regain his bearings. The table was too far for David to easily lunge across, and even if he tried, there were two armed guards standing behind Esfahani.

David tried to shake off the sedatives. He could hear Esfahani talking, but the first few sentences made little sense. It had to be the drugs, but two things were clear: Esfahani was responsible for this whole fiasco, and he was not apologizing.

"The entire planet is about to change."

It was the first sentence that made any sense to David. His head was beginning to clear. But he did not like what he was hearing.

"We are about to live in a world without America and without Zionism," Esfahani continued. "Our holy hatred is about to strike like a wave against the infidels. We don't trust anyone. We can't trust anyone. The enemy is moving. He is among us. We must be careful."

"That's it?" David asked, a burst of anger and adrenaline now helping to give more clarity.

"What do you mean?" Esfahani asked.

"That's all you're going to say?"

"About what?"

"You had me tortured. You had me waterboarded."

"We could not take a risk that you worked for the CIA or the Mossad. Now that we're convinced you don't, we can get back to work."

"Back to work?" David shot back. *"Are you out of your mind? Why would I want to do anything for you at this point? What happened today is completely unacceptable."*

"Mr. Tabrizi, you're not leaving this country until we get all the phones."

"How am I supposed to get the phones if you won't let me go get them?"

"We don't think you'll ever come back."

"Really? Whatever would give you that idea?"

"You said you wanted to work with us, Mr. Tabrizi. You said you wanted to serve Imam al-Mahdi. Were you lying?"

"Of course not. I've been doing everything you asked."

"Not fast enough."

"As fast as possible."

"That's where we disagree."

"So your idea of how best to motivate me is to torture me?"

"You were being vetted."

"Vetted?"

"Yes."

"For what?"

"You wanted to be part of the Group of 313, did you not?"

David was stunned. Was he hearing this correctly? "Yes, of course," he said cautiously. "But I—"

"How were we supposed to know if we could really trust you? We had to know for certain. Now we do."

"So what are you saying?" David asked.

"It is simple, Reza—you get us the rest of the phones in the next seventy-two hours, and you're on the team."

David didn't really know what that meant, but he knew better than to ask too many questions for now. "I'll do my best."

"I'm sure you will."

"Now, you have to understand, it's not going to be easy to get these phones shipped in. It may cost more money."

"Then that will come out of your wallet. Not ours. We've already paid you handsomely."

"I know, but I am taking great risks here, Mr. Esfahani. I mean, I don't have to remind you that these satellite phones can't be legally purchased by Iran under the UN sanctions."

"Technically, we're not buying them. You are."

"Which just further proves my point. I'm taking enormous risks."

"We're all taking great risks," Esfahani countered. "But the fact is this: we cannot build the Caliphate if the Promised One cannot communicate with his top commanders. And this cannot happen until we have all of the phones. That is the end of the matter."

With that, Esfahani got up and left the room. His bodyguards followed him after sliding a small box across the table, leaving David in the room by himself.

Curious, he opened the box. It was one of the satphones he had just brought with him. It was clear what he had to do—and clear what the consequences were if he did not.

★ ★ ★ ★ ★

OAKTON, VIRGINIA

Najjar Malik's heart was beating wildly.

He had never driven in the US before. He had never even been to the States before. He had no idea where he was or where he was going. He just knew that he had to get as far away from the safe house as rapidly as possible without getting caught.

He glanced at the gas gauge. There was half a tank. In a Corolla, he figured that would keep him going for quite some time. What he needed was money and a map. At a stoplight, he checked the glove compartment but found only a stack of manuals, the car's registration, a wad of napkins, and some toy cars. He glanced in the backseat—nothing but fast-food wrappers, two car seats, and some loose change on the floor. In the compartment between the front seats, though, he found a GPS unit. It wasn't exactly like the one he had back in Hamadan, but it was close. He quickly powered it up, scrolled through various points of interest, and chose the nearest pub-lic library, only a few miles away.

Once there, he was greeted by a helpful young librarian who hap-pily guided him to a bank of computer terminals and even showed him how to log on to the Internet. He thanked her, waited for her to go off to help someone else, then pulled up Google and typed in "Farsi language TV stations in Washington, DC." That didn't work. He typed in several other variations and soon came up with three possible options for getting his message into the Middle East. The first was BBC Persian. Launched on January 14, 2009, BBC Persian struck Najjar as the best option. It wasn't run by Muslims. It was accessible from Washington. It had a large Farsi-speaking audience, and it had strong credibility inside Iran. He had never watched the network himself for fear of being branded a traitor by his father-in-law or his colleagues in the nuclear program. But he figured he was a unique case. He knew that the Hosseini regime was constantly denouncing BBC Persian, which meant it was watched and paid attention to by not only the elites in Iran but the masses, who often loved to do the exact opposite of what their leaders told them to do.

The second option was Al Jazeera. True, it was only available to the region in Arabic, but many Iranians spoke Arabic and watched the network. What's more, the network was well watched and respected throughout the Islamic world and would be monitored by Iranian jour-nalists and bloggers who, he hoped, would pick up his story.

The third option was the Persian Christian Satellite Network, a Farsi-language Christian TV company based out of Los Angeles but with studios in New York and Washington. This was a rogue network if there ever was one, broadcasting the gospel through Bible teaching and Bible dramas into Iran in Farsi twenty-four hours a day, seven days a week. It certainly didn't have the ratings of the other two, but according to the website, it was respected by a wide range of Iranians searching for an alternative to Islamic teaching and state-run news. Most importantly, Najjar figured PCSN would be the most sympathetic to his story and perhaps, therefore, willing to give more airtime than the others.

He decided to aim high. He went back to the car and used the cell phone he'd taken from the neighbors' house to call BBC's headquarters in London, where he was transferred to a Farsi-speaking producer. He explained that he was a senior Iranian nuclear scientist who had defected to the United States. He briefly described his background and said he wanted to give someone an exclusive story about the Iranian nuclear program and the CIA's efforts to stop it. Was the BBC interested?

The conversation didn't go quite as Najjar had hoped. The producer asked a lot of questions, but to Najjar, she sounded skeptical, though she promised to talk to her editor and get back to him.

Najjar hung up the phone and stared out at traffic passing by. Then he closed his eyes and bowed his head. "O Father, thank You for saving me and making me Your child," he prayed. "Please lead me now. Please guide me. Am I doing the right thing? Am I taking the right approach? As You promise in Psalm 32, please instruct me and teach me in the way I should go, and please counsel me with Your eye upon me, O Lord. Thank You again, Father. I trust You. And please bless Sheyda and Farah and my little one. You know where they are. You alone can protect and comfort and encourage them. I entrust them and myself entirely to You. In Jesus' holy and powerful name I pray. Amen."

Najjar opened his eyes again. He didn't see a vision. He didn't hear an audible voice. He did, however, feel a peace he couldn't explain, and that was enough for him. The Lord had told him to talk to his country, to be a watchman to alert his people. Satellite television seemed the right way. He was open to other avenues, but for now he sensed he should keep trying.

He opened the cell phone again, dialed PCSN's Washington bureau, and was again transferred to a producer. Once more he briefly shared his story, but this time he shared a little of the spiritual journey he was on as well.

The reaction was completely different. The producer was ecstatic. He asked a few more questions and seemed to grow more excited with Najjar's every answer.

"Where are you?" the producer asked.

"Oakton."

"How quickly can you get into the city?"

"I can come there now."

"Thirty minutes?"

"I really don't know," Najjar conceded. "I've never driven it before."

"Okay, let's say an hour. Get on the road now, and I'll call you back in a few minutes with several of my colleagues to ask you more questions."

Thrilled, Najjar agreed. He entered PCSN's address into the GPS and soon found himself merging onto Interstate 66 toward the nation's capital, singing to the Lord in Farsi as he drove.

Until a terrible thought hit him: what if the CIA was monitoring the call?

★　★　★　★　★

JERUSALEM, ISRAEL

It was an hour's drive back to the Defense Ministry.

But Levi Shimon wasted no time. Sitting in the backseat of the bulletproof sedan, he opened a small leather journal he called the Book of Death. It was here that he scribbled notes, dreamed up new projects, sketched out initial war plans, and jotted down page after page of operational questions that he needed to answer or get answered by his general staff. He pulled out a fountain pen, noted the date and time, and made a new entry.

- PM: no other way to protect Israel—we must attack Iran.
- Time is short—wants operation to be ready in forty-eight to seventy-two hours.
- Objectives:
  1. Destroy all Iran's nuclear weapons
  2. Destroy key nuclear facilities
  3. Destroy missile production facilities
  4. Destroy Iranian naval assets in the Med and the Gulf
  5. Assassinate top nuclear scientists
  6. Hit key targets in Tehran—Ministry of Defense, IRGC hq, intelligence hq

7. Be ready for missile blitzkrieg
8. Be prepared to neutralize retaliatory capacities in Lebanon, Syria, Gaza—be ready with ground forces, if necessary
9. Minimize IDF casualties/loss of equipment, Israeli citizen casualties

- How do we maintain element of surprise?
- How do we keep the US on our side?
- What is the likelihood that Egypt or Jordan will enter the fray? What level of influence does the Twelfth Imam have there?

Back at the Defense Ministry, he had a full war plan in his safe. He and the generals had been working on it for years. They had been refining it for months. But it was just beginning to dawn on Levi Shimon that this was finally the moment for which they had been preparing for so long. Unless something dramatic happened to change the strategic dynamic, the duly elected leader of the State of Israel was going to authorize him to use all means necessary to neutralize the Iranian nuclear threat in the next few days. It was going to be the most dangerous and difficult operation in the history of the IDF, and the stakes could not be higher. They were either going to lose their country or transform the Middle East forever.

There were so many details to finalize. There were so many ways this operation could go terribly wrong. What worried Shimon most, however, was that their success or utter failure depended on one man. Not him. Not the prime minister. Not any Israeli citizen, in fact. Their fate was now in the hands of one asset the Mossad had recruited years before, deep behind enemy lines. He was an asset who had provided extraordinarily accurate information in the past. He had helped plant the Stuxnet computer worm responsible for shutting down more than thirty thousand computers throughout Iran, particularly those running key Iranian nuclear facilities, and his involvement had never been detected. He had planned the assassination of Dr. Mohammed Saddaji, the clandestine leader of Iran's nuclear weapons program, and hadn't been caught. He had provided the Mossad with detailed readouts from the Iranian nuclear weapons test just the week before, readouts proving beyond the shadow of a doubt that not only had the test gone well—it had gone far better than expected.

But now the asset had gone dark.

They had asked him for the exact location of each and every nuclear warhead in Iran. He was uniquely positioned to know that information, or at least find it out. But they hadn't heard from him since, and they didn't dare try to communicate with him again. What had gone wrong? Had he been compromised? Had he been arrested or executed? Shimon had no idea. All he knew was their most important asset was missing, and time was running out.

★ ★ ★ ★ ★

WEDNESDAY
MARCH 9
(IRAN TIME)

30

TEHRAN, IRAN

The Mahdi was calling.

It was the wee hours of the morning, Iran time, but Javad Nouri dutifully rushed to his master's quarters.

"Yes, my Lord?" Javad said, bowing low.

"Call your cousin."

"Now?"

"Of course. Tell him to go to the bank. Call him home."

It was their exit strategy, a safe-deposit box at a Citibank in Queens. Javad knew where to get the key. Inside were new passports, credit cards, and cash.

"Yes, my Lord."

"Tell him to take Jamshad and get out of New York, get to Canada, get back here as soon as possible. Tell him to route through Venezuela, if he needs to. He'll know why."

"My Lord, I will do whatever you ask, of course, but . . ."

"But what?"

"Well, I . . . You have all wisdom, of course, my Lord . . . but I'm just curious—isn't that too risky, at least right now? Why don't we have him just hunker down where he is until the storm passes? After all, we don't really need him here right now, do we?"

"You're missing the point," the Mahdi said. "I want you to call on your satellite phone. I want to see if these phones are really clean. If they are, Jamshad and your cousin should have no problems. You'll see them

209

back in Tehran in a few days, before the war begins. But if the phones are bugged, then we'll know for certain before we launch."

★ ★ ★ ★ ★

David asked for a cab to take him to a nearby hotel.

Instead, Esfahani sent word that he would provide him a car and driver. David gathered the satphone, his briefcase, and his luggage, stepped out of the conference room, and was escorted from the building. Only then did he realize where he was. He stopped for a moment and marveled at the buildings and the campus, illuminated with floodlights in the middle of the night. Architecturally, they had no value or attraction, but he had seen them before. Indeed, he knew every inch of their layout and much of their history. He was now standing outside the headquarters of the Quds Force, one of the most-feared intelligence and special forces units of the Iranian Revolutionary Guard Corps. He was, therefore, standing outside the former US Embassy in Tehran, which the Quds Force had made its own after the Islamic Revolution.

David looked around at the former chancery, at the home where the American ambassador once lived, at the house where the deputy chief of mission used to live, along with the old consulate and the warehouse that had been dubbed "Mushroom Inn." He tried to imagine what it all would have looked like on that fateful day—November 4, 1979—when Marseille's father, Charlie Harper, had been standing right there in that very spot. What had it been like to be there, watching thousands of enraged, armed, militant students rushing the embassy's gates, scaling her walls, storming her grounds, seizing her people? What would it have been like to be working undercover for the Central Intelligence Agency inside Iran during those chaotic, historic days?

It was all so quiet now.

David's escorts put him in a black sedan that pulled up in front of the gates, most certainly driven by a Quds Force operative. Yet at that moment, all David could do was stare back at the facilities of "Henderson High," as the former embassy had once been called, and think about how the fate of his family and the Harpers had become forever intertwined in that very place. If the embassy hadn't been taken over and the American diplomats had never been taken hostage, David realized, then Charlie and Claire Harper would never have been in such danger. They never would have had to flee Iran or ask David's parents for help, a request that eventually set into motion the CIA's operation to rescue not only the Harpers from Iran but the Shirazis as well. And who had masterminded the rescue plan? None other than Jack Zalinsky.

What were the chances, he wondered, that Mohammad and Nasreen Shirazi's youngest son would now be back in Tehran, working under-cover for the CIA, working for Jack Zalinsky, and in love with the Harpers' only daughter, even if the possibility of ever seeing her again was shrinking rapidly? What were the odds? A million to one? A billion to one? It couldn't be random. It didn't feel like coincidence or hap-penstance. It felt like fate. It seemed like destiny. Was it possible that there really was a God, a loving God, a God who had a plan for him? For the first time in his life, he began to think the answer might be yes.

★ ★ ★ ★ ★

WASHINGTON, DC

It had finally arrived.

After being alerted to the phone intercept, the president had been expecting it since Sunday. And it was finally here, a personal message from the Mahdi sent via the French defense minister and the US defense secretary to the White House.

Alone in the Oval Office, Jackson couldn't help but wonder why the Mahdi had bypassed the secretary of state and the entire American diplomatic system. Was that to ensure the message's secure delivery or to be able to deny its existence if publicly exposed?

He opened the sealed envelope and found the message as brief as the CIA had described. Sure enough, the Mahdi expressed his personal condolences to the president for this "terrible tragedy." He promised a thorough investigation to determine who was responsible. But his main message was that he wanted the president to know that "now is the time for peace, not more bloodshed." As anticipated, he asked for a phone meeting with the president the following Tuesday, after he finished his initial tour of the Middle East.

"I do not see the wisdom in resuming formal relations between the Islamic Republic of Iran and your country for the foreseeable future, under the current conditions," the Mahdi wrote bluntly. "You have not spoken favorably about the new Caliphate I am building. You do not demonstrate an understanding of Islam's power or emerging role in the world, nor has your government expressed the requisite repentance for past offenses. Still, we have crossed a threshold. We have entered a new age, and it seems the better part of wisdom to speak soon. Perhaps our representatives should meet to discuss issues of mutual concern, including a matter you keep proposing, a regional peace accord. It remains to be seen whether such an accord is possible, given your policies toward the oppressed peoples of our region and your financial, military, and political support for those who oppress them most. But since you have requested a meeting, I will not oppose one. I have come to bring peace. That is my mission. If you truly seek peace, then let us move quickly, before the moment passes forever. As the ancient Persian proverb says, 'A promise is a cloud; fulfillment is the rain.'"

Was it a threat or a true open door? Jackson wondered. It certainly wasn't the most warmly worded communiqué he had received since taking office, but it was, after all, coming from an enemy, not a friend. The Mahdi had taken a clear shot at America's relationship with Israel (aka the oppressors) and made a clear allusion to the nuclear weapons he now controlled ("we have crossed a threshold"). Still, the Mahdi seemed to want a back channel. He was reaching out. He wanted to talk, if only by phone.

Jackson reached into the top right drawer of the *Resolute* desk, pulled out a fountain pen and a piece of thick White House stationery, and began drafting his reply.

★ ★ ★ ★ ★

Najjar wiped the perspiration from his hands and forehead.

He was relieved to have finally made it to the Washington bureau of the Persian Christian Satellite Network. He hadn't gotten lost. He'd found parking quickly. The staff had welcomed him warmly. He sensed the Lord was with him and that he was doing the right thing. Yet between the heat of the TV lights and the cramps in his stomach, he was struggling to stay focused.

A young man clipped a microphone to his shirt while a young woman put some makeup on his face, and then it was time.

"Now, remember, this isn't live," the producer said. "It's too early in Iran right now to go live. So we're going to tape this for now. That way, if you feel like you've messed up, you can always start an answer over again, and we can take care of that in editing. Okay?"

Najjar nodded. He had never been on TV. He had never wanted to be on TV. He had never even imagined being on TV. But there he was, wondering exactly what he was going to say and wondering what Sheyda would say if she could see him right now.

"At this point," the producer added, "we're planning to run this tomorrow evening as a full hour-long special at prime time, probably in the seven o'clock hour, Tehran time, or 10:30 a.m. Eastern. Is that okay?"

Najjar nodded and asked for a glass of water.

"Excellent," the producer said. "Now, do you have a website you want to direct people to?"

"No, of course not. Why do you ask?"

"People are going to be absolutely fascinated with your story, Dr. Malik. Believe me. This is what I do. I help Iranian believers tell their stories to Farsi speakers all over the world—in Iran, of course, but all through Europe, North America, wherever. Our network has a very high viewership. And I always encourage our guests to have a website where people can go to learn more."

Najjar didn't know how to respond. "It's all happened so quickly. I don't have anything like that."

"How about a Facebook page?"

"Sorry, no."

"Myspace?"

Najjar shook his head.

"Okay, wait here," the producer said. "I have an idea."

He ran to his office and came back a minute later with his laptop. "Have you ever used Twitter before?"

Najjar stared at the young man. "I've been building nuclear reactors and weapons all my life. I haven't even learned how to use a mobile phone for more than calls and e-mail," Najjar answered.

"So no tweeting?" the producer asked.

"I'm sorry," Najjar said. "I don't even know what that means."

"It's okay. I'm setting up an account for you right now, and we're going to tell people throughout the show to sign up to follow you. Don't worry. I'll explain it all after we're done."

A production assistant brought Najjar a bottle of water while the crew made final adjustments. Soon they were all ready, and the red light of the lead camera came on. Najjar tried to relax, tried to look calm, but he was holding the arms of his chair so tightly his knuckles were white.

"Let's start at the beginning," the producer said. "Please tell us your name, your background in Iran as a high-ranking nuclear scientist, and why you were once a follower of the Twelfth Imam but have now become a follower of Jesus Christ."

31

TEHRAN, IRAN

David found a hotel and checked in.

Once his "minder" had driven off, he went up to his room, locked the door behind him, closed the curtains, and sat down on the bed. He opened the box that held the satellite phone and took the phone apart piece by piece. He could not take a chance that it was bugged.

When he was convinced it was clean, he put the phone back together and dialed the Munich Digital Systems branch office in Dubai. No one answered, so he left a message with his manager, letting him know he was safe in Tehran and would be checking in with the technical team the following morning. Next, he called the MDS headquarters in Munich and left a cryptic message on Eva's line, saying he needed to "accelerate" the arrival of the "shipment we discussed" and see if it could be rerouted to his office in Tehran. His goal was to be doing what Abdol Esfahani had asked him to do, on the satphone Esfahani had given him to use for that very purpose. If somehow someone was listening, David needed them to hear what they expected to hear. Nothing more. Nothing less.

That done, however, David pulled out his own Agency-modified Nokia N95, the company's top-of-the-line smartphone, which worked more like an iPhone than a BlackBerry. He took that one apart as well, since from the moment he'd been subjected to interrogation, it had been out of his hands. Had it been tampered with in any way? The process of pulling it apart and reviewing every microchip and wire took nearly an hour, and he was grateful for the first time for all the training Langley's techies had given him—and that he was remembering it all.

Convinced everything was fine, he now had to put it all back together without messing up any of the special improvements the technical division had made. The phone had a special GPS function that allowed Zalinsky and the Agency to track his location in real time without anyone being able to detect that such tracking was going on. It had also been preloaded with the names and contact information of people David would be expected to know in his job as a technical consultant for MDS. What's more, special software securely uploaded any new names, phone numbers, and e-mail addresses he added to his contact directory to Langley's and NSA's mainframe computers and alerted both agencies to hack in and begin monitoring those phone numbers and e-mail addresses as new high-priority targets. Most important, while his phone typically operated on standard frequencies, allowing foreign intelligence agencies to listen in on his calls and thus be fed disinformation if needed, a proprietary encryption system could be activated to enable him to make secure satellite calls to Langley or to other field agents. This was only for rare cases and extreme emergencies, because whenever the software was activated, those monitoring David's calls would know immediately that he had gone secure, potentially risking his cover as a consultant for Munich Digital Systems.

This, however, was one of the rare cases. He had to talk to Zalinsky and tell him what had happened so far—the waterboarding, the invitation to join the Group of 313, and the urgent request for the rest of the phones. But he didn't feel comfortable making the call from his room. He still hadn't gone through everything in his briefcase and his luggage to make sure no bugs had been planted. Esfahani had said he was clean, but they were clearly concerned enough that he might be a spy that they were applying extraordinary measures. At this point, he couldn't be too careful.

He ducked out into the hallway. Then he found the stairwell, headed up to the roof, and made the call.

"I don't know," Zalinsky replied after hearing Esfahani's demand for the rest of the phones. "I'm not sure I'm comfortable giving the Mahdi and his team a full communications network right now. We're too close to war, and we don't have the manpower to track all those calls in real time."

"What if you send a hundred or so for now," David suggested, "but have most of them be 'damaged in shipping'? That would make it look like I was trying hard, but it would also buy us time."

"It's a good idea," Zalinsky said, "but it's risky. What if Esfahani explodes?"

"I'll tell him it's his own fault," David replied. "He should have let me go get them in person."

Zalinsky agreed, then asked if David was still okay, all things considered.

"I'm in some pain," David replied, "but that's not what worries me."

"What does?"

"I don't have a single lead on these warheads, and events are moving too fast. Jack, I don't know how I'm going to find the warheads in time, and even if I do, the president won't take action to destroy them."

"Don't worry about the president," Zalinsky countered. "You just find those warheads, and when you do, believe me, I'll find a way to take them out. On that you have my word."

"Thanks, Jack."

"What you're doing isn't in vain. Now listen—do you remember a guy named Javad Nouri?"

"Of course. He's the guy I delivered a bunch of phones to. Works for the Supreme Leader, I think."

"Actually, we've determined he's the personal aide to the Twelfth Imam."

"Wow, that's huge."

"He keeps popping up on the call intercepts, and we now have video of him traveling with the Mahdi in Mecca and Beirut. Now here's the thing: do you know anything about his family?"

"No, why?"

"We believe he has a cousin, Firouz, who was the cell leader for the attack on the president at the Waldorf on Sunday night. We think he's still in the States, probably still in New York. We have a huge manhunt under way right now. The problem is we don't have a picture. If you can get one, we need it."

David had to shake his head. "So I was right."

"You were."

"The cell was Iranian, not al Qaeda or the Brotherhood."

"That's true," Zalinsky confirmed. "The guy the Secret Service shot and killed is Rahim Yazidi. He's a member of the Revolutionary Guard Corps. The guy we have in custody is Navid Yazidi, Rahim's kid brother, also part of the Guard. Eva got Navid to give up Firouz Nouri. His father is Mohammed Nouri. He's a mullah in Qom, big in the Twelver community, apparently. He's written several books on the Twelfth Imam. Anyway, see what your friend Birjandi can tell you about the family. We need everything we can get. I don't have to tell you how much pressure the Agency is under to get this guy, Firouz. The president is off the charts about us not seeing the Manhattan attack coming. We need a success, and we need it fast."

★ ★ ★ ★ ★

LANGLEY, VIRGINIA

Eva Fischer popped her head into Zalinsky's office.

"Got something you need to see."

Zalinsky was typing furiously on his laptop. "Close the door," he replied without looking up.

Eva complied and took a seat.

"Is it Malik?"

"No, but we're doing everything we can to find him."

"Then why haven't we?" Zalinsky asked. "Murray's handling this reasonably well, under the circumstances. But the director—who's still in Israel—is furious. They haven't told the White House yet, but they're going to have to soon. But that's not the worst of it."

"What is?"

"The director is asking if there's any chance Malik is a double."

"Absolutely not," Eva said categorically.

"You're sure about that?"

"You've read the transcript," Eva replied. "Does he come off as a double agent to you? I mean, the guy renounces Islam and claims he saw a vision of Jesus Christ, for crying out loud. Not exactly typical behavior of an Iranian mole."

"Wouldn't that throw us off all the more?"

"He's not a double, Jack. He's scared. He's lonely. He misses his wife. He misses his daughter. And we had him confined to a house all alone, but for the armed guards."

"Some good it did us."

"Look, Jack, everything he's told us has checked out. Everything. And we're doing everything we can to find him. What else can we do? In the meantime, I've got a new intercept for you."

Zalinsky sighed and put on his reading glasses as Eva handed him the translation of a recent call.

VOICE 1: Code in.

VOICE 2: "This ill cannot be healed, neither can the serpents be uprooted. Prepare food for them, therefore, that they may be fed, and give unto them for nourishment the brains of men, for perchance this may destroy them."

VOICE 1: Cousin, is that really you?

VOICE 2: It's me, Javad.

VOICE 1: Are you all right?

VOICE 2: Yes, yes, thanks to Allah, I'm safe—for now, at least.

VOICE 1: Are you alone?

VOICE 2: No, Jamshad is with me.

VOICE 1: What about Rahim and Navid? Are they safe too?

Zalinsky looked up from the transcript. "Is that really Firouz Nouri?"

"Yes."

"So they're actually cousins."

"Apparently."

"What's the code he uses?"

"It's a few lines from a Persian poem."

"Which one?"

"*The Epic of Shahnameh* by Ferdowsi."

"What's the significance?"

"I don't know yet."

Zalinsky kept reading. "They're in Queens?"

"So it seems."

"Who's Shirin?"

"Firouz's sister. We're working on all the connections. The point is, I just got this to the FBI, and I'm having them intensify their manhunt in Queens."

"Okay, good work. And, Eva, make it crystal clear to the Bureau—we need this guy and Jamshad fast, and we need them alive."

★ ★ ★ ★ ★

TEHRAN, IRAN

David slept for a few hours and awoke early Wednesday morning.

He showered, dressed, grabbed his phone, and headed down to the lobby, half-expecting to see an intelligence goon waiting for him. But the lobby was empty. The restaurant was still closed. All was quiet.

Heading out to the street, he hailed a cab to the Iran Telecom operations center on the south side. Given the typical but unbearable Tehran rush-hour traffic, the six-mile ride took him nearly an hour. Once there, he spent the next several hours catching up with his MDS technical team, finding out how their work was going, and answering their many questions. By no means was it what he wanted to be doing, and he didn't feel it was the best use of his time. But he had no choice. He knew he was being watched. He had to maintain his cover. What's more, the senior executives back in Munich, the ones who paid him a salary and generous benefits each month, had no idea he worked for the CIA. They had hired him to help them rebuild Iran's antiquated mobile phone network, and they were expecting him to deliver.

32

The military helicopter touched down at noon.

It landed in an open field across the street from the home of Dr. Alireza Birjandi as it did once a month. The neighbors didn't like the noise or the sight of armed men taking up positions on their street, but they certainly didn't complain. They lived in the Islamic Republic of Iran, and they knew better.

Two soldiers knocked on Birjandi's door. The old man was ready and waiting as always with his white cane in hand. They helped the blind, eighty-three-year-old cleric down his steps, across the street, and into the still-running chopper, without saying a word. It was routine now. Each man knew his place and did what he had to do, and soon they were airborne again, gaining altitude and airspeed en route to the Qaleh.

For Birjandi, it did not really matter where he met the Supreme Leader and the president. Their monthly luncheons had not begun in the Supreme Leader's private mountain retreat center in the early years. They had originally occurred in Hosseini's residence on Pasteur Street, not far from the German and British Embassies. However, six months earlier, Hosseini had invited Birjandi up to his compound in the mountains, and they'd been gathering there ever since. From what Birjandi heard, Hosseini was spending less and less time engaged in official functions in Tehran and more and more time in the mountains. Was it for security reasons? Or health reasons? Or just the peace and quiet that Mount Tochal afforded? Birjandi wasn't entirely sure, but he had his suspicions.

Hosseini was now seventy-six years old. He was alone in the world, having murdered his wife in 2002, and having sent all three of his sons to minefields to become martyrs during the Iran–Iraq War in the eighties. He had been a loyal disciple and deputy to Ayatollah Khomeini and had been at his side when the leader of the Islamic Revolution had passed away. Though he was not the first choice of the Assembly of Experts to replace Khomeini, Hosseini had eventually gained their favor and had now been the nation's Supreme Leader for over a decade. During that time, he had worked diligently to shore up his power base and solidify his control of the military, the Revolutionary Guard Corps, the Basij militia, and most of the ruling class, including the religious leaders in Qom and the business elite in Tehran. Now he was firmly convinced that both the end of his own days and the end of all days were rapidly drawing near. He did not seem to want to be bothered with the trivial pursuits of the mere mortals living down below. His eyes had been firmly fixed on the coming of the Twelfth Imam, and now that he was here, the Supreme Leader was consumed with pleasing the so-called Promised One. Hosseini seemed to think it was more spiritual to stay in the mountains and beneath him to attend to the needs of his people.

As the helicopter made its final approach to the landing pad at the Qaleh and finally touched down, a sadness settled on Birjandi's heart. He genuinely loved Hamid Hosseini. He abhorred the man's choices. He abhorred the man's religion. But the man was lost, utterly lost, and it grieved Birjandi. *Imagine,* he thought, *if a man like this became a follower of Jesus Christ. Imagine what joy and forgiveness he would experience. Imagine how much influence he would have on Muslims worldwide.* On his knees for hours at a time, Birjandi had begged the Lord to open the man's eyes to the truth of Christ's unfailing love and free gift of salvation. Birjandi chose to meet with Hosseini, as well as with President Darazi, because he was not sure there was a single other person in their lives who was a follower of Jesus Christ, who knew that the Twelfth Imam was a false messiah, and who was willing to risk his life to bear witness to those truths.

When he heard the chopper's engine shut down and the rotors slow,

Birjandi asked the Lord the same question he asked before every meeting: *Is today the day I should tell them I follow the true King of kings?* He had felt the Spirit's undeniable restraint each time they met. He wasn't sure why. He always listened to the men carefully and sincerely. He always answered their questions honestly. But they believed that they and he were kindred spirits, equally excited about the Twelfth Imam and equally devoted to serving him as the Lord of the Age. That had been true when they had first begun meeting, but it had not been true for some time now, and Birjandi prayed that today the Lord would give him an open door and a green light to tell these men the truth, for he had no idea how many more opportunities he would have to meet them face-to-face.

★ ★ ★ ★ ★

TEHRAN, IRAN

After a productive morning, David took the MDS team out to lunch.

At their strenuous request, he reluctantly agreed to meet several of them at one of Iran Telecom's switching stations near the city of Qom the following day to troubleshoot some software problems they couldn't seem to solve. He had never been to Qom before, and it was not in his game plan for the Agency. But at the moment he couldn't see a way around going, so he agreed and then said good-bye.

Promising to check in with them in the morning to finalize the arrangements, he left the upscale restaurant where he had splurged on them and walked for a few blocks, stopping occasionally to window-shop in various storefronts, really to see if anyone was following him. Unsure, he walked for another two blocks, then ducked into a crowded coffee shop, ordered a cup to go, and waited to see who came in behind him. No one looked suspicious, but he was taking no chances. After another ten minutes, he made his way to the back of the shop toward the restrooms, then ducked out the back exit into an alley, walked quickly around the corner, and bent down to tie his shoe. He glanced down the street to the north, then back to the south. No one appeared to be trailing him. Finally convinced, he hailed a cab.

"I need to get to the airport as fast as possible," he told the driver. "How long will that take?"

★ ★ ★ ★ ★

THE QALEH, IRAN

The three men gathered in the dining room.

Hosseini and Darazi were buoyant, explaining that the Caliphate was rising, oil prices were soaring—up another nine dollars a barrel overnight—and the annihilation of the Zionist entity was imminent. It wasn't the first time they had said such things, of course, but Birjandi privately noted the way they said them. They spoke with such conviction, such certainty, that the hair on Birjandi's neck stood on end and his entire body felt chilled.

"As we speak, Imam al-Mahdi is headed to Cairo," Hosseini said. "He should land at any moment. He's going to meet with the vice president and the supreme council of military leaders. By this time tomorrow, Egypt will be part of the Caliphate."

"That means we will have the Zionists almost completely surrounded," Darazi added. "We already have Lebanon and Syria, the Saudis, and several of the Gulf states. We have Sudan, Libya, and Algeria. With Egypt, the encirclement is almost complete. We still need Jordan, and we'll get it. The king is digging in his heels, siding with the Americans. Director Allen of the CIA will undoubtedly head to Amman at some point. But Jordan will soon be ours. If the king opposes the Mahdi, he will regret it."

Birjandi hadn't heard anything about the Cairo trip. He wondered if David Shirazi knew, though he had no way to contact him. "Is the Mahdi going to Amman?" he asked.

"I don't know," Darazi said. "Once the king sees what happens to the Jews, I think he will come begging us for mercy."

"How I will love that day," Hosseini said.

"How soon will the attack on the Zionists begin?" Birjandi asked.

"Any day now," Hosseini said. "It's up to him, of course, but I suspect everything will be ready by Monday at the latest."

"That is so soon. Is there anything I can do while we wait?"

"Imam al-Mahdi wants to meet you when he gets back from Cairo. Ahmed and I have been telling him about you and how helpful you have been, how devoted you are."

Inside, Birjandi cringed. He had no interest in being in the same country with the Twelfth Imam, much less the same room. He did not feel at liberty to say as much, though, so he nodded graciously and said he served "at the pleasure of my Lord." He meant the Lord Jesus, but he could accept, for the moment, being misunderstood. "There is much talk that the Israelis will launch a massive air strike before you can launch your attacks," he said.

"It's just talk," Darazi said. "The Americans won't let them do it. The Mahdi has sent the president a private message within the last few days. It requests a phone call with Jackson next Tuesday."

"And the president has accepted?"

"Not yet, but we believe it is just a matter of time. He has sent the director of the CIA to Jerusalem to meet with Naphtali. From what we can gather, the president is making the prime minister an offer he can't refuse."

Birjandi wasn't convinced. He turned to Hosseini, wishing he could make eye contact but hoping at least to make him pause. "Hamid, my friend, do not underestimate Asher Naphtali. He may be a friend of the president, but he is not his lackey. He saw your test. He hears your rhetoric. He hears what the Mahdi is saying. He is not stupid. He knows he's running out of time. He's going to strike soon, and millions of our people will suffer."

"That's why we confuse them, delay them, until we can strike first with the warheads we've just built," Hosseini replied.

"But what if the Israelis do launch first?" Birjandi pressed. "What if they destroy all our warheads before we can use a single one of them?"

"There is no need to worry, Alireza. Really. We are fine. The Mahdi has everything under control. All is going according to his plan."

"What does that mean?" Birjandi asked. "We dare not under-estimate the reach of the Zionists. They have spies everywhere. They killed Saddaji. They kidnapped Malik, for all we know. They nearly killed the Mahdi. How do you know they're not coming after you?"

"Ali, my friend, we have taken care of everything," Hosseini said. "First of all, we are safe up here. No one even knows we are here. Second of all, the warheads are all spread out. Not even Ahmed or I know exactly where all of them are. We know generally, but frankly we don't want the scientists who built them or the generals who control them to share every detail with us, for the very reason you cite. We don't want the Zionists—or the Americans, Allah forbid—to learn what we learn. But this I can tell you. You know that five of our warships will be passing through the Suez Canal later today, just about the time the Mahdi lands in Cairo?"

"Yes, I've heard this on the news," Birjandi said.

"I have not even told my closest advisors such things, but I will tell you, my friend—two of our eight warheads are aboard those ships as they head to the Mediterranean. They are attached to missiles, aimed at Tel Aviv and Haifa."

Birjandi prayed his face did not express his horror. "I thought we did not have the capacity to attach the warheads to missiles," he said. "That's what you told me last month."

"Last month we didn't," Hosseini replied. "Today we do."

33

TEHRAN, IRAN

David reached the airport and paid his cab driver in cash.

Inside the main terminal, he withdrew the maximum daily amount allowed from his Eurocard account and exchanged it for Iranian rials. Then he picked one of the rental car agencies and filled out the paperwork for a maroon, four-door Peugeot 407 sedan.

★ ★ ★ ★ ★

LANGLEY, VIRGINIA

Zalinsky's cell phone rang.

Disoriented, he sat up in bed, checked his watch, and groaned. It was only four thirty Wednesday morning, Washington time. Three decades of experience told him this couldn't be good. He groped for the phone on his nightstand and answered on the sixth ring.

"Jack, it's Eva. Sorry to call you so early."

"Who's dead?"

"Nobody."

"Then what's wrong?"

"I just got a call from my guy at NSA."

"Where are you?"

"At my desk."

"Didn't you ever go home?"

"No."

"You're sleeping on your floor?"

"I'm not doing much sleeping. But, Jack, listen. The NSA just sent me the transcript of a very interesting call."

"Go on."

"They intercepted a call from Javad to Firouz. It happened about an hour ago."

"That's fast. What happened?"

"Javad described a safe-deposit box at a Citibank branch in Queens. He said it contained two fake passports, one with a false identity for Firouz and another for Jamshad. He said there were passports for the other two terrorists, too. It had all been pre-positioned, just in case. He said there were also credit cards, cash, forged birth certificates, and whatnot. There's also four automatic pistols and plenty of ammunition. He gave Firouz the address of the bank and told him to be there precisely at ten o'clock, when the branch opens. They're supposed to retrieve everything, use the documents to get out of New York, then get to Toronto and back to Tehran as soon as possible. He suggested they route through Venezuela, if necessary, and that Firouz would know why. We've got them, Jack. I really think we've got them. I'm about to call the guys at the Bureau so they can set up a stakeout on the bank, but I wanted you to be the first to know—or rather, the third."

"You and the translator?"

"Right."

"You haven't told Murray?"

"No. I figured you'd want to."

"No," Zalinsky said. "We don't tell anybody. Not a one."

"What are you talking about, Jack? We can nail them. Right now. We can bag two terrorists. It'll be a huge coup for the Agency—well, for the Bureau, for the president."

"No, no, that's precisely what we don't want. This can't go beyond the three of us right now—and definitely not to Tom."

"Why not? That's crazy."

"Stop, Eva. Think. We can't arrest them. Not now. It's too obvious. If we take these guys down, Javad Nouri is going to know we can listen in on his calls. Then they're going to consider all the satellite phones suspect, and then everything we've tried to put in place will be for naught. No, we need to follow the trail and see where it leads."

Eva protested for another few minutes but finally backed down when Zalinsky reminded her of how much danger David would be in if the US government's ability to intercept the satphones were discovered by the Iranian regime.

"They already suspect him," Zalinsky said. "We can't take the risk that they'll bring him in again. Next time they won't waterboard him. They'll kill him."

"So what do we do?" Eva asked.

"Don't tell the FBI. Put one of our teams on the bank. Have them shadow Firouz and Jamshad for the next several days and await further orders."

★ ★ ★ ★ ★

THE QALEH, IRAN

"Ali, you don't look happy," Hosseini said after a while.

They had finished their salads and their salmon entrees and were being served steaming-hot cups of chai. Their conversation had been wide ranging, covering potential US and Israeli responses to an Iranian first strike, Darazi's belief that the American president did not have the will to launch another war in the Middle East—least of all to save Israel—and Hosseini's belief that Jackson might order air strikes but wouldn't let himself be drawn into a ground war like Operation Iraqi Freedom. The key, Hosseini said, was not specifically provoking the Americans by shutting down the Strait of Hormuz or attacking the Iraqi oil fields or directly confronting the US Navy.

Birjandi couldn't believe what he was hearing. He thought they were insane. He didn't disagree that this particular American president at this particular time didn't likely have the fortitude to take on the Islamic Republic militarily. But he was stunned by what he regarded as Hosseini's and Darazi's utter and foolish dismissal of Israel's capacities both to absorb a first strike and to launch an absolutely devastating second strike.

Nevertheless, Birjandi knew better than to try to debate them on geopolitics. They weren't going to listen to him. That wasn't why he was there, and they didn't consider him an expert on such matters. His value, in their eyes, was his knowledge about Islamic prophecy, the Shia perspective on the End Times, and how all of the events they were witnessing and leading would come together to reestablish the Caliphate. He had been listening to both of them for nearly ninety minutes now, only asking an occasional question for clarification. Now he sensed it was time to begin that for which the Lord had sent him. It was clear that Hosseini and Darazi did not have ears to hear nor eyes to see nor hearts to understand the gospel of Jesus Christ or a direct presentation of scriptural truths, as much as he had prayed that they would. But he sensed the Lord telling him to sow seeds of doubt in their minds about their own eschatology, doubts perhaps that the Spirit would reinforce in the hours and days ahead.

"I sincerely apologize for my countenance. I do not mean to burden you."

"It is no burden," Hosseini said.

"Still, I am hesitant to bother two important men such as yourselves with my own problems, as trivial as they may be." Birjandi spoke with great discretion and discernment, playing to the egos he sat with.

"Nonsense," Hosseini said. "We consider you our friend. What is troubling you?"

"It is probably nothing," Birjandi replied. "It's just that I am finding myself wrestling with a few questions in private to which I cannot seem to find answers."

"Like what?" Darazi asked.

"Really, I needn't bother you. You both have so much on your minds."

"Don't be silly, Ali. Tell us plainly."

"Well—and please take this in the spirit in which it is intended— merely a question, though a vexing one at that . . ."

"Of course, of course," they said.

"I just find myself wondering, where is Jesus, peace be upon him?"

There was dead silence. It wasn't a name that often got mentioned in the presence of the Grand Ayatollah and the president of the Islamic Republic of Iran.

"What do you mean?" Hosseini finally asked, audibly sipping his chai.

"I just mean, wasn't Jesus supposed to come back before the Mahdi? Isn't that what the prophecies said? Wasn't that supposed to be one of the signs?"

"I suppose."

"Then where is he?"

Neither Hosseini nor Darazi had an answer.

"You have both given sermons that Jesus would come back as the lieutenant to Imam al-Mahdi, right?"

"True."

"Then as I said, I find myself wondering, where is he?"

Darazi shifted uncomfortably in his seat and asked, "What exactly are you implying, Ali?"

"I am not implying anything," Birjandi replied calmly. "I am simply asking where I went wrong. Please don't misunderstand me. You preached that one of the signs preceding the Mahdi's return would be the coming of Jesus to require all infidels to convert to Islam or die by the sword. You did that because I taught you that. I taught you that because of a lifetime of studying the ancient texts and so many commentaries on the same. Yet Jesus is nowhere to be found. The infidels have not been warned. It's bothering me. Because that's not all. There are other prophecies that I have not seen fulfilled, and I am wondering why."

"Other prophecies?" Darazi pressed. "Which ones?"

"I hesitate to continue," Birjandi said. "I don't want to be misinterpreted. I'm just trying to be honest with the ancient texts."

"No, go on," Hosseini said. "Ahmed and I have always valued your insights. Now we value your questions as well."

"You are certain, my friend?"

"Most certain," Hosseini replied.

"Very well," Birjandi said. "If you insist." He paused a moment, then began again. "In my work done through the Bright Future Institute, I identified and outlined five distinct signs that would precede the arrival or the appearance of the Hidden Imam. The first sign was supposed to be the rise of a fighter from Yemen called the Yamani, who attacks the enemies of Islam. This actually does seem to have been fulfilled. There have been a whole series of violent attacks against Christians in Yemen in recent years and even in the weeks leading up to the appearance of the Mahdi."

His listeners said nothing, but Birjandi sensed them nodding, silently encouraging him to continue.

"The second sign is the rise of an anti-Mahdi militant leader named Osman Ben Anbase, who will also be known as Sofiani. This figure is supposed to be joined by another anti-Mahdi militant called Dajal. Many Muslim clerics liken this figure to the Christian notion of the Antichrist. The uprising of Sofiani was supposed to precede the reappearance of the Mahdi in Mecca by exactly six months," Birjandi observed. "These two forces were supposed to occupy Syria and Jordan and advance from there. Did this happen? When? Where? I never saw it. When were the forces of good led in battle by the man from Khorasan? When was the epic battle that was prophesied to happen near the city of Kufa, in the Shia heartland of southern Iraq? Did I miss it? Did you?"

Neither Hosseini nor Darazi replied.

"The third distinct sign," Birjandi continued, "is to be voices from the sky, the most prominent of which is supposed to be that of the angel Gabriel, gathering the faithful around the Mahdi. That seems to have just happened in Beirut. It was only one angelic voice, to be sure, not multiple voices or a host of angels, but still, I think it's fair to say that this prophecy was fulfilled, or at least partially so. But that should have led to the fourth sign, the destruction of Sofiani's army. However, since Sofiani never seems to have come, never seems to have raised an army, and certainly hasn't seized control of Syria or Jordan, I do not believe this prophecy has been—or can be—fulfilled. And the question I keep asking myself is why."

Still no response. Birjandi continued anyway.

"The fifth sign is supposed to be the death of a holy man by the name of Muhammad bin Hassan, called Nafse Zakiye, or the pure soul.

The Mahdi is supposed to appear in Mecca fifteen days after this fig-ure is killed. I have been pondering this for days, but I can't see how this prophecy was fulfilled. Granted, the Mahdi's army is supposed to begin with 313 faithful Muslims and grow into ten thousand, fifty of whom will be women. This is in the process of happening, so that's noteworthy. But some of the other minor details of the Mahdi's com-ing haven't come to pass either. He doesn't appear to be wearing a ring that belonged to King Solomon. Nor is he holding the wooden stick that Moses held when he parted the Red Sea. Does it matter? Maybe not. But I feel a great sense of responsibility. I have been studying the Last Things most of my adult life. I have been preaching and teaching these things for as long as you have been gracious enough to give me the freedom to do so. But something isn't adding up. Something's wrong. And I keep asking: what?"

34

Najjar was awakened by the cell phone ringing.

He had slept in the Toyota in an underground parking garage all night because he had nowhere else to go and had been too embarrassed to ask the staff at the TV station for help. Now his neck and back ached and he scrambled to find the phone and check the caller ID. He was afraid it might be the neighbors or, worse, the police but was startled to see it was a call from London.

"Hello?" he asked cautiously.

"Is this Dr. Najjar Malik?"

"Who's calling?"

"My name is Nigel Moore. I'm the senior producer for BBC Persian. Do you have a moment?"

Najjar sat up, rubbed the sleep from his eyes, and checked his watch. It was just after seven on Wednesday morning, Washington time, half past three back in Iran. He suddenly realized he was famished.

"Yes. How can I help you?"

"Honestly, my colleague whom you talked with yesterday was quite skeptical about your story. But we spent most of the night doing our homework and talking to sources, and we're much more interested now."

Najjar tensed. Was he being set up? "I'm not sure I'm interested any longer, but thank you for calling."

He was about to hang up the phone, but the producer pleaded with him to stay on the line.

"You were absolutely right," Moore said. "This would be a huge story, unlike anything we've done in quite some time. You've got a very compelling story to tell, and it should be heard. We're grateful you considered us."

"I'm not interested in being played, Mr. Moore," Najjar responded. "I've got governments trying to arrest me and people trying to kill me, and I was hoping for more understanding from the BBC, of all places."

"You have it now, Dr. Malik. I'm very sorry. I know you have to be careful. I understand that. I do. But please understand that we have to be careful too. We can't just let anyone come on the air. People try to play us every day. I'm sure you can imagine."

"I guess that would be true."

"Listen, Dr. Malik, rumors are flying that a war is going to break out any moment between Iran and Israel or between the US and Iran. Have you heard the news this morning?"

"No. What?"

"President Jackson ordered a second aircraft carrier battle group into the Persian Gulf, but the *Washington Post* says the White House has been engaged in secret discussions with the Twelfth Imam and that the president has accepted the Mahdi's invitation to talk by phone next Tuesday."

"He's stalling."

"Who?"

"The Mahdi."

"What do you mean?"

"He's going to launch the warheads, probably this weekend, but no later than Monday," Najjar said.

"How can you say that?" Moore asked. "Based on what?"

"Mr. Moore, the Mahdi has control of eight nuclear warheads. Someone just tried to assassinate him. Maybe it was the Americans. Maybe it was the Israelis. But it doesn't really matter. He wants revenge. He wants to destroy Judeo-Christian society once and for all. And he's about to try."

"He keeps saying he wants peace."

"If he were really interested in peace, he'd be on the phone with the president right now. Why wait six days? There's only one reason. To stall until he can launch."

"Come onto our network and say that," Moore said. "The world needs to hear your perspective. We'll tape an hour-long special. Maybe even a two-part series, if you'd like. This is an incredible moment, Dr. Malik. Remember, you came to us first. We did our due diligence. Now we're ready. What do you say?"

This was the moment of truth. He had to decide. He'd already shared with the Christian network his story of seeing the vision of Jesus Christ and renouncing Islam. BBC Persian was a huge opportunity. Plus, Moore was right; he had come to them. Najjar glanced in the rearview mirror. He looked horrible—unshowered, unshaven, bloodshot eyes. But he felt the Holy Spirit prompting him to say yes. He had asked for an opportunity to share the gospel with his people and to warn them war was coming. This was another open door, and a significant one at that.

"Okay, Mr. Moore, I will do it," he finally replied. "But only on one condition."

"What's that?"

"I'm not going to do it taped. It has to be live, and it has to be now."

"The BBC doesn't take well to conditions," Moore replied.

"Fair enough; then I pass."

"No, wait."

"Yes?"

One of the BBC's most senior producers was calculating the payoff on a huge risk. "I can't get you on before ten Eastern. But if you can get to our DC studio by nine thirty, we'll get you into makeup, walk you through a few logistics, and do a full-hour live interview from ten to eleven."

"No," Najjar said. "The interview must be no longer than twenty minutes. That's all the time I can afford. I can't allow the authorities to track me down."

"Twenty minutes, fine. Starting at ten, okay?"

"That's six thirty in the evening in Tehran, right?"

"Right," Moore said. "And we'll put together a promo and start running it right away."

"No," Najjar said. "You can't do that."

"Why not?"

"People are looking for me, Mr. Moore. A lot of people. I'm taking a big enough risk as it is. I can't give the Iranian intelligence services or the Americans a head start on finding me."

"I understand, but we'd really like to promote this thing, and—"

"No, I'm sorry. That's nonnegotiable."

There was a long pause. "Okay, fine. Anything else?"

"Yes, one more thing."

"What's that?"

"Promise me you won't identify where I'm being interviewed from— nothing that would indicate that I'm in DC or even in the US."

There was another long silence, so long, in fact, that Najjar began to wonder if they had been disconnected.

"And that's it—that's all your requests?" Moore asked.

"Yes, that's all," Najjar said.

"Deal," Moore said, then gave Najjar directions to the BBC's studios in Washington, not far from the White House.

★　★　★　★　★

LANGLEY, VIRGINIA

A storm was rolling in over northern Virginia and the District.

Thunder rumbled in the distance as a light rain began to come down. Traffic on the George Washington Memorial Parkway was slow, but Marseille Harper had left in plenty of time, and she pulled onto the grounds of the George H. W. Bush Center for Central Intelligence ahead of schedule. Dressed in a conservative gray suit and equipped with a golf umbrella she'd bought in the hotel gift shop, she cleared the guard station, parked in the visitor lot, entered the main building, and went through security, receiving a temporary badge.

While she waited to be escorted up to Deputy Director Tom Murray's office, she tried to soak in all the atmospherics. The enormous seal of the CIA embedded in the gray-and-white marble floor in the Agency's main lobby. The wall of stars, one for each employee ever killed while in the Agency's employ. The large American flags and the various works of art. What surprised her most, however, was the Bible verse prominently displayed on one of the lobby walls, defining the mission of the entire Agency.

"And ye shall know the truth, and the truth shall make you free."
JOHN 8:32

A lump formed in her throat. That was all she wanted—the truth about her father.

★ ★ ★ ★ ★

WASHINGTON, DC

"Mr. President, you have the CIA director on line two."

Jackson nodded and excused himself from a meeting with his chief economic advisors. He stepped out of the Roosevelt Room and back into the Oval Office, where he took the call in privacy.

"Roger, how did this leak?" he bellowed, a copy of the *Washington Post* in his hands.

"I have no idea, Mr. President," Allen began. "We're doing everything we can to find out, but honestly, sir, I'm not optimistic."

"I want someone's head on a platter. We're on the verge of war here, Roger. This is a very sensitive moment. I'm engaged in extremely delicate diplomatic maneuvers with the Mahdi, with Israel, with the Egyptians, and with the rest of our allies. And this is a huge blow."

"I know, sir. And believe me, it hasn't helped the situation here."

"Please tell me you've made progress."

"A little, sir. But I've spent most of the last two hours on the phone with one of my oldest friends, listening to a rant on why you shouldn't be engaging in back-channel discussions with the Twelfth Imam, of all people."

"Let me guess the number of times the words *Hitler* and *Chamberlain* and *appeasement* have been used."

"A few."

"And you're telling me the prime minister of Israel doesn't want my government to pursue every possible road to peace, to exhaust every option short of war?"

"I'm telling you the Israelis think we don't have the foggiest idea who the Twelfth Imam is, what he really wants, or how far he will go to get it. I'm telling you they think we're about to get sucker punched because we don't truly understand what kind of enemy we're facing."

Jackson rubbed his eyes and changed the topic. "What about my offer?"

"I've discussed it with him."

"And?"

"I've discussed it some more."

"What's there to discuss?" the president snapped. "I said it wasn't open for negotiation. It's take it or leave it. Period."

"I reiterated that," Allen said, "and he says he needs clarifications on several issues."

"Like what?"

"The top concern is what happens if Iran—or one of its proxies or allies or a combination—launches a first strike against Israel. What precisely will the US do for Israel in such a case?"

"What did you say?"

"I reiterated that we would keep all of our obligations to Israel. We'd accelerate shipments of already-purchased arms. We'd rush in additional Patriot missile batteries. We'd continue to coordinate on intelligence matters, and so forth."

"And?"

"It wasn't enough."

"Why not?"

"Naphtali needs assurances—written, signed, Congress-approved guarantees, mind you—that the US would declare war against Israel's enemies within twenty-four hours of the first attack, use US air superiority to help Israel punish the aggressors, and be willing to send in US ground forces alongside Israeli ground forces to overthrow any regime who participated in the attacks."

"That's negotiating, Roger, and I won't have it."

"That's not how they see it, Mr. President."

The president swore. "I don't care how they see it! I don't work for Asher Naphtali, and I'm not going to let him tie my hands or the hands of my government in the event of a future attack on Israel."

"I hear you, Mr. President," Allen said calmly, "but to be fair, he's trying to get clarification on two of the key points in your offer. He said, first of all, that he's grateful for your 'pledge of aggressive US support for Israel to join NATO as a full member in the next six months.' And second of all, he deeply appreciates your 'pledge for the US to sign a full alliance treaty with Israel should the NATO deal stall or be denied, promising to go to war alongside Israel if the Jewish State were ever attacked by Iran.' But he needs to know precisely what that means."

"He's trying to box me in," Jackson said, pacing.

"Again, he doesn't see it that way."

"I think anyone would say I'm being exceedingly generous. No American president has ever offered the Israelis what I'm offering, starting with the Los Angeles–class submarines alone, not to mention everything else."

"The prime minister seems genuinely appreciative of the offer, in my view. However, he told me repeatedly that the devil is in the details and that there was simply no way his Cabinet would ever agree to such a deal, as generous as it is, without more clarity on just how far you and future American governments are willing to go to defend the Jewish people from a second Holocaust."

Increasingly exasperated, Jackson decided to shift gears again. "Are you picking up signs that the Israelis are preparing for a preemptive strike?"

"Not as such," Allen replied. "There is a lot of activity on the homeland security side. The government is urging the people to be prepared for any eventuality. They are issuing gas masks. They are deploying antimissile defenses. They're stocking bomb shelters with food, water, diapers, and other essentials. Magen David Adom has just launched a massive blood drive. But the prime minister and his entire government are being very disciplined. They're not hinting at an Israeli first strike. In fact, they keep saying they are doing everything they can to avoid war. But they are warning their people in no uncertain terms that war could be coming if Iran and the Twelfth Imam try to make good on their many threats."

"Are they calling up the Reserves?"

"Not formally, though the Ministry of Defense has put all Reservists on alert."

"Any unusual air activity?"

"Nothing out of the ordinary. But of course, the Israeli Air Force has been training heavily and aggressively for months, so it might be hard to distinguish what was accelerated activity at this point."

"You think he'll do it?"

"Asher?"

"Yes."

"Do I think Asher will order a first strike?"

"Right."

"If we don't do more, and fast, then yes, Mr. President, I think he's leaning that way."

"What more can we do?"

"Honestly, sir, I think you should come over here and negotiate this thing yourself."

"Right now?"

"When else?"

"You want me to drop everything I'm doing and fly to Jerusalem for the day."

"I think it would send a powerful message to the Israeli people that the US is standing by our most stable democratic ally in the region. And I think it would send a powerful message to the Mahdi and his advisors that they'd better not play with fire. Because right now, sir, I think people over here are getting mixed signals."

"I can't, Roger; not right now."

"Why not, sir? The entire region is on the brink."

"I know that. Of course I know that, but I just sent a message back to the Twelfth Imam. I told him that the United States is committed to peace in the region. We're supposed to talk on Tuesday, once he finishes his tour of the region. Apparently, he's supposed to be in Cairo today.

Tomorrow he'll be in Damascus. After that, who knows where? But how is it going to look if I show up in Jerusalem right at the point when we're trying to establish a relationship?"

"May I speak candidly, sir?"

"Of course."

"It will look like you're standing with an ally, while he stands with his. Look, Mr. President, Naphtali is asking me why you haven't commented on the Twelfth Imam's vow to build a new Caliphate. He and his aides are asking what the US position is on the Caliphate. I said we're watching the situation very closely."

"And?"

"They took that for what it was—a dodge. Mr. President, the Middle East is being radically reshaped as we speak. The Twelfth Imam has the initiative. By the time you talk to him on Tuesday, he could be in charge of everything from Egypt to Pakistan. I can't tell you what to do. But my job is to tell you what I think is going to happen next, and I'm telling you we are losing the epicenter and we don't have to. Naphtali insists the Sunni regimes are terrified of the Shias being in charge. He's right. We have leverage, if we'll use it."

"Where would you start?"

"Look, I'm in the region. Send me to Amman today. I'll talk to the king ahead of his meeting with the Mahdi. I'll take his temperature and reassure him that you're standing with him. Then I'd like to fly to Islamabad to see President Farooq. We know he's hesitant about the Mahdi. I showed you that intercept. Let me go talk to him, reassure him that you won't let his regime fall, that there's an alternative to joining the Caliphate. Then, with your permission, I'd recommend I double back to Baghdad and then Cairo to meet with Vice President Riad and Field Marshal Yassin. Let me see how they're doing after their meeting today with the Mahdi, see if we can help them build a Sunni alliance against him. I can't promise all this will work. I don't know that. But I know one thing: if the US does nothing, we're going to lose everything."

"Do it," the president said without hesitation.

"The whole trip?" Allen clarified.

"Yes. I think you're right."

"And what should I tell Naphtali? Are you open to coming to Jerusalem in the next few days?"

"I don't know," Jackson said. "I need to give that more thought."

"Time is short, Mr. President. I can't stress that enough."

"I understand, Roger. Believe me—I understand."

"Miss Harper," a secretary said, "would you please follow me?"

Marseille glanced at her watch. It was precisely 9 a.m., just as promised. She stood, smoothed the wrinkles out of her skirt, took a deep breath, and forced herself to smile as she followed the secretary into the office of the deputy director for operations.

"You must be Marseille," Murray said, shaking her hand and encouraging her to take a seat. He asked her if she wanted anything to drink.

"Thank you, Mr. Murray. I'll have some water, if that's okay."

"Please, call me Tom," he said warmly, asking his secretary to bring back a pitcher of water and some glasses. "What a joy to meet you. I'm so sorry about your father. I was a big fan of his. He really served his country well."

"That's very kind of you, Mr. . . . um, well, sir," Marseille replied. "I'm sorry; I don't know why, but I'm feeling very nervous."

"Well, you don't need to be. You're practically family here. I actually knew both your parents. Oversaw your father's training at the Farm. Selected him to go to Tehran in '79. And to be honest, had to work very hard to make sure your mom never knew I worked here but thought I was with State. She was a very bright woman. I would have loved to have recruited her to work for us too, but your father was dead set against it."

"Why was that?"

"He said Claire—er, your mom—didn't have a poker face. 'The woman can't lie,' he said. 'It's like genetic or something. She just can't do it.' Said she couldn't cook, either. But I never had the chance to find out."

Marseille smiled shyly. He was right about that.

She pulled out the yellowed, slightly ripped letter of commendation that Murray had once written to her father and slid it across the desk.

"My goodness, that was a long time ago. But he deserved this. He was a real asset to us."

"Why? What did he do?"

"Well, I'm afraid most of that is classified. But yesterday I checked with our personnel office and with our ethics officer to see what I could tell you. There are a few things."

He opened his desk and pulled out a manila folder, which he slid over to her.

As Marseille leafed through it, she found a copy of her father's original application to join the Agency, copies of his college transcripts, his original background check, his pay records, a stack of performance evaluations (some of which contained redacted classified material that was blacked out), three other letters of commendation for his work in France, Italy, and Switzerland in the early 1980s, and various other pieces of paperwork. "Am I able to keep these?" she asked.

"I'm afraid not," Murray replied. "But after our meeting, I can put you in a room and let you take however long you need to read through it all. I know it's a lot to absorb, but I think you'll find it fascinating. I skimmed through a lot of it last night, and it brought back good memories."

Marseille set the folder down and looked around the office. Books lined the shelves. There was an array of framed photographs of Murray and various presidents and Agency directors. What was missing, she noticed, was any evidence of Murray's family.

"May I ask you a personal question, Mr. Murray?"

"Of course, Marseille. But again, please call me Tom."

"Are you married?"

"Why? Are you looking?" He laughed, then seemed to realize she didn't find it funny. "Sorry. Well, uh, I was—twice. But no, I'm divorced. Why do you ask?"

"I imagine it's hard to be married and work a job like this—long hours, all the secrecy, all the danger and stress."

"Yes, I'm afraid it is. Some guys handle it well. Your dad seemed to. I guess I never did."

"I'm just wondering what it was like for my mom to be married to my dad and never know he worked for the Agency."

"It's a good question. My first wife didn't know. Still doesn't. My second wife was my secretary. She worked here. We . . . She knew the stresses, but she . . . Well, anyway, your mom was a saint, Marseille. She loved your dad very much. She talked about him constantly. He talked about her constantly. They were like high school kids. Always holding hands. Sending each other little notes. You obviously don't remember, but I was at your mother's funeral."

"Really?" she said. "You were there?"

"Of course. Jack and I went together."

Marseille was startled. "Jack who?" she asked cautiously.

"Jack Zalinsky," he replied. "The two of us and your parents were quite close."

"And Mr. Zalinsky worked for State as well?"

"Well, officially, yes, but . . ."

"But what?"

"I really can't say more about it."

"Because it's classified?"

"Something like that."

"But Mr. Zalinsky was the one who helped organize my parents' escape—and the Shirazis' escape—from Tehran, wasn't he?"

"Uh, look, I really can't say, Marseille."

"Why not? It happened three decades ago."

"I just . . . I can't."

"But David told me all about it—the fake film company, the office in Hollywood, the Canadian passports, everything. David said Mr. Zalinsky and my father masterminded the whole thing."

"David told you that?"

"Yes."

"David Shirazi?"

"Yes, we've been friends since we were kids. My parents never talked about their time in Iran. It was all too painful, especially with my mom's miscarriage. But David . . ." Marseille stopped talking when she saw the perplexed look on Murray's face. "What's the matter?"

"Nothing, I just . . ."

"Just what?"

"I just wouldn't have . . ." His voice trailed off again.

"Wouldn't have what, Mr. Murray?"

"When was the last time you saw David?"

"Sunday morning. We had breakfast in Syracuse."

"And did you talk about any of this?"

"Of course," Marseille said. "I showed him your letter. We talked all about it."

Murray turned and stared out the window, shaking his head.

"What's the matter?" Marseille asked.

"That's not good."

"What's not? What's the problem?"

Murray turned back and looked her in the eye. "The problem is I thought David knew better," he said with an edge of annoyance, or perhaps even anger, in his voice. "The problem is I thought he was a professional. I thought I could trust him. I certainly never expected him to tell you about your father being in the CIA or working for me, or why he joined the Agency himself and the irony of him working for me as well. But maybe I should have seen it coming. You're a big part of the reason he's doing all this, after all. I guess he couldn't help himself, but it's still a major security breach, and I . . ."

Murray suddenly stopped talking, and Marseille wondered if she looked as stunned as she felt. "Excuse me," she said, desperately trying to process what she thought she had just heard, "did you just say that David works for the CIA?"

★ ★ ★ ★ ★

CAIRO, EGYPT

Javad Nouri had never been to Cairo.

He knew that with some nineteen million people, the metropolitan area was one of the largest in the world, as well as the political and economic capital of the Republic of Egypt. A proud and historic city, it was also the home of Al-Azhar University, the Harvard of the Middle East, and it was the intellectual epicenter of the entire region. This was the place where the vast majority of the Middle East's books were published, films produced, and TV programs created and distributed. He also knew full well that Abdel Ramzy had ruled this city and this country for decades with an iron fist and that an enormous political vacuum had now been created by his death. Javad had no doubt that the man he was traveling with was the man to fill it, but it would not be easy.

In so many ways, Egypt and Iran could not be more different. Egypt was ethnically Arab and religiously Sunni. Iran, by sharp contrast, was ethnically Persian and religiously Shia. Traditionally, Arabs and Persians hated each other. So did Sunnis and Shias. They had warred against one another throughout the ages. But as the Mahdi had explained it to Javad en route to Cairo, this was a different moment. This was the dawn of an Islamic Awakening. Now Egypt and Iran had to come together for two strategic reasons: first, to surround Israel, destroy the Jews, and capture Jerusalem for Islam; and second, to surround the Arabian Peninsula, finish bringing down the apostate Saudi regime, and solidify control of the holy places of Mecca and Medina.

"No Iranian leader in history has been able to persuade the Egyptians to unite with Iran and rebuild the Caliphate," the Mahdi had told Javad. "That is because, by definition, every Iranian leader has been a Persian. I, on the other hand, am an Arab. I come from Mesopotamia. I have a great love for the Egyptian people. I speak their language. I love their culture. I see their plight. And I have come to liberate them from their oppressive masters. Watch and see, Javad. A new day is dawning."

Had that day truly arrived? Javad hoped so, but privately he battled skepticism and cynicism, though he felt terribly guilty for such feelings and feared they were dangerously close to apostasy in and of themselves.

The Mahdi and his security entourage—nearly double in size since the attack in Beirut—arrived at Abdeen Palace, the sumptuous official headquarters of the Egyptian president and his most senior advisors, located on Qasr el-Nil Street in historic downtown Cairo. Javad had never seen anything like it, with its nineteenth-century French architecture, five hundred rooms and parlors, expansive and exquisite gardens, and solid gold fixtures, clocks, and assorted adornments. But he and his boss weren't there for the grand tour. Instead they gathered in the state room, where they were greeted by Vice President Fareed Riad and Field Marshal Omar Yassin—the commander in chief of the Egyptian military—and the other nineteen members of the Supreme Council of the Armed Forces. As per protocol, Javad hung back and let the principals connect, but he was stunned to see the vice president merely shake the Mahdi's hand and not bow, as every other leader had in Javad's experience. Field Marshal Yassin, on the other hand, showed far greater deference, as did the generals at his side, not only bowing, but keeping their faces to the ground until the Mahdi thanked them and expressed what an admirable job the field marshal was doing keeping order in the wake of the president's untimely death. At that point, everyone took a seat around a massive, ornately decorated conference table.

"I will not waste your time, gentlemen," the Mahdi began. "Allah invites you to join the Caliphate. I am not here to discuss terms. A simple yes or no will suffice."

"Well, that is very kind, Your Excellency," Vice President Riad said. "I imagine we all have some questions."

Riad looked to Yassin, who shook his head. He then looked around the rest of the room but found no one interested in asking a question. So he took it upon himself. "Very well, then; I have many questions."

"I have one as well," the Mahdi said. "Why did you not bow to the ground in my presence?"

From Javad's angle, though he was halfway across the room, it seemed the blood drained from Riad's face. His hands began quivering, and he stammered when he replied. "I . . . Well . . . we just met, and I thought that . . ."

"You will bow to me, or you will cease from my presence," the Mahdi said.

"But I . . . You have come to . . . We are colleagues. We are . . ."

Riad never finished the sentence. Suddenly his eyes glazed over. He began vomiting uncontrollably. Then he collapsed to the ground, twitched several times, and went limp. A moment later, he was dead. But no one rushed to his side. No one called for help. For several minutes no one moved. No one spoke. No one made a sound. And then all of the generals in the room suddenly fell to their knees and worshiped the Twelfth Imam. All of them loudly and repeatedly pledged to follow him forever.

"I will take that as a yes," the Mahdi said when it was over. "Welcome to the Caliphate."

★ ★ ★ ★ ★

LANGLEY, VIRGINIA

"Mr. Murray, you're not answering my question."

"Marseille, I'm sorry; I can't say anything else."

"What are you talking about?" she countered. "You have to. You can't say something like that and then let it drop."

"Look, I've obviously made a mistake here—a serious mistake—and I apologize. But I—"

"No, that's not good enough," Marseille said, cutting him off. "You just said David Shirazi works for you, for the CIA, just like my father did. And you thought I knew that, right? You thought he'd told me that, right?"

There was a long, uncomfortable silence, but Marseille could see in Murray's eyes that she was right. "Well, just so you know," she continued, "he didn't."

Her mind was reeling. She thought David worked for some company in Europe, traveling constantly. They'd never really talked about it. Now that she thought about it, she hadn't really even asked him for any specifics. There had been too much else to talk about and too little time.

"I was talking about my dad," she said, looking down at the folder in her hands. "I was telling David how shocked I was to find your letter as I went through my dad's personal papers, wrapping up his affairs and everything. I was going to ask him for his advice, whether I should try to track you down, or Mr. Zalinsky, when he got a phone call from his boss and suddenly had to leave right away."

She looked up at Murray, who appeared increasingly uncomfortable. "Was that you who called?"

Murray didn't reply.

"Not that it really matters, I guess. It's just that . . . well, David said he had to go back to Europe and would be gone indefinitely. But given all that's going on . . . I mean, he's in Iran, isn't he?"

Murray looked down, cleared his throat, then walked around the desk and sat next to Marseille. "Listen, your father was a good man," he told her gently. "One of the best operatives we ever had while he served in the Clandestine Service, and perhaps an even better analyst when he left the Agency full-time and became a consultant. Few people understood Iran or Shia Islam better than your dad, which was particularly amazing to me since he'd never even been there until he and your mom went to work in our embassy in Tehran just as the Revolution was building steam. But as good as he was—and like I said, we were very close friends and remained so pretty much until the end—I'd have to say one of the most important things he ever did for our country was help rescue the Shirazi family out of Tehran. He and your mom didn't do it because I asked him to or because Jack did. They didn't do it as part of their jobs. In fact, to be completely honest with you, Marseille, it would have been a lot easier for them to have left the Shirazis behind, to use them as assets and then cut them loose, but they couldn't. It just wasn't in their nature. The Shirazis saved their lives, and they felt obligated to save theirs. Your father couldn't possibly have known that one of the Shirazis' boys would grow up to join the Agency, to do what he did. Nor could he have possibly known that same boy would turn out to be the single most effective undercover operative the Agency has ever had in Iran. But life is funny that way, Marseille. Sometimes you do the right thing—sometimes you take a huge risk—when everyone else tells you you're crazy, and sometimes it pays off big. That's what your father did. I think he was too distraught about your mom's death to see all that he had accomplished—for this Agency, for this country, and for you. But I agreed to see you because I've always loved your family, and now you're all that's left of it. And I wanted you to know as much as possible about who you are and where you come from. I thought maybe it would be helpful as you decide where to go from here. I shouldn't have let slip the information about David. I've been in this business for far too long. But maybe you were meant to know."

"Maybe," Marseille said. "Thank you."

"You're welcome. But listen—you cannot tell anyone what you suspect about David."

"I won't. I promise."

"Seriously, I can't even tell you how much danger he's in now or how much worse it would be if anyone found out what he's doing. I could never forgive myself if something happened to him because of a mistake I made, however innocent."

"I understand," Marseille said.

"I hope you do."

"May I just ask you one question?"

"You can ask. I can't promise that I'm allowed to answer it."

"Fair enough. It's just that . . ."

"What?"

"I don't know. It's just . . . well, a moment ago you said that I was the reason David was doing all this. And you said you guessed he couldn't help himself from telling me. But the thing is, Mr. Murray, when we were growing up, I didn't know my dad worked for the CIA, so I never could have discussed it with David. And he certainly hasn't told me about it since, nor has he even hinted about it. So I'm just wondering what you meant by that. How could I possibly be the reason for him to work for you? It doesn't make any sense to me."

Murray sighed. "I've said too much already, Marseille. You want my recommendation? Ask David next time you see him."

"But that's what scares me most, Mr. Murray," she said, her eyes filling with tears. "I'm afraid I'm never going to see him again."

36

David finally arrived.

He pulled up in front of Dr. Birjandi's little bungalow on the outskirts of Hamadan but was surprised to see several other cars parked out front. He debated going in, but the truth was he had nowhere else to go and no time to come back. Deciding he had nothing to fear—it was Abdol Esfahani, after all, who had first connected the two men and encouraged David to learn everything he could about the Twelfth Imam from the nation's foremost expert on the subject—he scooped up the two bags of groceries he had brought as a gift, strode up the steps, and knocked. Moments later, the octogenarian sage came hobbling around the corner with his dark sunglasses and white cane and opened the door.

"Dr. Birjandi, it's me, Reza Tabrizi," he said, using his alias mostly for the benefit of whoever else was in the house, since the old man knew his real name.

"Reza, is that really you?"

"Yes, it is. And I've brought you some fresh bread and rice and vegetables."

"Thank God. I have been thinking about you all day and praying for the Lord to reconnect our paths. Please, please, my friend, come in."

Birjandi headed into the living room, and there David found himself struck once again, as he was the other time he visited, by what a voracious scholar Birjandi was. The walls were lined with shelves so packed with books that they appeared bound to collapse at any moment. Books were stacked up on the floor and piled on chairs, together with boxes of scholarly journals and other publications. Birjandi had once told David that his late wife, Souri, had read all of these books to him, marked them up, and taken copious notes on all of them, as they discussed them for "hour after blessed hour." Now Souri was gone, but the books remained.

Sitting on the floor of the living room were a half-dozen young, robed clerics—all apparently in their late twenties and early thirties—surrounded by still more piles of open books, talking animatedly and scribbling furiously in their notebooks.

Birjandi cleared his throat and got the young men's attention. "Gentlemen, allow me to introduce a surprise visitor but a wonderful young friend, Reza Tabrizi."

They all greeted him, though David thought he detected some suspicion or at least reticence in their eyes. Then the old man led David into the kitchen, where they put away the food.

"I'm so sorry to interrupt," David said. "I didn't expect you to have company. Should I come back later?"

"Nonsense. Where would you go? Besides, we must talk. I have much to tell you."

"Good. I have much to tell you as well," David said in a whisper. "But perhaps . . ."

"You needn't worry about these lads. They are all very trustworthy. Indeed, you should spend some time with them, get to know them."

"I'm not sure I'm in the mood for anyone new right now."

"You would like them. Really, you would. They are all sons of leading Shia mullahs from Qom or parliament members from Tehran. Their fathers are some of the most famous and powerful men in Iran. And guess what?"

"What?"

"They're all secret believers!"

"In what?" David asked.

"What do you mean?" Birjandi replied, visibly perplexed.

"What do they secretly believe?"

Birjandi smiled. "They are all followers of Jesus, David. They've all secretly renounced Islam and become Christ followers."

David was stunned. "Really? Is that true?"

"Of course it's true. Their stories of coming to faith are absolutely amazing. Each of them is a miracle, a true miracle. I love these young men. They come to meet with me every Wednesday morning for Bible study and prayer. We've been gathering faithfully for the last two months. Of course, today we had to push our meeting back a bit because of my lunch with Hosseini and Darazi, which I must tell you about. How long can you stay?"

"Not long, Dr. Birjandi. Maybe an hour. I need to get back to Tehran. Events are moving very rapidly."

"More rapidly than you know," Birjandi agreed. "Okay, make us some tea. I will go talk to the lads and give them an assignment to keep them busy for a while. Then I will meet you in my study."

★　★　★　★　★

CAIRO, EGYPT

Javad looked out over the masses gathered in Tahrir Square.

It was a raucous group, singing and dancing and celebrating the arrival of the Twelfth Imam. The Cairo police chief leaned over to Javad and said he thought the crowd numbered over one million. Javad thought the man might actually be underestimating. What he saw was a sea of humanity, radiating out in every direction, and the moment the Mahdi stepped onto the specially built platform, raised six feet off the ground and surrounded by bulletproof glass, Javad braced for the expected roar. It never came. Instead, it became unnaturally quiet, save the sound of every person dropping to his knees and bowing before the Mahdi in reverent worship. A strange sensation ran through Javad's body; then he, too, dropped to his knees and bowed, as did the chief of police and all of the Mahdi's security detail.

"The formation of a New World Order is of prime importance, and I tell you today that we have taken another major step forward," the Mahdi began. "The leaders of Egypt have requested my permission to join the Caliphate, and I was most pleased to give my assent."

Now the crowd roared, as if from one end of Cairo to the other.

"This is just the beginning. The day of the oppressors is over. The age of liberation has come. Full victory is near."

★ ★ ★ ★ ★

HAMADAN, IRAN

David checked his watch again.

He paced around the dining room that doubled as Birjandi's study. There was so much he needed to convey and so many questions he needed to ask, and there wasn't nearly enough time to accomplish it all. It was Birjandi who had told David to find Najjar Malik, saying that Najjar was the key to unlocking Iran's nuclear secrets. David had never even heard of Najjar Malik before that day, but how right Birjandi had been. Yet David hadn't even had a chance yet to tell him how he had found Najjar, much less all that had happened to get him out of Iran and back to the States. Nor had he been able to tell Birjandi of the treasure trove of information Najjar had proven to be. Still, all that seemed like ancient history now, given everything that had happened since.

David pulled back one of the tattered curtains and stared out a window that needed to be washed. The sun was beginning to set on a gorgeous spring day, with the temperature in the midseventies, a light, warm, westerly breeze, and perfectly blue skies marred only by the contrail of a jet plane to the east. All the trees were budding, the red roses—Iran's national flower—were in bloom, as were tulips of a dozen different shades, and the yards were all green, thanks to the generous winter rains. How sad, he thought, that this dear man spent his life cooped up in this damp, creaky house. How sad, too, that he had even more bookshelves here, lining the walls, sagging with the weight of hundreds if not thousands of dog-eared books, none of which the man would ever read.

In one corner, Birjandi's desk was piled high with mail that couldn't be read, while in another corner stood a television that couldn't be watched. In some ways, it all seemed a testament to the brilliance of the man but also his irrelevance. What hope was there for a scholar who could not read and had no one to help him study, write, or publish his ideas? What more was there for a man who had lost the wife of his youth, the love of his life, and now lived alone in utter darkness?

Yet the more David thought about that, the more he realized just the opposite was true. Birjandi was certainly blind, but wasn't he seeing more clearly than anyone else in the country? He was without question a widower, but he certainly wasn't alone, was he? He had experienced devastating losses in his life, but hadn't he found hope that was transforming his life? In fact, David couldn't think of a single person in his life who seemed to have more joy, more insight, more wisdom or zest for life than Birjandi. Certainly not his parents or his brothers. Certainly not Zalinsky or Eva or Tom Murray. Only Marseille had that same spark in her. Why? What was it they had that he didn't?

★ ★ ★ ★ ★

WASHINGTON, DC

Breathless, Najjar Malik finally made it to the BBC's studios.

He'd had to park several blocks away and had to run for fear of being late. He was met at the door by a young production assistant and an armed security guard, who quickly whisked him directly into a studio where a cameraman, sound technician, and makeup artist were waiting to put him on the air.

"Put this in your ear," the sound guy said, handing Najjar a wire with a little rubber nub at the end.

"What is it?" Najjar asked.

"An IFB."

"A what?"

"It lets you hear . . . It doesn't really matter—just do it fast. You're about to go live."

Najjar stuck in the little earpiece, and the technician showed him how he could increase or decrease the volume with a small knob by his seat.

"Dr. Malik, can you hear me?"

Surprised, Najjar looked up to see where the voice was coming from.

"This is Nigel Moore, in London. We spoke earlier."

"Oh yes, of course. How are you?"

"I'm fine and glad you're with us. But more importantly, how are you?"

"A little nervous."

"First time on live television?"

"I'm afraid so."

"Well, there's nothing to worry about. I'll be talking you through the entire process. Now I want you to look straight into camera one, that one right in front of you."

Najjar complied.

"Good, now just keep looking straight into that camera. Our anchor will come on in a few minutes. You won't see him, but you'll be able to hear him through your IFB. Don't look around the studio. Don't let anything distract you. Just keep looking straight into the camera, and it will look just right, like you're looking right at the anchor. When we break, I'll let you know. Then you can have some water or look around or whatever. Okay?"

"Yes, thank you."

The production assistant called out, *"Sixty seconds."*

"Now, just a few more things before you're on. How would you like to be identified on-screen?"

"What do you mean?"

"Can we use your name, your title? We can certainly not mention your name, or we could give you a pseudonym, but of course anyone in Iran who knows you will recognize you. You didn't ask that we electronically disguise your voice or put your face in shadow."

"Thirty seconds."

"No, no, that's fine. You can use my name, my title, anything—just please don't say where I am."

"Agreed. Now, I know you want to talk about your faith, and we'll get to that, but we're going to start with your work as a nuclear scientist, why you've chosen to defect to the US . . ."

"Twenty seconds."

"No, please say 'to the West.'"

"Fine, 'to the West.' And then the anchor will ask you why you believe war is coming soon—what you base that on, and how soon is 'soon.'"

"Yes. Thank you for having me on."

"Thanks for doing this."

"Ten seconds."

"Oh, one more thing," Najjar blurted out.

"Yes, what's that?"

The theme music for the BBC Persian special report swelled, and out of the corner of his eye, Najjar could see a monitor with the network's distinctive graphics and video opening sequence.

"Five seconds."

"Can you post my Twitter account on the screen below my name?"

★ ★ ★ ★ ★

LANGLEY, VIRGINIA

"Satellite photos show increased activity at Iranian air bases."

Zalinsky, having just been summoned to Murray's office, slid the latest reconnaissance photos across the desk to show his boss. "We're also seeing increased activity at Iranian missile bases," he added.

Tom Murray carefully reviewed the photos with a magnifying glass. "Did I tell you Marseille Harper dropped by to see me?" he asked without looking up.

"What? Charlie's daughter? You're kidding."

"No, she just left a half hour ago."

"How did that come about?"

"It's a long story; I'll tell you later," Murray said, sliding the photos back to Zalinsky. "But she asked about you, actually."

"Me? Really?"

"Yep."

"Why? We've never even met."

"She's heard stories."

"From who? Charlie always said he didn't want her to know he'd worked for the Agency."

"He didn't, but David told her a little, and she found an old commendation letter that I once wrote to—"

Eva burst into Murray's office.

"Eva, what are you doing?" Murray snapped, unaccustomed to staff coming in without an appointment or his personal summons.

"I'm sorry, but you're not going to believe this, either of you," she exclaimed, turning on the television, punching in the coordinates for the BBC Persian channel, and letting Najjar Malik do her explaining for her.

"What worries me most," Najjar was saying, "is that too many world leaders—including in the US, Great Britain, and throughout the EU—don't seem worried enough. I am the highest-ranking Iranian nuclear scientist who is still alive. I know the program inside and out. I've spent all of my professional life inside it. My father-in-law, Dr. Mohammed Saddaji, ran the weapons side. I ran the civilian energy side. And I can tell you categorically that the Twelfth Imam is telling the truth when he says that the Islamic Republic of Iran has tested a nuclear weapon. I can tell you that warhead was operational. I can tell you there are eight more just like it. And I can tell you there are detailed plans to use those warheads and a dozen more that are currently in production to attack the United States and Israel in the coming days."

"Are you telling this to the government officials where you've sought political asylum?" the anchor asked.

"Of course."

"And what do they say?"

"It is like they are asleep," Najjar said. "They hear me, but they are not listening to me. They are not taking any of this seriously. They have all the facts, but they are not taking action."

"Tell me this is not happening," Murray said. "How long has he been on?"

"Ten minutes," Eva said. "Maybe fifteen."

"Why didn't anyone tell me sooner?"

"We weren't monitoring the network."

Zalinsky picked up the phone. "Get me the FBI—counterterrorism division."

Murray turned to Zalinsky. "What are you doing?"

Zalinsky held up his hand for Murray to wait.

Najjar kept talking. "Just today we learned that the president of the

United States wants to negotiate with the Mahdi. Excuse me, but this will not work. This is a dangerous mistake. The Mahdi is just trying to buy time so that he can strike first. I will explain this in more detail in my interview on the Persian Christian Satellite Network. I'm doing a full hour with them, and I will explain everything more carefully, and in Farsi."

"This is Jack Zalinsky at Langley. I need the director immediately."

"Jack, what are you doing?" Murray pressed.

"Hello? Yeah, it's Jack. We found him—he's at the BBC bureau in DC. *Get your men moving, now.*"

37

David was impatient, but Birjandi suggested they go for a walk.

"Maybe we should just stay here," David said. "We have a lot to cover and very little time."

"Nonsense," the old man said. "You need a little fresh air, and so do I."

Birjandi led the way, and soon they were outside, slowly making their way up Birjandi's quiet street. There were no sidewalks.

"I need to ask you a question," David began. "Have you ever heard the names Jalal Zandi or Tariq Khan?"

"I have not. Who are they?"

"Nuclear scientists. Worked for Saddaji on the warheads."

"High-value targets."

"They are."

Birjandi cocked his head and turned his face to the setting sun. "It smells like a beautiful day," the old man said, one hand on his cane, the other on David's arm.

"Yes, it is," David said.

"Of course, it belies the storm that is coming."

"War?"

"Yes."

"How soon?"

"By Monday at the latest."

David stopped in his tracks, taken aback by Birjandi's specificity. "Why do you say Monday? How do you know?"

"You heard about the *Washington Post* story?"

"The back-channel discussions between the president and the Mahdi?"

"Yes."

"I heard it on the radio while driving here," David said.

"A very foolish mistake by your president," Birjandi said. "The Mahdi is never going to talk to President Jackson. He has come to annihilate the United States, not make peace with her. This is the final ploy."

"What do you mean?"

"The Mahdi is buying time to launch a nuclear strike against Israel. I honestly thought the strike would have already come. But there must be some final technical issues causing a delay. That delay is giving the Israelis an opening. Naphtali could move first, and this would be devastating to the Mahdi's plans. The only leverage on the Israelis is your president. And the Mahdi senses weakness in Mr. Jackson, so he's exploiting it to the fullest. He's offering peace. But it is a lie. It's a smoke screen. That's why I say if the phone call is supposed to be Tuesday, the Iranian attack against Israel will come sooner. Indeed, it could come at any moment."

"Are you certain?" David pressed. "Or are you just guessing? Did Hosseini or Darazi say anything specific at lunch?"

"This is precisely what they said. That's why I'm telling you. You must tell your president before it's too late."

"They specifically said Monday?"

"Yes. I asked, 'How soon will the attack on the Zionists begin?' And Hamid said, 'Any day now. It's up to him, of course, but I suspect everything will be ready by Monday at the latest.' Then they told me that two of their eight nuclear warheads are on board the Iranian warships that are passing through the Suez Canal today, bound for the Mediterranean. They said the warheads are attached to missiles aimed at Tel Aviv and Haifa."

"Wait a minute; I thought your country didn't have the capacity to attach the warheads to missiles."

"That's what I said."

"And?"

"And they said, 'Last month we didn't. Today we do.'"

★ ★ ★ ★ ★

JERUSALEM, ISRAEL

The rotors were whirring at full speed, and it was time to leave.

On cue, Prime Minister Asher Naphtali stepped gingerly out of the ready room, crossed the tarmac, boarded an IDF chopper, and waved at the press corps. At his side was Defense Minister Levi Shimon, taking his boss for a quick trip north to visit the Ramat David air base, not far from Megiddo in the lush and strategic Jezreel Valley. It was a well-publicized trip, the first since the attack in New York, and a transport helicopter filled with reporters and photographers was tagging along. Yet unlike the speculation of some initial wire service reports, the prime minister was not going to review the Israeli Air Force's ability to project long-range force. Instead, as Naphtali's spokesman had made clear just before their departure, the PM was going to visit an American-operated Patriot surface-to-air missile battery. The message: with American support, Israel was ready to stop anything and everything Iran was preparing to launch.

On board and in the air, however, Naphtali put on his headphones and turned to his defense minister to restate his intentions. "We need to go this weekend, Levi."

"I understand, sir. We're making final preparations while trying not to let the press—or the Americans—see what we're doing."

"So far, so good."

"Yes, it would appear that way."

"You had a final meeting with Roger."

"I did. I said you were seriously reviewing the president's offer but you could not make a final decision until you had clarifications. He said he had conveyed that to the president, and then he left about an hour ago for Jordan to meet with the king."

"Do you expect any answers quickly?"

"Honestly? No. Not before the president's phone call with the Mahdi next Tuesday."

"Which should give us justification, shouldn't it?"

"You haven't accepted his request. But you haven't rejected it either. And you've made it clear we're running out of time."

"Good," Naphtali said. "Now, have we heard from our man in Tehran?"

"No, not yet."

"Why not?"

"I don't know, sir."

"So we don't have a final fix on the warheads?"

"No, I'm afraid we don't."

"Can we go if we don't hear from him?"

"I'm not sure that would be wise, but yes, we can. We've been running additional satellite passes over all the known targets on our high-priority list. We're finalizing the target packages now. I'm ready to do a full briefing for you in the morning, if you're ready."

"I will be," the prime minister said, shifting in his seat.

"What's wrong?"

"Nothing, it's just that . . ."

"What?"

"I need to know who our source is in Tehran."

"You already know his code name, Mordecai—our eyes inside the Persian palace."

"No, not his code name," Naphtali said. "Who is he? What's his real name? What does he actually do? What's his rank? Does he have a family? Why do we trust him?"

"Mr. Prime Minister, please, it is better if you do not know such specifics—safer for our asset, safer for you."

"Levi, I have to know. How am I supposed to make final targeting decisions based on what he says, assuming we hear from him quickly, which I pray to God we do? How am I supposed to trust someone I know nothing about?"

"Asher, listen, I can't tell you now, here, flying up the Jordan Valley. But even if we were alone, it's not a good idea. Mordecai has always been accurate, has always steered us in the right direction, up to and including the Saddaji assassination. I have full faith in this asset, my friend. You should too."

"That was good enough until now," Naphtali countered. "But this is different. I am facing the most dangerous moment in the history of the modern State of Israel. No prime minister—not even Ben-Gurion or Eshkol—had to make a decision like this. The weight of the world is on my shoulders, Levi. I have to know whom I'm listening to."

Shimon looked out the window as they flew over the farmlands of Samaria. "I need to think about it overnight," he said at last.

"Very well," Naphtali said. "Have breakfast with me tomorrow morning, and we'll discuss it then."

★ ★ ★ ★ ★

HAMADAN, IRAN

"Do you believe them?"

"I have no reason not to," Birjandi said. "They are brimming with confidence, David. They are acting like men who have the wind at their backs and believe Allah is on their side and they are about to see a great victory for the Muslim people. They are so blinded. They are about to bring great suffering to the Muslim world. But I believe the Lord is allowing it all to happen, to shake Islam to its core, to persuade Muslims to abandon Islam and start following Jesus Christ, the only hope for any of us."

"I need to get this back to my government," David said.

"Of course," Birjandi said. "I would have told you sooner, but I realized that I had no way to get in touch with you."

"I brought you a present to take care of that."

"What kind of present?"

"It's a satellite phone. It's in my trunk. I'll give it to you when we get back to your house. It's totally secure. You can call me at any time, day or night. Will you see them again soon, before Monday, at least?"

"Actually, they want me to meet the Twelfth Imam."

"When?"

"In the next few days. Maybe this weekend. They're going to call me."

"That's good," David said, brightening slightly. "Actually, that's amazing. You'll be in the room with the Mahdi. You'll know exactly what he's thinking."

"No," Birjandi said curtly. "It's out of the question."

"What are you talking about? We need this. You have to go."

"There is nothing he can tell me that I don't already know, David, or that the Lord cannot tell me Himself if I really need to know. Which brings me to the most important topic—have you been thinking about what we discussed last time?"

"Which topic?" David asked. "There were so many."

"The gospel. Have you been thinking about the gospel?"

"Yes, a little, but much has happened since I saw you last. That's part of what I want to tell you."

"David, you need to take this seriously. You need to make a decision to receive Jesus Christ as your Savior or reject Him forever. The Scriptures say, 'But as many as received Him, to them He gave the right to become children of God, even to those who believe in His name.' But you're running out of time, and honestly, I'm scared for you. I pray for you night and day."

"Whoa, whoa, wait a minute," David replied. "Let's not get off the subject."

"That *is* the subject, David. Now is the day of salvation. Now is the appointed time of God's favor. You may not get another chance. You don't know what tomorrow holds. None of us does. You need to humble yourself and repent of your sins and receive Christ into your heart before something terrible happens."

"We'll get to all that," David said. "I promise you. But right now we need to get you in the room with the Mahdi. And then you need to call me and tell me what he said. Do you realize how much hangs in the balance?"

"David, you're not hearing me. I've been in the room with Jesus Christ. He is the King of kings and the Lord of lords. He told me that you were coming to see me before I had even met you, remember? He told me that David was your real name. He told me you worked for the CIA and that you were in love with a girl named Marseille and that I was supposed to tell you things I had never told anyone else. Do you remember all that we spoke of?"

"Yes, of course."

"Then you, of all people, should know that I'm telling you the truth. You've got your eye on the wrong person. You're fixated on the Twelfth Imam, on all the death and destruction and chaos he is planning. But Jesus Christ is the one you need to focus on. He's the one you need to hear from, not the Twelfth Imam. The Mahdi comes to rob, kill, and destroy, my friend; but Jesus came that you might have life, and have it abundantly. That's what the Holy Scriptures say, and it's true, if only you have the ears to hear it and eyes to see it."

"Look, Dr. Birjandi, I appreciate your concern for my soul. I really do. And I have been thinking a lot about what you said, and I'd love to talk about it. But not right now. My country sent me here to stop the Mahdi, to stop Hosseini and Darazi. I need to track down all eight warheads, and I only have a few hours—at most a few days—to do it. If I fail, then one of two things will happen. The Mahdi will fire the weapons at Israel, and a second Holocaust could occur. Or Israel will launch first to thwart a genocide, but we could see the entire region go up in flames. Our only hope is to find these warheads and destroy them before any of that happens. And for that, I desperately need your help."

Birjandi stopped walking. He turned to David and took both his hands. "Young man, I am doing everything I can to help you. But honestly, you're not listening to me. Now go, call your superiors. Tell them about the two warheads on the ships. But as for going to meet with the Mahdi, I simply cannot do this."

"But why? Can you at least tell me that?"

"Because my Lord told me not to."

"What do you mean?"

"I told you before, when you first came to see me. The Twelfth Imam is a false messiah. I suspect he is possessed by Satan. He is certainly guided by demonic forces. And in Matthew chapter 24, the Lord Jesus warns His followers that there will be false messiahs who arise in the last days. Three times in the same chapter He makes this warning. What's more, He says these impostors will deceive many. He even says some of these false messiahs will be able to do 'great signs and wonders, so as to mislead, if possible, even the elect.' But He is crystal clear that 'if anyone says to you, "Behold, here is the Messiah," or "There He is," do not believe him.' And 'if they say to you, "Behold, He is in the wilderness," do not go out, or, "Behold, He is in the inner rooms," do not believe them. For just as the lightning comes from the east and flashes even to the west, so will the coming of the Son of Man be.'"

"I hear you, Dr. Birjandi. I do. But I'm not asking you to believe that the Twelfth Imam is really the messiah. You know he's not. I know he's not. So it's not a matter of believing in him. It's a matter of meeting with him, eliciting information from him, so we can defeat him, so we can save Iran and the United States and Israel and everyone in between."

Birjandi turned and started hobbling back to his house. "You are a good boy, David. I like you very much. And I know you are passionate about your work, your mission. But there is a false messiah on the planet. He is deceiving millions. He wants to deceive me as well. So when my Lord tells me not to go meet him, I am going to obey. I'm not that bright, David. I cannot outfox the devil. All I can do is listen to the words of Jesus, and if I love Him, then I will obey Him. And I love my Jesus more than life itself. How could I disobey Him, especially when He is coming back so soon?"

David was about to take one more run at the old man, however futile it appeared to be, but just then, one of the young clerics came bursting out Birjandi's front door.

"Uncle, uncle, come quickly. There is a man on television. You must hear what he is saying!"

•

38

DC Metro police cars flooded the zone.

Within minutes of Zalinsky's call, the BBC's Washington bureau was surrounded and all roads sealed off for two blocks in each direction. Then two dozen heavily armed FBI agents—led by a counterterrorism SWAT team—stormed the offices and studios.

"Get down! Get down!" shouted the lead agent, wearing a bulletproof vest and carrying an MP5 machine gun, as one team moved through the front entryway and past the secretarial staff.

"Go, go, go," another shouted as a second team burst through the back doors and sealed off the only other avenue of escape.

Guns drawn, they moved quickly and methodically through the five thousand square feet of rented space. But Dr. Najjar Malik wasn't there.

★ ★ ★ ★ ★

HAMADAN, IRAN

David couldn't believe what he was seeing.

What on earth was Najjar Malik doing on television? Why was he telling his story to the world? Didn't he know how seriously this jeopardized David's mission?

Feeling angry and betrayed, he watched Najjar's interview on the Persian Christian Satellite Network. He tried to imagine how Eva and her team could have allowed Najjar to escape in the first place. Then he racked his brain to come up with a reason why Najjar would put himself, his family, and the CIA's primary operation inside Iran at risk by going on worldwide television. Was Najjar going to expose the CIA's tradecraft, how they got him out of Iran, the safe house in Karaj, the safe house in Oakton, the communications gear they used? Was he going to name names? Was he doing this out of vengeance, to settle personal scores? David was about to storm out of the house and call Zalinsky immediately and find out what in the world was going on, but he found himself struck by the young clerics, who were glued to Najjar's every word.

"God bless him!" one of the young men suddenly shouted out.

"Yes, yes, praise God for such a brave brother as this!" another exclaimed.

"It's incredible," *a third said.* "How great is our God, that He would reach down and save such a one as this!"

As Najjar continued talking about his newfound faith and why he had chosen to renounce Islam (he promised to talk more about the Iranian nuclear program and the growing threat of war later in the broadcast), David couldn't help but notice that the young men started taking detailed notes. They were writing feverishly. They were whispering to one another in animated tones. Occasionally one would shout, "Amen!" or erupt in applause. Then one by one, each grabbed his mobile phone and began texting furiously.

It all struck David as odd and disorienting at first. The young men looked like future mullahs and ayatollahs. Some wore white turbans; some wore black. All wore the flowing robes of Shia clerics, and all but one had full-grown beards. Yet they were, as Birjandi put it, secret believers. They were apparently true revolutionaries—of a spiritual nature, at least, if not a political. Each of them had renounced Shia Islam and chosen Jesus over jihad, and they weren't alone. Birjandi said there were over a million in Iran just like them, and their numbers were growing every day. They had no formal leader. They had no physical headquarters. They operated in the shadows, as dissidents, as rebels with a cause. But now, all of a sudden, one of their own had broken free. He had a name. He had a face. He had a voice. He was telling his story, which, David figured, was probably much like their own. He was explaining the gospel without fear, without compromise, and in Farsi. He wasn't an outsider. He wasn't a foreigner or a missionary or a "tool of imperialism," as Hosseini and Darazi liked to call Western Christians. Najjar Malik was one of them, a native-born son, and he had standing. Najjar, after all, had been helping run Iran's nuclear program. The man's father-in-law was the father of the Persian Bomb. And now he had turned—not on his country but on her rulers, on "the tyrants" and "the madmen," as Najjar was putting it so passionately, who threatened the very existence of the Persian nation.

"Who are you texting?" David finally asked the group.

"Everyone we know," one said.

"Why? What are you saying?"

"We're telling them to turn on this channel and hear what this man is saying."

"But don't you risk being exposed as Christians?"

"No, of course not. I'm telling all my friends a lunatic is on television. That way they'll tune in for certain."

"I have a database of 150,000 current and former seminary students," another said, explaining that his father was the head of some Iranian clerical student association. "I just sent them all a message saying an enemy of the Mahdi is on television, which is true. Believe me, right now the vast majority of them are dropping everything they are doing and tuning in, or trying to find a TV connected to a satellite dish. And I guarantee you, if they miss the show, they'll watch the YouTube clips later tonight and tell their friends and have a debate over what this man is saying. This Dr. Malik fellow, he is going to spark a national conversation, and that is good. We don't need to let people know that we believe what he believes. Not yet. But we can fan the flames."

Several others said things similar, but one stood apart. "It is time."

"Time for what?" David asked.

"To stand up and be counted as a follower of Jesus," said the youngest of the group, a man who looked barely able to shave, much less teach or help lead a revolution. "I'm telling everyone I know that I agree with Dr. Malik."

Every head turned.

"Why?" David asked.

"Because he's right. And I do. And Uncle Birjandi taught us what the apostle Paul said in his letter to the believers in Rome: 'I am not ashamed of the gospel, for it is the power of God for salvation to everyone who believes.'"

"But couldn't saying that publicly get you in trouble?" David pressed.

"It cannot cost me more than what my Savior paid," the young man replied. "Jesus gave me His life. Shouldn't I be willing to give mine for Him?"

★　★　★　★　★

LANGLEY, VIRGINIA

"What do you mean he wasn't there?" Zalinsky yelled.

Murray and Fischer had been glued to the television. Now both turned to their colleague as he hollered into the phone.

"You've looked everywhere? . . . That's impossible. Look again. . . . Then send a team over to the other Persian channel. . . . I have no idea—just look it up and go there now!"

Eva's cell phone rang. It was the Global Operations Center.

"Are you watching this?" the watch commander asked.

"On the Persian Christian station?" she asked. "Yes, of course."

"No, no, on BBC Persian again."

"What do you mean?"

"Switch back," the watch commander said.

"What are you talking about?"

"Just switch back. They've picked up the feed from the Christian station, and they're showing it live."

Eva grabbed the remote off of Murray's coffee table and switched back to the BBC Persian channel. Sure enough, the BBC was simulcasting the feed from the Christian satellite network. Whether they were pirating it as a "news event" or had some sort of deal with the network, she had no idea. But it didn't really matter. The point was that millions of Iranians were watching this thing. She didn't yet know the repercussions for herself or her team, but she feared Najjar was making a horrific mistake and was going to pay dearly.

★ ★ ★ ★ ★

HAMADAN, IRAN

"War is coming, my dear brothers and sisters," Najjar said finally.

The hour was coming to a close, and he was almost pleading with his fellow Iranians to listen to him carefully as he stared into the camera.

"Humanly speaking, war can no longer be avoided. Only God can stop this war, and not the god of Islam. Not the Twelfth Imam. Not the mullahs or the ayatollahs. Their god—the god of Islam—wants a war. He wants to rob, kill, and destroy all that we know and love and hold dear to our hearts. But the One True God—the God of the Bible, the God of our Lord and Savior Jesus Christ—He is the Prince of Peace. He came to bring us life—eternal and abundant and fruitful and meaningful."

David found himself transfixed, as were the others in the room. He had read Najjar's story in the transcripts of his conversations with Eva. He knew the basic trajectory of Najjar's conversion. Yet there was something about seeing a man tell such a story at such a moment on worldwide television at the risk of his life—and at the risk of being taken down by the FBI on the air—that David found more compelling than he would have thought. He found himself impressed by Najjar's earnestness and drawn to the depths of his conviction.

"Jesus Christ is the only one who can stop this war," Najjar concluded. "Pray to Him. Get on your knees—get down on your faces—and ask Him to forgive you, beg Him to save you, implore Him to redeem you and your family and your nation. For Jesus Christ is all that stands between us and an eternity in hell. He may not spare us from war. He may let this war come to punish us for our wickedness. But He will save you individually if you ask Him. Jesus said, 'I am the resurrection and the life; he who believes in Me will live even if he dies, and everyone who lives and believes in Me will never die.' My friends, now is the time. This is the day. This is the time of God's favor. Receive

Jesus Christ by faith and receive the free gift of eternal life before it is too late."

David glanced at Birjandi and wondered how it could be that he and Najjar were reading from the same playbook.

"Did any of you write down Dr. Malik's Twitter account address?" asked the oldest of the group, a guy named Ali, who had been the quietest in the room thus far.

"Yes, here it is," said the youngest, Ibrahim, the guy who had just outed himself as a follower of Christ. "I just signed up myself."

They all signed up, even David, who was embarrassed at not already having a Twitter account, something he had never even considered before. But how could he not follow everything Najjar was telling the world? Wasn't he supposed to be in the intelligence business? How could he let twentysomethings in Iran know more than he did? He doubted Roger Allen or Tom Murray were going to track Najjar, and he wondered if Zalinsky had even heard of Twitter.

"Do you guys all think he's right?" David asked the group. "Do you think that 'humanly speaking, war can no longer be avoided'?"

They all did.

"Why?" David pressed. "I mean, is it just for the reasons Dr. Malik said? Is it a gut instinct? Or something else?"

"The Israelis are going to hit us," Ibrahim said. "They're not going to wait. They've heard what the Mahdi and our Supreme Leader and our president have said. They've heard all the threats, and they're going to strike first. You mark my words."

The cleric next to Ibrahim vigorously disagreed. "You're wrong, Ibrahim. The Americans will hold back the Israelis. That's why they sent the CIA director to Jerusalem. That's why the president is going to talk to the Mahdi. The Americans think the Mahdi can be reasonable. They have no idea who they're dealing with. When the war comes, and I believe it will come any day, it will be because the Mahdi initiated it. And it's going to be bloody. Many, many will die."

"You're misreading the Israelis," Ibrahim countered. "They're close to the Americans, yes. But at their core they are driven by their memories of the Holocaust and their determination to never allow another one to occur. Don't you remember how the Israeli Air Force hit Saddam's nuclear facilities in 1981 at Osirak? Don't you remember how they hit Assad's nuclear facilities near Damascus in 2007? The Israelis are coming here next. To think the Americans could offer them anything to dissuade them from defending themselves against what they perceive is an impending second Holocaust is fantasy."

Then Ali weighed in unexpectedly. "I wish the Americans could do something—anything—to stop this war," he said with a deep sense of sadness in his voice and in his eyes. "But it's coming, and fast. Ibrahim, my friend, you are wise beyond your years. You have insight and knowledge that make me envious. But in this case you are wrong. The Israelis will never get the chance to strike first because the Tehran Initiative is now in motion, and it cannot be stopped."

"What's the Tehran Initiative?" David asked.

"The Tehran Initiative is the Mahdi's doomsday scenario," Ali said.

"Meaning what?" David pressed.

"Yeah, what are you talking about?" Ibrahim asked.

"To destroy Israel and wipe out all the Jews," Ali explained. "I don't know all the details. I just know what my father told me. He said he can't be at my son's birthday party on Saturday because he has been summoned to the Qaleh for a final strategy meeting for the Tehran Initiative. That was all he said, and then he hung up the phone."

"When was that?" Ibrahim asked.

"This morning, just after breakfast," Ali said. "I can't even tell you how ticked off my wife is at him. She's been planning this party for weeks, and my dad promised to attend. But my mom says it's not just him. Faridzadeh and Jazini have ordered all of their senior commanders to be there. They've canceled all military leaves, at least in the air force and the missile command units. This morning they began issuing orders to call up the air combat reserves. I don't know what's happening with the army, but my mom said the rumor is all the families of the air force senior commanders are going to be moved to special bunkers starting tomorrow. My point is, Dr. Malik is dead-on. War is coming, and the Mahdi is going to start it."

The whole group erupted in discussion, and David wasn't sure how to proceed without looking too interested. He didn't know them, and they didn't know him. He had to tread carefully. He trusted Birjandi, and Birjandi clearly trusted these young men. But they didn't know he was CIA. They thought he worked for a phone company. He couldn't suddenly be asking questions that were too probing or too detailed. Ali was saying that Iran's minister of defense and the commander of the Iranian Revolutionary Guard Corps were making final preparations to attack Israel. David assumed that to be true, but how would Ali know such things, and who was his father?

As if reading David's mind, Birjandi leaned over and whispered, "Ali's father is a highly decorated general in the Iranian Air Force. Flies F-4s. Last I heard, he commands Tactical Air Base number six."

"In Bushehr?" David whispered back as the rest of the group buzzed about the new details Ali had just provided.

Birjandi nodded. "That's the one."

David leaned into Birjandi and asked as quietly as he could, "Is what he's saying credible?"

"Ali has no reason to lie," the old man said. "He's the leader of this group. He's the quietest among them but the most influential. He knows each one of these guys. He came to Christ before any of them. He recruited them one by one and then brought them to me and begged me to meet with them once a week. He has his father's gift of leadership, I'd say."

"Is his father a Christian?"

"I wish," Birjandi said. "No, I'm afraid he is a committed Twelver."

★ ★ ★ ★ ★

CAIRO, EGYPT

Javad had never seen a man in such a rage.

They had just taken off from Cairo International Airport en route for Amman and were barely at cruising altitude, but the Mahdi was already out of his seat. He was cursing at the top of his lungs, smashing glasses and demanding the pilots reroute the plane to Iran instead.

Javad cowered in his seat, keeping his head down, trying not to make eye contact but fearful the Mahdi was going to turn his wrath on him. The man was demanding to know how Najjar Malik could have been allowed to escape from Iran at all. How could he have been lured away by the Americans? How much did he know? Had Saddaji's computer ever been found, the one he'd kept in his home? What information had been on that computer? How much of Iran's nuclear program had been compromised? How much had the Americans told the Zionists? The questions kept coming one after another, and Javad didn't have the answer to a single one.

★ ★ ★ ★ ★

WASHINGTON, DC

Marseille drove into the District.

It was still raining, but she didn't care. She parked near the Washington Monument, grabbed her bright-red umbrella, stuffed some quarters into the meter, locked her car, and looked around, wondering where to go. To her right was the White House. Behind her was the Capitol building and some of the Smithsonian museums. Straight ahead, beyond the Washington Monument, was the World War II Memorial. To her left was the Bureau of Engraving and Printing and the Holocaust Memorial Museum.

Traffic was getting snarled by drivers anxious about the increasingly slick roads. An ambulance was approaching from a distance, trying to snake its way through the congestion. There were hardly any tourists out, of course. Who would be stupid enough to get soaked in such a downpour? But Marseille literally didn't know where to turn.

For no particular reason, she started walking up the Mall toward the Capitol, but though she hadn't seen these sites since she was about thirteen, she wasn't really absorbing any of them now. She was still trying to process the news that David worked for the CIA and, though Murray hadn't completely confirmed it, the likelihood that he was now in Iran. Of course David hadn't told her when they'd met for breakfast. How could he have? He loved his country. He always had. He'd never thought of himself as an Iranian. He'd always wanted to be a red, white, and blue American. And he was nothing if not loyal. He'd been a loyal friend and a loyal son. She was certain he was loyal to the Agency, and it was no surprise that Murray had said he was very good at what he did. That's just who David Shirazi was.

Whatever he was doing, Marseille knew, it had to be undercover. The US didn't have an embassy in Tehran anymore, nor any consulates. So that meant he had to be caught up in all that she was reading about in the papers. Had David been responsible for trying to assassinate the Twelfth Imam? She hoped not. She harbored no doubts about how evil this so-called Islamic messiah was, but she didn't want to think of her friend as a killer. Maybe David was the intermediary between the president and the Twelfth Imam. It was certainly possible, but wasn't that almost as bad? It might even be worse. If the Twelfth Imam really was the Antichrist, he was possessed by Lucifer. He had the ability to deceive all whom he encountered. From her cursory reading of Bible prophecy, she didn't see how the Antichrist could be stopped by anyone but God Himself. She prayed silently that David wasn't anywhere near the Mahdi and wouldn't go near him. And she prayed once again that the Lord would open David's eyes and draw him to His heart.

The winds were picking up, and the rain was now coming in at an angle. Her tailored suit was nearly soaked, despite her umbrella. She felt cold and sad and utterly alone. It was not true, she reminded herself. The Lord had promised never to leave her, never to forsake her, but she wanted someone to talk to. She loved the Lord—loved to talk to Him in prayer and listen to Him as she read His Word—but sometimes she wanted a friend she could see, a friend who could hold her and comfort her and tell her everything in her life was going to be all right. She thought of her fellow teachers back in Portland and her principal and his wife, who had always been so kind. She pictured the darling faces of the children she had the joy of teaching every day. On some dark, hard mornings, they were the only practical reason she could think of to get out of bed. And there was Lexi, of course, whom she worried for now more than ever. Israel had seemed like such a dream place to take a honeymoon. Now every new headline threatening imminent war in the Middle East brought new worries that her best friend and her bridegroom could get caught in a disaster. She made a mental note to text Lexi as soon as she got back to her car. She wanted to make sure they were okay and that they were coming home early.

But all of that brought her back to thoughts of David. Where was he? Was he okay? And abruptly she realized she missed him so much it almost physically hurt.

★ ★ ★ ★ ★

HAMADAN, IRAN

David had heard enough for now.

He excused himself and stepped into Birjandi's study. There, he pulled out his phone, punched in his secure code, and hit speed-dial. He had to get all this to Langley.

Zalinsky answered on the first ring. "Code in."

David did.

"Zephyr?"

"Yes, it's me."

"What are you doing in Hamadan?"

David was caught off guard by the question. "How did you know?"

"We're tracking the GPS signal in your phone."

"Right, of course," David said, having regretted the foolishness of the question the second it had crossed his lips. "Look, I came to see Chameleon. You're sure we're secure?"

"Absolutely. Why?"

"I have news."

"I'm listening."

"The Iranian warships that just crossed through the Suez Canal . . ."

"Yeah?"

"Two of the warheads are on board. They're attached to missiles, and they're programmed to hit Tel Aviv and Haifa."

Zalinsky cursed. "I thought—"

"I know; we all did," David said. "But apparently Saddaji wasn't told what the missile scientists were capable of. Maybe he was just behind the curve. Maybe those above him were compartmentalizing. I don't know. The point is, the warheads are missile ready—two of them at least—and they're now about three hundred kilometers from Israel's largest city."

"You're absolutely certain about that?"

"It comes directly from the top."

"Hosseini?"

"And Darazi."

"They told that to Chameleon, or is he inferring it?"

"They said it directly to him. Obviously, we need to get it verified. . . ."

"We'll get right on it."

"Good, and there's more. The Mahdi is going to launch the war by Monday at the latest. I can't say which day. It could come at any moment. But I'm told specifically it will come before President Jackson's call with the Mahdi. I've also learned that the senior air force commanders are meeting at Hosseini's private retreat center, the Qaleh, on Saturday. They're having a 'final strategy meeting' for something that's being called the Tehran Initiative."

"What is that?"

"It seems to be the war plan to hit Israel."

"This also comes from Chameleon?"

"No, but it comes from a source he trusts."

"Who?"

"The oldest son of the general who commands Tactical Air Base Six."

"Protecting Bushehr?"

"Right. Apparently, Faridzadeh and Jazini have ordered all of their senior commanders to be there. They've canceled all military leaves for the air force and the missile command units. They've also begun calling up the air combat reserves, and there is a rumor that all the families of the air force senior commanders are going to be moved to special bunkers starting tomorrow."

"So the Mahdi could launch by Sunday, or even Saturday?" Zalinsky pressed.

"Theoretically, yes."

"That doesn't give us much time to find the other six warheads."

"No, it doesn't."

"Any leads on those?"

"Not yet—this is all I've got so far."

"Any progress on Zandi and Khan?"

"Nothing."

"What's your gut tell you?"

"That we're going to blow this thing. That we're going to be too late. The president isn't even preparing to hit Iran, is he?"

"No. He thinks diplomacy still can work."

"What do you think?"

"I think you need to find me those other six warheads before they get launched."

"Easy for you to say."

"What's your next move?" Zalinsky asked.

"I honestly don't know, Jack. I'm racking my brain, but I don't know what to do next. By the way, are you watching this thing with Najjar?" David asked.

"It's a disaster."

"How did this happen?"

"We still don't know. We've got a full manhunt on for him right now. But I've got to hand it to him. He's pretty clever."

"Why do you say that?"

"Because he actually taped the Christian station interview first—then only did twenty minutes live on BBC. By the time the FBI stormed the BBC studios, he was gone. And when the FBI team stormed the Christian station's studios, they learned the show was taped."

"So you have no idea where he is at the moment?"

"Not a clue."

"And Sheyda?"

"She and the family are fine. But they haven't heard from him. They have no way to hear from him or get in touch with him. But Sheyda couldn't be more proud of Najjar or excited about the reaction."

"What reaction?"

"You haven't heard?"

"No, what happened?"

"Ayatollah Hosseini just issued a fatwa."

"Against Najjar?"

"Against his whole family," Zalinsky said. "Here, I'll read it to you verbatim. 'I would like to inform all the intrepid Muslims in the world that Dr. Najjar Malik and his entire family are hereby sentenced to death. I call on all zealous Muslims to execute them quickly, wherever they find them, so that no one will dare to insult Imam al-Mahdi, Islamic sanctity, or the new Caliphate now emerging. Whoever is killed doing this will be regarded as a martyr and will go directly to heaven.'"

"He's a dead man," David said.

"If we don't find him before they do, yes," Zalinsky agreed. "And that's not going to be easy. The Ayatollah just put a $100 million bounty on his head."

40

The Airbus jumbo jet would be back in Tehran in less than an hour.

But the Twelfth Imam could not wait. Still seething at the incompetence of the Iranian intelligence services for having let Najjar Malik slip through their fingers and broadcast his heresies to the world, he summoned Javad to his luxury cabin in the front of the aircraft. Javad rose from his seat in the back of the plane and made his way forward, dreading every step. After taking a deep breath and removing a handkerchief from his pocket to wipe his perspiring hands, he knocked twice and was told to come in. He complied and bowed low.

"Have you heard from Firouz and Jamshad?" the Mahdi asked.

"Yes, Your Excellency," Javad replied. "I just got a text message from Firouz a little while ago."

"Are they safe?"

"Yes, they are."

"They weren't arrested?"

"No."

"Were they watched?"

"They don't think so."

"Where are they now?"

"Caracas."

"They've gotten to Venezuela? Good. So they are coming home now."

"Yes, they figure they should be home by tomorrow night."

The Mahdi nodded and stared out the window, pondering

something, but his expression was inscrutable, and Javad was in no mood to ask questions.

"Get Ali Faridzadeh on the line," the Mahdi commanded without looking back at Javad.

Javad was surprised, not so much that the Mahdi wanted to talk to the Iranian defense minister—that was to be expected given how close they were to zero hour—but that the Mahdi evidently wanted him to use one of the satellite phones not for a text message or two but for an actual conversation. Thus far, he had been suspicious of their ability to speak securely on the phones and deeply reluctant to use them except when absolutely necessary, such as the call with the Pakistani leader, Iskander Farooq. But such decisions, Javad decided, were above his pay grade. He pulled the satphone from his pocket, dialed Faridzadeh's personal satphone number, and handed the phone to the undisputed leader of the Islamic world. He wondered if he should return to his seat, but he had not been dismissed, so for now he stood still, his stomach in knots.

"Where are you?" the Mahdi asked. "Good. I will be on the ground in about an hour and at the location we discussed in less than two. I will meet you there. Just make sure everything is in place and ready—everything—when I arrive."

★　★　★　★　★

HAMADAN, IRAN

David needed to get to Qom.

He was exhausted and wanted to ask Dr. Birjandi if he could crash there overnight, get up early, and make the three-hour drive to the holy city at sunrise the following morning. Yet something in him felt uneasy about that plan. He sensed he needed to be in Qom, fresh and ready, when the day began. He had no idea why, but he had learned to trust his instincts.

Pulling out his laptop, he looked up hotel options and found a website called AsiaRooms.com, which gave him a selection of higher-end facilities.

"The Qom International is one of the best hotels in Iran," one entry read. "The building has a lovely glass frontage with attractive lights. There is a marbled reception area and a cozy lounge with elegant Persian carpets. The Qom International in the historic city of Qom offers complete privacy, security, and comfort to its guests." The lavish description went on from there.

It was a little pricey for David Shirazi, but it was exactly the type of place Reza Tabrizi would stay. He booked a single room with a king-size bed for one night, then closed the laptop, packed up his car, and took Dr. Birjandi into the kitchen, away from the others. There he gave the old cleric his own satellite phone, the gift he had promised him, and quickly explained how to use it and how to charge it.

"Please don't hesitate to call me," David said. "If you learn something, anything—even if you're not sure if it's useful or you think maybe I already know it—please call me, no matter when. Okay?"

"That's very kind, my friend," Birjandi replied. "Thank you."

"You're welcome," David said. "But really, it's no good to me if I don't hear from you. So promise you'll use it."

"You have my word."

"That's good enough for me. Thank you for everything, Dr. Birjandi. I don't know what the future holds, but I'm very glad to have met you and deeply grateful for all you've taught me and all you've shared with me so far."

"You're welcome, David. Now I have a gift for you."

He padded over to a cabinet next to the refrigerator and opened the top drawer. From it he drew a slim volume with a green cover and put it in David's hands. It was a Farsi New Testament. Internally, David recoiled. His heart started racing. He tried not to give any evidence of his anxiety to the man standing next to him, but he had never owned his own Bible. He had barely touched one in all his twenty-five years. He had been taught by the mullahs in Germany during college that to read one would sentence a Muslim to the fires of hell on the Day of Judgment. And he dared not be caught by Abdol Esfahani, or really anyone else in the country, with a New Testament, especially now with the fatwa issued against Najjar Malik and the government crackdown surely coming against the followers of Jesus Christ throughout Iran.

And yet it was a gift from a man who had become a dear friend and his most important asset. David did not want to seem ungrateful or unwilling, so he simply said thank you, as sincerely as he knew how.

"I know you do not want to take this," Birjandi said quietly, as if he could read David's every thought. "You're scared of the words in this book, and you should be. The apostle John wrote his letter to the secret believers and said plainly, 'He who has the Son has the life; he who does not have the Son of God does not have the life. These things I have written to you who believe in the name of the Son of God, so that you may know that you have eternal life.' If you desire eternal life, David, you will receive Christ as your Savior, and you will read this book every moment you have the chance. If you choose to spend eternity separated from Him in hell, then reject Christ and don't bother reading this book. It's your choice. But I am warning you, son, you do not know when your life will be required of you or when you will stand before the Lord God Almighty. Choose well, and choose quickly."

★ ★ ★ ★ ★

TEHRAN, IRAN

Faridzadeh sent an urgent secure text message to Jalal Zandi.

Are the last two cakes baked?

A few minutes later, Zandi—now the most senior nuclear scientist in Iran after Mohammed Saddaji's assassination and Najjar Malik's defection—replied. Baked, yes, but T has had trouble with the candles. Has been working on this around the clock for the past few days. Literally putting finishing touches on it now.

T, Faridzadeh knew, referred to Tariq Khan, Zandi's senior deputy. Questions are being asked, the increasingly impatient defense minister texted back. Need answers immediately. When will the cake be finished?

Within the hour, T believes, came the reply.

It can then be transported to other factory and readied for delivery?

Yes.

Are you with T?

No—preparing other cakes for delivery.

How is that coming?

Delicate process. But making progress.

Why are these cakes taking so much longer than the first two?

Difficult question to answer by text.

Try.

Short version: originally told first two cakes were for special delivery. Told we had more time to get the others ready. Party date has shifted multiple times. Doing best we can.

Bottom line—will they all be ready?

Nearly two minutes passed before Zandi finally replied. If the party is Sunday, we should be ready by Saturday, midday at latest.

Faridzadeh turned to Mohsen Jazini, commander of the Iranian Revolutionary Guard Corps. The two men stood in the war room in the bunker ten stories below the Ministry of Defense in downtown Tehran. Faridzadeh showed Jazini the exchange. "What do you think?"

"I pray to Allah that Zandi is right," Jazini said. "Or heads will roll."

"My thoughts exactly. If we don't start this party by Sunday—and the earlier in the day the better—I fear the Zionists will beat us to the punch."

"You don't buy Darazi's argument that the Americans will find a way to restrain Naphtali from launching a preemptive strike?"

Privately, Faridzadeh thought Darazi was an uneducated, pretentious fool, boastful, arrogant beyond words, and basing his case purely on emotions—on what he hoped the Americans would do—not on reason or intellect or pure facts. "President Darazi is a fine and able man," Faridzadeh said cautiously. "But respectfully, I have a somewhat-different perspective."

"Go on," Jazini said.

"Look," the defense minister said, "the Israelis almost certainly assassinated Saddaji, and they almost certainly were the ones behind the attempt to kill the Mahdi as well. Naphtali is willing to take risks. He's proven that. But he's running out of people to kill our nuclear program and strangle the Caliphate in its cradle. He and his air force are coming after the warheads next. You know it. I know it. The Mahdi knows it. I suspect the Ayatollah knows it as well. That's why they're pushing us so hard to accelerate the timetable. But what can we do? Until all the final technical glitches are resolved and the six remaining warheads are successfully attached to missiles, we are all at the mercy of the scientists and the engineers. And you know me, Mohsen—I don't like to be at the mercy of anyone."

41

David thanked Birjandi and his study group of young clerics.

He said good-bye, then hit the road for Qom. From Hamadan, it was a 283-kilometer journey. He estimated it would take about two and a half hours. As soon as he was under way, he put on his Bluetooth headset, pulled out his phone, and speed-dialed Eva on the secure channel.

"Hey, it's me, checking in," he began.

She seemed glad to hear his voice and asked him how he was feeling. It felt good to talk to a friend, and he confided he was still battling physical discomfort and flashes of panic, both from the waterboarding and from the car crash in Tehran the week before. But soon he shifted quickly to the real reason for his call. "Have you mailed the phones yet? Please say no."

"Why?"

"I need them rerouted."

"Well, you're in luck," Eva said. "The phones actually just arrived from technical, all one hundred, most of them damaged, just as you requested."

"Do they really look like they were beat up in shipping? It has to be believable."

"Don't worry," she assured him. "These guys are pros."

"Good. Look, don't send them to my address in Tehran."

"Why not?"

"I'm not going to be there tomorrow. Change in plans. I'm heading to Qom right now. Can you overnight them there?"

"Of course. Where to?"

He gave her the address for the Qom International Hotel on Helal Ahmar Street.

"Done," she said.

"Thanks. Any luck hunting down Najjar?"

"None. It's a nightmare. He's the gift that keeps on giving."

"How in the world did he escape?"

"Please don't go there."

"I'm just asking."

"I don't know how it happened, all right? I wasn't there. I was coming back from New York at the time, but I can't tell you how many people who outrank you I've had that conversation with."

"I'm not blaming you," David said.

"You'd be the first."

"I was just asking—really."

"How about you? Any leads on the nuclear scientists, the location of the bombs, on any of your objectives?"

He could see he'd made a mistake asking about Najjar's escape. "Okay. Let's change the topic. What did you think about Egypt joining the Caliphate today?"

"I'd expected Riad and Yassin to hem and haw and tell the Mahdi they needed to think about it and they'd get back to him," she answered.

"Like Farooq?"

"Exactly."

"I thought the same. How can we expect to build a Sunni alliance against the Caliphate with Egypt, Jordan, Pakistan, and hopefully some others, if Egypt fell so quickly?"

"The director is furious. So is the king. They met in Amman today."

"Did it go well?"

"Not after the news out of Cairo."

"What happened in the meeting?"

"Which one?"

"The one between Riad, Yassin, and the Mahdi."

"I've got nothing on it yet."

"Let me know when you hear something," David said. "Fareed Riad didn't bide his time as vice president and carry Abdel Ramzy's water all these years to gain the reins of Egypt one day and then hand them over to the Twelfth Imam the next. Something doesn't add up."

"You're right," Eva said. "And it was odd, too, because Riad wasn't standing with the Mahdi in Tahrir Square when he gave his big speech. The field marshal was there and some of the other generals, but not Riad."

David needed to get off the phone, but Eva asked him one more question. "Any news on your mom?"

There was a long silence. "No," David said quietly. "Not yet."

"Keep us posted, okay?"

"I will. Thanks for asking."

"Sure. See you soon."

"Okay. Oh—one more thing. Are you still there?"

"Yes," Eva said. "I'm here."

"Could you send some fresh flowers to my mom's room from me?"

"Sure, anything you need."

"Thanks. I appreciate it." David signed off and hung up the phone. He glanced at the clock on the dashboard of his rented Peugeot. It was getting late. There was almost no traffic on Route 37 as he headed north for the junction with Route 48, which would take him most of the way to Qom. He yawned and rubbed his eyes and scolded himself for not asking Birjandi for some coffee to take on the road.

He was grateful for Eva's friendship and for how good she was at her job. She was an incredible researcher and an even better interrogator. Her Farsi was flawless, her judgment was solid, and she always bent over backward to help him do his job better. She was a first-rate intelligence operative, which was why her questions to him had stung. She was right—he didn't have any leads on Khan or Zandi or the other six warheads, and he was running out of time and options.

★ ★ ★ ★ ★

NATANZ, IRAN

Jalal Zandi sent an urgent page to Tariq Khan.

Less than a minute later, he felt his own pager vibrate, checked the incoming numeric code, and immediately excused himself and logged on to the Iranian singles chat room that he and Khan often used to send classified messages to one another outside normal communications channels.

u still at the bakery? Zandi asked under the user name Mohammed.

yes—y? Khan replied under the user name Jasmine.

need the cakes—are they done?

almost.

can't start without u.

soon.

u keep saying that.

really—just putting on the icing—you'll like it.

friends need 2nite—urgent.

u sure?

positive—bridegroom coming—wants 2 know if everything is ready.

okay—where do u want them?

send 2 party house in K—urgent.

fine—will you b there 2 take delivery?

no—preparing other cakes for delivery—got 2 go.

no problem—they will be on road shortly.

good—c u soon.

★ ★ ★ ★ ★

HIGHWAY 37, EN ROUTE TO QOM

David pulled up Abdol Esfahani's personal mobile number.

But he hesitated before dialing. It was so late. Yet he had to be up. The man was quickly moving up in the Twelfth Imam's circle of allies, and he would want to know the phones were on the way. Maybe he'd have a tidbit of intel David could squeeze out of him, something—anything—to point him in the right direction. He finally hit Send but got no answer and had to leave a message.

Next, he called Esfahani's secretary, Mina, at home. She wouldn't be happy with a late-night call, but she'd always been helpful. She was single. She lived alone. So he wouldn't be getting a husband or a father.

He'd tell her the truth, that he was trying to find her boss to talk about the delivery of the satellite phones, but maybe he could elicit some valuable information from her as well. After seven rings, however, he got voice mail, so he left a message and asked her to return his call as soon as possible.

As he continued driving north in the darkness, he began to have second thoughts. Even when they called back, what were they really likely to know? And if they did know something useful, why would they tell him? His doubts were rising rapidly and with them a growing sense of anxiety that all this effort wasn't going to work, that he wasn't going to be able to find these scientists or these warheads or stop this war in time, yet he might actually get killed trying. The waterboarding had shaken him more than he was willing to concede to Zalinsky or Eva. He had always told himself he was ready to die for his country, but now he was not so sure. He was giving this job, this mission, all he had, but what if it wasn't enough? How far was he willing to go, how much was he willing to put on the line, if in the end all the effort achieved little or nothing at all? What would be the point of making the ultimate sacrifice if he didn't make a lasting difference?

That said, was he really going to give up now? How could he? He was deep inside enemy territory. He had given his word. He was fully committed. And he reminded himself that he ultimately wasn't doing any of this for Zalinsky or Murray or Allen or the president. He was doing it for Marseille, for his parents, to protect them if possible but also to honor them in a way he had a hard time explaining. He hoped someday they would understand.

David passed through the town of Veyan and soon approached the junction for Route 48. There still wasn't much civilian traffic, but he was struck by the number of military vehicles now on the road: troop transports, jeeps, and even tanks being transferred from one place to another on flatbed trucks. He wondered whether this was some sort of anomaly in this area or whether Jack and Eva and Tom were getting reports of more military movement around the country. He made a mental note to report what he was seeing on his next call to Langley, for he suspected it was probably widespread. Iran was getting ready for a war that could commence within days. It certainly made sense that they were making final preparations.

Suddenly he found himself thinking of a line on intelligence gathering from Sun Tzu's classic tome, *The Art of War*: *"Foreknowledge cannot be elicited from spirits, nor from gods, nor by analogy with past events, nor from calculations. It must be obtained from men who know the enemy situation."* Wasn't this why Zalinsky had sent him inside Iran on this particular mission in the first place? The satellite phones were supposed to be giving them the ability to eavesdrop on the very men who knew the enemy's situation, who were planning and executing that situation. They had certainly had some important successes so far. But why weren't they getting *more* phone intercepts? Why weren't they being deluged with more details and insights than they could keep up with?

David pondered that for some time. Most of the regime leadership's conversations were probably via secure e-mail, a system they had not yet been able to tap into but which they would more likely be able to compromise once all of MDS's advanced telecommunications software was installed nationwide, though that was still months away. But the prime reason had to be that the Iranians at the highest echelons of the regime did not trust the satellite phones yet. Given their previous experience of buying satphones from the Russians and later finding them all bugged by the FSB, that certainly made sense. And what had Esfahani just said? *"We are about to live in a world without America and without Zionism. Our holy hatred is about to strike like a wave against the infidels. We don't trust anyone. We can't trust anyone. The enemy is moving. He is among us. We must be careful."*

Wasn't that why they had tortured him? Wasn't that why Javad had called Firouz and Jamshad using his satphone and spoken so openly about where to pick up their fake passports? They were testing, probing, trying to determine whether anyone was listening in, trying to determine whom and what they could trust.

Had the phones now passed the test? David guessed the answer was yes. That was why Esfahani was pushing him so hard to get the rest of the phones. He suspected, therefore, that call usage was about to soar. He certainly hoped so, but even that wasn't going to be enough.

Langley was relying far too heavily on SIGINT, signals intelligence, and more specifically on COMINT, communications intelligence. No one in the world was better at either than the US intelligence community, as David knew firsthand. But that wasn't why Zalinsky had recruited him, to bolster the Agency's already-strong hand. Zalinsky had specifically recruited him to help rebuild the Agency's weakest link, HUMINT, human intelligence. For the $80 billion they spent a year on spying, the US was doing far too little of it. They weren't putting nearly enough NOCs fluent in Farsi, Arabic, Urdu, and other Middle Eastern languages into the field to befriend or buy off men who knew the enemy situation. They had him, but David realized he had to aim higher. If he had any shot at truly being useful, he had to be talking to insiders, which led him to one name: Javad Nouri.

It was high risk, and he was not specifically authorized by Zalinsky to make contact with the Twelfth Imam's right-hand man. But what choice did he have? Javad likely knew more about the enemy's plans than any single individual, aside from the Mahdi himself. True, David had only met the guy once, when Esfahani had told him to collect the first satellite phones David had smuggled into the country. They had spoken only briefly. But David was desperate. So he pulled up Javad's number—not the satphone number, but his mobile—and dialed.

"I'm not here right now, or I'm on the other line. Please leave me your name, number, and a brief message, and I'll get back to you as soon as I can."

The recording didn't give a name, but the voice was unmistakable.

"Javad, hey, this is Reza. Sorry to bother you, but I couldn't get in touch with our mutual friends, so I thought I'd just call you directly. By tomorrow, I should have most of the gifts you guys requested. Still trying to get the rest but thought I should get you these right away. Please call me and let me know how best to get them to you. Thanks."

David gave his own number and hung up. "Three strikes and you're out," he sighed as he passed another military convoy on the road to Qom.

42

The president was headed to the Situation Room.

Surrounded by a phalanx of Secret Service agents, he left the Oval Office and walked directly to the five-thousand-square-foot complex of conference rooms, private offices, the "watch room," and the "surge room," on the lower floor of the West Wing, that was collectively referred to throughout the White House as the Sit Room. There, Jackson was met by the vice president and the rest of the National Security Council, who stood as he entered.

"Be seated," Jackson said as he took his own seat at the head of the mahogany table and quickly scanned the six flat-screen televisions lining the walls, two of which now provided real-time video feeds from a Predator drone monitoring the Iranian naval flotilla in the Med, while three provided live feeds from US spy satellites monitoring Iranian nuclear facilities in Hamadan, Natanz, and Esfahān. CIA director Allen was on the sixth screen, in a secure videoconference mode from the US Embassy in Amman.

"What have you got, Roger?"

"Mr. President, things are worsening at a fairly rapid clip over here," Allen began. "Have you had a chance to read the memo I just sent over to the NSC?"

Jackson hadn't, and he took a moment to scan the document.

>>TOP SECRET–EYES ONLY<<

TO: President, Vice President

CC: National Security Council

FROM: Roger Allen, Director, Central Intelligence Agency

RE: Warning of Possible Imminent Attack on Israel

New reporting indicates possible imminent attack on the State of Israel by forces under the command and control of the Twelfth Imam (TTI).

Credible intel puts two (2) nuclear warheads on Iranian naval vessels in the Mediterranean, both operational, both attached to high-speed ballistic missiles aimed at Israel, and both reportedly to be fired before Tuesday next.

We are sending a UAV with an externally mounted high-resolution scintillation detector to scan the naval flotilla. This will allow us to determine if high-energy gamma radiation is emanating from any of the ships. We should have results by late Thursday.

In the meantime, the Agency assesses the likelihood of two (2) warheads being on board, operational, and attached to high-speed ballistic missiles aimed at the State of Israel at 80 to 85 percent.

Six (6) additional nuclear warheads also believed to be operational. Locations currently unknown. Aggressive efforts to pinpoint them under way.

Other signs of probable imminent attack on Israel:

TTI canceled his trip to Jordan.

TTI making emergency return trip to Iran.

TTI told Iran's minister of defense to "make sure everything is in place and ready—everything—when I arrive."

We are now seeing increased activity on Iranian air bases.

We are now seeing increased activity on Iranian missile bases.

TTI has enlisted Egypt, Lebanon, Syria, and Saudi Arabia into Caliphate, effectively surrounding Israel.

Agency assesses that TTI now has means, motive, and opportunity to launch attack on Israel.

At this time, Agency assesses TTI has motive but not means or opportunity to hit the US homeland directly. Nevertheless, we recommend US move to DEFCON 3 and immediately put additional radiological sensors at border crossings, shipyards, and airports.

Finally, Agency assesses a growing Pearl Harbor threat to US Navy's Fifth Fleet and Central Command personnel and facilities in Bahrain. Should TTI choose to close the Strait of Hormuz and shut down oil shipments to the West, he has several options.

TTI could order a surprise attack against our ships and forces in Bahrain.

TTI could incite the Shia majority (almost 70 percent) to overthrow the Sunni ruling family—so far the king is sticking with us, but violent protests have rocked the capital in the last week and calls for the kingdom to join the Caliphate are rising.

At present, the Agency believes Israel is the main target for TTI and his allies, and TTI will not want to draw the US into a direct conflict unless or until Israel is destroyed or effectively neutralized. Nevertheless, we recommend putting all US naval forces in the region at FPCON CHARLIE.

The president turned his attention first to Jordan. "Does the king concur with this assessment?" he asked Allen.

"I didn't discuss this specific intelligence with him, Mr. President, or this specific memo," Allen replied. "You all are the first to get this. But there's no question the king is convinced war is imminent, and he is terrified, frankly, of Jordanians being killed in the cross fire of a missile war between Iran and Israel. He's making an emergency request for Patriot missile batteries to be deployed on Jordanian soil. He's asking that US fighter jets hold an immediate joint exercise with the Royal Jordanian Air Force. And he is asking that you make an immediate visit to Amman this weekend as a show of American commitment to him and the survival of his regime."

Jackson winced. That was the last thing he was prepared to do. Rather than respond immediately, however, he poured himself a glass of water and nodded to the secretary of state to reply.

"How did the king respond to the president's proposal that Jordan join a US-backed Sunni alliance against the Twelfth Imam and the Caliphate?" asked the secretary, freshly home from a whirlwind tour of NATO capitals. "The Europeans are skeptical that such an alliance can be built. Of course, they don't want to see the entire Middle East and North Africa under the control of one man either."

306 ★ TEHRAN INITIATIVE

"Well, let me just say that the king was more supportive of the idea before the Egyptians joined the Caliphate," Allen said. "Now he fears he'll be left all alone. If the Paks join us too, that would help. That's why I think my trip to Islamabad will be critical. But at the moment, the king is noncommittal until he sees tangible support for Jordan's security."

The president asked the defense secretary if they could put several Patriot missile batteries on the ground in Jordan in the next seventy-two hours.

"We certainly can," the SecDef said. "But I need to caution everyone here that the Patriot isn't perfect. It can take down tactical ballistic missiles, cruise missiles, and advanced fighter jets, but it's not going to get everything. Especially if hundreds of missiles are inbound."

"When are you supposed to meet with the king next, Roger?" Jackson asked.

"It's just past midnight here, sir. We're supposed to have breakfast at seven tomorrow. But the defense minister said I could call him at any hour once I heard from you. How would you like to proceed, Mr. President?"

That was the problem. Jackson didn't know. He hated being forced to react to events and requests. He wanted to be proactive, but try as he might, he couldn't seem to get out in front of the crisis.

"Say yes to the Patriots," he said at last. "Get Defense to take the lead on those details. But say no to the joint air exercise—it's simply too provocative at the moment."

"That could prove decisive on whether the king will help start a Sunni alliance against the Caliphate," Allen said.

"I understand, but it's too provocative," the president replied. "I don't want a show of American force. That would be throwing kerosene on a bonfire."

"And a quick trip over here by you?" Allen asked. "You could be here by tomorrow, then stop in Israel, too. Sir, I think it would mean a lot to both countries, knowing you are standing with them in this crisis."

"Even with your memo that war is imminent?" Jackson asked.

"Especially given that," Allen replied.

"I'm sure Secret Service will want to weigh in on that," Jackson quipped.

He solicited input from the rest of the NSC, which proved to be split down the middle, but he had already made up his mind.

"Tell the king I deeply appreciate his offer and look forward to visiting sometime soon but that my doctors say I cannot travel right now," the president said. "Look, gentlemen, I still think I can get through to the Mahdi and find a peaceful way out of this thing. I have to believe that. And I don't want to do anything provocative or incendiary that could jeopardize our discussions. In fact, I'm going to send a back-channel message to the Mahdi to see if we can move our phone call up from next Tuesday to tomorrow. In the meantime, tomorrow I'm going to call for an emergency session of the UN Security Council, and I'm going to suggest that the secretary-general invite the Mahdi to meet with the council and discuss his concerns at his earliest possible convenience."

There was a hum of agreement around the table.

"Mr. President, this is Roger again in Amman."

"Yes, Roger."

"Sir, no one appreciates your commitment to peace more than me. But every indicator we have is that the Mahdi is ready to launch a nuclear strike on Israel at any moment. He just told Defense Minister Faridzadeh to 'make sure everything is ready.' None of my senior staff believe the Mahdi is open to negotiations. We believe he is buying time to finalize his preparations for war."

"So what are you saying, Roger?"

"Mr. President, I'm saying that any window for diplomacy has closed. I think we need to seriously consider taking military action against the Iranian nuclear sites and naval vessels we know of before the Mahdi can use those warheads and before the Israelis can strike."

The president turned to the SecDef. "You have your plan ready, right?"

"Yes, sir, Op Plan 106," the SecDef replied. "We've secretly positioned additional air assets in Greece and Cyprus, and we have the USS *Enterprise* and the bulk of the Sixth Fleet in the eastern Med. Meanwhile, we have the USS *Dwight D. Eisenhower* battle group patrolling the Gulf. Our stealth bombers are on alert at Whiteman in Missouri. The moment we get confirmed coordinates on those eight warheads, we can launch cruise missiles within two hours and execute the entire plan in less than six."

"Good. We need to keep all options on the table," the president said. "So your point is noted, Roger. That said, I couldn't disagree with you more. I don't think another US-led war in the Middle East is going to solve anything. I firmly believe diplomacy is the way forward, in close consultation with the UN and our NATO allies. So, Roger, I'd like you to come home immediately after your breakfast meeting with the king. State will take over from here. I'm sending the secretary to Islamabad tonight instead of you. I want you to focus exclusively on finding those warheads and keeping us apprised of any Israeli and Iranian moves toward war."

Allen had just been benched. He looked deflated, but he knew his place. "Yes, sir, Mr. President. Just a quick point of clarification on that."

"What?"

"Would you like the secretary to brief Prime Minister Naphtali on our latest intelligence on the Iranian nuclear threat, or should I proceed with that?"

"I will call the prime minister myself in the morning," the president said.

"But, sir, respectfully, we are assessing an imminent attack," the CIA director noted. "The Israelis need to know immediately."

"I'll call them in the morning, once you have confirmed whether there are any warheads actually on those Iranian missile boats," the president said. "I don't want to traffic in rumors, and I certainly don't want to give the Israelis an excuse to launch a first strike. That is all, gentlemen."

And with that, Jackson stood and walked out of the Sit Room.

★ ★ ★ ★ ★

THURSDAY
MARCH 10
(IRAN TIME)

43

David had been on the road for more than an hour.

His eyelids were getting heavy, and the Iranian folk music he was listening to on the radio to pass the time wasn't helping. But he was making progress. He had just fueled up in the village of Kalle Dasht and was now rapidly approaching the town of Saveh and the junction with Route 5. There, he would turn south until he reached the interchange at Garangan, where he would take Route 56 directly into Qom. At this rate, he expected to reach the hotel by around 2 a.m. and be in bed no later than 2:30.

His mobile phone rang. He glanced at the caller ID but didn't recognize the number. Hoping it was Zalinsky or Eva with some good news, he took the call anyway.

"Reza?"

"Yes, this is he."

"This is Javad Nouri. I just got back to Tehran and got your message."

A surge of adrenaline instantly woke David up. "Hey, good to hear from you."

"I hope it's not too late to call you, but whatever you've got, we could use."

"It's no problem," David replied. "Thanks for getting back to me. I expect to have a hundred of what we were discussing by late in the afternoon tomorrow—er, I guess today. They're being shipped to me in Qom. That's where I'm heading now to meet some of my tech team later this morning at some switching station that's having a problem. Are you guys going to be in Qom by any chance?"

"No, we're not," Javad said. "But I have a better idea. Could you bring them directly to us? Our mutual friend has heard many good things about you and would like to meet you in person. Would that be acceptable?"

David was stunned. The only mutual friend they could possibly have was the Twelfth Imam. Was he really being invited to meet with him in person?

"Of course. That would be a great honor; thank you," David replied.

"Wonderful," Javad said. "Our friend is deeply grateful for your help, and he personally asked me to apologize for the vetting process you were subjected to. He hopes you understand that we cannot be too careful at this stage."

"I understand," David said, trying not to sound as ecstatic as he felt. "Abdol Esfahani explained everything. I'll survive."

"Good," Javad said. "Be in Tehran tonight at eight o'clock at the restaurant where we met before. Come by cab. Don't bring anyone or anything else with you, just the gifts. I'll have someone meet you there and bring you to us. Okay?"

"Yes, of course. I'm looking forward to it."

"So are we. I've got to go now. Good-bye."

Thrilled, David hung up the phone. He had to call this in to Langley. But just as he was about to, he suddenly remembered Dr. Birjandi's stern warning that the Twelfth Imam was a dangerous false messiah. Birjandi believed the Mahdi was possessed by Satan and was "certainly guided by demonic forces" to deceive the unsuspecting. He had even gone so far as to quote some End Times prophecy from the Bible, saying, *"'If anyone says to you, "Behold, here is the Messiah," or "There He is," do not believe him.' And 'if they say to you, "Behold, He is in the wilderness," do not go out, or, "Behold, He is in the inner rooms," do not believe them. For just as the lightning comes from the east and flashes even to the west, so will the coming of the Son of Man be.'"*

A chill ran through David's body as a deep sense of foreboding came over him. No one knew more about the Twelfth Imam than Dr. Alireza

Birjandi, and Birjandi had been adamant that he would not meet with the Mahdi under any circumstances, fearful that even a man of his wisdom and experience could be drawn to the Mahdi and lose his reasoning. But this was an intelligence operative's dream come true—and in many ways it was the very reason he had been sent to Iran.

★ ★ ★ ★ ★

ARLINGTON, VIRGINIA

Marseille finally got back to her hotel room in Crystal City.

She showered and changed and ordered room service for an early dinner, then checked the latest headlines from Iran. The *New York Times* and *Washington Post* websites were filled with the latest rumors of war, plus full coverage of the Mahdi's speech in Tahrir Square and analysis of why Egypt had unexpectedly joined the Caliphate. The *Wall Street Journal* noted oil and gas prices were both up significantly again in overnight trading as the crisis in the Middle East worsened, while the Dow had plunged 11 percent in the last week and the NASDAQ was being hit even harder. The *Jerusalem Post* website covered CIA director Roger Allen's visit to Jerusalem and Amman and Prime Minister Naphtali's photo op with an American Patriot missile battery in the Jezreel Valley, noting the US was rushing additional Patriot batteries to both Israel and Jordan. One headline read, "Tens of Thousands Gather at Wailing Wall to Pray for Peace As Crisis with Iran Heats Up." The more she read, the more worried she became for David and for Lexi and Chris. That reminded her to check her e-mail. One from Lexi caught her eye.

Dear Marseille,
Thanks so much for your very sweet note and for all your prayers! Chris and I so appreciate them. Keep them coming! I know the whole world thinks there's going to be a war over here soon, but aren't they always saying that? I mean, my parents have refused to go to Israel— and refused to take us kids—all of our lives because "it's just not safe." I can't tell you how blessed I am to have married Chris.
His motto: Fear not.

So we're trying not to read the papers, and we can't understand most of what's on the radio anyway. But we've been everywhere— all through Jerusalem and Bethlehem and Jericho, to the ruins of Caesarea, to a beautiful church on the top of Mount Carmel, to the Church of the Annunciation in Nazareth, to the McDonald's just down the road from Armageddon. (I'm not kidding! I've attached a picture of Chris and me in front of it. It's hilarious!) I even bought you some wine in Cana—a bottle of red and one of white!

I'm taking a bazillion pictures and writing furiously in my journal. I'll post everything on my Facebook when I get a chance, but Chris and I are having too much fun to post photos just now!

We just arrived in Tiberias and are staying at an amazing hotel on the shores of the Sea of Galilee. You have to come here. YOU HAVE TO!

Tomorrow, we're taking a boat ride on the Sea of Galilee— they call it the Kinneret here—and then going to the Mount of Beatitudes.

Anyway, the embassy is texting all Americans, encouraging us to leave the country immediately. But Chris and I don't want to miss a single minute, and everything goes so much faster when there aren't so many tourists here! So, Lord willing, we're staying through Sunday and should get back on Monday.

Sorry for such a long message. Did you get a flight back to Portland yet, or are you still stuck in DC? Go see the monuments and the art galleries!

Love you lots.

See you soon!
Lexi

★ ★ ★ ★ ★

LANGLEY, VIRGINIA

Tom Murray knew he wasn't going home that night.

He ordered a sandwich and soup from the commissary and sent his

JOEL C. ROSENBERG ★ 315

secretary downstairs to get it. Just then, his phone rang. It was the watch commander in the Global Operations Center.

"They're leaving now?" Murray asked, instantly alert. "How many? . . . Do you have the coordinates? . . . Hold on, let me grab a pen. . . . Okay, go ahead. . . . Got it. Do you have a Predator any-where close that can keep tracking them? . . . Do it now and keep me posted. We'll get this to our man on the ground and let you know. Good work."

★ ★ ★ ★ ★

EN ROUTE TO QOM

David took Zalinsky's call on the first ring.

Increasingly conflicted about the meeting with the Twelfth Imam, he had hesitated to call it in, but now he figured this was as good a time as any. Zalinsky, however, had his own news. "You need to turn around," he ordered.

"Why?" David asked. "What are you talking about?"

Zalinsky explained the Mahdi's intercepted call from Javad's phone to Faridzadeh and the order to put final details in place. Then he explained that an NSA Keyhole satellite had just picked up a convoy leaving Hamadan, an 18-wheeler flanked by two SUVs.

"We need you to intercept the convoy and follow it."

"Can't you task a Predator to do that?"

"We don't have one over Hamadan right now."

Incredulous, David asked why not.

"The one we had there was having mechanical problems," Zalinsky said. "I sent it back to Bahrain to be checked out. We've got another one going in, but it's going to take a few hours to get there."

David briefly explained his situation.

"Really, a meeting with the Mahdi?" Zalinsky said. "That's huge."

"I know," David said. "So shouldn't I stay on track for that?"

"When do you need to be back in Tehran?"

"By eight tonight."

"Then you should have plenty of time. Find the convoy, follow it, and report back every half hour. That's priority one right now. Then we'll make sure you're back to Tehran by eight."

"Are you really sure it's carrying warheads?" David asked.

"No, but the convoy left Facility 278 in the dead of night, and the fact that this is the first convoy to leave the facility at all since the nuclear test seems significant. There are several military bases along the main highway south, and we need to know for certain where they're headed. Anyway, this is our best lead right now. Actually, this is our only lead. We need to see where it takes us."

"Fine, but let's say the convoy does have a warhead. What am I supposed to do about it? I'm unarmed and alone. Is there a special forces team nearby?"

"I'm sending in two paramilitary teams," Zalinsky replied, "one to the safe house in Karaj and the other to the safe house in Esfahān. But they are HALO jumping into the country and won't be there until lunchtime at best."

David was startled. "I thought you already had teams on the ground. That's what you told me."

"We did. The White House had us recall them."

"When?"

"After the president heard from the Mahdi."

"But why?"

"All I can say is that the Agency is under enormous pressure not to do anything too provocative."

David couldn't believe what he was hearing. He was furious and felt hung out to dry. He was risking his life inside Iran, and the administration didn't want to do anything too provocative? What was wrong with them? Didn't they see what they were facing? There were times he wished he worked for the Mossad.

"Look," Zalinsky said, "I know how you must feel right now."

"Do you?"

"Yes, but I need you to do this for me. I'm sending the paramilitary teams in without the director's permission. I haven't even told Murray. I will when the time is right, but not now."

"Why?"

"I made you a promise. I told you I'd back you up, and I will. But in the meantime, I need you to get on this target and stay on it until we get more people into place and figure out what to do next."

David held his tongue. He had plenty to say, but there was no use unleashing on the one guy who was helping him.

"So," Zalinsky said, "can I count on you?"

David took a deep breath. "Sure. Which way are they heading?"

"South on 37."

"That's directly parallel with me, but ninety minutes away," David said, adjusting his GPS system to get a wider view of the area. "If I turn around, I'll never find them. I'd be better off taking a right on 56, cutting through Arak, and trying to intercept them at Borujerd."

"How long will that take you?"

"An hour and a half, maybe less if I hit the gas. An hour fifteen if I'm lucky."

"Do it," Zalinsky said. "And keep me posted."

44

Nasreen Shirazi abruptly stopped breathing.

Her husband frantically began giving her CPR and screamed for help. Azad had just stepped into the hallway to take a call from Saeed, but when he heard his father's yells and an urgent Code Blue message over the hospital's loudspeakers, he came rushing back in. Seconds later, a team of doctors and nurses rushed in as well. They took over from Mohammad Shirazi and worked feverishly to save Nasreen. But nothing they did worked.

Twenty minutes later, Mrs. Shirazi was pronounced dead. Her husband collapsed in a chair in the corner sobbing while Azad tried in vain to comfort him.

★ ★ ★ ★ ★

JUNCTION OF ROUTES 56 AND 37, OUTSIDE BORUJERD, IRAN

It was 2:30 a.m. in Iran when David reached the junction of 56 and 37.

He pulled his Peugeot to the side of the road, put on the parking brake, grabbed a flashlight from the glove compartment, got out, and popped the hood as if he were having car trouble. He had not passed the convoy coming through the city of Arak or any of the smaller towns and villages along Route 56, so there were now only two possibilities. His best-case scenario was that they had not reached the junction yet. If that was the case, they should be coming through any minute, and he could pick up their trail. If they had just passed through, then he was in trouble. It meant they were still heading south on 37 until they hit a fork. At that point, they could either go west through Khorramabad, a city with about a third of a million people, or continue south on 62 toward Esfahān, Iran's third-largest city with more than a million and a half people. At that point, it would take a miracle to find them.

David called Zalinsky to report that he had nothing to report except that he was freezing. Strong winds were gusting across the western plains and making the already-chilly March air even colder. David promised to check in again soon, hung up, then opened the trunk and pulled out his coat. The moon was just a sliver, and there were no streetlights or houses or shops to be seen for miles, so it was dark and barren and David felt a stab of deep sadness. He was anxious to find the convoy, to be sure, and worried all his efforts so far would be for naught if the Iranians launched their War of Annihilation against Israel or against his own country. But it was more than that. He felt very much alone, as if something precious to him had just been ripped away.

He thought about praying. He sensed that God might have the answers that he so desperately needed. But he felt guilty turning to God now, when he had been resisting Him for so long. For weeks, it seemed, God had been trying to get his attention—years, actually, but especially in the past few weeks. Through Marseille. Through Najjar Malik. Through Dr. Birjandi, and now through meeting his six secret disciples. Through one near-death experience after another. The car crash. The gun battle. The waterboarding. Through it all, God had been protecting him, watching out for him, providing for him even though he didn't deserve it. Yet had he taken time to really process what he thought about God, what he thought about Jesus? He knew the answer, and his guilt became all the more crushing.

Just then, David heard a truck coming south. He whipped around, but it was only a pickup, and it was alone. He went back to tinkering with his engine.

As he did, he began to ponder all that he had seen and heard and wrestled with in recent weeks. He did believe in God, he decided. Actually, he was pretty sure he always had. How could he not? He knew deep in his soul that God had been revealing Himself in ways large and small ever since he was a child.

What if his parents had stayed in Iran and he had been born here? He'd never have known freedom, never have met Marseille, never have had the incredible opportunities he had today. He might even be serving in the Iranian Revolutionary Guard Corps at this very moment, he realized. He might be serving the Twelfth Imam and be a full participant in the great evil now unfolding. Hadn't God spared him from all that?

Or what if Jack Zalinsky had never come to see him in the Onondaga County juvenile detention center when he was sixteen? What if he'd been sentenced for a more serious crime, given a longer sentence? What if his record hadn't been expunged and he'd never gone to college? Wasn't God's hand rescuing him then, too?

Yes, David was sure that a God existed, one who had a plan for him and was trying to get his attention. He was certain of this now. But he was also certain of something else: the god of Islam was not Him. David wasn't naive enough to think that Muslims were the only people to do horrific violence in the name of their god. Throughout history, people calling themselves Christians had done terrible things too. The difference, David concluded, was that the Muslims waging violent jihad were actually *obeying* the Qur'an's commands to kill the infidels, while people who said they were Christians but killed or mistreated Jews, Muslims, and others were explicitly *disobeying* the teachings of Jesus.

It was Muhammad, after all, who told his followers things like "Jews and Christians are the ones whom God has cursed, and he whom God excludes from His mercy, you shall never find one to help and save him" and "Kill them wherever you may come upon them, and seize them, and confine them, and lie in wait for them at every conceivable place."

Yet it was Jesus who told His disciples, "You have heard that it was said, 'You shall love your neighbor and hate your enemy.' But I say to you, love your enemies and pray for those who persecute you."

A few more cars passed. No military convoy.

David began to think more about Najjar. He still couldn't believe how radically the man had changed in just a month or so. He had grown up a devout Twelver. Over the course of his life, Najjar had even met the Mahdi several times and had seen him do signs and wonders, for crying out loud. Yet now he had turned his back not just on Shia Islam and the Twelvers but on all of Islam. Now he was telling his story on worldwide television, preaching the gospel, and telling his people that "Jesus Christ is calling you to Himself because He loves you—so receive Him by faith while you still have time."

Was Najjar right? Was it true? Did Christ really love him? Was Jesus really calling him to follow?

David had read the transcripts of Najjar's conversations with Eva three times, and now he'd even watched on the Christian satellite channel as Najjar told the story of meeting Jesus on the road to Hamadan. He practically knew the story by heart, but had he really thought about what it meant?

Najjar said he'd seen a man wearing a robe reaching to his feet. Across his chest was a gold sash. His hair was white like the snow that surrounded them. His eyes were fiery. His face shone. At that point, Najjar said he fell at the man's feet like a dead man, but the figure had said, "Do not be afraid."

"Who are you?" Najjar had asked.

"I am Jesus the Nazarene," the man had replied. "*I AM* the first and the last and the living One. I am the Alpha and the Omega, who is and who was and who is to come, the Almighty. Come and follow me."

Najjar said the first sentences were uttered with a measure of authority such as he had never heard before, not from any mullah or cleric or political leader in his entire life. Yet the last four words were spoken with such gentleness, such tenderness, that he could not imagine refusing the request.

Najjar went on to describe seeing the holes where spikes had been driven through Jesus' hands. As a devout Muslim, he had never considered the possibility that Jesus had been crucified at all, much less to pay the penalty for all human sins. No Muslim believed that. At that point, Najjar's mind had been filled with questions, and for David, Najjar's questions were his own.

How could Jesus be appearing as a crucified Messiah? If the Qur'an were true, wouldn't it be impossible for Jesus to have nail-scarred hands?

One thing seemed clear to David, just as it had to Najjar: Jesus wasn't claiming to be the second-in-command to the Mahdi. He was claiming to be God Almighty.

"I am the Way, and the Truth, and the Life," Jesus had said, "and no one comes to the Father except through Me. I am the Light of the World. He who follows me will not walk in the darkness, but will have the light of life. For God so loved the world, that He gave His only begotten Son, that whoever believes in Him shall not perish but have eternal life."

At that point, Najjar said, he had fallen to the ground and kissed the scarred feet of Jesus. He said that at that moment, something inside him had broken. "I wept with remorse for all the sins I had ever committed. I wept with indescribable relief that came from knowing beyond the shadow of a doubt that God really did love me and had sent Jesus to die on the cross and rise from the dead for me. I wept with gratitude that because of Jesus' promise, I knew that I was going to spend eternity with Him."

In some ways, David wanted to dismiss the story as a fairy tale, an anxiety-induced hallucination from a deeply disturbed individual. But nothing about Dr. Najjar Malik seemed mentally imbalanced or unstable. The guy was not only one of the most highly respected scientists in all of Iran but a man willing to face a $100 million bounty on his and his family's heads to tell the world what he believed to be true. He clearly wasn't doing it to get rich. He wasn't doing it for power. Though it cost him everything, Najjar Malik was now a follower of Jesus, a most unlikely turn of events.

And in the darkness and the solitude of that night, David realized that he, too, believed. Najjar was right. It was all true.

David had not seen a vision or had a dream or any other sort of supernatural experience. But maybe not everyone had to. David was an intelligence operative, wasn't he? He was supposed to hunt for the truth and follow the evidence wherever it led him. And the evidence pointed to the fact that Jesus was who He claimed to be. Not only that, David knew that Jesus was asking him to come and follow Him, whatever the cost, however high the price. In some ways, it was hard to imagine coming to this point. One moment he did not believe, and the next he did. He couldn't explain it, but he knew with absolute, inexplicable certainty that it was true, all of it, and that he believed it.

In the stillness of the moment, David looked up into the night sky, at the twinkling stars sprinkled across the heavens. He tried to imagine what God looked like, tried to imagine meeting Jesus face to face one day. And then, feeling compelled in his spirit, he got down on his knees on the pavement of Route 56 and put his forehead on the ground.

"O God in heaven, One True God, most kind and merciful God of the universe, maker of heaven and earth, my Creator, my Master, please have mercy on me tonight. I am the worst of sinners. I have been given so much, but I have squandered it all. You have been calling me, but I have been going my own way. I have been resisting You for so long, yet You have not given up on me. Thank You, O Lord. Thank You so much. Please forgive me for everything I have done in my miserable, godless, selfish life. I am so sorry. I know You are there. I know You are calling me. My heart is racing. I can feel Your hand on my life."

David looked up briefly as two trucks went by, but they were not the ones he was looking for. So he bowed down again to keep praying.

"But far more important than what I feel, O Lord, is that I now know that the Bible is Your Word. I know it alone contains the true words of life. And I know, too, that Jesus is Your Son and the only true Messiah. I know it because You have revealed it to me. I don't pretend to understand it all right now. But I believe. And if You will accept me, I want to follow You. Please accept me, O God. I believe Jesus died on the cross for me. I believe He rose for me. I see what He has done—what You have done—to save my friends Najjar and Dr. Birjandi, to change them so completely, and I want what they have. I want to know that I'm going to heaven when I die. I want to know that all my sins are forgiven. I want the joy and peace and sense of purpose and direction they have, even when life is hard—especially when life is hard."

He was quiet for a moment. All was quiet.

"I don't know what else to pray, Lord. I just want to say that . . . well . . . I love You, and I need You. . . . And as of tonight, I promise to follow You forever, so long as You will help me and lead me all the way. Amen."

There were no angels singing. There were no flames of fire. But David knew God was listening and had answered his prayer.

45

Suddenly three vehicles raced past, headed south.

David was so deep in thought, he almost missed them. But it was a truck with two SUVs. It was the convoy.

He slammed his hood, tossed the flashlight onto the passenger seat, removed the parking brake, and peeled out onto 37.

Once on the road, he speed-dialed Zalinsky. "Jack, I've got them."

"You're sure?"

"Yes."

"Don't get too close," Zalinsky warned. "Keep your distance, but don't lose them."

"Don't worry, Jack. You trained me well."

"Good. I'm heading to the Ops Center so I can see your location and track your progress. Call me back in a few minutes."

"Will do, Jack. How far away is the Predator?"

"Still another hour at least."

"Get it here fast. I have them now, but I have no idea what's ahead of me."

★ ★ ★ ★ ★

ARLINGTON, VIRGINIA

Marseille set her dinner dishes out in the hallway and locked the door.

Then she flopped on her bed, bored and alone. She'd had enough of

Facebook and couldn't take any more headlines from the Middle East. The weather reports from Portland were still depressing. The snow had stopped, but they'd gotten so much of it, the schools weren't going to be open until Monday at the earliest. What's more, United didn't have any flights heading to the Northwest until Friday, and they were all full, though they had her on standby for a Saturday flight, first thing in the morning.

She wanted someone to talk to, someone to hang out with and play a game or go to a movie with. She was half-tempted to call Lexi until she realized it was the middle of the night in Israel. So she sipped a bottle of water and flipped on the TV. Hoping for something light and funny, maybe a romantic comedy to relax with, she conspicuously avoided all of the cable news channels as she roamed the dial. She passed on the third in the Lord of the Rings series, then passed on *Gladiator* and *Saving Private Ryan*, too, and couldn't help but think of David, who had once told her that these were some of his favorite movies. Her spirits lifted slightly when she found a BBC production of *Pride and Prejudice* just beginning on PBS. She preferred the one with Keira Knightley but reminded herself that beggars could not be choosers.

She closed the curtains, lowered the lights, slipped into her nightgown, and went to power down her computer. Just then, however, she noticed a new e-mail. She clicked on it and was surprised to see it was a group e-mail from Dr. Shirazi's account, though written by his daughter-in-law, Nora.

Dear friends,
Thank you so much for your thoughts and prayers for our family during this terrible time. I'm so sorry to be the one to share this news, and to do it so impersonally, but it is with great sadness that I inform you that Mrs. Nasreen Shirazi passed away this evening.

She went without struggle. It was just her time, though far too soon. Dad and Azad were at her side. Unfortunately, I'm still on bed rest and back in Philly with my mom and the baby. Saeed is on his way from Manhattan. David is in Europe on business.

We are trying to track him down now and are hoping he can get back to us soon.

There will be a memorial service at 11:00 on Saturday morning. There will also be viewing hours on Friday evening. Azad is working on the details. I'll send them as soon as they're set.

Thanks for all your kind notes, e-mails, letters, and of course, for all the yellow roses that keep pouring in. Those were definitely her favorites, and she was so grateful for all your acts of kindness, as we have been.

For now, Azad and I would ask that you not call Dad directly. As you can imagine, he is overwhelmed by the loss of his beloved wife of more than three decades. I'll be handling all of his e-mails for the time being. It's the least I can do since I'm stuck in bed and up at all hours of the night. Thanks.

Love, Nora

★ ★ ★ ★ ★

ROUTE 37, IRAN

David slowed the Peugeot and speed-dialed Zalinsky again.

"You still with them?" Zalinsky asked.

"Yeah, but I'm hanging back a bit more. We're about thirty kilometers from Khorramabad, in the Heroor Pass."

"Good. I can see your GPS tracking signal."

"They just turned in to the Imam Ali military base. Isn't this an IRGC missile base?"

Eva's voice came on the line. "It is," she said. "They have Shahab-3 ballistic missile launchers there. We also believe they produce missiles at a facility on the base."

"Are you sure you haven't been spotted?" Zalinsky asked.

"Unless they're watching from the air, I should be good," David said. "But what do you want me to do now?"

"Good question. Find a place to stay out of sight. We'll get back to you in a few minutes."

★ ★ ★ ★ ★

ARLINGTON, VIRGINIA

Tears filled Marseille's eyes as she read the e-mail again.

She didn't want to believe it could really be true. She felt terrible for Dr. Shirazi and all that he had been through so far, and she was suddenly overwhelmed by bad memories from when her own mom had died. The line that pained her most, though, was the one that said David was in Europe and they were trying to track him down, hoping he could get back in time. She knew he wasn't in Europe, and given the headlines, she seriously doubted he could possibly be back in time, and it made her even sadder.

She clicked off the TV, picked up the phone by her bed, and dialed the United reservations number she now knew by heart. She booked a flight back to Syracuse the following day and a return flight to Portland for Sunday. Then she called the Sheraton on the SU campus where she and David had had breakfast just the Sunday before and reserved a room for a three-night stay.

★ ★ ★ ★ ★

OUTSIDE IMAM ALI MILITARY BASE, IRAN

Twenty minutes later, David called Zalinsky.

"They're moving again."

"The whole convoy?"

"No, just one of the SUVs with five men inside."

"Could they see you?"

"No, I'm off on a side road, tucked away in some bushes. They just drove past. I can stay here for a while. But if a patrol comes by, I could be toast."

Zalinsky directed him to follow the SUV. David warned that the semi could leave again and go someplace else and they'd have no eyes to track it, at least not until the Predator arrived from Bahrain. They also couldn't be 100 percent certain that the five men were connected to the convoy. But Zalinsky didn't want to take the risk of leaving David potentially exposed near such a vital military base. What's more, he said he was now more convinced than ever that the semi had just delivered a warhead, and perhaps the men in the SUV could "shed some light on the situation."

David needed to follow the SUV, figure out a way to isolate one of the men inside, interrogate him, and find out exactly what was in the semi and what was happening inside the Imam Ali missile base. He accepted the mission without hesitation, though he had no idea how he was going to pull it off.

He followed them along the front range of the Zagros Mountains into the city limits of Khorramabad, then into the downtown area. There, he stopped on a side street as he watched the SUV pull into a three-story parking garage by a small hotel called the Delvar, across from the post office and next door to a restaurant and an auto parts shop. He waited twenty minutes or so to make sure the vehicle didn't double back and leave the garage and to give the men plenty of time to check in and clear out of the lobby. Then he cautiously pulled into the garage. He spotted the SUV in the corner on the first level but drove up all three levels to get the lay of the land. Returning to the first level, he parked several spots away from the SUV, grabbed his suitcase, and headed into the lobby.

This was no Qom International Hotel, where he was supposed to have checked in by now. There was no marbled reception area, no elegant Persian carpets, no cozy lounge. There were three worn couches and three overstuffed chairs in the lobby that appeared as if they hadn't been replaced since the seventies. There was a dust-covered chandelier, but half of its lights had blown out. There was a wooden rack of tourist brochures that looked like they hadn't ever been touched. He doubted there was a Jacuzzi in the entire city, much less in this hotel, but David did notice a small, antiquated video surveillance camera over the front door, pointing back into the lobby, and another small camera mounted on the wall behind the reception desk. He made a note of both and went to check in.

Not finding anyone immediately, he rang a small silver bell on the counter. Soon a drowsy, disheveled, sixtysomething clerk appeared from a back room. He was a short, balding, thin man, nearly gaunt, with bushy gray eyebrows, wearing a wrinkled yellow shirt with a brown stain that almost matched his wide, frayed brown tie.

"May I help you?" he asked.

"I'm looking for a room for tonight and possibly tomorrow," David replied. "Do you have anything?"

"Only a few left, actually," the clerk said. "Never seen so much business in thirty years. You working at the base, too?"

"No, just passing through. Why do you ask?"

"Oh, no reason. Just lots of activity over there the last few nights. More than I've seen in quite some time. People keep checking in. People I've never seen before. Hard for a guy to get any sleep."

David smiled, but the old man wasn't kidding.

"ID?" the clerk asked.

David tensed. With everything else going on, he hadn't thought about the fact that he was going to have to hand over his passport. Now wasn't the time to let someone trace the name Reza Tabrizi to Khorramabad, of all places, when there was no legitimate reason to be there and he had already told Javad Nouri (among others) that he was going to be in Qom. But he had no other choice. Had he been thinking clearly, he would have parked down the street and slept in the car. But there was no turning back now. Reluctantly, he surrendered his passport and filled out the requisite paperwork, then paid for the first night in cash, since he certainly wasn't about to use a credit card.

Getting his key, he took the elevator up to the third floor and found room 308 down the hall and on the left, facing the parking garage. His room was small and cramped and smelled like mothballs, but he didn't expect to be spending much time there. He washed his face and brushed his teeth but didn't change and didn't unpack. Instead, he set the alarm on his phone for a half hour and caught a catnap.

Thirty minutes went by far too fast.

Nevertheless, David forced himself to get up, grabbed his suitcase, and took a back stairway to the first floor, where he cautiously poked his head out. Seeing no one around, he moved as quickly and quietly as he could down a side hallway, though he nearly crashed into a room service tray filled with dirty dinner dishes that apparently hadn't been cleared from the night before.

Reaching the end of the hallway, he glanced outside and again saw no one. It was five in the morning. There wasn't likely to be anyone around, but he couldn't take any chances. Confident it was all clear, he headed back to the parking garage and put his suitcase in the trunk. If he needed to move quickly, he didn't dare take the risk of leaving behind the only possessions he had with him in the country.

He reentered the hotel and decided to check on the clerk. Sure enough, his instincts were right. The old man was slumped in a chair in the room behind the reception desk, sound asleep and snoring, with an old black-and-white Persian war movie playing on TV. With no one else around and the hotel completely silent, David wasted no time. He slipped behind the desk, found the registration forms for the five men, and snapped a picture of each with his phone. Then he found the video surveillance system—an old VHS system he couldn't believe still worked—and rewound the two tapes covering the lobby. Using the video feature on his phone, he recorded the images of the five men entering the hotel and checking in. He rewound both tapes again, this time to the beginning, and hit Record on both decks. By the time anyone asked to see this footage, the images on them, including those of him checking in, would be recorded over and gone forever. Then he made sure everything was back in its place and hightailed it back to room 308.

There, he quickly uploaded the photos and the videos to Langley via his secure satellite channel and called Zalinsky to give him another update. Zalinsky promised to get Eva analyzing the images and told David the Predator drone was finally in position over the missile base. If the convoy left or if any other vehicles arrived, he said he would notify David immediately.

★ ★ ★ ★ ★

LANGLEY, VIRGINIA

Eva speed-dialed Zalinsky from her office.

It had only taken an hour. She explained that by cross-scanning the photos with the computer files from Dr. Saddaji that David and Najjar Malik had recently smuggled out of the country, she had tracked down the identities of four of the five suspects David was now tracking. She had names, birth dates, and personnel records on each of them. All four were experienced military police officers in the Iranian Revolutionary Guard Corps, assigned to Facility 278 in Hamadan. They were all excellent marksmen, two had received letters of commendation, and each had a top-secret security clearance. One had been the deputy director of perimeter security prior to Saddaji's assassination. She concluded that they fit the profile of a security force that could be tasked with transporting a warhead. She couldn't be certain, she said, but there was a strong probability.

Zalinsky agreed. It was circumstantial but increasingly compelling evidence that they had found another warhead. But before they could take it to Director Allen or the NSC, they needed more. He told her to call David right away and brief him on what she had found. She agreed but was concerned about Zalinsky. He didn't sound well.

"Jack, is everything all right?" she asked.

He didn't answer, but he didn't hang up either.

"Jack, what's the matter?"

Zalinsky cleared his throat. "It's about David."

"What? Is he all right? Did something happen?"

"No, no, it's not that," Zalinsky said. "It's not him directly. It's his mom. She passed away tonight."

Eva gasped. "That's terrible. When?"

"Just after six."

"How did you hear?"

"We've been monitoring Marseille Harper's calls and e-mails."

"Who?"

"You know, Marseille Harper? I helped her parents and the Shirazis get out of Iran during the Revolution. She and David were childhood friends, and she met with Tom Murray this morning."

There were too many dots to connect all at once for Eva. Marseille Harper? She remembered the name. She remembered that the Harpers had a daughter about David's age and that the death of Mrs. Harper in the 9/11 attacks was a huge turning point in David's life. But what was Marseille doing in DC? And here, at Langley? It didn't make sense. "What was she doing here?"

"It's a long story."

"But why would we monitor her? I mean, it's illegal for the CIA to monitor American citizens on US soil. You know that."

"It's not us directly," Zalinsky assured her. "We tipped off the FBI, they got a court order, and they've been keeping an eye on her."

"But why? I don't understand."

"Look, I don't have time to go through it all now. I'll fill in the blanks for you later. The bottom line is, Tom let it slip that David works for us. Marseille signed a nondisclosure form, but Tom's worried she might say something anyway."

"Let it slip?" Eva asked, incredulous. "How is that possible?"

"Just call David and brief him ASAP."

"Fine," Eva said. "But you owe me."

"Don't worry. I'll tell you everything. I promise. Apparently, there's history between them. I'm not exactly sure what. But I get the sense it's just flared back up."

Eva was speechless. Zalinsky was right. She'd had no idea, and she wasn't thrilled about it either. She hadn't felt such a strong flash of jealousy in years, and the intensity caught her by surprise. Still, she figured, she was the one in direct contact with David, not Marseille.

"Anytime," Eva said coolly. "I'm all ears. In the meantime, I'll tell David about his mom when I call him."

"No, not right now."

"Why not?"

"We can't distract him," Zalinsky argued. "There's too much on the line. Let's get through the next few days and see where we are."

Eva strongly disagreed but kept silent.

★ ★ ★ ★ ★

KHORRAMABAD, IRAN

David's phone rang.

He stepped out of the icy shower—the Delvar Hotel apparently didn't have any hot water that morning—and checked the caller ID. It was Eva. He grabbed a towel and took the call. She quickly briefed him on each of the four men she had identified so far.

"And the fifth?" David asked.

"No idea, but I'm guessing it's just another MP."

"Then why wouldn't his personnel records be in the files we got from Saddaji?"

"I'm just telling you what I know," Eva said. "But look, I'm sending you back still images of guys we've identified for certain. The rest, my friend, is up to you. And I don't need to remind you that—"

"—the clock is ticking."

"Sorry—guess that's why they pay you the big bucks."

"Oh, right."

"Getting any sleep?"

"Hardly."

"Well, take care of yourself. I'll say a prayer for you."

"Thanks, I'll take it," David said. "By the way, where are my guardian angels?"

"I heard they just landed at Desert Alpha about fifteen minutes ago and linked up with their local contact and got their vehicles. They're actually moving faster than expected. They should be to you in less than three hours."

David could tell by her tone that she was trying to encourage him. But at that moment, the news had just the opposite effect.

"We don't have three hours."

★ ★ ★ ★ ★

NATANZ, IRAN

Jalal Zandi was startled awake by the shrieking ring of his mobile phone.

He rolled over, checked his watch, and took the call.

"The cakes arrived safely," said a voice that was electronically muffled.

"Good," he said, trying in vain to rub the fatigue out of his eyes. "Get them ready for delivery."

"We've already started."

★ ★ ★ ★ ★

KHORRAMABAD, IRAN

David got dressed quickly and headed down to the lobby.

He was going through caffeine withdrawal and hoped the desk clerk either had made a pot of coffee or could point him in the right direction posthaste. Fortunately, even before he got off the elevator, he could smell the answer. He reached the first floor and made his way directly to a small table where a fresh pot had just finished brewing. He poured himself a large cup, tossed in a few sugars for good measure, then noticed that the hotel actually had a gift shop and that it was open. He was surprised he hadn't noticed it a few hours earlier, but then he'd had other things on his mind. He went in, bought a local newspaper, and sat down on one of the forty-year-old overstuffed chairs in the lobby to wait.

About twenty minutes later, a young man in his thirties wearing khaki pants, a blue dress shirt, and a black leather jacket stepped off the elevator and rang the silver bell at the front desk. He was unshaven but well built, about five feet ten inches tall, with closely cropped hair. David recognized him instantly but took a quick check of the still photos Eva had sent just to make sure. Slowly the barely awake clerk padded out from the back room.

"Yes?" he groaned.

"I want to buy some gum, and I need some petrol for my truck," the young man said.

The clerk mumbled something about the gift shop and gave the young man directions to a gas station "two blocks down that way and one block to your left."

David stood, folded his paper, gulped down his coffee, and nodded politely as the young man headed into the gift shop. The moment the man was out of sight, David moved quickly down the side hallway toward the exit. Seeing the room service tray still in the hallway, he scooped up a used steak knife as he passed by and then bolted for the parking garage.

It was still early. There were only a few cars on the street and no one in the garage.

After verifying that there were no security cameras in the garage, David headed directly for the black SUV, then plunged the knife into the right rear tire several times. Within seconds, the tire had deflated. Next, David walked over to his Peugeot, opened the trunk, tucked the steak knife into a side pocket of his suitcase, and placed the suitcase on the floor by the front passenger seat. Then he grabbed the tire iron out of the trunk and pried off his license plates, first in the back and then in the front. He stuffed these in his suitcase as well and returned to the open trunk.

Soon the young man in the leather jacket came strolling into the garage. He was whistling until he saw the flat tire; then he started cursing up a storm.

"What's wrong?" David asked innocently, preparing to close his trunk.

The man pointed to the tire and just stared at it, cursing some more. David walked over to take a look.

"Need some help?" he asked, approaching the man from behind.

Still grumbling, the man turned toward David. Just then, David sucker punched him in the face full force with the tire iron in one violent motion. The man flew back against the SUV, and David smashed him over the head with the iron, sending him crashing to the pavement, bleeding and unconscious.

David looked around. There was still no one in sight, but that might not last for long. He checked the guy's pulse. He was still alive. Then he quickly looked inside the guy's coat and, as he'd expected, found a holster with a silencer-equipped pistol. He removed the pistol and tucked it into the back of his own trousers. He picked the man up, carried him over to the Peugeot, and set him in the trunk. He quickly fished through the guy's pockets, removed his wallet, car keys, room key, IRGC ID badge, mobile phone, and an extra magazine of 9mm ammunition, and put all those in his own pockets. Satisfied that the young man was picked clean, he closed the trunk and locked it. Then he got in the car, started the engine, and pulled out of the parking garage, heading east on Route 62.

47

David put on his Bluetooth headset and speed-dialed Zalinsky.

He got Eva instead. "Where's Jack?"

"In a meeting."

"I need him, fast."

"He's in with Tom. They don't want to be disturbed. Jack told me to take your call. Where are you?"

"I'm heading east toward a town called Alamdasht. I saw a dusty side road not far from there. I have a guest with me."

"A guest?"

"Morteza Yaghoubi."

He briefly explained, then found the side road, pulled off the highway, and drove another couple of miles until he found a small stand of trees surrounding a tiny pond that seemed, at least for now, well out of view of any human being. He backed the car beneath the trees and turned off the engine. There, he opened Yaghoubi's mobile phone, pulled out his SIM card, stuck it into his own phone for a moment, and uploaded all of the data to Eva. Then he replaced his own SIM card and restored Yaghoubi's phone. Next, he riffled through the guy's wallet, snapped a photo of his driver's license and another of his IRGC ID, and uploaded those to Eva as well.

"So what's your plan?" Eva asked as she downloaded all the data, half a world away.

"Motivate this guy to talk. See what he knows."

"Motivate, huh?"

"Hey, it's not like I can send him to Gitmo just now."

"No, I guess not."

"What do we know about him so far?"

There was a pause as Eva pulled up his file. "Morteza Yaghoubi, thirty-four years old, born in Tehran, unmarried, no children, has served in the intelligence division for twelve years," Eva began. "So far, he sounds like me."

"Very funny," David said, not laughing. "Keep going, come on."

"Okay, hold your horses. I'm getting there," she said, pulling up more data. "Started out in the al-Quds Force. Trained Hezbollah suicide bombers in the Bekaa Valley. Supplied IEDs to the Mahdi Army in Iraq. Trained Mahdi Army insurgents how to wage ambushes against US forces in Fallujah and Mosul. Was wounded in a botched attack on a Red Cross convoy outside of Baghdad. Was then assigned to the military police unit at Facility 278 two years ago. From what it says here, it would seem he was part of the personal security detail for Dr. Saddaji. Expert marksman. Twice decorated."

"Sounds like a prince. Anything else?"

"Yeah, I wouldn't let him out of the trunk."

"Good point."

"I'll cut and paste what seems relevant and e-mail it to you."

"Thanks. Now let's go through his phone."

"I'm already on it," Eva said. "My computer is cross-checking any names and numbers in his phone directory with our database."

"Any hits?"

"Well, not surprisingly, he's got the phone numbers for the other three MPs back in that hotel—if they're still there."

"E-mail me those," David said. "That could come in handy. What else?"

"He's got all of Najjar's numbers in Hamadan."

"Makes sense."

"The rest look like friends, family, other colleagues, but no one else we have in our records."

"Do me a favor and search for Javad Nouri."

"I already have," Eva replied, explaining that she had already searched for any of the names and numbers David had previously given them.

"What about Firouz Nouri and the other guy, Jamshad? I don't have those."

"He doesn't either."

"Okay, that's enough. I'm going to open the trunk and pour a bucket of water over this guy's head."

"Be careful."

"Don't worry."

He picked up the pistol off the passenger seat beside him and made sure the safety was disengaged. Then he chambered a round and got out of the car.

"You still there?" he asked.

"Of course," Eva said.

"Good. Stay on the line. If this goes bad, at least you'll know what happened and where to find my body."

He walked to the water's edge and looked for something he could fill with water. "You can never find a good bowl or a hat when you need one," he said, rooting around the area for anything he could use.

"Story of my life," Eva quipped.

"What's that supposed to mean?"

"I don't know. I'm getting a little punchy. Give me something to do. I can't just sit here and wait until this guy jumps out of the trunk at you with a meat cleaver or something."

"Thanks. Fine. Look up some more numbers."

"Which ones?"

"I don't know," David said. "Hey, look, I found an old pop can. Maybe this will work."

He filled it with pond water and had a thought.

"Try Jalal Zandi," he said, carrying the pop can of water back to the trunk.

"Sorry," Eva said. "Nothing."

"Okay, how about Tariq Khan?"

He had just gotten back to the Peugeot and was about to open the trunk when Eva's tone changed completely. "That's it, David. We got a hit."

"What do you mean?"

"Tariq Khan," she said. "He's got his mobile number and e-mail address in his phone."

"You're kidding."

"I'm not."

"Can you run a trace through the Iran Telecom system and find Khan's phone?"

"I'm doing that now. Hold on."

David set down the pop can and studied the pistol. He was glad to have it but hoped he didn't have to use it. He had trained for all eventualities, and he was ready if he needed to be. But he had just killed men for the first time the week before in Tehran, and it was still haunting him. He'd be fine if he never had to do that again.

"Got it," Eva exclaimed.

"Can you triangulate its position and tell me exactly where Khan is?"

"I don't believe this," Eva said.

"You got him?"

"You're not going to believe this either."

"Why? Where is he?"

"The Delvar Hotel," Eva said. "He's on the second floor."

★ ★ ★ ★ ★

JERUSALEM, ISRAEL

Naphtali was set to meet with his Security Cabinet.

But as promised, he met first with Levi Shimon for a light breakfast of coffee, yogurt, and some fruit.

"The answer is no," Shimon said immediately as they sat down.

"Levi, that's not acceptable."

"I'm sorry, Asher, but I can't tell you the details of our asset in Tehran. It goes against all IDF and Mossad protocols and it's dangerous, and you know it. Look, either you trust me or you don't. And I'm telling you, I trust Mordecai. He's been right every time. We've tested and challenged him in a dozen different ways. If he was a double, we'd know it. If he was a fraud, we'd have figured that out by now. He's the real thing, Asher. Like Mordecai in the book of Hadassah, he has been chosen by Yahweh Himself to save us from the Persians. What does the Tanakh really tell us about Mordecai, right? We know he was a Jew in Susa, the capital of the empire at that time. We know he was the son of Jair, the son of Shimei, the son of Kish, a Benjamite who had been taken into exile from Jerusalem by Nebuchadnezzar. We know he was Hadassah's older cousin but that he raised her as his own daughter. We know he was wise and resourceful and that the Lord gave him unique insight into the mind of the enemy and how to counter him. That's it. That's all we know. Yet isn't that enough?"

"Not for Hadassah," the prime minister countered. "She didn't trust him blindly. She knew everything about Mordecai because she was raised by him, which is why she listened to him. And besides, he was Jewish, just like her. He was in exile, just like her. They had a common heritage. They were facing a common threat and the same fate. What about your Mordecai, your man in Susa, as it were? Is he Jewish?"

"Of course not."

"Is he going to perish with us if Iran fires eight nuclear warheads at us?"

"No."

"Then why should I trust him?"

★　★　★　★　★

NEAR ALAMDASHT, IRAN

David jumped back in the car and started the engine.

"Reposition the Predator over the hotel," he told Eva.

"I can't do that."

"You have to. I'm going back to the hotel, and I'm going to need as much intel as I can get."

"Only Jack is authorized to retask the Predator."

"Then get him," David ordered as he drove down the dirt road.

"He's in a meeting."

"Pull him out."

"He's in a knock-down, drag-out fight with Tom."

"Over what?"

"The president is refusing to let Roger share with the Israelis what we've learned about the two warheads the Iranians have in the Med."

"We're not talking to the Israelis about it?"

"No."

"Why not? That's crazy. They're the best ally we have over here."

"That's Jack's point. He's trying to tell Tom we have a moral obligation to tell the Israelis—off the record, at least—what we know, even if the president has forbidden any official briefing, but Tom's not buying it."

David pulled onto Route 37 again, heading west into Khorramabad. He was infuriated with the president and with Murray, and he was fearful for the Israelis, who were in growing danger of being blindsided. But at the moment, he didn't have time for politics. "Eva, I don't care how you do it. I need that Predator over that hotel in the next ten minutes. Just make it happen. I'm counting on you."

He hung up and sped back to the hotel, trying to develop a plan. His first problem was that Morteza Yaghoubi was going to be waking up soon in his trunk. The guy was a trained killer. What exactly was he supposed to do with him? If he left him in there, Yaghoubi would soon be screaming bloody murder until someone came to get him or until David put a bullet in his forehead. But he didn't want to kill him. Not unless he had to. The man was the enemy, but David was now a follower of Jesus. Wasn't he supposed to love his enemies? Still, he couldn't just dump him at the side of the road. If he got to a phone and alerted anyone, David was a dead man. That said, Yaghoubi was the least of his worries.

David was about to take on three IRGC operatives who were equally vicious, each of whom was armed and incredibly dangerous. Even if he could figure out a way to isolate Khan and get him away from the others to interrogate him—something he still wasn't sure how to do—he couldn't figure out how to do it without killing at least one of the four operatives, and maybe all four. Again, if even one of them made a phone call to the missile base, he was a dead man. If a hotel guest overheard any of them fighting or struggling or even raising his voice, he was a dead man.

David assessed his options, but there weren't many. He had no way to tie up any of the men or keep them quiet, and the CIA special forces team was still two hours away.

He got back to the hotel and pulled into an alley on the opposite side of the building from the parking garage. His phone rang. He took it on the Bluetooth again so there was no chance of Yaghoubi overhearing.

"It's done," Eva said. "I'm streaming the live feed to your phone now."

He opened the video feature on his phone and punched in a passcode that allowed him to receive a video stream rather than send one. A moment later, he was looking at pictures directly from the Predator, three miles above them.

"Can you switch to thermal imaging?" he asked.

"Sure, one second. . . . Okay, there—can you see it?"

"Yes—got it."

He could now see two of the Revolutionary Guard security men in room 203. He could also see Khan and another security man in room 201, though he couldn't tell which was which. What was the best way into 201? He could pose as a room service guy, but that had risks. He'd have to wait for them to order, and he'd have to intercept the actual hotel employee, and what would he do with him? David immediately ruled that out. Another option was posing as a maintenance man. But under what pretext could he try to do repairs in room 201 so early in the morning without raising suspicions? He ruled that out as well.

Even if he could get the men in 201 to open the door, was there a way to get Khan out without alerting the men next door? He had a silencer. But he'd have to kill the security man, and what if he screamed? What if Khan yelled? And which one *was* Tariq Khan? He'd never even seen a decent image of the man. True, he had photos of all the IRGC operatives, but he couldn't take the risk that he'd kill Khan by mistake or in the cross fire.

He remembered he had Yaghoubi's key. Maybe it was to room 201. He reached into his pocket and pulled it out. No such luck. It was stamped with the number 203. So that was that.

David turned off the engine. He took the pistol off the passenger seat and put it in his jacket pocket, got out of the car, and locked the door. Then he reentered the hotel through the side hallway, carefully stepping over the room-service tray. The lobby was empty and quiet, and the clerk was nowhere to be seen, so he ducked into the stairwell and double-timed it to the second floor, pausing at the exit door to draw his weapon and make sure again the safety was off.

48

David had never felt guilty holding a pistol before.

Now he did.

He'd had no time to think through what his newfound faith meant to his job, and there was no one to ask, at least not now. What would Birjandi tell him? What about Marseille? Then again, Charlie Harper might be the closer analogy. He'd been an NOC. He'd been trained at the Farm to kill without a moment's hesitation. He'd surely been told again and again, "This is war, and you're the good guy, and he's the enemy—never confuse the two." It was true, even wise, as far as it went. But had Charlie been a follower of Jesus when he'd served in the CIA? David seriously doubted that. His life, sadly, showed no evidence of having been changed. And he hadn't raised Marseille to love Jesus. She certainly hadn't been a true follower of Christ when they'd been together in Canada. Marseille seemed to have come to faith in college, or maybe late in high school, but not as a child. Maybe Charlie Harper was no help at all.

He peeked through the small window in the exit door. There was no one in the hallway. He was free to move. But when he glanced down at his phone, he noticed a new complication. As he looked at the thermal images from the Predator, it appeared as if the men in rooms 201 and 203 were passing through walls, back and forth. It took him a moment, but then he realized that the door between the two rooms, which were side by side, had to be open. Now he was even more at risk of killing Khan by accident.

"We have a problem," he whispered.

"You don't know which one is Khan," Eva replied as if reading his mind.

"Right. I don't want to go in there and pull out the wrong guy or accidentally blow him away."

"Actually, you've got another problem," Eva said.

"What?"

"I've got NSA covering all the phones in those two rooms. They say Khan just took a call from someone at the missile base. They need him back immediately. They're not going to be in those rooms for long."

Yaghoubi's phone began to vibrate in David's pocket. They were looking for him to get the truck and take them back to the base. David was out of time. He had to move now.

"Do you see which one is making a call right now?" he asked.

"Yes," Eva said.

"Is that Khan's phone?"

"No. Why?"

"Whoever it is, he's calling Yaghoubi. They're about to leave. This is my last chance. What should I do?"

Eva had an idea. "Call Khan," she said.

"What? Are you crazy? He doesn't know who I am."

"No, use Yaghoubi's phone. Dial him just before you enter the room. Whoever's on the phone when you go in will be him."

"Okay, that's good. Now, look, can NSA jam or cut off the other mobile numbers so none of those guys can call out?"

Eva said yes, but it would take a few minutes.

"Do it now. Yaghoubi's phone is ringing again. They're getting desperate. I have to move."

David was about to head down the hall.

"*Wait!*" Eva yelled.

Startled by her vehemence, he stopped, backed into the stairwell again, and pressed against the wall, not knowing why. A moment later, the door to room 201 opened, and someone came out.

"Who is that?" David whispered.

"I don't know."

"It can't be Khan," David said. "They wouldn't let him move by himself."

Whoever it was came down the hall, pushed the button for the elevator, and waited. David debated what he'd do if the man came into the stairwell. At least he'd have the element of surprise.

But it didn't happen. The elevator bell rang, the door opened, and the security guy got in.

That created a new problem. Once he got to the parking garage and found the tire flat and didn't find Yaghoubi, he'd know something was wrong. He'd alert someone, and then what would David do?

There was nothing left to think about, David decided. This *was* war. These people weren't innocent civilians. They were terrorists. They were working for an apocalyptic, genocidal regime. They were working for a false messiah. They were trying to kill six million innocent civilians in Israel and 300 million more if they could ever reach the United States. He didn't want to kill them, but they were armed and hostile, and if he had to do it, he wasn't going to feel guilty about it. He didn't have the luxury.

He glanced back down the hall. It was clear, so he adjusted his headset and moved quickly and quietly through the exit door, the pistol in his right hand, his left hand dialing Khan. It started ringing. He pulled out the key and slowly inserted it into the door of 203.

"Hey, man, where are you?" Khan said.

"I'm here now," David said, muffling his voice slightly and turning the key.

"Where?"

"You ready?"

"What?"

David shoved the phone in his jacket pocket. Then he turned the handle and kicked the door in and entered the room quickly. One of the security detail wheeled around. The look of shock on his face registered instantly. He went for his weapon and David put two rounds into his forehead, dropping the man instantly. The second man dove through the open door between the two rooms, shouting in Farsi, *"Get down!*

Get down!" David saw him jump on Khan and pull him to the floor between the beds. Khan's phone went flying.

David pivoted around the corner and squeezed off a shot, but it missed and shattered a lamp on the nightstand. He pulled back behind the wall as the security man fired two shots, then two more. David waited a fraction of a second, then spun around the corner again and squeezed off two shots of his own. Someone screamed out in pain. Blood splattered all over the wall and the bedspreads. David didn't hesitate. He charged into the room and saw the security man grabbing his shoulder and writhing in pain. But at that moment, the man turned and saw David's face. His eyes went wide. He raised his weapon again and David double-tapped him in the head.

Now Khan was screaming.

David couldn't tell if he, too, had been hit, but he pointed the pistol at Khan's face, which was covered in blood.

"Silence," he commanded in Urdu, *"or you're next."*

Khan appeared stunned to hear his native language and shut his mouth. David, suddenly grateful for the trips into Pakistan when Zalinsky had him working with Mobilink and hunting al Qaeda operatives, pointed to the pistol on the floor and told Khan to kick it to him. Khan did as he was told. David picked up the pistol, removed the magazine and put it in his pocket, then tossed the gun.

"Get up—*move,*" he ordered.

Khan stood to his feet, trembling.

"Use a pillowcase. Wipe the blood off your face and hands."

Khan complied.

"Now get your phone—and keep your hands where I can see them."

Khan walked over by the desk and picked up his phone.

"Toss it to me." David caught the phone and put it in his jacket pocket. "Now stand there for a moment."

Again, Khan obeyed. David now backed into Room 203 and glanced at the two dead men on the floor. They weren't moving, but he put another round into each of them, just to be sure. Neither so much as twitched. He quickly cleared their weapons, took their magazines, wallets, keys, and IDs and put them in a pillowcase, tied the end of the case in a knot, and tossed the bundle to Khan.

"Come here," David ordered, careful to keep his voice down.

Khan cautiously stepped into 203. His hands were trembling.

"Stop." He checked to make sure his Bluetooth was still on. It was. "Where's the fourth man?" he asked Eva.

"He's at the SUV, checking out the tire, looking around," Eva replied.

"His phone is jammed?"

"Yes."

"Good. Is the hallway clear?"

"It is for now."

"Okay, we're coming out."

David looked at Khan. "Move. Now. Or I will put a bullet through your skull. Open the door. Turn right. Go quickly down to the end of the hall and into the stairwell. I'll be right behind you."

Khan opened the door, and they started moving rapidly. David practically pushed the man through the exit, then down the stairs. They burst out onto the first floor, and to David's shock the lobby was full. A tour bus was parked outside, and dozens of senior citizens were milling about. What stunned David most, though, was the sight of two uniformed military officers checking in at the front desk. The noise of the stairwell door opening so quickly and slamming against the wall shocked everyone and drew their attention, including the officers. Their eyes went wide and David assumed they were staring into Khan's terrified eyes. This was not going as planned.

Instantly the officers drew their weapons. David fired two rounds at each, felling one of them but only wounding the other. He pushed Khan down the back hallway.

"Go, go, go!" he yelled in Urdu, then heard the explosion of a .45-caliber pistol behind him.

The rounds went high, but David couldn't take any chances. He pushed Khan through the exit door, then wheeled around and tried to fire back at the officer, but he was out of ammunition. He hit the deck as the man shot two more rounds, and he could hear the bullets whizzing over his head. He quickly scrambled out the back exit, pulling a second magazine from his pocket, ejecting the spent magazine, and reloading. He reached the Peugeot just as the officer crashed through the door. David ducked behind the trunk of the car, then popped out and put four rounds in the man's chest.

With no time to waste, he grabbed Khan, unlocked the car, and threw him in the backseat.

"Get on the floor, facedown, and don't get up!" he ordered, again in Urdu.

He hadn't thought of how to keep Khan restrained or quiet. He had nothing to tie his hands, nothing to stuff in his mouth. He couldn't afford the risk of Khan knocking him out as he drove or seizing him by the throat or, God forbid, jumping out of the moving car. He needed this prisoner alive above all else. He needed to interrogate him quickly and find out everything he knew about the warheads and their locations. But under no circumstances could he let Khan escape or take the initiative.

He didn't want to do it, but he had no time and no choice. He fired a bullet into the back of Khan's right knee.

The man screamed in pain, but he wasn't going anywhere.

49

A bullet sizzled over David's head.

Then another. Both smashed into a brick wall behind him.

David ducked behind the car. He peeked around the side and saw the fourth man running flat out from the parking garage, gun in his hand. David squeezed off two rounds. He missed but sent the man diving for cover. He didn't have time for more. He jumped into the front seat, slammed his door shut, and started the engine.

The back window exploded. The man was firing again.

David lowered his head, hit the gas, and raced down the alley. The security man was running hard behind him, firing again and again. Tires screeching, David peeled out onto the main street, narrowly missing the tail end of the tour bus in the process. The Peugeot was fishtailing. Fighting to regain control, he turned the wheel hard to the right, then back again to the left. He was about to accelerate when a pickup truck filled with crates of vegetables suddenly pulled out onto the street in front of him. David swerved hard to the right to miss it but clipped the back of the truck and spun out.

He jammed the car into reverse and started backing away from the pickup, but as he looked into his rearview mirror, he saw the final Revolutionary Guard operative dragging a businessman out of a silver Mercedes W211 at gunpoint, throwing him to the street, and jumping into the driver's seat. David maneuvered away from the pickup as quickly as he could, then slammed the car into drive again and tromped on the accelerator on a straightaway through the center of the city. He was gaining speed—*forty kilometers per hour, fifty, sixty, seventy*—but the Mercedes was accelerating as well and rapidly closing the gap as the man continued firing at the Peugeot. David could hear round after round hitting the trunk, what was left of the back window, and the rear bumper.

"Stay down!" he ordered Khan.

As their speeds kept accelerating and the security operative kept firing, David now feared the man's objective might not be to run him down as much as to kill the man he was sworn to protect, to prevent him from talking.

Swerving in and out of oncoming traffic, David knew it was only a matter of time before someone called the police. He had to lose this Mercedes, ditch the Peugeot, and get Khan someplace safe and quiet to find out what he knew and get it back to Langley before they were both dead. He glanced in his rearview mirror. The Mercedes was weaving in and out of traffic as well, but not as quickly. David could see he was actually gaining some ground, but it wasn't enough.

He glanced into the backseat. Blood was everywhere. Khan was writhing and screaming in pain. In the rush of adrenaline, David hadn't even heard the man for the last few minutes; he'd been focused on not crashing the car or being overtaken by the Mercedes. But now he realized he had even less time than he thought. If Khan didn't get a tourniquet on that leg soon and some medicine, he was either going to black out or bleed out. Either would render all of this worthless. His mind was racing, but he was coming up with nothing.

"You still there?" he yelled as he passed a tractor trailer at a speed now topping 120 kilometers an hour and heading fast toward 140.

"I'm here," Eva said.

"You sure this guy's phone is jammed?"

"Absolutely—ever since he stepped out of the hotel."

"He hasn't made a single call."

"No, he hasn't."

"Because if this guy calls for backup, that's it. You know that, don't you?"

There was a momentary pause; then Eva replied, "David, the whole hotel is calling the police now."

Now that they were out of the congested traffic of Khorramabad and onto Route 37 heading east through towns David had never heard of before, he knew he was in trouble. The Mercedes W211 behind him was a newer, sleeker, and vastly more powerful car than his Peugeot 407 rental. It had a five-liter V8 engine, compared with the Peugeot's three-liter V6. It was no surprise the Mercedes was now gaining on him.

It wasn't a complete straight shot back to the fork with Route 62. There were some curves in the roads and a few hills. There were moments when David could see the Mercedes, but they were fewer and farther between now. Unfortunately there were no useful exits and few decent side roads for another forty kilometers.

"David, come on, man—lose this guy," Eva urged.

"I can't," David said. *"He's too fast."*

"Do something," Eva pressed.

"I'm doing everything I know."

"He's almost on you."

David could hear genuine fear in her voice—whether it was for him or the mission, he didn't know; probably both—but either way, it unnerved him. Eva was usually the steadiest on their team, cool under pressure, logical and methodical. If she was this scared, he was in even more trouble than he thought.

"Then take him out," David shouted at last.

There was silence on the other end of the line.

"Did you hear me?" David repeated. *"Take him out."*

"What do you mean?" Eva asked, sounding back in control of her emotions.

"You've got a Predator. It's got missiles. Take this guy out now before Khan and I die."

"David, I can't."

"Of course you can."

"No, you don't understand; I can't," she said again. "I wasn't authorized to retask this Predator in the first place, much less order it to fire inside Iran. Murray will have my head."

"Are you kidding me?" David yelled. *"I've got the number two nuclear*

scientist in the country in my backseat, and the entire Iranian Revolutionary Guard Corps is about to come down on me. Now take this guy out—NOW!"

David went whipping through a few light turns. As he rounded the last one, he could see a clear, open stretch of road ahead of him for at least five or six kilometers. No turns. No hills. Not much traffic. It was a kill zone for either the Mercedes or him.

He pressed the pedal to the floor and gripped the steering wheel for dear life. The car was now pushing 140 kilometers an hour. Then 150. Then 160. Then 165. He knew the car's top speed was 117 miles—about 190 kilometers—per hour. He'd never imagined pushing such a car to its limit, but what choice did he have? The Mercedes could top 200 miles—or about 320 kilometers—an hour.

David glanced again in his mirror. The Mercedes was about a quarter mile behind and closing fast. All kinds of options flashed through his mind. He could slam on the brakes and hope the guy raced right by. But that was more likely to flip the car, he figured, and kill them all.

He could slow down more gradually and try to engage his pursuer in a gun battle. How much additional ammo could the guy possibly have on him—one mag, two, three at most? Yaghoubi had only been carrying one extra. That was most likely. David now had the one in the pistol (Yaghoubi's spare) and the three he'd picked up in the hotel room. Still, slowing down and getting out of the Peugeot also meant the guy could stall for time until backup arrived. There was no question it was coming. It was just a matter of how soon.

Then again, what if he slowed down, spun the car around, and played chicken? Of course, then he'd be driving right back into Khorramabad, about the last place in the world he wanted to be just then.

He glanced back again. The Mercedes was now only a few hundred meters behind. A few moments later he was only one hundred meters back, and David still had no better plan than the Predator, though he certainly didn't want to be anywhere near the Mercedes if and when fire came raining down from the sky.

"Where are you?" he yelled.

But no one answered.

★ ★ ★ ★ ★

What David didn't know was that death was already on its way.

At an altitude of 17,429 feet, the CIA's $4.5-million, state-of-the-art unmanned aerial vehicle known as the MQ-1 Predator had already received its encoded orders. They had come from the Third Special Operations Squadron at Cannon Air Force Base in Clovis, New Mexico, after originating from the Global Operations Center at CIA headquarters in Langley.

Now, a five-and-a-half-foot, one-hundred-pound AGM-114 Hellfire air-to-ground missile was sizzling through the crisp morning air at Mach 1.3. The entire journey took barely eighteen seconds.

Suddenly the Mercedes behind David erupted in an enormous ball of fire. It scared Tariq Khan half to death, but David thanked God for answering his prayer.

50

The PM's motorcade arrived at the Defense Ministry.

Flanked by an enhanced security detail, Asher Naphtali and Levi Shimon made their way to the strategic planning center, five levels down. Even more than the White House Situation Room, the IDF's "war room" was a high-tech wonder, looking more like a television network control room than a corporate boardroom. Some two dozen mid-size video monitors and electronic maps lined the side walls, while large flat-screen plasma monitors were mounted at either end of the room. A control panel at the head of the table allowed whoever was running the meeting to transfer images from any of the individual monitors to the larger screens and to manage secure videoconferences with live feeds from every Israeli military base in the country and any Israeli diplomatic facility around the world.

Upon entering the room, they found the Security Cabinet already assembled and waiting. In addition to the PM and the defense minister, this typically included the vice prime minister, the minister of foreign affairs, the minister of internal security, the finance minister, the minister for strategic planning, the justice minister, and the chief of staff of the Israeli Defense Forces. That morning, it also included the directors-general of Shin Bet and the Mossad and the prime minister's military secretary, as well as senior commanders from the army, the air force, and the navy.

Naphtali took his seat at the head of the table and began immediately. "At present we face a moment unlike any other in the modern history of the State of Israel. This is not comparable to 1948 or '67, or even '73. This is 1939, and we are on the brink of annihilation.

"As you know, we have confirmed that Iran has eight nuclear warheads. Our latest intelligence indicates that at least several of these warheads have been attached to high-speed ballistic missiles and that this madman, the Twelfth Imam, intends to launch these warheads at us in the next few days, by Monday at the latest. I don't have to tell you, gentlemen, that if he authorizes such an attack, he could do in about six minutes what it took Adolf Hitler nearly six years to do, and that is to kill six million of us.

"The difference between then and now is that we have a state. We have an air force, and we have strategic weaponry; our parents and grandparents did not. History will never forgive us, my friends, if we do not act with courage and foresight before it is too late.

"Now, I am sorry to say that our assessment of the Jackson administration is that they do not seem to understand the gravity of the situation. I have had lengthy personal conversations over recent months and even in the last week with President Jackson. Levi and I have had extensive conversations with the president's most-senior national security advisors, including CIA director Allen. Some of them understand the stakes, but it is clear to Levi and me that the president does not. I think our foreign minister here can attest to the fact that most of the leaders of NATO and the United Nations don't see the crisis clearly and are not ready to take decisive action."

The foreign minister, already stricken with a grave countenance, nodded.

"So we are at a moment of decision, one we must not take lightly," Naphtali continued. "As you know, from the moment I took office, I instructed all of you to be working on a comprehensive war plan that we have code-named Operation Xerxes. It is time for us to put this plan into motion. I have asked Levi here to brief us on some of the final operational details.

"First, however, let me say this is not the first time the Jewish people have been faced with the threat of annihilation by the leaders of Persia. In the Ketuvim, we read the story of Hadassah and Mordecai facing the wicked Xerxes, king of the Medo-Persian Empire, and his arguably more wicked deputy, Haman, Persia's president or prime minister at the time. We read in the ancient text that our ancestors faced a very dark hour. They faced certain destruction of the entire Jewish race. To whom, then, did they turn? To the American president? To NATO? To the UN Security Council? No. They turned to the God of Abraham, Isaac, and Jacob through prayer and fasting, and they mobilized other Jews to do the same. And though the name of the Lord is never mentioned in the entire book, we can see His fingerprints everywhere. For clearly the God of Israel heard and answered their prayers. Xerxes changed his mind. Haman was hanged. The regime was fundamentally changed. The war still came. The Jews still had to fight. But the Lord was with them, and they prevailed in one of the most spectacular victories recorded in the Tanakh."

Naphtali looked around the room and leaned forward in his seat.

"We have been praying for a miracle, for a regime change, for Hosseini to change his mind and Darazi to die, or some combination thereof. Thus far, those specifics have not happened, but I am confident that the God of Israel is still with us and that He is answering our prayers in ways that we do not yet see. One thing is clear: it is time for us to fight. Indeed, we have run out of time for anything else if we intend to survive. And, gentlemen, that is my intention. This will not be easy. In fact, I believe it will be the most difficult mission our nation and our armed forces have ever undertaken. Israel will suffer. The region will suffer. The Iranian people will suffer. But I see no other way, and in the end, I believe good will triumph over evil, and I hope to God that you do too."

★ ★ ★ ★ ★

NATANZ, IRAN

Jalal Zandi took the urgent call in his office.

Having been up most of the night overseeing the missile technicians, he was bleary and bloodshot and had just poured himself another large cup of thick, black coffee.

"Missing?" he asked between sips. "How long? . . . Gunshots? You're absolutely certain? . . . No, you've done the right thing. . . . What? . . . No, get this thing contained—I'll let the leadership know. . . . Yes, absolutely. . . . Okay, call me the minute you know more."

Zandi hung up the phone in disbelief. Tariq Khan was gone. Dead bodies were all over the scene. What did that mean? Who had done it? And were they coming for him next?

★ ★ ★ ★ ★

TEL AVIV, ISRAEL

Naphtali turned the meeting over to his defense minister.

"Thank you, Mr. Prime Minister," Shimon began. "As you know, gentlemen, we have multiple assets inside Iran who are feeding us detailed information. We are hopeful that in the next twenty-four to forty-eight hours, we will have precise targeting information to take out those eight warheads. But I must stress that I am advising the prime minister that we must be willing to attack by the beginning of Shabbat at the latest even if we do not have this information, or we will lose the initiative and, most importantly, the element of surprise.

"Surprise, of course, is a relative term. There is much concern inside Iran and around the world that we may be preparing for a strike. We have, therefore, been doing everything we can to make final preparations as discreetly as possible, as per our discussions here in this room over the last few months."

Shimon directed the attention of the Security Cabinet to the large flat-screen monitors as he walked them through a highly classified PowerPoint presentation on Operation Xerxes.

"We recently ran an exercise in which we sent some four hundred planes on a practice bombing run to Greece, given that Greece is roughly the same distance from Israel to the west as Iran is from us to the east," Shimon continued. "This was the second such exercise of its kind, though the first one involved only about a hundred planes. The purpose of this exercise was severalfold, but let me focus on two critical elements. First, we needed to see if we really could pull off such a massive air attack. I'm pleased to report that while we had numerous glitches, all of them have been fixed, and the IDF and I believe the answer is now yes, we could, if we were so asked. Second, we needed to get the Iranians—and the rest of the world—thinking that we are planning for a much larger-scale air attack than they had previously considered. This was done to confuse our enemies and our friends alike, to have them watching for grander preparations. But the truth is, we believe a smaller strike force is prudent. Let me explain."

For the next thirty minutes, the defense minister provided a detailed picture of what the IDF and IAF were preparing to unleash. Using satellite photos, maps, and pictures taken by assets on the ground, he identified sixteen Iranian facilities that would be targeted, ranging from nuclear research-and-development facilities and missile-production-and-launch facilities, to the Iranian Defense Ministry and the regime's intelligence headquarters in downtown Tehran. He noted that fourteen of the targets had been subjected to extensive surveillance and detailed attack planning for nearly eighteen months. Two, however, were new in the last few days—the Iranian naval flotilla steaming through international waters in the Mediterranean, and something called the Qaleh, the Supreme Leader's mountain retreat center, only recently uncovered by a Mossad asset within the regime.

"Rather than send a massive armada of four hundred planes that could be detected by every intelligence agency in the region the moment it left the ground," Shimon explained, "the idea is to send small squadrons taking different routes to attack each of the individual sites. We'll also need additional fighter jets for security to accompany those carrying the bombs, as well as refueling tankers, electronic warfare planes, and so forth, but the pilots have been practicing for months, and we feel confident that they can move with little or no notice, once the prime minister gives the word."

The questions came fast and furious.

"What is the total number of aircraft you plan to use?" the foreign minister asked.

Shimon explained that they were looking at using between 116 and 168 planes, depending on the final targets chosen. In the low-end scenario, he said, they would deploy fifty-two fighter jets if each jet were dropping two bunker-buster bombs on its target. These would be guarded by an additional fifty F-16I fighter jets for air escort and fighter sweep missions and to suppress enemy air-defense systems. In addition, they'd be using twelve KC-130 and KC-10 refueling tankers, plus two Gulfstream 550 electronics jets.

In the high-end scenario, he explained, they would need to deploy 104 fighter jets, if each jet carried a single bunker-buster bomb to its target. These would need a similar assortment of support aircraft.

"What kind of attrition rate are you projecting?" the finance minister asked.

"Between 20 and 30 percent."

"You're planning for losing up to 30 percent of our planes?"

"Planning for it? Yes," Shimon replied. "Expecting it to actually happen? No. I believe our pilots are better than that, but war, as you well know, is unpredictable, and I'm trying to be conservative."

"So at the low end, you're saying that losing between twenty-three and thirty-five planes is acceptable?" the justice minister asked. "And at the high end, you are okay with losing between thirty-three and fifty planes, each of which cost about $20 million without ordnance, fuel, or electronics upgrades?"

"Compared to losing six million citizens? Yes."

Shimon noted that the war plan also included measures to minimize the loss of Israeli pilots. They would, for example, deploy fifteen UAV drones, each armed with two Hellfire missiles. In addition, they anticipated firing roughly two dozen cruise missiles from Israeli submarines as well as numerous torpedoes to take out key Iranian naval vessels.

"And when our boys go down in enemy territory, what's the plan to get them back?" the vice prime minister asked.

"We have twenty search-and-rescue helicopter teams on standby," Shimon explained, putting some of the data up on the screens. "About a month ago, we pre-positioned quite a few of these teams in Azerbaijan. They are very well trained. They are highly motivated. I have reviewed these teams personally, and I am confident they can get the job done."

At that, the prime minister stepped back into the conversation. "Just after the first of the year, as you'll recall, I went to see my friend Jilan Kazarov, the president of Azerbaijan," Naphtali said. "We met in his gorgeous villa in Baku, on the shores of the Caspian Sea. He was very gracious. He has seen the Iranian threat for a long time. He understands it. I gave him my list of requests, including more electronic listening posts near the Iranian border and the ability to pre-position these SAR teams, and he gave me everything I asked for."

Naphtali paused briefly. He waited for people to stop jotting notes or looking at the video monitors and for all eyes to be back on him.

"Levi and I and the IDF chiefs have looked at this thing a thousand different ways, gentlemen, and we've concluded that hitting these targets isn't the hardest part. It's going to be very hard—extremely hard—don't get me wrong. But it's not the hardest part. The real problem is after our planes get home and the full-scale retaliation begins. The Iranians have at least a thousand ballistic missiles, most of which are aimed at us. Hezbollah in the north has at least fifty thousand rockets and missiles aimed at us. The Syrians have theirs. Hamas has theirs. Succeeding with our first strike isn't what worries me. Riding out their first wave is."

51

"You did what?"

Zalinsky's face was so red it was almost purple. There were veins in his neck and forehead that looked like they were going to burst at any moment. Eva had known the man for years, and she had never seen him so angry. He was shouting at her in the middle of the Global Operations Center, and almost two dozen more CIA staff were watching.

"I didn't have a choice," Eva responded, trying to maintain her composure. "It was a split-second call—a life-and-death decision—and you weren't available, so I made the call."

"You retasked the Predator away from the missile base to help an agent in trouble?"

"Absolutely," Eva said. "And I'd do it again."

"You weren't authorized to do it the first time," Zalinsky shouted, *"and there isn't going to be a next time."* He turned to the uniformed security guards by the main door. "Guards, I need Eva Fischer taken into custody immediately."

Eva was incredulous. "You're having me arrested?"

"We operate within a chain of command around here, Ms. Fischer. You don't get to break it. No one gets to break it." He addressed the guards, who were now putting Eva in handcuffs. *"Get her out of my sight."*

★ ★ ★ ★ ★

ROUTE 56, IRAN

David was driving as fast as he dared.

He was heading east on 56, toward Arak. Khorramabad was far behind him, but that wasn't making him feel any safer. He feared he had already pushed his luck too far. He needed to find a place to interrogate Khan, hide the Peugeot, and regroup. Khan wasn't shrieking anymore, but David feared he was losing him. He had to move fast.

David suddenly remembered his meeting in Qom. The road he was on would get him there eventually. He was a little more than an hour away. But he certainly couldn't go now, not with Khan and Yaghoubi and with a car that had been shot to pieces. He speed-dialed the MDS technical team leader and apologized profusely.

"Look, I'm very sorry, but something has come up," he said. "I'm going to be late, probably this afternoon at the earliest. . . . You sure? . . . Okay, I'll check in when I'm almost there and give you an update. . . . I know, I owe you. . . . What? . . . Very funny. . . . Okay, see you soon—bye."

He hung up and kept driving. About fifty kilometers outside of Arak, he saw an exit for the Lashkardar Protected Area, one of Iran's national forests. Seeing no cars behind or in front of him at the moment, he took a left and headed north for about fifteen minutes, past five or six impoverished homesteads, until he found the forest and a parking lot nestled alongside a row of small, rustic cabins surrounded by thousands of pine trees and hiking trails leading off in every direction. The lot was empty. It was far too early in the season for camping. So David parked and told Khan to stay quiet.

He rechecked the pistol, making sure it was fully loaded, then moved quickly to the first cabin. It was empty. So were each of the others, though all of them were locked. He kicked through the door of the cabin nearest the Peugeot, then ran back to check on his two prisoners. He had no idea what he was going to do with Yaghoubi. He just hoped he didn't have to kill him.

Switching off the safety, he prepared to pop the trunk with his keys.

It was the first chance he'd had to see how much damage had been done by the gun battle at the hotel, and he counted no fewer than seven bullet holes in the crumpled bumper and the badly dented trunk. Now he aimed the pistol, stepped back a few feet, and hit unlock. The trunk slowly opened, and David braced himself for Yaghoubi's move. But the man didn't stir.

"Come on, let's go—out," he said.

But the man still did not move, and then, as David looked more closely, he realized that Yaghoubi had been hit several times by bullets that had penetrated the back of the car. He checked for the man's pulse, but there was none. He felt a twinge of guilt, or at least sorrow for the man, then realized that Yaghoubi had ended up serving as a human shield. Had he not been in the trunk, those rounds might very well have killed Tariq Khan.

★ ★ ★ ★ ★

TEL AVIV, ISRAEL

Was it time to call up the Reserves?

The debate around the table had been raging for a quarter of an hour and was still unresolved. The proponents held that there was no time to waste. If they were going to launch Operation Xerxes in the next forty-eight hours and the Israeli people were going to be subjected to a massive missile attack as retaliation, then the prime minister had to order a full mobilization within the hour. They needed to get the Reservists on the road and to their bases before missiles were inbound or risk having key bases undermanned and key positions poorly defended amid a full-blown war.

The opponents—led by the foreign minister—said they should wait a bit longer so as not to take actions that would look provocative to the Mahdi or the rest of the world. To buttress his case, the foreign minister read cables from the Russians, the Chinese, the Germans, the French, and the British, all strongly warning Naphtali and the Israeli government not to launch or provoke a new regional war lest they risk condemnation by the UN Security Council. The American secretary of state, he added, wasn't being quite as blunt but was warning Jerusalem not to take any "noteworthy action" without "consulting us."

The vice prime minister was incensed by the threat of UN action, calling it meaningless blather and downright anti-Semitic. This was seconded by several others, but not by Naphtali.

"Let's not kid ourselves," the prime minister told his colleagues. "No matter what we do, the world is going to condemn us and say it's our fault. This is nothing new. That's not the question here. And I'm sad to say, I am bracing for the Americans turning against us as well—not the people, probably not even Congress, but the president for certain. The weight of his administration will be soundly against us. The only question for those of us sitting here is whether we want the Jewish people to survive the Islamic nuclear onslaught or be remembered as the people who weren't 'too provocative'—when perhaps they should have been a little more."

He had decided. He was calling up the Reserves, effective immediately. He would let the defense minister decide which ones and how many, but the number had to be significant, though they would put out a statement saying it was purely for defensive purposes.

★ ★ ★ ★ ★

LASHKARDAR PROTECTED AREA, IRAN

David checked his watch.

He didn't have time to regret this man's death. He opened the back door and helped Khan out. There was blood everywhere. Khan couldn't stand upright. David tossed the pistol on the grass near the cabin and put Khan's arm around his neck, then essentially dragged him across the pavement, through the grass, and into the cramped hut, setting him in a weathered wooden chair. Then he stepped outside, picked up the pistol, reentered the cabin, and opened the window shades to let in the morning sunshine. It was time.

"Talk," he said in Urdu.

"No," Khan replied in English.

David aimed the pistol at the man's other knee. *"Talk."*

"I have nothing to say to you," Khan shot back, again in English. "You are CIA, but you're probably a Jew. May you all die and go to hell."

"Right now, I'm the only friend you have, Tariq. Now, I can get you out of this country alive. Or I can let your Farsi-speaking friends find you bleeding out by the side of the road, with a mobile phone in your pocket filled with Mossad phone numbers, Hebrew e-mails, and details of a Swiss numbered account with cash transfers coming in from Tel Aviv. How do you think the Mahdi will like it when he finds out you're the Israeli mole, that you're the one who gave up Saddaji?"

"That's a lie! I have never worked for the Jews, and I never would!"

"That's not how it's going to look, Tariq. Your cell phone is off right now. No one knows where you are. But they're all looking, and when I turn it back on and download everything I just told you, they're going to be here in less than ten minutes. You don't think they're going to wonder why your phone was off for the last hour or so?"

"Then kill me," Khan insisted.

David smiled. "Nice try, Tariq. I have no intention of killing you. I'm going to let the Revolutionary Guard do that, after they've tortured you far worse than anything I could dream up. You'll be begging them to believe that I work for the CIA, but all the evidence is going to prove to them you're lying."

"You wouldn't do that," Khan said, his flash of anger now giving way to fear. "I have a family. For Allah's sake, I have children."

"Two daughters, of course. And guess where they're about to get their college tuition this semester? A bank in Haifa, that's right. And imagine what Iranian intelligence is going to do when they realize the Israelis are taking care of your family."

"Please don't. Please. I beg you—kill me, but don't do anything to my family."

"I'm not doing anything to your family, Tariq. It's your choice what happens from this point forward. I'm just saying in ten seconds you're not going to have a second kneecap unless you start cooperating. It's up to you."

David took the silencer off the pistol, cocked the hammer, and started counting.

Ten, nine, eight, seven, six . . .

Without warning, he pulled the trigger, though aiming slightly to the side at the last moment. The explosion terrified Khan and seemed to shatter his already-frayed nerves. He began weeping and resumed begging David not to hurt him or his family.

"What do you want?" he cried. *"Just tell me, what do you want?"*

"How long have you been working on Iran's nuclear weapons program?"

"On and off for six years."

"What do you mean, 'on and off'?"

"At the beginning, when the Iranians bought the plans from my uncle . . ."

"A. Q. Khan?"

"Right—when they bought them, my uncle sent me to Tehran and then to Bushehr, just for a few months to help them get organized. Then I went home and didn't come back for a few years. Then, about five or six years ago, they asked me to come for a month at a time."

"Who did?"

"Mohammed Saddaji."

"How did you know him?"

"I didn't. My uncle did. I first met him in Karachi, then in Tehran on that first trip, and we have worked closely together ever since. He was a hard man, but we got along well."

"And then?"

"When Darazi became president, that's when things really accelerated."

"How so?"

"When you Americans went into Iraq, Hosseini got nervous. He decided not to pursue the Bomb, at least not for a while. But when Darazi came to power, they started talking more and more about the coming of the Mahdi. They started believing they had to build the Bomb to prepare the way for him to come."

"Aren't you Sunni?"

"Yes."

"Then you don't believe in the Mahdi."

"I didn't, not when I first started coming here from Pakistan. I was just coming for the money—they pay very well—and because my uncle told me to."

"But now?"

"What can I tell you? The Twelfth Imam is here."

"So now you're a Twelver?"

"I don't know what I am. I'm just trying to get my work done well and on time."

"Have you met Imam al-Mahdi?"

"No. They keep us away from anyone political. Actually, they keep us away from almost anyone."

"When was the last time you saw your family?"

"I see them by Skype."

"What about in person?"

"Two years."

"Really? Why don't you go visit them?"

"They won't let me. They say it would be a security risk."

"Why can't your family come here to stay, or to visit at least?"

"That's what I ask, but they say that's a security risk too."

"What if we get your family and bring them to the States?"

Khan had a startled look on his face. "Would you do that?"

"If you cooperate, absolutely."

"Really?"

"Of course."

"I could see my wife and my daughters?"

"They couldn't ever go back to Pakistan, of course."

"That's okay. Just to have them with me. Just to hold them in my arms again. Is it really possible?"

"Yes," David said. "Tell me where the warheads are, and I'll get the ball rolling."

Khan hesitated. David wanted to push him but restrained himself. The guy was talking. He just needed a few minutes. David reached into his coat pocket and found his phone and immediately patched back into the Global Ops Center at Langley. He said nothing, just let the team listen.

"You can't ever go back—not to the missile base, not to Tehran, not to Pakistan," David said gently. "You know that, right, Tariq? I'm never going to let that happen. And as we speak, I'm putting a new SIM card into your phone that is going to load all the Mossad material I told you about earlier."

Tariq watched in wide-eyed horror as David reached into his jacket, tore a piece of the inner lining, and took out a SIM card that had been taped inside. Then he removed the SIM card in Tariq's phone, put the new card in, and taped Tariq's original SIM card back into the lining of his jacket.

"You are now officially a Mossad agent," he smiled. "All that's left is to turn it on."

But Tariq would have none of it. The fear in his eyes told the story, and he began to talk.

52

Jalal Zandi tried to tell himself to calm down.

He walked the floor of the 120,000-square-foot missile-assembly facility in the middle of a poverty-stricken neighborhood on the periphery of the Iranian city of Arak—a facility most locals thought built construction cranes because, in fact, half of the massive plant did—and tried not to hyperventilate. Looking scared would only make him look guilty, and looking guilty right now would be a death sentence. Inside, uniformed IRGC were everywhere. Outside, plainclothes agents acted like factory workers, truck drivers, and maintenance men, but they were all armed and beyond paranoid. They knew what had happened to Saddaji. And they knew what had happened to the nuclear facilities built by Saddam Hussein and Bashar al-Assad. They had all met the same fate, a fate none here was eager to share.

But telling oneself not to look scared or be scared hardly removed the fear, and Zandi was terrified. Hadn't he given them everything they had asked of him so far? Hadn't he done what he had promised? He hadn't demanded or accepted much money, just enough not to feel like he was giving his valuable services away for free. After all, there weren't a lot of people who did what he did or knew what he knew. All he'd ever wanted was peace of mind. He'd have done it for free, actually, if they'd asked him. All he'd wanted was not to be killed and for his family to be safe as well. It hadn't seemed too much to ask. Until now.

He checked in with two shift supervisors and answered a few technical questions. He gave some instructions as they made final adjustments to the second of two Shahab-3 (or Meteor-3 or Shooting Star–3) ballistic missiles, an adaptation of the North Korean Nodong missile. The variant they were finishing was stronger and faster than its predecessors, with a speed of Mach 2.1 and an extended range just shy of 2,000 kilometers, or about 1,200 miles. Typically, the 2,200-pound warhead held five conventional "cluster warheads" that could break away from the missile upon reentry and hit five entirely different targets with standard explosives. But in this version, and in the others like it being finalized around the country, the standard nose cone holding the warhead was being retrofitted to hold a single nuclear warhead and all the electronics and avionics that went with it. They were using the Pakistani designs both for the nuclear warhead itself and for its attachment to the missile, the designs the Iranian regime had purchased from Tariq Khan's uncle for a ghastly sum.

Now Dr. Saddaji was dead. Najjar Malik had defected. Khan was missing. Zandi feared for his life, but he wasn't sure what to do next. He knew he was supposed to report any anomalies in the program up the chain of command. He had direct access, twenty-four hours a day, seven days a week, to Mohsen Jazini, commander of the Iranian Revolutionary Guard Corps, on his personal mobile phone and on his home phone. And Jazini had been clear that if there were ever an emergency and he couldn't reach him, he should immediately contact Ali Faridzadeh, the minister of defense, whose personal mobile, home, and office numbers Zandi had been given as well. But calling either man terrified him. They were under enormous pressure from the Twelfth Imam to deliver completed, operational missiles and to get them into the field, ready to be fueled and launched as soon as possible. It had been a miracle to get the first two missiles ready for the navy, but those were entirely different kinds of missiles and far easier to complete.

Zandi cursed himself. He should never have agreed to such an accelerated timetable. He and his men were barely eating or sleeping. They never saw their families and hadn't had a day off in months. They were being driven too hard. They were about to break. In many ways, he had broken long before, and the news about Khan weighed heavy on his soul. He walked up the metal stairs to his temporary office over-looking the production floor and stared at the phone. What exactly was he supposed to tell Jazini?

★ ★ ★ ★ ★

TEL AVIV, ISRAEL

Naphtali made another critical decision.

He had to start calling up the IDF's Reserves. At the same time, he needed to confuse the enemy and cause them to think they had more time than they really did. To ensure this, he ordered the foreign minister to issue an immediate statement to the press that "the prime minister is pleased to accept the gracious invitation of the UN secretary-general to come to New York for a series of high-level meetings with other world leaders on how to achieve regional peace." The statement would further say that "the prime minister will depart on Friday morning for the US, where he will appear on NBC's *Meet the Press* on Sunday morning and address the AIPAC policy conference at their gala banquet on Monday night."

At the same time, he instructed the foreign minister to leave immediately for Ben Gurion airport and fly to Washington and simultaneously sent the deputy foreign minister to Brussels. "On the way, tell any journalist who will listen that you and I believe there is one last chance for peace, but after this week there can be no guarantees."

★ ★ ★ ★ ★

LASHKARDAR PROTECTED AREA, IRAN

David's phone rang.

It was Zalinsky. He was livid. He tore into David for the foolish risks he was taking and for having the temerity to request that the Predator over the missile base in Khorramabad be moved to save him. Who did he think he was? Zalinsky fumed. Was he more important than the national security of 300 million American people? Hadn't Zalinsky taught him better than that?

David was caught off guard by his mentor's rant—and infuriated as well. He was risking his life every day. A little gratitude might be in order. But he held his tongue. There was no point arguing with the man when he was like this. All he could do was ride it out.

"You finished?" David asked when the tirade began winding down.

"Are you being sarcastic?" Zalinsky shot back.

"I have something for you, but I don't want to interrupt."

"That's not funny."

"I'm not trying to be."

"Then what?"

David took a deep breath and forced himself to stay focused. He was excited about what he'd accomplished, proud even, and he wasn't going to let Zalinsky ruin it all now.

"Got a pad and a pen?" he asked calmly.

"Why?" Zalinsky countered.

"Do you have a pad and pen?" David repeated.

"Hold on. Okay. What is it?"

"Take this down; it's a list. Ready?"

"Yes."

"Good. Natanz—two. Arak—two. Khorramabad—two. Med—two. Plus the one already tested."

Zalinsky didn't respond.

"Jack, you still there?"

It was quiet for another few moments.

"Yes, I'm here," Zalinsky finally replied. "Is this for real?"

"As real as it gets," David said.

"You're sure."

"I'm just telling you what Khan told me. But I'm still pointing a pistol at his good knee. If you don't believe him, just say the word."

David wasn't smiling. Khan's eyes went wide. David put his finger over his mouth and made it clear Khan should remain silent.

"Give me more," Zalinsky demanded. "What else did he say?"

"He confirms that he and Zandi and Saddaji and their team built nine nuclear warheads using the designs from his uncle. He confirms that one of the warheads, as we thought, was tested in Hamadan."

"When you say 'confirms,' do you mean you're telling him what we know and he's confirming that, or what?"

"No," David said. "I haven't told him anything. I just told him I was going to blow off a second kneecap and expose him to his friends as a Mossad agent, and he started spilling his guts. But those first pieces are consistent with what we were learning from our other sources."

"This is incredible. Keep going."

"He says that he and Zandi worked closely with the IRGC's missile engineers to attach two of the warheads to an Iranian variant of the Russian KH-55 cruise missile. Obviously the 55 is typically air launched, but he says last year the Iranians adapted some 55s they originally bought from Ukraine in 2006 to be fired off Iranian missile boats. He says as far as he knows, the two they worked on are currently on either the *Jamaran* missile frigate or the *Sabalan* frigate, both of which he says are part of the Iranian naval presence in the Med."

"Those are the two lead ships that passed through Suez yesterday," Zalinsky said. "We're hoping to confirm in a few hours whether they're carrying nuclear warheads, but the circumstantial evidence is certainly adding up."

"It is," David said. "He says the adapted cruise missiles have a speed of Mach 0.75, are GPS guided, and are accurate to between twenty and thirty feet of their target. He says he doesn't know precisely what target package was loaded into them—that wasn't under his purview—but Tel Aviv and Haifa were the cities that kept getting mentioned most. And there's more."

"Keep going."

"He says he was overseeing two nuclear warheads being attached to Shahab-3 missiles at the facility in Khorramabad. He said they were initially having some technical problems with part of the trigger, but that he got that resolved even before they left Hamadan. He said the warheads are being attached to the missiles now and are supposed to be finished by Saturday morning, or lunchtime at the latest."

"And the others?"

"Two are at the Iranians' main nuclear research facility in Natanz. They're supposed to be attached to their missiles by Friday night at the latest. Two more were under Zandi's supervision in Arak. As far as Khan knows, one was to be fully operational by nightfall and loaded onto one of the mobile launchers. He wasn't sure where they were going to take it. Another is supposed to be ready by Saturday morning. He's given me all kinds of technical details on the warheads and the missiles and a quick rundown on their schedule to produce more warheads within the next month. I don't know how much you want right now. You tell me."

"Do you have a laptop handy?"

"No, why?"

"I need you to write up everything you have—especially the precise facilities, buildings, and sections of buildings where Khan says the six warheads and missiles are located, the ones not out at sea—and get that all to me ASAP."

"Jack, I'm in the middle of nowhere. I need to give it to you over the phone."

"Not right now. I need to get the basics of this to Murray and Allen and then to the president."

"Fine," David said. "Put Eva on. I'll dictate the rest to her."

"That's not possible. She can't. She's doing something else for me right now. I'll get someone else—hold on."

Doing something else? This was everything they had trained and prepared for. What could Eva possibly be doing that was more important than this? But just then, he heard two vehicles pulling up the dirt road.

"Jack, I'll call you back in five minutes. I need to go."

David hung up the phone and crouched low. He made it clear to Khan that he needed to keep his mouth shut. Then, keeping the pistol close to his chest, he moved to one of the windows and peeked out.

They had company. Lots of it.

53

The Twelfth Imam did the live broadcast from the Qaleh.

No one knew where the program was originating from. The Mahdi hadn't wanted to go all the way back to Tehran just to use the Supreme Leader's personal television studio, so Javad brought in a bare-bones crew, a helicopter full of cameras, lights, and sound equipment, and put together a makeshift studio in the dining room. The Mahdi refused to wear makeup, so he was ready when the crew was.

"We interrupt our regular programming to bring you this live special report," an announcer said back at the main control room in Tehran. "And now, His Excellency, Imam al-Mahdi."

The red light on the lead camera turned on, and they were under way.

"I praise the merciful, all-knowing, and almighty God for blessing me with another opportunity to address my people all across the globe on behalf of the great Caliphate that is rising and to bring a number of issues to the attention of the international community. I also praise the Almighty for the increasing vigilance of peoples throughout the world, their courageous presence in different international settings, and the brave expression of their views and aspirations regarding global issues. Today, humanity passionately craves acknowledgment of the truth, devotion to God, commitment to justice, and respect for the dignity of human beings. Rejection of domination and aggression, defense of the oppressed, and longing for peace constitute the legitimate demands of the peoples of the world, particularly the new generation of spirited youth, who aspire to a world free from decadence, aggression, and injustice and replete with love and compassion. The youth have a right to seek justice and truth, and they have a right to build their own future on the foundations of tranquility. And I praise the Almighty for this immense blessing."

Javad stood off to the side, behind the lights and the crew, marveling at the Mahdi's eloquence, all without notes, without a teleprompter, without a speechwriter or assistance of any kind.

"I address you today because a serious threat to world peace is growing, and growing rapidly. As you know, as I have repeatedly stated, and as I have repeatedly demonstrated in all of my public actions, I have come to bring peace and justice and tolerance for all peoples and all religions and all persuasions everywhere, even while calling every man, woman, and child to submit themselves to the will of Allah and to become good and faithful Muslims before the Day of Judgment. I am reaching out to all of the leaders of this region and visiting them personally when I can. I have even reached out to the American president and offered a hand of unity, if he will but accept it. Despite the enormous gulf between our two peoples, I believe that making peace means that we must discuss our differences and that one must be willing to lay aside one's doubts and submit to a greater good.

"Yet today I have received disturbing reports that the Zionist forces are preparing for war. They are mobilizing their military. They are calling up their reserve soldiers. They are sending their air force on one so-called preplanned exercise after another. And all the while, their leaders speak lies to the world. They accuse me of preparing for war. But nothing could be further from the truth. I have come to seek peace. How many ways must I say it? Yes, I have control of weapons to defend the Muslim people from aggression and humiliation, but these are for defensive purposes only. Yet the Zionists are hungry for blood—our blood, Muslim blood. We have not reciprocated, but we will not be intimidated.

"That said, I am encouraged by a call I received last night from the United Nations secretary-general. He has asked me to come and address the General Assembly in a special session next Wednesday. I will tell you what I told him. If it can advance the cause of peace, then I would be delighted to go to New York and meet him and address that august body. We Muslims have nothing to fear from frank and open dialogue among the peoples of the earth. For the Caliphate is rising. The Zionists cannot stop us. No one can stop us. This is the will of Allah. The day of Islam has come. Let those who seek peace take note."

The Mahdi finished the broadcast, removed his microphone, and summoned Javad to him.

"Yes, my Lord?"

"What are these reports of Naphtali going to New York as well?" the Mahdi asked.

"I'm just hearing this myself, Your Excellency," Javad said. "Reuters is reporting that Naphtali is leaving for New York in the morning. And Al Jazeera is reporting that the foreign minister is heading to Washington as we speak. They say there's just 'one last chance for peace.'"

"Our call for peace and the surprise engagement with the Americans are putting the Zionists on the defensive," the Mahdi said with a faint smile on his lips. "They are having to react to us. This is good. Perhaps our plans are working."

"Yes, my Lord," Javad said. "I'm sure they are."

Javad felt his phone vibrating. He excused himself and stepped aside for a moment. A text message was coming in from Defense Minister Faridzadeh. It was marked *URGENT* and contained just three ominous words: Khan is missing.

★ ★ ★ ★ ★

TEL AVIV, ISRAEL

"How ready are we for the retaliation from our neighbors?" the justice minister asked.

Others could have addressed this, but Naphtali answered the question himself. "As ready as we can be," he replied. "Obviously, we have the Patriot missile batteries in place. We have the Arrow system on full alert as well as our Iron Dome system. The Arrow and the Patriot systems will be focused primarily on taking out Iranian missiles, since they are more powerful, more precise, have relatively sophisticated guidance systems, and could have chemical or biological warheads, or even nuclear warheads we don't know about. The Iron Dome system will be deployed in the north near the border with Lebanon and in the south along the border with Gaza. We will do what we can, but I think you all know by now that we're not going to be able to stop every missile, much less every rocket or mortar. We'll stop what we think are the most serious threats. The rest we'll have to let through, which means people may have to live in shelters for several weeks. I don't have to remind you that the Second Lebanon War lasted for thirty-four days, and a million Israelis fled from the north or lived in bomb shelters. That said, the shelters are all stocked with several weeks' supply of food, water, and basic necessities—even diapers. Every Israeli has a personalized, fitted gas mask now. We've been running scores of homeland-defense drills. We're stocked up on blood supplies and medicines. All the hospitals are on full alert. But that's all defensive. I want Shimon here to talk about our offensive plans."

The defense minister stood and prepared to walk the Security Cabinet through a new IDF plan, Operation Black Viper. "Our air force—as good as they are—can only do so much," Shimon said. "What we learned from the Second Lebanon War and Operation Cast Lead in Gaza is that we cannot rely on air power to stop the rockets and missiles. Ultimately, we will have to launch massive ground campaigns, and we have been planning, training, and preparing for just this. Upon the prime minister's orders, we will launch lightning-fast ground incursions into Gaza and into southern Lebanon, up to—but probably not going past—the Litani River. Our objectives will be clear: to destroy Hamas and Hezbollah rocket and missile launchers and to capture or kill Hamas and Hezbollah forces. If the rockets and missiles stop, it means we're succeeding. If not, we must keep going. We're not going to get a second shot at this. We need to clear and hold these territories and stop the missile barrages at their source."

"What about Syria?" the vice prime minister asked. "What about Jordan?"

"We have contingencies for both," Shimon said. "At the moment,

I'm not worried about Jordan. We are in close contact with the king and his officials. They don't want a war with us. If they're toppled, that's a whole other story. But that's not my immediate concern."

"What is?"

"Damascus. If the Syrians choose to join in, we are going to have a real problem. Their missiles are much more powerful and precise than anything Hezbollah and Hamas have. We'll use air power, but I must warn you—we may have to move the IDF into Syrian territory as well if the missiles keep coming."

"You're talking about an invasion of Syria?"

"I'm talking about stopping Syria's rockets and missiles if they fire. I don't want to do it. We are privately sending messages to the Syrians not to get involved if a war does start. I just don't want any of you caught off guard. It is a real possibility. We have planned for it. Let us pray it doesn't come to that."

Now the minister of internal security had a question. "Any danger from Egypt now that they have joined the Caliphate?"

Shimon looked at Naphtali.

"Egypt is the wild card," the prime minister said. "The last forty-eight hours have been very troubling. They don't have a significant rocket or missile force. But they do have a decent air force. They've got 240 advanced American F-16 fighter jets, after all. So we'll have to keep a close eye on our southern skies. It's another reason we're not launching four hundred planes at Iran. We need enough in reserve to stop an Egyptian air assault."

Then Naphtali had a question of his own. "Any word from Mordecai?"

The head of the Mossad simply shook his head.

★ ★ ★ ★ ★

CAPE MAY, NEW JERSEY

The waves of the Atlantic lapped rhythmically upon the shore.

But Najjar Malik paid them no attention. He was riveted to the Twelfth Imam's speech, and he burned with anger. He needed to write.

He needed to send a new message to his Twitter followers—more than 647,000 of them, nearly all Farsi speakers—in Iran and around the world. But first he had to calm down, get his mind focused back on the Lord, and ask the Lord what He wanted him to say. For if it were up to Najjar, he would have unleashed a thousand bitter rants against the Mahdi, 140 characters at a time.

He needed to walk. He needed to clear his head. So despite the late hour, he got up, put on his jacket, and stepped out the back door of the gorgeous, two-level, five-bedroom beach house. As he walked past the pool and down to the beach, he was overwhelmed by God's gracious provision. When the producer of the Persian Christian Satellite Network said he had a friend who loved to make his home available for missionaries on furlough, pastors on sabbatical, and secret believers escaping from persecution, Najjar hadn't even really understood the first two categories. But he recognized that he fit into the last category and accepted the offer without hesitation.

He had been thinking of a couch in someone's basement or a cot in someone's attic, not a multimillion-dollar beach house all to himself on the Jersey Shore. It was off-season, to be sure, and Cape May was freezing cold and largely depopulated—though he heard it was a madhouse in the summer—but it was honestly more than Najjar could have hoped for or even imagined. But of course, he felt guilty for being there without Sheyda and Farah and his sweet little daughter.

Najjar walked for a while, staring out at the dark and endless ocean and asking the Lord for guidance. He listened to the waves and felt the bitter-cold winds on his face.

Then the words came to him, as they always did. He ran back to the house, powered up the laptop the producer had lent him, logged on to his Twitter account, and wrote the following: Don't be deceived, dear friends. The Mahdi is a false messiah. He wants not peace, but war. Turn to Jesus Christ while there is time.

54

LASHKARDAR PROTECTED AREA, IRAN

David's heart was racing.

Two large vans pulled up and stopped abruptly. The back doors of both burst open, and heavily armed men jumped out and took up positions around the cabins, forming a perimeter. At first he counted six, but soon he had revised his count upward to eight, plus the two drivers, who were now turning the vans around and backing them into position, clearly preparing to make an escape. None of the men wore fatigues—they had on street clothes instead—but each carried an AK-47 and a backpack David had no doubt contained grenades, tear gas, and plenty more ammunition. They didn't look like typical Revolutionary Guard Corps members. They had to be al-Quds commandos. How had they found him? Then again, what did it matter? They had. They were coming for Khan and for him.

He had a choice to make and only seconds to make it.

★ ★ ★ ★ ★

THE QALEH, IRAN

Javad Nouri made certain the Mahdi was not in need of anything.

Then he moved quickly down the hall to find a quiet place. He stepped out onto the large stone porch overlooking the mountains and the city of Tehran in the valley below. He pulled out his satellite phone and speed-dialed the defense minister, trying in vain to stay calm. "It's Javad," he said when the man answered. "What do you mean he's missing?"

"I just talked to Zandi," Faridzadeh said. "There's been some kind of ambush."

"Where?"

"The hotel in Khorramabad. Details are still sketchy. But there are dead bodies and one missing bodyguard, and Khan is missing too. There's a report of a large explosion east of Khorramabad too. The local police have some leads. They're moving on them now. But that's all I know."

"And the . . . ?"

"They're safe."

"All of them?"

"Yes."

"You're sure?"

"Believe me, we are taking precautions."

"Because I cannot go in there and tell the—"

"I know. I know. Don't worry. The cakes are safe."

"What about Zandi?" Javad asked. "Is he safe?"

"He is for now. But he's scared."

"Wouldn't you be?"

"Of course."

"We should move him," Javad said. "Bring him here. He'll be safer."

"No, that is not wise," the minister countered. "Not right now."

"Why not?"

"The Zionists are here. Or the Americans. Or both. We're doing everything we can to hunt them down. We'll know more soon. But right now we're not entirely sure whom we can trust. And we cannot proceed without Zandi. We need to keep him locked down."

"I want to talk to him."

"Javad . . ."

"I will ask Imam al-Mahdi how he wants to proceed, but I need to talk to Zandi immediately. The base commander there has one of the satellite phones, doesn't he?"

"Yes, but—"

"Then get it to Zandi and have him call me within the hour."

★ ★ ★ ★ ★

CAPE MAY, NEW JERSEY

Najjar followed his first message with a second.

> Jesus said, "I am the door; if anyone enters through Me, he will be saved . . . I came that they may have life, and have it abundantly."

What kind of eternal impact were his messages having? He had no idea. He could only keep praying and fasting and trusting the Lord to move in His might and His sovereignty, as He had done in Najjar's own life. But Najjar couldn't help but be amazed by how many people around the world were tracking every word he said and by how many were passing them along to others, especially inside Iran.

★ ★ ★ ★ ★

LASHKARDAR PROTECTED AREA, IRAN

The choice was not easy, but it was simple.

Under no circumstances could he allow himself to be taken alive, David told himself. He was not scared of dying. Not anymore. For the first time in his life, he knew he was a forgiven man, that when his life was over, he was headed to heaven to be with the Lord Jesus forever. Of this he had absolutely no doubt, and that assurance gave him new reserves of courage.

It wasn't dying that scared him. It was torture. The Iranians knew how to inflict pain in ways that made a man want to die but never quite make it there. They would do everything in their power to squeeze information out of him, to get him to turn against his friends, against the Agency, against his country, and they would have no mercy. How long would he last? He honestly had no idea, and he did not want to find out. That said, however, he would not turn his gun upon himself. He would not commit suicide. That was his redline, David decided.

He scrambled to the back of the cabin and peered out the window.

He could see two men in the bushes to the right. Two more were in position off to the left. When he saw one of them had a sniper's rifle, he quickly hit the deck and rolled to the front windows. They were moving. They were closing in. He had a clear shot at one of them and a decent shot at another. But then what?

David's phone rang. It was Abdol Esfahani, finally returning his call. David ignored it and looked at Khan. The man was sweating profusely. But he also seemed to have a glimmer in his eye, as if he sensed the tables were about to be turned. The captor was about to become the captive. A week ago, David would have had no qualms about killing the man right now. He was the architect and one of the chief engineers of eight remaining weapons of mass death and more to come. How could David let him go back into the service of the Twelfth Imam? He looked down at the pistol, then back at Khan. He wasn't sure he could do it. But why not? He hadn't hesitated back at the hotel. How dare he hesitate now? Millions of innocent lives were on the line.

"David Shirazi!" a man with a distinct Tehran accent shouted from the front yard. *"We know you're not alone. We know you're armed. Throw your weapons out and walk out slowly with your hands on top of your head. You've got three seconds."*

This was it, the moment of truth. He wasn't going out there. They were going to have to come in to get him. He moved over to Khan and put the pistol to the man's temple.

"No," Khan whispered. "You promised me. You said I would be safe. You said you'd protect my family."

"I did," David said. "And I meant it. But I was wrong. It's too late."

★ ★ ★ ★ ★

THE QALEH, IRAN

Javad expected a tirade.

It did not come.

"Khan was expendable," the Twelfth Imam said when Javad briefed him on the missing-and-presumed-dead status of the Pakistani scientist. "So was Saddaji. But nothing has happened to the warheads, right?"

"Right."

"And six will be ready by Saturday to fire at the Zionists?"

"Two are ready now. A third by nightfall."

"Perhaps we should keep these other two—the two Khan was working on—in reserve."

"We could," Javad said. "Whatever you wish, my Lord."

"More warheads are being built?"

"Well, my Lord, the uranium is being enriched, and we'll begin building the next set of warheads next week, *inshallah*."

"And Zandi will oversee all that?"

"Yes."

"Who would oversee that if Zandi were killed or captured?"

"It would be a very serious setback, my Lord," Javad said. "That's why I believe we should bring Zandi to us, but Minister Faridzadeh strongly disagrees."

"You are correct. Bring Jalal Zandi to me. Besides, I would like to meet this brave hero of the Revolution."

"Yes, my Lord. I shall take care of it at once."

"Very well. Now summon Hosseini and Darazi to me. Have them meet me on the porch. I have a topic of great importance for them."

★　★　★　★

ARAK, IRAN

There was a knock on the office door.

"Come in," Zandi said, looking up from his computer.

It was the base commander. "You are instructed to call Mr. Nouri," he said, handing Zandi a satellite phone and a slip of paper. "Here is the number. Return them both the moment you finish."

"But I have never spoken to Mr. Nouri by phone," Zandi said. "Only by secure e-mail."

"It's okay," the commander said. "These phones are new and secure. No one will be able to listen to what you say—not even me." The man smiled, shut the door, and left.

Jalal Zandi stared at the phone in one hand and the slip of paper in the other. He could practically hear his heart beating in his chest. He was surprised the base commander hadn't heard it too.

Zandi glanced at his watch, then at the clock on the wall. There was so little time. He logged back on to his laptop, which timed out every five minutes. He entered four completely different passcodes and pulled up the most highly classified document in the Iranian government, bearing the precise specifications and work history details of each of the nine warheads. Beside the two warheads in Khorramabad he added a notation with the date, the time, and the words "Khan missing. Project status: Unknown."

He hit Save. Then he powered up the phone and dialed the number the commander had given him.

"Hello?"

"Yes, I'm, uh . . . I'm looking for Mr. . . . um . . . Mr. Nouri," Zandi stammered.

"This is he."

"Yes, hello, uh . . . this is, um . . . Jalal Zandi. . . . I . . ."

"Oh yes, Jalal, thank you for calling."

"My pleasure," Zandi lied, his voice quivering. "How, uh . . . how can I help you?"

"I'm sending a chopper to pick you up and bring you to us. The Mahdi would like to meet you and hear a briefing on your work and next steps."

"That . . . that would be . . . a great honor . . . yes."

"Excellent. See you soon."

The line went dead. Zandi shuddered with fear. Why was the Twelfth Imam summoning him? Nouri made it sound like an honor.

He set down the paper and dialed another number from memory. It began to ring. Once. Twice. Three times. Four. And then the line connected. Zandi swallowed hard.

"Code in," the voice said in perfect Farsi.

"Zero, five, zero, six, six, alpha, two, delta, zero."

"Password?"

"Mercury."

"Authentication?"

"Yes, uh, this is Mordecai. I have very important information to pass on, and I have only a few minutes."

★ ★ ★ ★ ★

LASHKARDAR PROTECTED AREA, IRAN

David pressed the pistol into Khan's temple.

The man was shaking, begging him not to.

He switched off the safety and took a deep breath. He steadied himself. He was out of time. But just as he was about to pull the trigger, his phone rang. Startled, David clicked on his Bluetooth and took the call.

"David, it's me, Jack. Don't do it."

"What do you mean?"

"I'm watching a thermal image of you from the Predator. Don't kill Khan. We need him."

"It's too late, Jack."

"No, it's not."

"What are you talking about?" David asked.

"The men outside," Zalinsky said. "They're not Iranians. They're ours."

55

Tom Murray had never been to the White House so late.

In fact, he rarely went to the White House at all. Typically, it was Roger Allen who briefed the president, especially on such sensitive matters, but Allen was still en route from Amman and had told Murray by secure phone that he had to wake up the president and brief him immediately.

The Secret Service took his sidearm and phone, then had him empty his pockets and walk through the magnetometer. A uniformed agent then walked him from the West Executive Avenue guard post into the West Wing. There he signed in and waited until two plainclothes agents took him up to the residence. To his surprise, he was ushered into the solarium and was told the president would meet him there in a few moments.

Murray adjusted his tie and picked lint off his blazer. He checked his breath for a third time, then opened his black binder and reviewed his notes several more times. A few moments later, the president entered. Murray stood at attention. Jackson made no small talk and didn't shake his hand. He looked tired and annoyed, and Murray was certain from his slightly disheveled appearance that he had awoken and dressed hurriedly only moments before.

"Roger says you have news."

"Yes, sir."

"Well, what couldn't wait until morning?"

"We've received a report from our man in Iran."

"Zephyr?"

"Yes, sir."

"And?"

"He has another senior nuclear scientist in custody—Tariq Khan, nephew of A. Q. Khan, the father of the—"

"—the Pakistani Bomb, yeah, I got it—so what?" the president snapped.

"Khan gave up what he knows—the locations of the warheads, the missiles. We have everything, sir."

"Everything?"

"Yes, sir."

"And it's all confirmed?"

"Well, we're working to verify it all now, sir. But several of the key facts he gave us check out 100 percent. And other critical pieces he gave us confirm other inside sources we have. Bottom line: we believe we've got what we need, Mr. President."

"For what?" Jackson asked.

"Well, for an air strike, sir."

"An air strike?"

"Yes, sir."

"Now the CIA is giving me policy advice."

"No, sir. I'm just saying that—"

"I know what you're saying, Mr. . . . What did you say your name was?"

"Murray, sir—Tom Murray."

"Right, whatever. Listen, I'm the commander in chief. You're a spy. You give me data. I make the decisions. Not you. Not Langley. Is that clear?"

"Yes, sir."

"And you think I'm going to launch a new war in the Middle East with one source?"

"With all due respect, sir, it's not just one. It's the latest one."

"Right, right, but in terms of nailing down the precise locations of these warheads, how do we know this guy isn't lying? You tortured him, right?"

"Not exactly."

"Don't lie to me."

"I'm not, sir. But, yes, Khan was wounded in the operation."

"Wounded?"

"Yes."

"Severely, I imagine."

"Yes, sir."

"In a cross fire?"

"No, sir."

"By one of our agents?"

"Yes."

"Tortured, then."

"Disabled."

"Disabled?"

"Yes, sir. I'll have a full report for you in the morning. The point is—"

"The point is he would have said anything to keep this Zephyr guy from putting a bullet through his head."

"As I said, Mr. President, many of the key details have already been verified or corroborate what we know from completely independent, unrelated sources. And as the director's memo to you earlier today stated, the evidence is mounting that the Twelfth Imam is preparing for imminent attacks against Israel. We don't have much time, Mr. President. If we don't act quickly on the information we have, it could all be useless to us after a few days."

"Well, I need more."

"More?"

"Yes, Mr. Murphy, more. Did you see the Twelfth Imam's speech?"

"I read the transcript."

"Then you know he's reaching out to us," the president said, pacing about the room now. "He's clearly saying he wants peace. He's telling us to keep the Israelis contained until we can talk on the phone and in person at the UN next week. And he's right. There's too much at stake here. I'm not going to let the Israelis drag us into a war. And I'm sure not going to start a war based on a single source."

"It's not just Zephyr and Khan, Mr. President. There's Chameleon as well."

"Chameleon is secondhand. It's hearsay." Jackson sniffed. "Khan might be legit. I'll grant you that. But there's another scientist, too, isn't there? What's his name?"

"Jalal Zandi."

"Right, Zandi—isn't he just as important as Khan?"

"We believe so, yes."

"Then get him, too. Get them both. Let's see if their stories match. Only then will I decide if there are going to be any air strikes."

The president said good night and walked out, and Murray stood there alone, looking over the South Lawn and at the Washington Monument, lit up in the distance. He had no words to explain how disoriented and alone he felt at that moment. He and his team had risked their lives to give the president the best chance at stopping a nuclear holocaust, and the man had kicked the can down the road. What's more, he had now given them a near-impossible task that would put more American lives at risk, not to mention all of Israel. How had the character of American leadership sunk this low?

★ ★ ★ ★ ★

LASHKARDAR PROTECTED AREA, IRAN

"Mr. Shirazi, my name is Torres. I'm your ride home."

Marco Torres broke out in a wide grin and shook David's hand. David gave the special forces team leader a bear hug in return and started breathing again. The two men stood in front of the cabin and compared notes, while a medic attended to Khan inside the cabin.

Torres was six foot three, twenty-nine years old, and a former Marine sniper from San Diego. He'd joined the CIA after two tours in Afghanistan. Torres apologized for how long it had taken him and his team to get into the country from Bahrain, link up with their Agency contacts, and track him down, but for David, there was no need for apologies and no time for small talk. He was glad to see so many friendly faces and so much firepower, and it was time to get moving.

"Our orders are to get you and Mr. Khan to the safe house in Karaj and then fly you out in the morning," Torres said.

"Well, your orders have changed," David replied. "Have your second squad take Khan, fix him up, and get him out of the country for further interrogation. The rest of you need to hustle. We're going to Qom."

★ ★ ★ ★ ★

THE QALEH, IRAN

The Twelfth Imam gathered with his inner circle.

Javad had made certain they were all assembled on the porch of the Qaleh. Now they were sipping tea and discussing what might have happened to Tariq Khan and what this meant for the rest of their war plans, but when the Mahdi came out, they all bowed to worship him until they were released.

"Gentlemen, as I told Javad here, I am not worried about Mr. Khan," the Mahdi began. "He was expendable. Allah's plans cannot be thwarted. So you needn't worry. Mr. Khan is not why I have gathered you. The bigger issue is Jerusalem. Namely, what shall be done with it?"

Javad noticed the surprise in each of the men's eyes. He saw Darazi look to Hosseini and then over to Faridzadeh. As he expected, however—indeed, as the Mahdi had privately predicted to Javad just moments earlier—Hosseini was the first to speak, and he took no position at all.

"It does not matter what we believe, my Lord. What is Allah's will concerning the future of Jerusalem?" the Supreme Leader said.

"I'm not asking for your advice or your recommendations," the Mahdi said. "I'm asking for your understanding from all the ancient writings about the future of Jerusalem."

The men seemed taken aback by the question, but at the Mahdi's urging, they took a few minutes to discuss it among themselves. When they were finished, Hosseini spoke again.

"Well, of course, Jerusalem is not spoken of directly in the noble Qur'an," the Ayatollah said, looking weary and heavy laden with the magnitude of events now unfolding around them. "But we do see it alluded to in the blessed Night Vision, when the angel Gabriel took the Prophet Muhammad, peace be upon him, on the winged, horse-like beast for a journey unlike any other. In Sura 17, verse 1, we read, 'Glory to God, who did take His servant for a journey by night from the Sacred Mosque to the Farthest Mosque whose precincts we did bless, in order that we might show him some of our signs: for He is the One Who hears and sees all things.' The ancients clearly taught that the Sacred Mosque—Al-Masjid Al-Haram—was the holy Kaaba located in Mecca, while the Farthest Mosque—Al-Masjid Al-Aqsa—was the 'mosque in the corner,' or the holy house in Jerusalem, where today stands the Al-Aqsa Mosque alongside the Dome of the Rock. That is the location where Muhammad, peace be upon him, knelt twice and prayed to Allah, and then he was taken up to the Seven Heavens to confer with the saints."

"Very good," the Mahdi said. "Continue."

"Not all of the ancients, however, believed that the Al-Aqsa Mosque was in Jerusalem. Some said it was actually in heaven."

"Who?"

"The Sixth Imam, Ja'far Ibn Muhammad Al-Sadiq, for one."

"Precisely. And what did he say?"

"Well, he was once asked, 'What about the Al-Aqsa Mosque?' And someone said, 'They say it is in Jerusalem.' But his response was curious. He said the mosque in Kufa was superior to the mosque in the corner."

"Was it superior?" the Mahdi asked.

"Only you would know, my Lord; aren't you going to reign from Kufa? Isn't that where we are all eventually going, not long from now?"

"Very good, my son," the Mahdi said to Hosseini. "A very discerning answer. The rest of you would do well to learn from your brother Hamid. He is a good man and a good student. Now, I ask you, Ahmed, what are the implications of such truths?"

To Javad, the president looked petrified. He boasted of being a great scholar of Islam, but he was quaking now under the Mahdi's tutelage.

"We are to conquer Jerusalem, are we not?" Darazi said. "Are we not to reclaim it for Islam and rule it forever?"

"No," the Mahdi said with a vehemence that sent a chill through all of the men, Javad included. "You were not listening, Ahmed. You were not paying attention. Jerusalem means nothing to me, nor to my forebears. It was never the center of Shia Islam. It was never even the center of Sunni Islam. It is holy only to the Jews and the Christians, not to us. We conquered it once but never again. Jerusalem must be crushed, not conquered. It must be vanquished, not reclaimed. Islam was born in Mecca and Medina, but it came to full glory in Kufa in Iraq, the apple of Allah's eye. Jerusalem has been infected forever with the stains of the Zionists. Those who have taught otherwise have been misled or were misleaders themselves. The future of Jerusalem, gentlemen, is fire and bloodshed, and now we are just hours away."

56

An aide slipped a message to the director of the Mossad.

He glanced at the heading, then immediately handed the note to Levi Shimon, who sat back in his chair with an astonished expression.

"What is it, Levi?" the prime minister asked.

"You're not going to believe this," Shimon said.

"What?"

"It's from Mordecai. It's everything we asked for."

"What does it say?"

Shimon read the message in its entirety, slightly less than two pages. In it, Mordecai provided precise details—including GPS coordinates—on all the warheads' current locations and what kind of missiles they were attached to or about to be attached to. Then he begged for mercy for himself and his family, saying he did not want to end up "like the others" and that "that's not what I signed up for." He concluded by warning them in no uncertain terms: "I can guarantee you the warheads are where I say they are as I speak. But I can make no guarantees where they will be even a few hours from now. Events are moving rapidly here. I fear I will soon be exposed. This will be my last communiqué. I have done all that I promised, but I cannot do any more."

Naphtali looked around the table. Every man was as stunned and sobered as he was. Most concerning was the report of two nuclear cruise missiles on some of the five Iranian vessels just off of Israel's shores. They'd known it was a possibility but had no direct evidence of it, nor any indication from the Americans, who had far more sophisticated means to determine if a ship was carrying nuclear material. He turned to Shimon. "Levi, I need your assessment."

"This is deeply disturbing, Mr. Prime Minister," Shimon said, scanning the message again. "If this is disinformation planted by the Iranians, then they have to know they are inviting a preemptive attack. But I don't believe that. Far more likely this is the real thing. It was clearly communicated by a man under extreme stress. He's cutting off all contact, which suggests he's either going into hiding or thinks they're onto him. We're not going to get another chance like this. I think it is time to go. I don't see that we have a choice now."

"Any dissent?" Naphtali asked the others.

He got none. They were all in agreement.

"Then this is it, gentlemen," Naphtali said, his voice calm and firm. "We have supported American and European diplomacy toward Iran. We've supported multiple rounds of international economic sanctions against Iran. We've encouraged our allies to take covert operations against Iran's nuclear program, and to their credit, several of them have taken significant action. We have launched multiple covert operations of our own, some of them successful, some of them less so. I think history will show we did everything we could. We forced the Iranians to take almost three decades to build the Bomb, when it took us less than eight years. We urged the world to do more to stop Iran. We especially urged the Americans, up to and including the last few days. But there comes a time in every nation's destiny when it must act alone for its own survival. This is one of those times. I say this with neither joy nor malice. It is simply a fact. We are out of other options, and we are out of time. We must act in defense of the Jewish people and in defense of all of humanity. The world will hate us for what we are about to do, but I for one will be able to lay my head on my pillow every night in peace until I rest with my fathers, knowing I did the right thing. I hope you will too. I hereby authorize the commencement of Operation Xerxes. May the God of Israel be with us."

★ ★ ★ ★

THE QALEH, IRAN

"My Lord, may I say something?"

Mohsen Jazini lowered his head and did not make eye contact until he was called upon.

"Yes, of course, Mohsen," the Mahdi said. "What is it?"

"I realize that you are not concerned about the disappearance of Tariq Khan, and of course I fully respect—and agree with—your reasons, Your Excellency," Jazini said. "Still, until we know more, it would be safer if you were in one of the fully secure underground command centers in Tehran rather than up here."

"You mean *you* would feel more secure," the Mahdi said without expression.

"Allah is with you, without question, my Lord," Jazini replied. "But I am concerned that we pose too great a target all together and exposed like this. It doesn't strike me as prudent, but of course I completely defer to you, Your Excellency."

"Isn't the Qaleh unknown to the Zionists and the Americans?"

"Hopefully," Jazini said. "But we thought Dr. Saddaji and Dr. Khan were too. I just don't want us to take any chances. Moreover, I no longer think it is a good idea to bring all of the air force and missile commanders together up here on Saturday. It would take only one cruise missile and—"

"Very well," the Mahdi said, holding up his hand for Jazini to stop. "You have a missile command center north of Tehran, do you not?"

"Yes, we do, my Lord."

"Then let us go there. But don't tell the commanders about the change in plans. Give the chopper pilots the new location at the last possible moment."

"Yes, my Lord. Very good."

The men bowed again and were dismissed to get their personal possessions and head to the helicopter pad. Javad took the Mahdi aside and asked what he should do about the satellite phones.

"You are scheduled to get more tonight, are you not?" the Mahdi said.

"Yes, another hundred. Won't we need them for the commanders?"

"We will. Call your contact. See if you can meet him in an hour. Then come meet us at the command center."

★ ★ ★ ★ ★

ROUTE 56, EN ROUTE TO QOM, IRAN

David and Captain Torres were racing for Qom.

With them in the van were five of the CIA's most experienced paramilitary commandos. David brought them up to speed on some of the events of the last few days and what he had learned from Khan. Torres, in turn, briefed him on the kind of tools the team had with them, from electronic eavesdropping equipment to ground laser target designators. Then David's mobile phone rang. He checked the caller ID. It wasn't Zalinsky. It was Javad Nouri. He quieted everyone down, waited a beat, and took the call.

"Are you alone?" Javad asked.

"Yes," David lied.

"Change in plans."

"Whatever you need."

"Do you have the phones?"

David hesitated. He was tempted to lie and say yes. But what if something had happened to the shipment? What if Eva's package had never arrived? With everything else that had happened, he had forgotten to call the hotel and confirm he had a package waiting for him.

"No, not yet."

"What? Why not?"

"I had to make a stop in Hamadan. It got later than I thought, so I stayed overnight. But I'm on my way now."

"How long?"

"I should be to the hotel in a half hour."

"Fine. Call me when you have the phones, and we'll plan a new place to meet."

★ ★ ★ ★ ★

ABOARD THE *LEVIATHAN*, PERSIAN GULF

Tension was high in the Combat Information Center.

Captain Yacov Yanit stepped into the blue-lit chamber and cross-checked data on multiple computer screens before him. He had just confirmed his new orders with the head of naval operations in Tel Aviv. Sonar had no contacts. So this was it. He and his men had trained hard for such a time as this. But it was hard to believe the time had actually come.

Yanit desperately needed a cigarette. Why had his wife made him promise to quit? He pulled a stick of nicotine gum from his pocket and stuffed it in his mouth. Then he turned to his XO and ordered the 1,900-ton Israeli Dolphin-class diesel submarine to periscope depth. He quickly scanned the surface in every direction. As expected, there were no ships visible, so Yanit ordered the XO to take the German-built *Leviathan* to the surface. They would be there for less than five minutes, but that's all he and his crew would need to fire all eight Popeye Turbo cruise missiles.

"This is the captain. All engines full stop."

"All engines full stop, aye."

"Kill track 89014 with Popeye."

"Kill track, aye."

"Mark time to launch."

"Mark time to launch, aye."

"Twenty seconds to launch."

"Twenty seconds to launch, aye."

The CIC grew deathly quiet.

"Five seconds to time of launch—*five, four, three, two, one. Fire.*"

On cue, Yanit's fire-control officer turned his ignition key from Off to Fire.

"Boosters armed. Missiles enabled. Popeye One away. Popeye Two away."

Suddenly the entire submarine shook violently. Two cruise missiles exploded from their launch tubes with a deafening roar and rocketed into Iranian airspace. Thirty seconds later, two more missiles screamed into the heavens, carrying conventional payloads but enormous firepower into the heart of Persia. Then a third time. And a fourth.

And as rapidly as the *Leviathan* had come, she sank back into the ink-black waters of the Persian Gulf without a trace.

★ ★ ★ ★ ★

HATZERIM AIR BASE, ISRAEL

Captain Avi Yaron steadied his emotions.

He wasn't scared. He was exhilarated. But he needed to stay calm and focused and not let the spike in adrenaline cloud his judgment.

Like he had done before every training mission, he muted his radio, closed his eyes, and prayed, *"Barukh atah Adonai Eloheinu melekh ha olam, she hehiyanu v'kiymanu v'higi'anu la z'man ha ze."*

Blessed art Thou, Lord our God, King of the universe, who has kept us alive, sustained us, and enabled us to reach this season.

Behind him sat Yonah Meir, his weapons systems officer, who tapped him on the shoulder to let him know he was ready to roll. As he had done on a thousand training missions, Avi throttled up his engines and carefully veered his F-15 out of its underground bunker, then taxied onto the tarmac and waited for clearance. Behind him, a half-dozen flight crews in Israeli-modified F-15s and F-16s also maneuvered across the Hatzerim Air Base toward the prime runway, not far from the city of Beersheva, the town where Avi had been raised. But this was no training mission. This was the real thing.

Operating under strict radio silence, the ground crew used hand signals to give him the *go* sign. Immediately Avi gunned his two engines and put his Strike Eagle in the air.

Rather than rocket to forty-eight thousand feet in less than a minute as he typically did, Avi—flight leader for Alpha Team—shot low and fast across the Negev Desert. Six other heavily armed fighter jets were right behind him. He prayed the Gulfstream 550 electronic warfare jet was already in place. He prayed the Israeli efforts to jam the Jordanian, Egyptian, and Saudi radars had worked. It wasn't clear to him what the

Jordanians would do if they picked up his scent. The king had given private assurances he would not interfere in this mission. But he had no doubt the Saudis and the Egyptians, now that they were on board with the Mahdi, would alert Tehran instantly if they detected Israeli planes moving through the southern route.

Weaving low through the mountains and wadis of the Sinai Peninsula, Avi reached his first critical turn and banked hard to the left. Seconds later, as he crossed into Saudi airspace, his jet hit Mach 2.5. If all went well, he would be over the Iranian nuclear facilities in Natanz in a little under an hour.

★ ★ ★ ★ ★

OFF THE SOUTHERN COAST OF IRAN

Two other Israeli submarines now surfaced, if only for a moment.

The first was positioned near the strategic Strait of Hormuz. The second was positioned about two hundred kilometers to the south in the Gulf of Oman.

One by one, they fired their cruise missiles as well and then slipped beneath the waves with barely a ripple.

★ ★ ★ ★ ★

RAMAT DAVID AIR BASE

Avi's twin brother, Yossi, throttled up his F-16.

Quickly taxiing out of the hangar at the Ramat David Air Base, not far from Har Megiddo, the mountain of Armageddon, he put the pedal to the metal, climbing to fifty-seven thousand feet in less than two minutes. Behind him, eleven more F-16s—all armed to the teeth with Python-5, Sparrow, and AMRAAM missiles and two GBU-28 bunker-buster bombs—lifted off in succession and raced to catch up with him.

As leader of Beta Team, Captain Yossi Yaron led the way through the northern route. Beta Team would arc out into the Mediterranean, bypassing Lebanon, then slice back through Syria, careful not to cross into Turkish airspace at any time. They would eventually cut across the

Kurdistan region of northern Iraq and then into Iran, where they would target the regime's nuclear facilities in Qom.

The first order of business, however, was to not get caught.

Yossi had been the strike force leader in the Israeli attack against a nuclear facility under construction in Syria in the fall of 2007. At the time, he had successfully penetrated Syrian air defenses, hit his target, and slipped back out before the Syrians had even known they were there. He'd been tempted to take a victory loop over Damascus but knew if he ever wanted to fly that route again, he must maintain the strictest discipline. And there was no doubt he'd wanted to fly that route again. But the game was not quite the same this time. Since then, the Syrians had bought and installed advanced air defense systems from both the Russians and the Iranians. Israeli technicians were confident they could penetrate and confuse those systems too, and they were about to find out.

With the glistening blue Med below him, he punched a series of controls on his dashboard. This allowed him to begin invading Syrian communications and radar networks. Soon he was hopping through their signals, unscrambling and decoding and digitally analyzing them until he found and locked onto the Syrian air force's command-and-control frequency. Now he could see what Damascus could see. A few more buttons, and Yossi was taking over the enemy's sensors. Soon he was transmitting false images to them, causing them to see clear skies in every direction rather than the Israeli onslaught that was overtaking them.

A hundred kilometers to the east, Yossi knew, an Israeli Gulfstream 550 electronics plane was simultaneously scanning Turkish and Lebanese frequencies and jamming those as well. What's more, they were monitoring his success—or lack thereof. If they detected a problem, they would alert him. But they hadn't—not yet, at least. So Yossi rocked his wings, alerting his teammates that they were a *go*, and shot into Syria, just above the town of Al Haffah.

57

David and his team finally reached the Qom International Hotel.

The modern, three-story, steel-and-glass building was far more impressive than the Delvar in Khorramabad, but they had no time right now to enjoy it or any of its business-class amenities. While Captain Torres and his men stayed out in the parking lot, David sprinted for the lobby, checked in, asked if a package had arrived for him, and waited for the clerk to find it.

His phone rang. It was Birjandi.

"Hello?"

"Reza, is that you?"

"Yes, it's me," David said. "Is everything okay?"

"No, something has happened," Birjandi said. "I can feel it in my spirit."

"What is it?"

"I don't know exactly. I've been praying and fasting for you, for Najjar, for the country. And something just happened, about an hour ago. I wish I could say I'd had a dream or a vision, but I haven't. It's just an instinct."

"What do you think it is?"

There was a long pause. Then Birjandi said, "I think the war just started."

★　★　★　★　★

TEL AVIV, ISRAEL

Naphtali took a deep breath.

He glanced at the various digital clocks mounted on the conference room wall, noting the times in key capitals around the world. It was 3:34 a.m. in Washington, 10:34 a.m. in Jerusalem, and just after noon in Tehran. Naphtali had stalled long enough. It had been nearly an hour since he'd given the *go* order. The first Israeli planes were now in Iranian airspace. They would soon be hitting their targets. If he didn't call now, the president was going to hear the news from the CIA or the Pentagon, not from him directly. US–Israeli relations were going to be difficult enough from this point forward. He couldn't make them worse by not giving Israel's closest ally a heads-up of what was coming.

He picked up the secure phone in the conference room and asked the Defense Ministry operator to put him through to the White House.

★　★　★　★　★

ARAK, IRAN

A military helicopter landed in the parking lot.

Flanked by six heavily armed Revolutionary Guards, Jalal Zandi was rushed outside wearing a flak jacket and a helmet and carrying his laptop. There he presented his identification and answered several questions to convince the pilot and security crew on the chopper that he was who he said he was. Then he was loaded into the chopper, the door closed, the parking lot was cleared, and they lifted off and headed north.

★　★　★　★　★

QOM, IRAN

"I've heard nothing like that," David said.

"Well, perhaps I am wrong," Birjandi said.

"Is this it?" asked the young clerk, carrying a large DHL box.

"Look, I'll see what I can find out and let you know," David told Birjandi. "But right now I have to go."

"I understand, my friend. May the Lord be with you."

"He is," David said. "He finally is."

"What do you mean?" Birjandi asked, a sudden air of hope in his voice.

"I can't really talk right now," David replied, "but I want you to know that your prayers and your counsel have meant a great deal to me. I am with you, on all of it. I believe now. And I'm so grateful."

He hung up, wishing he could tell Birjandi more about how he'd given his life to Christ—and wishing even more that he could ask the man his many and growing questions. For now, however, he turned his attention to the clerk and the box. It was severely beat up, dented in places and actually ripped in others. The whole thing looked like it had been run over by the delivery truck. But it was definitely addressed to Reza Tabrizi and was marked as being shipped from Munich, though David knew full well it had just come from Langley. He had no idea how Eva had pulled that off, nor did he have the luxury to care.

"Yeah, this looks like mine, but what happened to it?" he asked, feigning annoyance.

"I don't know," the clerk said. "That's just how it came."

"What if I want to file a complaint?"

"I don't know, sir. You'll need to take that up with DHL. Just sign here to say you received it."

David protested slightly, then signed, took his package and his room key, and headed back to the van. There he handed the box to Torres, pulled out his phone, and dialed Javad, who picked up on the first ring.

"I'm at the hotel," he said. "The box arrived."

"You have it?" Javad asked.

"It's in my hands," David said. "Where should I meet you?"

"What better place?" Javad said. "I'll meet you in front of the Jamkaran Mosque in ten minutes."

"Done."

It was not ideal; it was public, and it would be crowded. But they didn't have any other choice. David hung up the phone and quickly told the others his plan. First he told them he was going to take a cab to the world-famous mosque. Torres and his team should follow close behind. It was midday on a Thursday; there shouldn't be much traffic.

But what he told the paramilitary team next caught all of them off guard. It was a high-stakes gamble. It could get him killed. It could get them all killed. But if it worked . . .

★ ★ ★ ★ ★

Four F-15s lifted off from the Tel Nof Air Base near Rehovot.

They blazed west over the Med, then banked sharply to the south. Within seconds, they had the Iranian-flagged *Jamaran* missile frigate and her sister ship, the *Sabalan* frigate, on radar. Both were now 450 kilometers from the Tel Aviv shoreline, flanked by three Iranian destroyers.

★ ★ ★ ★ ★

David handed his pistol to Torres and cleaned out his pockets.

Then, carrying the package, he left the van, hailed a cab, and directed it to the Jamkaran Mosque. On the way, he put on his Bluetooth headset and called Zalinsky. "Is something happening?"

"What do you mean?" Zalinsky asked.

"I'm getting a weird feeling," David said, "like something has started."

"No, it's all pretty quiet right now," Zalinsky said.

"Is the boss going to move?" David asked cryptically so as not to draw the attention of the cab driver.

"Not yet."

"Why not?"

"Murray went to the White House. The president isn't satisfied. He wants another source."

"There's no more time. We got him what he asked for."

"He wants more."

"Like what?"

"He wants Jalal Zandi."

David laughed. "Is he kidding?"

"No, he's dead serious."

"How are we going to do that in the next twenty-four to forty-eight hours?"

"I don't know. What about Khan? He and Zandi worked closely. He has to know where he is."

That was true, David thought, but he hadn't asked Khan much about Zandi and couldn't now. Then he remembered Khan's SIM card in his jacket lining. "Wait," he told Zalinsky. "I'm uploading something to you."

He opened the back of his Nokia phone, inserted the SIM card, and did a search. There it was, all of Zandi's contact information. He was angry with himself for not thinking of it sooner, but he quickly uploaded everything to Langley and got Zalinsky back on the line.

"Got it?" he asked.

"Got it," Zalinsky replied. "Great work. We'll get right on this. Where are you now?"

"I'm in a cab on the way to the Jamkaran Mosque."

"Not sure this is the best time for sightseeing."

"I'm meeting a friend."

"Who?"

David couldn't say openly without attracting the attention of his driver. "I'm delivering the package he asked for."

"You're going to meet Javad Nouri?" Zalinsky said. "I thought that was later tonight."

"He moved it up."

"Why is he in Qom?"

"He's coming just to see me."

"What if you grab him?"

"I can't."

"No, seriously, David, the special ops team is following you, right?"

"Right, but—"

"Then take Nouri down," Zalinsky pressed. "Can you imagine what a coup that would be? Almost as good as getting Zandi, and maybe we can get him, too."

"Wouldn't that unravel everything?" David pushed back. "I mean, if he's gone, then wouldn't the whole project, you know, be compromised?"

David suddenly heard a commotion in the background.

"Something's happening," Zalinsky said. "I'll call you right back."

Frustrated, David checked his watch. They would be at the mosque in less than three minutes. He didn't have time to wait around.

★ ★ ★ ★ ★

WASHINGTON, DC

"Mr. President, I have Prime Minister Naphtali on line one."

Jackson forced his eyes open, grabbed his glasses off the nightstand, and stared at the clock. He turned on the lamp beside his bed.

"Put him through," he told the White House switchboard operator. "Asher, please tell me you have very good news."

"I'm afraid not, Mr. President."

"Of course not," Jackson said. "Good news can always wait until daybreak."

"Mr. President, I am calling to inform you that we have credible, actionable intelligence from inside Iran on where their warheads are. Two are on Iranian naval vessels off our coast. The rest are being attached to intermediate-range ballistic missiles. We have evidence that the Twelfth Imam intends to launch these missiles at us within the next forty-eight to seventy-two hours, and we cannot take the risk of being hit first. Therefore, just moments ago, I ordered the IDF to commence Operation Xerxes to destroy those weapons and neutralize the Iranian threat. I wanted you to be the first to know."

★ ★ ★ ★ ★

INTERNATIONAL WATERS, MEDITERRANEAN SEA

"Fox three, Fox three!"

The Gamma Team leader fired two AGM-84 Harpoon antiship

missiles at the *Jamaran*, while simultaneously jamming the ships' radar and communications. A split second later, his wingman fired two more Harpoons at the *Sabalan*. On cue, their colleagues fired upon the three destroyers.

Meanwhile, as the Harpoons were hurtling toward their targets at the speed of sound, an Israeli Dolphin-class submarine trailing the flotilla fired ten torpedoes in rapid succession.

★ ★ ★ ★ ★

WASHINGTON, DC

"I have to say I'm very disappointed, Asher," Jackson said.

"I understand your position, Mr. President," Naphtali replied. "But please understand mine. There was no more time. We were facing annihilation and are exercising our God-given—and UN–recognized—right to self-defense. We can do this operation alone, if we must. But I am calling not just to inform you but to ask for your country's assistance. The Mahdi and his nuclear force are not just a threat to us. They are a threat to you and to the entire free world."

★ ★ ★ ★ ★

INTERNATIONAL WATERS, MEDITERRANEAN SEA

"Captain, Captain, we're being fired upon!" the Iranian XO cried.

"Deploy countermeasures," the captain of the *Jamaran* shouted back, racing for the bridge.

The sirens on the ship immediately sounded.

"Man your battle stations! Man your battle stations!"

But the attack came too fast. The men had no time to react. The first Harpoon hit the bridge. The second pierced the top of the deck at almost the exact same moment. Both erupted with enormous explosions that incinerated most of the crew within seconds, while below the water, two torpedoes tore massive holes in the underbelly of the ship. Thousands of gallons of icy seawater flooded the lower quarters, and the frigate began to sink almost instantly.

★ ★ ★ ★ ★

The officers and crew of the *Sabalan* had a few seconds more.

And that made all the difference. The captain and XO knew instantly that they were going to die. They weren't going to be able to stop the inbound missiles or torpedoes. But just before the first impact, they were able to reach the fire control panel and launch all of their missiles.

58

"I don't like being put in a corner," the president said.

"Neither do we," the prime minister replied.

"What kind of help do you expect, now that you've launched a war without US consent?"

★ ★ ★ ★ ★

One by one, the sub-launched cruise missiles hit their marks.

Three smashed into the fully staffed Defense Ministry headquarters in Tehran just after lunch, nearly bringing the building down and killing most of those inside.

Minutes later, three other missiles hit the top, middle, and ground floors of the Intelligence Ministry headquarters in Tehran, decimating the building and setting it ablaze.

Another high-priority target for a salvo of Israeli cruise missiles was Facility 311, the nuclear-enrichment facility in the town of Abyek, about sixty miles northwest of Tehran. One minute the complex and its 163 scientists and support staff were there; the next minute they were not.

In the south, no fewer than five cruise missiles obliterated the research and support facilities surrounding the light-water nuclear reactor in Bushehr, while leaving the reactor itself untouched. Without question, this had been the most controversial target for Israeli military planners and senior government officials. Should they hit a nearly active reactor site, particularly one built and partially operated by the Russians? The risks of striking Bushehr were high. So were the risks of leaving the site alone. A Mossad analysis noted that in the first full year of operation, the reactor could generate enough weapons-grade uranium to produce more than fifty bombs the size of the one dropped on Nagasaki. Naphtali had personally made the decision that it had to be neutralized.

★ ★ ★ ★ ★

TEL AVIV, ISRAEL

"Missiles in the air!" the war room's watch commander shouted.

Defense Minister Shimon and the IDF chief of staff immediately rushed out of the conference room into the war room and to the commander's side. Live images were streaming in from the four F-15s out over the Med. Other data were pouring in from the Israeli subs and other naval vessels stationed off the coast.

"Sound the alarms," the commander ordered.

An aide complied immediately, triggering a command sequence that would soon result in air-raid sirens being sounded throughout the country, not knowing yet which cities were targeted but not wanting to take a chance.

"How many do you have?" Shimon asked.

"I count six—no, eight!" the watch commander said.

Naphtali turned to see what was happening. "Mr. President," he said, "I must go. Our country is under attack."

He hung up the phone and headed into the war room only to see the radar tracks of eight ship-to-surface ballistic missiles inbound from the *Sabalan*. As the telemetry poured in, supercomputers calculated the missiles' size, speed, trajectory, and likely points of impact. It wouldn't have taken a genius to guess that most were headed for all of the major population centers along the coast. But Naphtali was stunned to see one of the missiles heading for Jerusalem.

★ ★ ★ ★ ★

QOM, IRAN

David's phone rang just as the cab was nearing the mosque.

"You were right," Zalinsky said, coming back on the line. "Something is happening."

"What?"

"The Israelis have just attacked the Iranian naval flotilla," Zalinsky exclaimed. "The Iranians were able to fire off a salvo of missiles at Tel Aviv and Jerusalem. NSA indicates Israeli cruise missiles are hitting targets all over Iran. Israeli jets are in the air. I need to brief the director. He just got in. But grab Nouri if you can, get to one of the safe houses, and hunker down. I'm guessing most of the Israeli Air Force is going to be on top of you any minute."

★ ★ ★ ★ ★

TEL AVIV, ISRAEL

"Fire the Arrows—now!" Naphtali ordered.

Shimon and the IDF chief of staff barked orders at military aides, who relayed them by secure phone and data lines to commanders at air and missile bases throughout the country. But all of it took precious time.

Naphtali's fists clenched. He scanned the different visual displays in front of him and locked onto one piece of data above the rest. It indicated that the first missile impact would be in downtown Tel Aviv in less than ninety seconds.

★ ★ ★ ★ ★

IRAN

Ten Israeli F-15s swooped in over Hamadan.

They snaked through the mountains and took out the air defenses with little resistance. Then, turning around and taking one pass after another, each pilot fired two bunker-buster bombs on the

400,000-square-foot underground nuclear research and production complex and the administrative buildings on the surface that had been home for Saddaji, Malik, Khan, and Zandi for so many years. Facility 278 was no more. The bombs decimated all life for half a mile and shook the city so hard that many thought another earthquake was under way.

In Arak, four Israeli F-16s dropped GBU-10 bombs on all the buildings surrounding the heavy-water reactor. They were under strict orders not to hit the reactor itself and by God's grace did not. Within minutes, the sixty-thousand-square-foot aboveground complex was completely destroyed, and the reactor was rendered useless.

The pilots turned and headed home.

★ ★ ★ ★ ★

TEL AVIV, ISRAEL

The prime minister was actually wrong.

The Arrow wasn't designed to stop short-range missiles. Their only hope at this point was the Patriot. Fortunately, there was a Patriot battalion located at the air base at Tel Nof, just south of Tel Aviv, made up of a fire control center, a radar center, six mobile missile batteries mounted on the backs of specially designed semitrailers, and more than four hundred Israeli personnel running the highly complex operation.

But as Naphtali and Shimon watched the video feeds and listened to the encrypted radio traffic from their vantage point in the main war room at the defense ministry, they weren't sure if the team at Tel Nof was going to be able to react in time.

★ ★ ★ ★ ★

"I'm seeing three Tel Aviv inbounds," the on-site commander said.

"That's affirm—I have three," the tactical control officer said.

"Time to target?"

"First to hit in eighty seconds, sir. Do you certify inbounds are hostile?"

"I certify all are hostile. Select firing batteries."

"Batteries selected, sir."

"Go from standby to engage."

"System engaged," the TCO said, triple-checking his instrumentation.

"Illuminate the targets."

"Targets illuminated."

"Fire one and two—go!" the commander said.

The TCO flipped a switch and fired the first two PAC-3 missiles moments apart.

"Fire three and four—go!"

The TCO launched the second round of Patriots.

"Fire five and six—go!"

The third set of Patriot missiles exploded from their launchers and streaked into the sky.

★ ★ ★ ★ ★

"Get a lock on the Jerusalem inbound—now!"

To Naphtali, listening to the radio traffic, the thirty-one-year-old Patriot missile battery commander at the Palmachim Air Base near Rishon LeZion, just south of Tel Aviv, didn't sound nearly as controlled and professional as the commander at Tel Nof or the Patriot commanders in Ashdod or Haifa who were simultaneously ordering their men to identify, track, and fire at the inbounds. But Naphtali felt the young man's urgency. None of them knew which missile, if any, had the nuclear warhead, so they couldn't afford to let a single one through.

The Palmachim commander rapidly ran through the checklist of procedures with his tactical control officer. Then he ordered the TCO to fire on the single ballistic missile headed for the heart of Jerusalem.

Three PAC-3 interceptors burst from their canisters and raced upward at Mach 5.0. One of the video screens in the war room showed a live shot from a camera on the roof of the air base, and Naphtali could see the white contrails of the Patriots streaking toward their prey.

★ ★ ★ ★ ★

A massive explosion occurred in the skies over Tel Aviv.

Two seconds later, a second concussion could be heard and felt for miles. The first inbound missile had just suffered a direct hit from the lead Patriot interceptor. The second interceptor hit the missile's debris, and its explosion turned what was left into dust.

Back at Tel Nof, the fire control room erupted with wild cheering. The cheering intensified when the second set of Patriot interceptors hit their marks as well. But then the room went deadly quiet as the third set of PAC-3 interceptors missed their marks by less than thirty meters and ten meters respectively.

Horrified, the commander, the TCO, the radar operator, and the rest of the staff could only watch helplessly as the third Iranian missile accelerated to earth with no way for any of them to stop it. An instant later, it plunged through the roof of the sprawling Dizengoff shopping center in the heart of Israel's commercial capital, instantly killing more than four hundred shoppers and causing much of the building to collapse upon itself.

The people had never had a warning. Only seconds later did the air-raid sirens in Tel Aviv and throughout the rest of Israel begin to sound.

★ ★ ★ ★ ★

Naphtali saw it too.

He, too, was horrified. There was no indication the warhead was nuclear. But could it have been chemical? Biological?

Still, his attention quickly shifted back to the ballistic missile inbound for Jerusalem. The air-raid sirens were now sounding. But he knew it was all going to be too late. Scores of Israelis were about to die unless this missile was somehow intercepted. But it had already reached its apogee. It was beginning to descend. And the Patriots were still climbing.

★ ★ ★ ★ ★

IRAN

Esfahān was one of the more complicated targets.

All of the facilities were aboveground. None of them were hardened. But the site included four small Chinese-built research reactors and a yellowcake uranium-conversion facility in an area covering about 100,000 square feet. Three F-16s were tasked with this mission. Each fired two Paveway III guided bombs and a combination of Maverick and Harpoon air-to-ground missiles.

Simultaneously, a squadron of ten F-16s hit Iranian missile production facilities in Khorramabad, Bakhtarun, and Manzariyeh—all of which were not far from the heavy-water reactor in Arak—as well as missile production and missile launching sites near Natanz and in Hasan.

★ ★ ★ ★ ★

TEL AVIV, ISRAEL

All the other inbound Iranian missiles had been shot down.

But at the moment no one in the war room could take much solace.

"It's aiming for the Knesset!" Shimon shouted.

Sure enough, the Iranian cruise missile was now clearly bearing down on the parliament building, the heart of the Israeli democracy.

"Can't you stop it?" Naphtali demanded. *"Can't you do something else?"*

Even as he said it, Naphtali knew the answer and he couldn't breathe. The Knesset was in session. More than a hundred legislators were there right now, Naphtali knew, being briefed by the vice prime minister on Operation Xerxes. Hundreds of staffers and security personnel and visitors and tourists were there too. There was no way to warn them, no way to get them to safety in time.

QOM, IRAN

The cab finally pulled up in front of the Jamkaran Mosque.

David paid the driver but asked him to pull over to the side of the road and wait for a few minutes. David scanned the crowd but did not see Javad yet. It was hard not to marvel at the architecturally gorgeous structure, the mammoth turquoise dome of the mosque in the center, flanked by two smaller green domes on each side and two exquisitely painted minarets towering over them all. The site—revered since the tenth century, when a Shia cleric of the time, Sheikh Hassan Ibn Muthlih Jamkarani, was supposedly visited by the Twelfth Imam—had once been farmland. Now it was one of the most visited tourist destinations in all of Iran.

Over the last few years, Hosseini and Darazi had funneled millions of dollars into renovating the mosque and its facilities and building beautiful new multilane highways between the mosque and downtown Qom and between the mosque and Tehran. Both leaders visited regularly, and the mosque had become the subject of myriad books, television programs, and documentary films. After a sighting of the Twelfth Imam just prior to his appearance on the world stage and the rumor that a little girl mute from birth had been healed by the Mahdi after visiting there, the crowds had continued to build.

David watched as dozens of buses filled with pilgrims pulled in, dropped off their passengers and guides, and then circled around to the main parking lot, while other buses picked up their passengers and headed home. He estimated that there were a couple hundred people

milling about out front, either coming or going. There were a few uniformed police officers around, but everything seemed quiet and orderly.
Javad Nouri was a shrewd man. He had chosen well. Any disturbance
here would have scores of witnesses.

★ ★ ★ ★ ★

APPROACHING NATANZ, IRAN

Avi Yaron was still in the lead.

So far as he knew, his squadron had not been detected yet, but
his hands were perspiring in his gloves. Sweat dripped down his
face even though he had the air-conditioning in the cockpit on full
blast. He raced low across the desert, running parallel with Iran's
Highway 7.

He knew the maps. He knew the terrain. He knew Highway 7 would
take him straight into Natanz, if he wanted. But he couldn't run the risk
that someone driving along that road would see the Star of David on
the tail of his or his comrades' fighter jets and make a phone call that
would blow their element of surprise. So he stayed a few kilometers
to the north and kept praying that nothing would slow him, nothing
would stop him.

A moment later, he pulled up hard and quickly gained altitude. A
thousand meters. Two thousand. Three. Four. At five thousand meters
he cleared the highest peaks of the Karkas mountain chain. Then he
leveled out and accelerated again. Now the Natanz nuclear facility was
before him. He could hardly believe it. He had pored over the satellite
photographs. He knew every inch, every doorway, every ventilation
duct. Now he could actually see the six critical buildings aboveground,
the uranium separation plants, the research facilities, and the administration buildings covering some two hundred thousand square feet.
Those were important, but they would be hit by the next wave of IAF
pilots.

For Avi and his team, the mission was to decimate the underground
complex, the pearl of the Iranian nuclear program. It covered an area of
nearly seven hundred thousand square feet. It was seventy-five feet deep

and covered by a steel- and concrete-hardened roof. This was where the Iranians housed some seven thousand centrifuges. These centrifuges spun night and day, enriching uranium from the 3 to 5 percent needed to run a power plant to the 20 percent needed for medical experimentation. According to the latest intel from the Mossad's man in Tehran, this was also where the Iranians enriched the 20 percent uranium to weapons grade of 95 percent purity and higher.

"Now, Yonah, now!" Avi cried.

Behind him, his weapons systems officer fired the first of two GBU-28 bunker-buster bombs. Moments later, he fired the second.

Avi felt a surge of pride and quickly pulled up and away from the site. He imagined what it would have been like to fly over Hitler's Germany in the forties and wished he could tell his parents—both of whom were Holocaust survivors—where he was and what he was doing.

The precision-guided munitions dropped clean. They hurtled toward the center of the underground complex as Avi shot like a rocket into the brilliant blue sky.

★　★　★　★　★

TEL AVIV, ISRAEL

"Fifteen seconds to impact!" the war room commander said.

Naphtali couldn't bear to look. And what if the warhead was nuclear? What would they do then? This couldn't be happening, not on his watch.

"Twelve seconds."

Naphtali cursed himself. He should have launched the attack sooner. But he hadn't known for certain there were nuclear warheads on the Iranian ships. What else could he have done?

"Ten seconds."

The two PAC-3 interceptors were closing in, one from the south and one from the east. Until then, all Naphtali, Shimon, and the military commanders could see was the radar trajectory of the inbounds on a giant video screen. But now Israel's Channel 2 had live images shot from a news helicopter of the Iranian missile diving for the heart of the New City of Jerusalem and the two Patriot interceptors racing to take it out.

★　★　★　★　★

NATANZ, IRAN

Beep, beep, beep, beep, beep.

The missile warning light on his dashboard was going off. Seated behind him, Yonah confirmed they had two surface-to-air missiles racing toward them. Yonah immediately deployed countermeasures, firing flares and chaff while Avi rolled the F-15 to the left and raced toward the mountains. One of the missiles took the bait and exploded behind them. But the other sliced through the fireball and smoke and was rapidly catching up to them.

Below them, the earth was an inferno. Each of the Israeli fighter jets had successfully dropped its ordnance, and another dozen Israeli planes were five minutes behind them. So far they had accomplished their mission. They had achieved the element of surprise. They had dropped their bombs. They had obliterated much of the Natanz facility and had likely killed scores of Iranian nuclear scientists and engineers. But that was the easy part. Now they had to get home.

Avi banked hard to the right, then rolled to the left. The missile was still behind them. It was still gaining on them. Yonah fired off another round of countermeasures, but again they were unsuccessful.

★　★　★　★　★

TEL AVIV, ISRAEL

"Six seconds," the watch commander yelled.

At that moment Levi Shimon turned away, but Naphtali couldn't. He wanted to. He understood the instinct. But he kept watching, first the monitor with the radar track, then the live images coming in from Channel 2.

"Four seconds."

Suddenly the first Patriot interceptor clipped the tail of the inbound cruise missile. That knocked the missile off its course and sent it tumbling through the sky. A half second later, the second interceptor scored a direct hit on the warhead, turning it into a gigantic fireball crashing down to earth.

Everyone in the war room erupted in applause and cheering.

★ ★ ★ ★ ★

QOM, IRAN

Four fighter jets suddenly roared over the mosque.

They were so low, most of the crowd instinctively ducked down. David did as well, as stunned to see the jets as anyone else. The crowd cheered, assuming they were Iranian pilots training for a showdown with the Zionists. After all, the TV and newspapers were filled with talk of imminent hostilities, even as the Mahdi proclaimed over and over again his desire for peace and justice.

But David could see these were not Russian-built MiG-29s. Nor were they aging American-built F-4 Phantoms, bought by the Shah before the Revolution. These were F-16s. President Jackson hadn't sent them. Which could only mean one thing: the Israelis were here.

★ ★ ★ ★ ★

Yossi Yaron tried not to think about the mosque.

If it were up to him, he would have dropped his ordnance on the cherished site of the Twelvers and obliterated it forever. But Israeli military planners would have none of it. Israeli pilots would not be bombing religious or civilian targets under any circumstances, they repeated over and over again. They would not be bombing water or electrical plants, bridges, industrial facilities, or other civilian infrastructure.

Their focus was narrow and their mission precise: to neutralize Iran's nuclear weapons program and protect the Israeli homeland. Could they completely wipe out the program? Probably not. But the defense minister believed they could set it back at least five to ten years, and that would buy the Jewish people desperately needed time. Yaron hoped the pilgrims at the Jamkaran Mosque had seen the Star of David on the tails of all four F-16s. He just wished he could see their faces when they realized what was happening.

★　★　★　★　★

Avi Yaron wanted to radio his men.

He wanted to make sure they were racing back for the Persian Gulf, not waiting around for him. The Iranian Air Force would be all over them any moment. None of them were worried about getting shot down by mere kids. The Iranian pilots were typically too young and badly trained and had little or no actual combat experience. Worse, they were flying jets more than twice their age, many of which were practically held together with superglue and duct tape since spare parts had long been banned by the international sanctions against the regime. No, the problem wasn't the Iranian pilots or their planes; it was the Israelis' own fuel supply.

The ground crews back in the Negev had stripped their F-15s and F-16s down to the bare minimum to add fuel tanks, giving them additional range. Once outside of Iranian airspace, they could get to safe zones where they could hook up with Israeli refueling tankers. But they had to get there first. If they had to engage in dogfights or outrun SAMs or triple-A fire, they were going to burn fuel they couldn't afford.

60

QOM, IRAN

David felt a tap on his shoulder.

He turned around, and there was Javad Nouri, surrounded by a half-dozen plainclothes bodyguards.

"Mr. Tabrizi, good to see you again."

"Mr. Nouri, you as well," David said. He wondered if Javad and his team had seen the jets.

"I trust you had no trouble getting here."

"Not at all," David said.

"Have you ever been here before?"

It seemed like an odd question, given the moment.

"Actually, I'm ashamed to say I have not."

"Someday I will have to give you a tour."

"I would like that very much."

★ ★ ★ ★ ★

KARKAS MOUNTAINS, IRAN

Reaching the mountains, Avi Yaron cleared the closest peak.

Then he pushed the yoke forward, diving into one of the canyons. Yonah craned his neck but couldn't get a visual, though the missile was still on his radarscope. They hadn't shaken it yet.

Snaking through the canyons, Avi kept pushing the plane faster and faster, burning tremendous amounts of fuel every second.

"Avi, it's right on us," Yonah shouted.

Avi accelerated still further and held his breath. Now it wasn't fuel he feared. Now it was the split-second decisions he was having to make every few hundred meters. One wrong move and they could plow into a mountainside. One wrong move and they could scrape against the top of a ridge, gutting their fuselage and rupturing their fuel tanks. Either way, they'd crash and burn. They'd never have time to eject, and even if they did, neither wanted to be captured by the Iranians. That was a fate worse than death.

★ ★ ★ ★ ★

QOM, IRAN

Javad looked at the box in David's hands.

"Is that the package we were expecting?"

"It is," David said, "but we have a problem."

"What is that?"

David glanced around. He noticed there were several more body-guards taking up positions in a perimeter around them. There was also a large white SUV waiting by the curb with a guard holding the back door open. Ahead of it was another SUV, presumably serving as the lead security car. Behind it was a third, completing the package.

"Most of the phones are damaged and unusable," David explained, handing the mangled box to Javad. "Something must have happened in the shipping."

Javad cursed and his expression immediately darkened. "We *need* these."

"I know."

"Now what are we going to do?"

"Look, I can go back to Munich and get more. It's what I wanted to do in the first place. But—"

"But Esfahani told you not to leave."

"Well, I—"

"I know, I know. Allah help me. Esfahani is a fool. If he weren't the nephew of Mohsen Jazini, he wouldn't be involved at all."

"What do you want me to do, Mr. Nouri?" David asked. "That's all that matters, what you and the Promised One want. Please know that I will do anything to serve my Lord."

The words had just fallen from his lips when he heard brakes screech behind him. Then everything seemed to go into slow motion. He heard the crack of a sniper rifle, and one of Javad's bodyguards went down.

Crack, crack.

Two more of Javad's men went down. Then Javad himself took a bullet in the right shoulder and began staggering. He was bleeding badly. David threw himself on Javad to protect him as the gunfire intensified and more bodyguards went down.

He turned to see where the shooting was coming from. He saw buses. He saw taxis. He saw people running and screaming. Then he saw a white van driving past. The side door was open. He could see flashes of gunfire pouring out of three muzzles. By now, an Iranian police officer had his revolver out and was shooting back. Two plainclothes agents on the periphery raised submachine guns and fired at the van as it sped away, weaving in and out of traffic and disappearing around the bend.

★ ★ ★ ★ ★

Yossi could now see his target just eight kilometers ahead.

The once top-secret uranium enrichment facility at Qom had been revealed to the world on September 25, 2009, but the Israeli Mossad had known about it since late 2007. Designed to hold three thousand centrifuges, there was no way that this center was for developing peaceful, civilian nuclear power, as the ayatollahs comically claimed. The complex was built deep underground. It was built underneath an Iranian Revolutionary Guard Corps base. It was heavily guarded and surrounded by a phalanx of surface-to-air missiles.

But not for long.

Two of the three F-16s behind him pulled even on his left. His own wingman pulled even on his right. Yossi took his weapons off safety and fired six AGM-65 Mavericks, one right after the other. A split second later, his comrades followed suit. For a moment, the air in front of Yossi was filled with a blaze of antiaircraft artillery.

At nearly the speed of sound, all twenty-four air-to-ground missiles screamed into the radar stations and the missile silos and the triple-A batteries surrounding the main facilities and blew them to smithereens. Yossi pulled back on his yoke to gain some altitude. He fired his first GPS-guided, two-thousand-pound bunker-buster bomb, then his second as well. The ground shook, writhed, and buckled, and soon everything Yossi could see below him was ablaze. It was time to gather his men and head for home.

★ ★ ★ ★ ★

David heard the deafening roar of the explosions, one after another.

He turned toward the mountains and could see enormous balls of fire and plumes of smoke rising into the sky and the Israeli fighter jets disappearing into the clouds. As the ground convulsed violently, the minarets began to totter. People were again screaming and running in all directions as the first tower came crashing down, followed by the second, and suddenly the turquoise dome of the mosque split in half.

David covered his head and made sure Javad was covered too. Then he turned and surveyed the carnage. Bodies were sprawled. Some were dead. Others were severely wounded. David turned Javad over. He was covered in blood. His eyes were dilated, but he was still breathing. He was still alive.

"Javad, look at me," David said gently. "It's going to be okay. Just keep your eyes on me. I'm going to pray for you."

Javad flickered to life for a moment and mouthed the words *Thank you*. Then his eyes closed, and David called for help.

"Somebody, help. My friend needs help."

Guns still drawn, three injured bodyguards rushed to his side as David carefully picked up Javad and carried him to the white SUV. Together, they helped lay Javad on the backseat. One security man climbed in the back with him. Another climbed into one of the middle seats. The third shut and locked the side door, then got in the front passenger seat.

"Wait, wait; you forgot these," David yelled just before the guard closed the door.

He picked up the box of satellite phones and gave them to the guard. "The Mahdi wanted these," David said. "They don't all work. But some of them do."

He pulled out a pen and wrote his mobile number on the box. "Here's my number. Have the Mahdi's people call me and tell me how Javad is. And tell me if there's anything I can do for the Mahdi himself."

The guard thanked David and shook his hand vigorously. Then the door closed. The motorcade raced off, and David stood there alone, staring at the billows of smoke rising from the air strikes just over the horizon.

He turned and rushed to the side of one of the severely wounded guards. He could hear police sirens and ambulances in the distance. They would be there soon. David took off his jacket and used it to put pressure on the man's bleeding leg, and as he did, he silently prayed over the man too, asking the true God to comfort him and even heal him. This man was an enemy, to be sure, but David figured God loved him anyway.

Emergency vehicles began pulling up to the scene, and medics had to push their way through the crowds that had formed to triage the wounded and get them to the nearest hospitals. In the commotion, David stepped back and blended in and soon slipped away, never to be questioned, much less exposed.

★　★　★　★　★

KARKAS MOUNTAINS, IRAN

The missile was bearing down on them.

Avi didn't know these canyons. Yonah knew he didn't know them. But faster and faster they went.

Avi pulled back on the yoke and shot straight up into the atmosphere. The missile stayed on them. Avi pulled harder, flipping the plane and doing a full 180 until they were sizzling through the narrow canyon walls again.

"Avi, watch out!" Yonah yelled.

Avi pulled up slightly and just in time, missing a ridge by less than twenty meters. Then he banked hard to the right, missing the side of another peak by even less. It was a gutsy move and a close one, but it now put them out in the open, away from the mountains, and there was nowhere left to run.

But just then both men heard an explosion behind them as the missile missed the turn and ran straight into the cliff. Avi felt the jet shake. He could actually feel the intense heat of the flames meant for them. Once again he had cheated death and couldn't describe the experience. It was exhilarating—intoxicating—and Avi hollered at the top of his lungs. Yonah joined him.

They were young and invincible and the new heroes of Israel, and they were headed for home.

★ ★ ★ ★ ★

FRIDAY
MARCH 11

(IRAN TIME)

61

It was early Friday afternoon.

Marseille hadn't imagined being back in Syracuse less than a week after leaving. But this had not been a normal week. The world seemed to be spinning off its axis. It had been difficult to take her eyes off the television reports since she awoke in DC on Thursday morning. She'd been glued to images of the Israeli air strikes in Iran and the Iranian response. Her best friend was on her honeymoon in Israel, her old friend David was in Iran, and she could reach neither. She watched helplessly as missiles were fired into Israel from north and south. She wept when she saw the images of Israelis forced to hide in bomb shelters and of parents desperately trying to put gas masks on their babies and small children. She could not believe it when her own president denounced Israel for its preemptive strike and demanded an immediate cease-fire. How could he not recognize the evil intentions of Iran or acknowledge Israel's right to defend itself?

The only good news was that none of the missiles striking Israel seemed to be nuclear, chemical, or biological, and under the circumstances that was actually miraculous. But she wished there were something more she could do than pray.

She was holding on to God and His Word as the new information and myriad questions unearthed in the past few days swirled in her head. During her Bible study that morning, she had read in Hebrews about the confidence followers of Jesus can have, based on what He has done for them, and she particularly loved the words "This hope we have as an anchor of the soul." It was this unchangeable truth that encouraged her as she looked out the window at the gray skies of upstate New York while the plane made its descent into Hancock Field.

★ ★ ★ ★ ★

KARAJ, IRAN

He was exhausted but alive and grateful to see some friendly faces.

It was nearly midnight on Friday in Iran when David finally made it to Safe House Six, the basement apartment the CIA owned on the outskirts of the city of Karaj, about twenty kilometers west of Tehran, in the foothills of the Alborz Mountains. Captain Torres and his men greeted David warmly. They immediately heated up some food for him and wanted to know every detail of his harrowing journey from Qom amid wave after wave of Israeli air attacks from fighter planes and sub-launched cruise missiles. But first David wanted to know about them.

"Are all your men okay?" David asked, taking a piece of naan.

"Yes, yes, we're all fine," Torres said. "The van was pretty shot up, but we ditched it and stole another."

"Good—and Khan, how is he?"

"He was pretty shaken up by everything, but he'll pull through," Torres said. "They flew him out yesterday, just before the air strikes began. He's in Bahrain now. They're doing more interrogations and a medical check. I expect him to be in Gitmo by this time tomorrow."

David nodded and chewed his Persian bread slowly. They offered him one of the cold beers the Agency kept stashed in the refrigerator, but he waved it off. He did not feel like celebrating.

True, in a narrow sense, his plan had worked. Following David's order to open fire as they had, Torres and his team had taken out key men around Javad Nouri. They had severely wounded Javad himself without killing him. They had, therefore, neutralized Javad's ability to serve as the Mahdi's trusted right-hand man at a time when the Mahdi would need him most. Most importantly, they had given David the opportunity to play the hero. By taking Javad to the ground and protecting him with his own body from further gunfire and then getting him quickly into the SUV and off to the hospital, David had proven his loyalty to the Mahdi. It was something Javad and his men would likely not soon forget. Indeed, David hoped it was something they would eventually reward.

That said, his overall mission had been a total failure. By God's grace—and there could be no other explanation for it—David had done nearly everything his superiors at Langley had asked of him. He hadn't captured Javad Nouri or found Jalal Zandi yet. But he had nabbed Tariq Khan. He had found the locations of all eight warheads. He had gotten the information back to Zalinsky and Murray before the Iranians had launched them. And he had put more phones in the hands of the Twelfth Imam's inner circle, which he prayed would bear more fruit in the days and weeks to come. But what had really come of any of it? At the end of the day, the president hadn't been willing to use all means necessary to stop Iran from getting the Bomb. It had all been too little, too late. So what was he supposed to do next?

David apologized to the men and excused himself. He took a long, hot shower and changed into some clean clothes, and as he did, he tried to make sense of the risks he was taking. He was more than willing to put his life on the line to protect his country. He was even more willing now that he knew for certain where he was going when he died. But if neither the Agency nor the president were going to act quickly and decisively on any of the information he was gathering, then what was the point? If they weren't going to take risks for peace, then why should he?

Exhausted and unable to process any more, he lay down and quickly fell asleep.

★ ★ ★ ★ ★

SYRACUSE, NEW YORK

The viewing would be that evening.

The funeral was set for the next morning at eleven. The Shirazis had offered to have her stay with them, but as much as she longed to see David's childhood home for the first time in years, she'd insisted on staying at a hotel and not burdening the family.

Marseille rented a car and a GPS system at the airport. Then she drove back to the University Sheraton, where she had stayed for Lexi's wedding. As she did, she pulled out her cell phone and called David's sister-in-law, Nora Shirazi. Nora, the wife of David's eldest brother, Azad, had been her contact point for the past few days. They had e-mailed back and forth several times, but it felt strange that Nora wasn't even going to be able to make it to Syracuse from their home outside of Philly. Nora was the only woman in the family now, filled as it was by the strong Shirazi men. Even Nora's newborn child was a little boy, carrying on the family name into the next generation. But it was little Peter, born only on Tuesday, who prevented Nora from attending the funeral.

Marseille had replied to Nora's e-mail as soon as she'd received the message about Mrs. Shirazi's passing on Wednesday night. She'd explained that she'd actually never left the East Coast and would very much like to be there for the funeral. She'd heard from Nora within the hour and several times on Thursday as the funeral arrangements were being made.

The call went through. "Hello?" a woman said at the other end.

"Nora?"

"Is this Marseille?"

"Yes, hi—I hope I'm not bothering you."

"No, no, not at all," Nora said. "I'm just feeding the baby. I actually thought you might be Azad. But I'm glad it's you. Did you get in okay?"

"I did, thanks. I'm heading to the hotel right now. I just wanted to see if there was anything I could do, you know, to be helpful in some way. I feel a little like, I don't know, like a stranger."

"Nonsense—you're practically family," Nora said with a genuine warmth that touched Marseille. "Heck, you've known the Shirazis longer than I have, and Dad for one is really eager to see you. Honestly, when Azad told him you were coming, he said it was the first time in days when Dad's spirits actually seemed to pick up a bit."

Then the baby started fussing. Nora apologized and said she had to go. Marseille said she understood and hung up, but as she drove, she wished they could have talked longer. It wasn't just that Nora was part of the Shirazi family or that Nora had to have known David far better over the last few years than she had. It was also the sinking feeling that at the moment, she really had no one else to talk to.

★ ★ ★ ★ ★

KARAJ, IRAN

David sat bolt upright in his bed.

He checked his watch. It was not yet dawn, but he couldn't believe he'd been sleeping for so long. He rubbed his eyes, then jumped up, splashed some water on his face, and quietly went out into the living room to find a laptop and log on to the Internet.

Once online, he checked his AOL account, hoping to write a quick note to his dad and to Marseille. What he found, however, were nearly a dozen e-mails from Azad and Nora and even Saeed, and when he learned that his mother had died some forty-eight hours earlier and his brothers were angry that he wasn't calling or e-mailing back, his heart broke.

There were e-mails about the viewing and e-mails about the memorial service and e-mails about the burial, all of them asking where he was and when he was coming.

What was he supposed to say to them? How could he possibly explain to them why he wasn't going to be there for his own mother's funeral or why he hadn't even had the decency to be in touch with them? No lie would suffice. And for David, at the moment, not even the truth sufficed.

★ ★ ★ ★ ★

SYRACUSE, NEW YORK

Marseille allowed herself extra time to get to the viewing.

Not wanting to be late, she wound her way through the neighborhoods near the university, crossed Erie Boulevard, and started up the hills into the northern neighborhoods, thankful for her GPS. Carter Funeral Home was a lovely white building set away from the road.

It looked welcoming. There were already several cars parked outside, though it was still thirty minutes before the visiting hours would begin.

Hoping to have some quiet moments with David's family, yet not sure if it was appropriate to show up early, she decided to just go in. The front doors were propped slightly open, and she could see a small group at the top of a short set of stairs. She suddenly worried that no one would recognize her and felt a flutter of fear and awkwardness. But as the older man in the center of the little knot of people glanced in her direction for a moment and she saw instant recognition light up his eyes, she sighed with relief and returned his smile.

"My dear Marseille, it is so wonderful that you are here," Dr. Shirazi said, wiping his tears and actually brightening. "I am so honored that you would come. To have such a longtime friend here with us means a great deal."

Dr. Shirazi came to her and embraced her, and she almost lost control of her emotions. To be in a father's arms, to smell the somehow-familiar scent of pipe tobacco and aftershave, was almost too much to bear.

"Dr. Shirazi, I am so glad to be here with you," Marseille said, sniffling. "But I am so sorry for all the sadness you are bearing, that all of you are bearing. And I'm so sorry that David can't be here."

Her voice faltered just then, and she suddenly wished she had waited for him to bring up David's name.

But Dr. Shirazi just patted her on the back. "Thank you, Marseille. The empathy of a friend is a treasure I do not take for granted. And I know you have had more sorrow than a young woman should ever be asked to bear. Thank you for sharing ours."

His words soothed her, and in her heart she thanked God for the kindness of this dear man.

"And as for David," Dr. Shirazi said softly and with an intensity that surprised her, "he is where he is needed most. I know it breaks his heart to miss this difficult time with the family. But my heart is not broken because he is a good son, because he sat with me and his mother for hours and cared for me, because he is a good man and this is the heart's desire of any father. Do not judge him, Marseille. It is not vanity or riches that have prevented him from coming. He is doing his duty, and I am grateful—and I know his mother would be, too."

Marseille was amazed by the firm words and will of Dr. Shirazi. She wondered how he could have such strength, such faith in David, unless he knew the truth about who David worked for and where he now was. But how could he?

"Come, now," he said, taking her by the arm. "Come say hello to my other two sons. It has been a long time since you've seen each other, no?"

David's father guided her over to greet Azad and Saeed, two strikingly handsome men with the same piercing brown eyes as their younger brother. They each embraced her, kissing her on the cheek, and she fell into easy conversation with them all until people began arriving and they needed to host.

★ ★ ★ ★ ★

SATURDAY
MARCH 12

(IRAN TIME)

62

David spent the day forcing himself not to call home.

He had returned all the e-mails from his family. He had told his brothers and Nora the best lie he could come up with, and he prayed to God his father could read between the lines and forgive him.

As for Marseille, he hadn't written her at all. He didn't want to lie to her. He would rather say nothing than deceive her. But having no contact whatsoever was more painful than he thought he could bear. Did she know about his mother? Had anyone in his family thought to tell her? What would she think of him when she learned he hadn't gone to the funeral, that he hadn't even been in touch? What could he possibly say to her to make it right?

Going stir crazy in the safe house, he called Zalinsky to check in. The news from Langley was mixed. Aside from the administration's denunciation of the Israeli strikes and the president's threat to support a UN Security Council resolution condemning the Jewish State for unprovoked and unwarranted acts of aggression, the early evidence suggested the Israeli operation had been far more effective than the Agency would have believed possible. It would still take days if not weeks to assess, but initial Keyhole satellite photography indicated that all of Iran's major nuclear sites had been destroyed, as had most of their missile production sites. The Patriot missile batteries had worked better than expected in defending the Israeli homeland. In fact, what the media didn't know yet, but the CIA had just confirmed, was one of the missiles shot down by a Patriot over

Jerusalem had, in fact, been carrying a nuclear warhead. Fortunately, the missile had been destroyed before the warhead could arm itself, and recovery crews had been successful in locating the warhead's uranium trigger before significant radiation could be released. What was more, it appeared the rest of the warheads had been taken out in the air strikes.

Also remarkable, Zalinsky said, was that Israeli losses had been so low. Director Allen had told the president that Agency analysts envisioned the Israelis losing forty to sixty planes if they ever embarked on a preemptive strike—one of the reasons Jackson didn't think Naphtali, in the end, would actually authorize such a mission. Actual planes downed, however, were far less. Only six F-16s had been shot down by ground-to-air missiles in Iran. Two more were lost to mechanical failures. A KC-130 tanker and an F-15 had suffered a midair collision over northeastern Syria during a refueling operation. But not a single Israeli plane had been shot down in combat.

That said, the Twelfth Imam had ordered a full-scale retaliation.

More than two hundred Israeli citizens had already been killed in the first twenty-four hours of missile attacks from Iran, Hezbollah, Hamas, and Syria, Zalinsky said, and the death toll was expected to keep rising. The injured were many multiples of that number, and Israeli hospitals were rapidly approaching their breaking point. Millions of Israelis had been forced into bomb shelters. All flights into and out of Ben Gurion International Airport had been canceled, yet thousands of tourists were still streaming to the airport, not knowing what else to do.

"The Israelis have launched massive air attacks against their neighbors," Zalinsky said. "And they seem to be gearing up for major ground campaigns within the next few hours."

"What do you want me to do?" David asked, his anger rising in proportion to his sense of helplessness.

"Nothing," Zalinsky said. "Just hunker down and stay safe until we figure out how to get you and your men out of there."

It was precisely what David didn't want to hear. He hadn't signed up to hunker down or retreat. He wanted a new mission. He wanted to make a difference, to stop the killing. But how?

★ ★ ★ ★ ★

SYRACUSE, NEW YORK

Saturday morning's memorial service was beautiful.

It was in a quiet and lovely room at the back of the funeral home, with Persian area rugs over green carpet and white upholstered chairs set in place. In the center of the room were several huge flower arrangements set around a framed portrait of Mrs. Shirazi. Marseille had been welcomed with open arms by David's father and brothers, and sitting in the room filled with coworkers and neighbors, she knew it was right to have come. She belonged.

She was grateful for her connection to this warm family, grateful for the memories of infrequent but memorable visits paid back and forth between Syracuse and New Jersey during her childhood before her own mother had died. Marseille remembered the vibrant, passionate Mrs. Shirazi from those years and smiled. Somehow, being here made her feel closer to her own parents. Azad stood with tears in his dark eyes and spoke of the faithful, loving mother Mrs. Shirazi had been. Saeed read from a book of Persian poetry. Then he translated the poem into English, and Marseille found the words strange yet beautiful.

Could be I know you for years,
As if You have been with me for centuries,
For Your strong presence,
Your now and then smiles,
Your gentle Heart,
Your sweet Voice,
*Yet are touchable for me!**

The Persian words were so evocative and fascinating. The land of Iran intrigued her, and her thoughts turned to David, as they had a thousand times that day. Was he okay? When would she hear from him again? How would he react when she told him what she knew? Would

---

* This poem was written by an anonymous Iranian blogger on August 8, 2007.

the Lord help her heart loosen its grip on thoughts of him? Marseille prayed for David as she had for years, that he would search for God and that Jesus would reveal Himself, that her old friend would open his heart to the Savior, and that Jesus would be at home in the heart of David Shirazi.

EPILOGUE

Ahmed Darazi brought tea to his colleagues in the command center.

The lighting was dim, the air was thick with cigarette smoke, and the atmosphere was solemn. This wasn't going as planned, and Darazi was at a loss to know why. How many times had the Twelfth Imam promised that the Zionists would be annihilated? How many times had he said the destruction of the Jews and Christians was imminent? How many times had Darazi himself repeated those words? Why wasn't it happening? What had gone wrong? What was more, why weren't all the prophecies coming true? What about all the questions that Alireza Birjandi had raised? Who had the answers?

Part of Darazi felt terrified even to think such thoughts in the presence of the Mahdi, yet he couldn't help it. His doubts were rising, though he dared not voice them. He wanted to live. It was as simple as that. Perhaps the answers would come in due course. For now, he decided, it was best to remain silent and play the servant.

That said, Hosseini was as angry as Darazi had ever seen him. The man wasn't going off in tirades or even raising his voice at all. But he paced the room constantly, demanding more information from Defense Minister Faridzadeh and the generals around him, all of whom sat behind a bank of computers and video monitors, working the phones and gathering intelligence from the field.

The Zionists' attack had caught them all completely by surprise, Darazi chief among them. He had been absolutely convinced that the Americans would be able to keep the Israelis in check. He had fully bought the lie on Thursday morning about Naphtali preparing to leave for the US on Friday. So had Hosseini, and Darazi guessed this largely fueled his anger.

The counterstrike was in motion, at least. They were pushing the enemy back on its heels. The Iranian Revolutionary Guard Corps was firing four to six ballistic missiles at Israel every hour. The Zionists' Arrow and Patriot systems were downing 75 to 80 percent of them, but those that were getting through were causing heavy damage in Tel Aviv, Haifa, and Ashkelon, though none had hit Jerusalem—at least not yet.

Hezbollah, meanwhile, was launching twenty to thirty rockets out of Lebanon every hour. A half dozen had hit the northern suburbs of Tel Aviv. Most were hitting Haifa, Tiberias, Nazareth, Karmiel, and Kiryat Shmona. Fires were raging in each of those cities and towns, but with so many rockets raining down on Israel's northern tier, it was extremely difficult for fire trucks and ambulances to respond quickly, if at all.

At the same time, Hamas terrorists in Gaza were launching forty to fifty rocket and mortar attacks an hour against the Jews living along the southern tier in places like Ashdod, Ashkelon, Beersheva, and Sderot. Even the community of Rehovot, south of Tel Aviv, had been hit by several Iranian-made Grad missiles.

But Darazi could see it was not nearly enough for the Twelfth Imam, meditating alone in the corner, quiet and contemplative. The Mahdi had not said anything for several hours. Nor had Darazi seen him eat or drink anything in more than two days. It was fitting, Darazi guessed, for the Promised One to be consumed in prayer and fasting, but the silence was unnerving.

Suddenly, without warning, the Mahdi opened his eyes. "Jazini. Where is he?"

"He went to check on the status of the Intelligence Ministry," Faridzadeh said. "He should be back in about an hour."

"Call him now," the Mahdi ordered. "He has news."

"How can we, my Lord?" Faridzadeh asked. "We're only using land-lines right now, and as I said, he's out in the city."

"Get him by satellite phone," the Mahdi insisted. "Just get him now."

"My Lord, please do not be angry, but we're concerned that those phones might be compromised after what happened when Javad met Reza Tabrizi."

"Nonsense," the Mahdi said. "I talked to Javad myself yesterday. He said Tabrizi saved his life. Now get me Jazini, and put him on speakerphone."

Darazi watched as one of the defense minister's aides connected Faridzadeh's satphone to a line running up through the bunker to a satellite dish on the roof. A moment later, General Jazini was on the line for everyone in the command center to hear.

"I was praying, and your face came before me, Mohsen," the Mahdi said. "Allah is with you, and you have news."

"I do, my Lord," Jazini said breathlessly. "I was going to wait and bring you the news in person, but is it okay to speak on this line?"

"Of course. Now speak, my son."

"Yes, my Lord. I have good news—we have two more warheads."

"Nuclear?"

"Yes, two have survived the attacks."

"How?" the Mahdi asked. "Which ones?"

"The ones Tariq Khan was working on. The ones in Khorramabad."

"What happened?"

"The moment Khan went missing, the head of security at the Khorramabad facility feared for the safety of the warheads," Jazini said. "He feared Khan might be working for the Zionists. Since the warheads weren't yet attached to the missiles, he decided to move them out of his facility and hide them elsewhere. I just spoke to him. He's safe. The warheads are safe."

The Mahdi stood and closed his eyes. "I thank you, Allah, for you have given us another chance to strike."

ACKNOWLEDGMENTS

It's an honor to publish another book with such a great team of people, and I'm deeply thankful to Mark Taylor, Jeff Johnson, Ron Beers, Karen Watson, Jeremy Taylor, Jan Stob, Cheryl Kerwin, Dean Renninger, Beverly Rykerd, and the incredible team at Tyndale House Publishers.

Thanks to Scott Miller, my excellent agent and good friend at Trident Media Group.

Thanks to my loving family—my mom and dad, Len and Mary Jo Rosenberg; June "Bubbe" Meyers; the entire Meyers family; the Rebeizes; the Scomas; and the Urbanskis.

Thanks, too, to my dear friends Edward and Kailea Hunt, Tim and Carolyn Lugbill, Steve and Barb Klemke, Fred and Sue Schwien, Tom and Sue Yancy, John and Cheryl Moser, Jeremy and Angie Grafman, Nancy Pierce, Jeff and Naomi Cuozzo, Lance and Angie Emma, Lucas and Erin Edwards, Chung and Farah Woo, Dr. T. E. Koshy and family, and all our allies with The Joshua Fund and November Communications, Inc.

And thanks especially to my best friend and awesome wife, Lynn, and our four wonderful sons, Caleb, Jacob, Jonah, and Noah. I love you guys so much and I love the adventure the Lord has us all on together!

ABOUT THE AUTHOR

Joel C. Rosenberg is the *New York Times* best-
selling author of six novels—*The Last Jihad*,
The Last Days, *The Ezekiel Option*, *The Copper
Scroll*, *Dead Heat*, and *The Twelfth Imam*—and
two nonfiction books, *Epicenter* and *Inside the
Revolution*, with some 2 million total copies
in print. *The Ezekiel Option* received the Gold
Medallion award as the "Best Novel of 2006"
from the Evangelical Christian Publishers
Association. Joel is the producer of two documentary films based on his nonfiction books.

He is also the founder of The Joshua Fund, a nonprofit educational and
charitable organization to mobilize Christians to "bless Israel and her
neighbors in the name of Jesus" with food, clothing, medical supplies,
and other humanitarian relief.

As a communications advisor, Joel has worked with a number
of U.S. and Israeli leaders, including Steve Forbes, Rush Limbaugh,
Natan Sharansky, and Benjamin Netanyahu. As an author, he has been
interviewed on hundreds of radio and TV programs, including ABC's
Nightline, *CNN Headline News*, FOX News Channel, The History
Channel, MSNBC, *The Rush Limbaugh Show*, *The Sean Hannity
Show*, and *Glenn Beck*. He has been profiled by the *New York Times*,
the *Washington Times*, the *Jerusalem Post*, and *World* magazine. He has
addressed audiences all over the world, including those in Israel, Iraq,

Jordan, Egypt, Turkey, Russia, and the Philippines. He has also spoken at the White House, the Pentagon, and to members of Congress.

In 2008, Joel designed and hosted the first Epicenter Conference in Jerusalem. The event drew two thousand Christians who wanted to "learn, pray, give, and go" to the Lord's work in Israel and the Middle East. Subsequent Epicenter Conferences have been held in San Diego (2009); Manila, Philippines (2010); and Philadelphia (2010). The live webcast of the Philadelphia conference drew some thirty-four thousand people from more than ninety countries to listen to speakers such as Israeli Vice Prime Minister Moshe Yaalon; pastors from the U.S., Israel, and Iran; Lt. General (ret.) Jerry Boykin; Kay Arthur; Janet Parshall; Tony Perkins; and Mosab Hassan Yousef, the son of one of the founders of Hamas who has renounced Islam and terrorism and become a follower of Jesus Christ and a friend of both Israelis and Palestinians.

The son of a Jewish father and a Gentile mother, Joel is an evangelical Christian with a passion to make disciples of all nations and teach Bible prophecy. A graduate of Syracuse University with a BFA in filmmaking, he is married, has four sons, and lives near Washington, DC.

To visit Joel's weblog—or sign up for his free weekly "Flash Traffic" e-mails—please visit www.joelrosenberg.com.

Please also visit these other websites:

www.joshuafund.net
www.epicenterconference.com

and Joel's "Epicenter Team" and the Joel C. Rosenberg public profile page on Facebook.

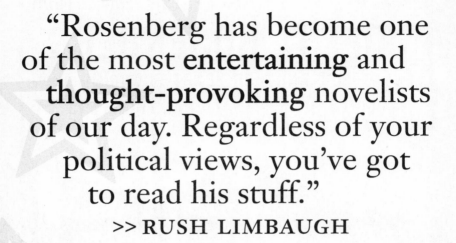

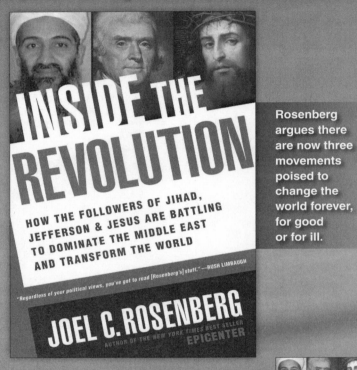